ANDY McDERMOTT

THE SECRET OF
EXCALIBUR

headline

First published in Great Britain in 2008 by
HEADLINE PUBLISHING GROUP

First published in paperback in Great Britain in 2009
by HEADLINE PUBLISHING GROUP

6

Cataloguing in Publication Data is available from the British Library

ISBN 978 0 7553 4550 2

Typeset in Aldine 401BT by Avon DataSet Ltd,
Bidford-on-Avon, Warwickshire

Printed in the UK by CPI Mackays, Chatham, ME5 8TD

Headline's policy is to use papers that are natural, renewable and recyclable
products and made from wood grown in sustainable forests. The logging
and manufacturing processes are expected to conform to the environmental
regulations of the country of origin.

HEADLINE PUBLISHING GROUP
An Hachette UK Company
338 Euston Road
London NW1 3BH

www.headline.co.uk
www.hachette.co.uk

For my family and friends

Prologue

Sicily

The little church watched over the village of San
Maggiori as it had every sunset for seven centuries.
The dusty road up from the village was steep and
winding, but the local faithful were proud enough of
their place of worship and its long history not to complain
about the trek. At least, not *too* frequently.

Father Lorenzo Cardella was the most proud of the
church. He knew pride was technically a sin, but this
place belonged to God, and surely even the Creator
would allow Himself a moment to appreciate it. Modest
in appearance and size, it had for all that withstood
weather and wars, invaders and insurgents, since the days
of the Holy Roman Empire. God, the priest mused,
clearly liked it enough to keep around.

He took a last moment to appreciate the splendour of

1

the setting sun before turning to the church's time-scoured oak doors. He was about to lock them when he heard the slithering crunch of a vehicle coming round the road's final hairpin. A large black SUV pulled itself through the turn, tyres scrabbling for traction even with four-wheel drive.

He suppressed a sigh. The truck – American, he guessed, from its sheer bulk and gaudy chrome – had a foreign registration plate. The idea that churches had opening hours just like any place of business always seemed to escape tourists, who treated the world as their own personal amusement park. Well, this group would have to go away disappointed.

The truck rumbled to a standstill. Father Cardella put on a polite face and waited for its occupants to emerge. The windows were tinted so darkly that he couldn't even tell how many people were inside. He held back another sigh. Who did they think they were, Hollywood stars?

The doors opened.

Definitely *not* Hollywood stars. While Father Cardella didn't want to be uncharitable, he couldn't help thinking it had been a long time since he'd seen such a concentration of ugliness. First out was the driver, a shaven-headed man with a sallow, almost sickly complexion. He had the look of a soldier – or a convict. From the other side emerged a giant, a mass of muscle unfolding himself with difficulty even from this oversized vehicle's interior. His wiry beard failed to camouflage a face pock-marked with scars, the biggest a gnarled knot of skin in the centre of his forehead. Whatever injury he had sustained there, he had been lucky to survive it.

The third person to exit was a woman, whom Father Cardella would have considered attractive if not for her hard, scowling expression and lurid blue-dyed hair, which seemed to have been more hacked than cut as if she had done it herself using a knife, without the aid of a mirror. She quickly turned in a full circle, eyes scanning the surrounding landscape before locking on to him with an uncomfortable intensity.

For a moment the three stood still, regarding him. Then the woman tapped twice on the SUV's window. The last occupant emerged.

He was older than the others, close-cropped hair grey, but had the same hardness to him, an armour forged by the batterings of a brutal life. Somehow, Father Cardella could tell this man was used to treating others as he had been treated himself. His nervousness increased as the man strode towards him, the others automatically falling in step behind like soldiers on the march. He backed up slightly, one hand reaching for the door handle. 'Can . . . can I help you?'

The leader's broad, almost frog-like mouth unexpectedly broke into a smile, though his piercing blue eyes remained as cold as ever. 'Good evening. This is the church of San Maggiori, yes?' His Italian was reasonably good, but he had a strong accent – Russian, the priest thought.

'It is.'

'Good.' The man nodded. 'My name is Aleksey Kruglov. We have come to see your . . .' He paused, frowning briefly as he struggled to find the right word. 'Your *reliquary*,' he finished.

'I'm afraid the church is closed for the night,' Father Cardella told him, still with one hand on the door handle. 'It will open again at ten o'clock tomorrow morning. I can show you round then, if you like?'

The humourless smile returned. 'That is not convenient for us. We want to see it now.'

Masking his rising concern with dismissiveness, Father Cardella opened the door and backed through it. 'I'm sorry, but the church is closed. Unless you want to make a confession?' he added, the words coming out unbidden in a failed attempt at levity.

To his horror, Kruglov's smile became genuine, a sadistic leer. 'Sorry, Father, but even God would be shocked by everything *I* have to confess.' His hand jabbed forward in a signal for action.

Father Cardella threw the door shut, closing the bolt as someone slammed against the wood. He leaned against the oak to hold it shut as he fought rising panic, trying to think. His mobile phone was in his small study at the back of the church; help from the village could be here in minutes—

Another blow to the door, so hard that Father Cardella was thrown to the ground as the bolt sheared in half. A gnarled, plate-sized hand reached around the edge to shove the door wider.

He kicked as hard as he could. The door crashed shut, smashing the hand against the frame. A low gasp came from outside, an intake of breath. He waited for the scream of pain.

It didn't come. Instead, he heard *laughter*.

He scrambled upright. Stumbling down the aisle, he looked back to see the huge man almost filling the doorway, bared teeth glinting in a demented smile.

Outside, the woman yelled something in Russian. Father Cardella raced desperately for his study.

'Get out of the way, Bulldozer!' shouted the blue-haired woman. 'And *stop laughing*, you retard!'

'That felt *good*!' growled the giant, ignoring her insult. He stepped back, examining his hand. A gash had been torn across its back, blood matting the thick hair covering it. 'Ha! The old man kicks like a donkey!'

Kruglov clicked his fingers impatiently. 'Dominika, Yosarin, get the priest.' He gestured to the giant. 'Maximov, come with me.' The woman and the shaven-headed man nodded obediently and ran into the church.

Maximov wiped the blood from the back of his hand with a final grunt of pleasure. 'Where are we going, boss?'

'The reliquary. If the German's research was right, what we want is in there.' He gestured through the door. Maximov grunted again, this time in acknowledgement, and ducked to go inside. Kruglov followed.

The priest had reached a door at the far end of the church, and slammed it shut. Kruglov frowned. Either he meant to barricade himself inside until help arrived, or . . . 'Dominika, if he gets outside, stop him,' he called, new strategies instantly clicking into place inside his head. 'Maximov, break the door down.'

Dominika turned and ran back the way she had come as Yosarin reached the other door. As Kruglov had expected, it was locked from inside. Maximov broke into a lumbering run down the aisle and barged into the wood shoulder-first. It was far less solid than the sturdy oak at the church's entrance – the force of the impact ripped it clean off its hinges. Man and door ploughed into Father Cardella's desk, tipping it over and spilling its contents across the floor.

Yosarin ran in after him, just in time to see the frightened priest scurry through another door at the rear of the study. 'He's gone out the back!' he warned Kruglov.

'Go after him!'

Yosarin took off, passing Maximov as he untangled himself from the wreckage of the desk. 'You want me to go too, boss?' the big man asked.

'No,' said Kruglov. 'Let's get what we came for.'

The phone was clutched tightly in his hand, but Father Cardella couldn't spare even the moment he needed to look down and punch in a number as he ran along the narrow path between the back of the church and the steep, rocky slope below.

He heard a bang – the door being thrown open. They were coming after him.

Who *were* they? And what did they want? The reliquary, the leader had said: they wanted something from the church's repository of relics. But why? The items there were significant only in regard to the church's history, not for their monetary value – at most they would be worth a few thousand euros.

Nothing worth coming all the way from *Russia* to steal . . .

He emerged from behind the church, risking a glance back as the path widened. The shaven-headed man was running after him, fists and feet pumping almost robotically. At the top of the road he saw the black truck, the woman throwing open the rear door and pulling out a long cylindrical case.

That escape route was blocked, then, but there was another, an old path winding steeply down through the woods to the village—

Heart thudding, he headed for the gap between the scrubby bushes marking the start of the trail. It had been a few years since he'd last taken it, but he knew the route well, and unless the man chasing him had the agility of a goat he too would find it tricky to negotiate. Father Cardella just needed him to be slowed for a few seconds, enough of a respite to use the phone. One call would bring the entire village to his aid; the people of San Maggiori wouldn't take kindly to strangers threatening their priest.

He reached the bushes. The hillside opened out below him.

Footsteps behind, getting closer—

Father Cardella leapt over the edge, black robes flapping behind him like a cape. His foot thumped down amongst the rocks and roots. The path was a blur, only memory guiding him. Arms flailing, he fought to bring his descent under control.

A shout from behind, a foreign curse followed by an explosive crackle of branches. Father Cardella didn't need to look back to know what had happened – his pursuer had slipped and tumbled into a bush.

He had the few seconds he needed.

Raising the phone, he stabbed at the keypad to bring up the directory. Anyone in the village would do. He selected a name, pushed another button. A message on the screen told him the phone was dialling. A few seconds to make a connection, another few to get an answer . . .

He looked back up the slope as he held the phone to his ear. It was ringing. The bald Russian was still entangled in the bush.

Come on, pick up . . .

Another figure at the top of the hill, a silhouette against the sunset. The woman.

A click in his ear, the phone being picked up. 'Hello?'

He opened his mouth to speak—

The fat cylindrical suppressor attached to the barrel of the rifle Dominika was holding reduced the sound of the gunshot to little more than a flat thump. It was so quiet that Father Cardella never even heard the shot that killed him.

★

The reliquary was a cramped chamber behind the altar, low enough to force Kruglov to duck his head. He ignored the inconvenience as he hunted for his objective. The other items in the reliquary, carefully arranged on blood-red velvet inside a glass-topped case, were little more than junk. A very old Bible, the Latin text illuminated by hand rather than printed; a silver plate with a crude illustration of Jesus etched into the metal; a golden cup . . . the rest of the pieces didn't even merit more than a cursory glance. He knew what he was looking for.

There it was. The last item, tucked away in a corner of the case as if even the priest considered it insignificant. It certainly looked it, just a shard of metal barely ten centimetres long, the broken tip of a sword. A circular symbol was inscribed on it, a labyrinth, marked with small dots. Apart from that, it appeared utterly unremarkable.

But the sight of it made Kruglov smile his cold smile once more. He had to admit that he'd believed the German was either a fraud or deluded, spouting nonsense. But Vaskovich thought otherwise . . . and only a fool would dismiss *his* beliefs.

He pointed at the case. Maximov, practically crouching to fit in the room, clenched his fist and banged it down on the glass. It shattered over the relics. The huge man's beard twitched with an involuntary smile, and Kruglov wasn't surprised to see a sliver of glass poking from his hand. He ignored it, long used to his subordinate's peculiarities.

Instead, he reached past him into the case, carefully prodding the glass fragments aside until he could lift out the sword piece. After everything Vaskovich had told him about it, he half expected something extraordinary to happen. But it was just metal, inert, cold.

Maximov plucked the glass from his hand, then looked more closely at the golden cup. 'Do we take the other things too?' he asked, already reaching for it.

'Leave it,' snapped Kruglov.

The scar on Maximov's forehead twisted with his look of disappointment. 'But it's gold!'

'You can buy better from any goldsmith in Moscow. This is all we came for.' He took a slim foam-lined metal case from inside his jacket, carefully placing the broken piece of the sword inside before closing it with a click. 'That's it.'

Dominika peered into the reliquary. 'I took care of the priest,' she announced in a bored tone.

Maximov's scarred forehead furrowed again. 'You *killed* him?'

She snorted sarcastically. 'Duh.'

'But he was a priest!' he protested. 'You can't kill a priest!'

'Actually, it's easy.' After rolling her eyes, she looked at the case in Kruglov's hand. 'Did you get it?'

'I got it. Let's go.' Kruglov looked past her. 'Where's Yosarin?'

Another eye-roll. 'He fell in a bush.'

Kruglov shook his head, then slipped the case back into his pocket and ducked through the low door. 'Start the fire over there,' he decided, pointing at the first row of pews. 'No need to make it look like an accident. The Sicilian Mafia will take the blame, it's their kind of thing.' He strode up the aisle as Dominika sprayed lighter fluid over the pew, then lit a match and tossed it into the puddle of liquid. Flames instantly leapt up with a whump.

The trio left the church, joining Yosarin and climbing back into their black SUV. As they drove down the winding road, the first curls of smoke drifted from the door of the little church, catching the last light of the dying sun as they rose.

1

Washington, DC: Three Weeks Later

'Nervous?' asked Eddie Chase, nudging his fiancée as they approached the door.

Nina Wilde fingered the pendant round her neck, her good-luck charm. 'Er, yeah. Aren't you?'

'Why? We've met the guy before.'

'Yes, but he wasn't the frickin' *President* then, was he?' An aide opened the door, and they were ushered into the Oval Office.

They were greeted by applause as they entered. Waiting for them were former US Navy admiral Hector Amoros, their current boss at the United Nations' International Heritage Agency; several White House officials and representatives of Congress; the First Lady . . . and Victor Dalton, the President of the United States of America.

'Dr Wilde!' he said, stepping forward to shake her hand. 'And Mr Chase. Good to see you both again.'

'Good to see you again too. Uh, Mr President,' Nina added quickly.

Chase shook hands next. 'Thank you, sir.'

The others took their seats while Nina, Chase and Dalton remained standing. Dalton waited for everyone to settle before speaking, standing half-turned to face the White House photographer recording the event as much as his guests of honour. 'Ladies and gentlemen,' he began, 'distinguished members of Congress, members of my Cabinet. It is truly a great privilege to present this award to a woman whose unflinching bravery in the face of extreme danger has saved countless lives, both in America and elsewhere in the world. And at the same time, a woman whose dedication to science and discovery has changed our view of history for ever, restoring to the world long-lost treasures that until now were thought only to be myth. In a way, she is responsible for protecting both our past *and* our future. I am honoured today to introduce Dr Nina Wilde, the discoverer of the lost city of Atlantis and the buried Tomb of Hercules, and also the saviour of this nation from a monstrous terrorist act, and to present her with the highest accolade this office can bestow – the Presidential Medal of Freedom.'

Nina blushed, simultaneously fighting the pedantic

urge to correct Dalton – Atlantis was the name of the *island*, not the city – as he carefully took a medal on a blue ribbon from a velvet tray. 'Dr Wilde, this nation is in your debt. I would be honoured if you would accept this symbol of our eternal gratitude.'

'Thank you, Mr President,' she said, lowering her head. Dalton raised the medal and placed it round her neck. He then shook her hand once more before turning her to face the strobing flashes of the camera, leaving her momentarily dazzled. The speech she had worked out earlier melted away to nothing under the onslaught of light and renewed applause. 'Thank you,' she repeated, struggling to come up with something intelligent to say. 'I'm . . . I'm very grateful for this award, this honour. And, um, I'd also like to thank my fiancé, Eddie –' She cringed mentally at that. *I'd also like to thank? This isn't the goddamn Oscars!* – 'without whom I'd probably be, well, dead. Several times over. Thank you. Everyone.' Cheeks now as red as her hair, she moved back.

'Dr Wilde stepped on my toes a little there,' said Dalton jovially, raising a polite laugh and making Nina wish the Oval Office had a secret trapdoor she could disappear down. 'But yes, the second person we're here to honour today is Eddie Chase,' he gestured for Chase to step forward and take Nina's place, 'who as a former member of the United Kingdom's elite Special Air Service has chosen to eschew public recognition for security reasons, which is a decision we can all respect. But this nation owes him as much as Dr Wilde a tremendous debt of gratitude for his role in preventing a terrorist atrocity.' He shook Chase's hand. 'Mr Chase, on behalf of the people of the United States of America, I thank you.'

'Thank you,' said Chase as the applause began again. When it became clear that he wasn't going to add anything else, the sound quickly died down. This time, only a single picture was taken: unlike the photos of Nina, which would be attached to a press release and sent out to news agencies worldwide within the hour, this was solely for the White House's official records. Dalton's slight turn away from Chase acted as an unspoken signal that the formal part of the presentation was over, and the audience stood, the politicians quickly seizing the opportunity to approach the President.

'So, that was your big speech?' Chase said quietly to Nina. 'Thought it was going to be all about "the wonder of great treasures from the past"?'

Nina's face screwed up at the reminder. 'Don't start. God, I was so embarrassed. You're lucky I managed anything more coherent than "*Duuuhhh . . .*"'

Amoros stepped up to them. 'Well, congratulations, to both of you. Eddie, are you *sure* you don't want any kind of recognition? I'm sure something could have been arranged.'

'That's okay,' said Chase firmly. 'I've pissed off a lot of people over the years – last thing I need is to remind them that I shot their scumbag brother or whatever by getting a medal.' He looked down at Nina's neck. 'Speaking of which, that suits you. You should wear it at the airport,

16

see if it gets us a free upgrade to first class.' Nina gave him a sarcastic smile.

'You're still rushing off to England tonight?' Amoros asked.

Chase nodded. 'Wednesday, meet the President of the United States at the White House. Thursday, meet my nan for tea and biscuits in Bournemouth. Not *quite* in the same league.'

'We've been engaged for nearly a year,' said Nina. 'We thought it was time I met Eddie's family.'

'*You* thought it was time,' Chase said pointedly.

Nina held back her response as Dalton joined them, hangers-on moving into position around him. 'So, Dr Wilde. You found Atlantis and the Tomb of Hercules – what's next on your agenda? Discovering the Temple of Solomon, or maybe Noah's Ark?' He finished the sentence with a small chuckle.

Nina didn't laugh. 'Actually, my current project for the IHA goes back much farther than anything I've done before – before Atlantis, even. What I'm trying to do is take advantage of the IHA's access to worldwide archaeological and anthropological data to track the spread of humanity around the world in prehistory.' The words came out faster as her enthusiasm mounted. 'The general pattern of the expansion of mankind out of Africa across Asia and Australasia, and then later into the Americas and Europe, is pretty well established. The lowering of sea levels during ice ages allowed ancient humans to travel overland and settle in places that are now under water – there's a very promising site in Indonesia we're planning to explore later in the year.'

'I can't wait,' said Chase. 'It'll be great to finally get out of the office and see some action!'

'Careful what you wish for,' Nina joked. 'But my goal is to pinpoint the *exact* origin of humanity; the cradle of civilisation, so to speak.'

Dalton raised an eyebrow. 'Sounds to me like you're looking for the Garden of Eden.'

'You could say that, yes. Although not in the Adam and Eve, talking snake sense. Actually finding the place where *Homo sapiens* branched off from other ancient hominids won't make the Creationists happy!' She realised Dalton had tensed slightly, and Amoros cleared his throat in a tone of soft but definite warning. 'Oh God, sorry, they're part of your – your "base", aren't they? Sorry.'

'That's okay,' said Dalton, smiling thinly. 'My base is broader than just the Creationist wing, fortunately. Why, some of my supporters even believe the earth revolves around the sun!' He forced a laugh, his entourage joining in; after a moment, Nina followed suit in a mixture of embarrassment and relief. 'It all sounds fascinating, Dr Wilde. Although it'll be a tall order to top discovering Atlantis and the Tomb of Hercules – and both before you were thirty! You turned thirty just recently, am I right?'

'Yeah, I did,' said Nina, not happy to be reminded of the fact.

'Well, I'm sure you've still got time for plenty more

18

accomplishments!' Dalton laughed again, as did Nina, though this time it was her turn to be forcing it.

He was about to turn away when Chase spoke. ''Scuse me, Mr President – can I ask you about something? Sort of in private?' He tipped his head to indicate a spot a few feet away from the rest of the group.

Dalton exchanged looks with his staff, then smiled and stepped over, the ever-present Secret Service agents watching from the side of the room. 'Of course. What can I do for you, Mr Chase?'

'I wanted to ask what's going on with Sophia.'

'You mean Sophia Blackwood?'

Chase very nearly replied, 'No, Sophia *Loren*,' but managed to hold back the sarcastic retort. The former Lady Blackwood – the UK parliament had recently stripped her of her title *in absentia* – was Chase's ex-wife . . . and also the mastermind behind the planned act of nuclear terrorism that he and Nina had just barely foiled. 'Yeah, Sophia Blackwood. Last I heard, she'd been moved to Guantánamo Bay. When're you going to put her on trial?'

'She was moved to Guantánamo for her own safety,' Dalton answered. 'If we put her in the normal prison system, she'd be dead long before we could hold a trial.'

'It'd save all those lawyers' fees. We all know she's guilty, and you're going to execute her anyway, right?'

Dalton gave him a cold smile. 'I have faith in the justice system to do the right thing.'

'Glad to hear it.' Chase raised his hand. 'Thank you, Mr President.'

'Thank *you*, Mr Chase.' The President shook the offered hand, then raised his voice. 'Now, if you'll excuse me, I have to take care of a small difference of opinion with our Russian friends. The *USS George Washington* is already on station, but hopefully a second carrier group will help make our point.' The muted laughter the comment provoked was very much of the dark kind: the ongoing disagreement between the West and Russia over the extension of the latter's territorial claims in the Arctic had taken an ominous turn just a few days earlier, when Russian warships forced an American survey vessel out of the disputed waters at the point of their guns. 'Dr Wilde, Mr Chase – and Hector,' Dalton added, nodding to Amoros, 'thank you.'

With that, Nina, Chase and Amoros left the Oval Office, a young aide escorting them through the White House corridors. 'Thought that went okay,' said Chase. 'Well, my bits did, anyway.'

Nina ground a fist against her forehead. 'Oh, God! I can't believe I made an ass of myself in front of the President!'

'Twice in two minutes, an' all,' Chase commented.

'*Not* helping!'

'Don't worry about it, Nina,' Amoros said reassuringly. 'You did fine.'

Chase waved a thumb at the medal round her neck. 'And you got a nice piece of bling out of it.'

'Eddie,' Amoros chided, 'the Presidential Medal of Freedom is *not* "bling"!'

Nina felt mildly affronted as well. 'Yeah, come on, Eddie. I wouldn't make fun of you if you got a medal from the Queen.'

'Who says I haven't?' Chase replied, deadpan.

Nina regarded him suspiciously. Even after having known him for over two years, she still wasn't quite able to tell whether he was being serious or, as he called it on the frequent occasions when he was doing so, 'taking the piss'. 'Nah,' she said at last. 'If you'd really got a medal from the Queen, you'd have told me by now. Even you couldn't keep that a secret.'

He shrugged. 'Suit yourself. I've got medals, though. I just don't make a big deal about them. They're in a box somewhere.'

'Well, maybe you can dig them out and show them to me when we get home. We've got time before the flight.'

Chase grinned. 'I didn't say the box was *here*, did I?' He flicked Nina's medal, making a faint metallic ting. 'I think you should wear that on the train back to New York. See if anyone recognises you.'

Nina was indeed recognised on the Acela high-speed train to Penn Station, but it wasn't because of the medal, which she returned to its presentation case before leaving the White House.

The discovery of Atlantis had not taken place under ideal conditions – the backer of Nina's expedition had ulterior, genocidal motives. So the Western nations behind the founding of the International Heritage Agency, under the auspices of the United Nations, had in large part set it up in order to devise a much more innocuous cover story.

Such a story had finally been agreed upon, and a carefully staged programme of media coverage arranged to reveal it to the public, with Nina, fittingly enough, at its head. As a result, she had recently been doing the publicity rounds in newspapers, magazines and even TV – hence her being spotted by a man who asked for her autograph. 'Bit more of this,' said Chase as they left the train, 'and you'll be in all the tabloids.'

'God, no! I don't want *that* much recognition,' Nina moaned. Though she had to admit, being recognised by a complete stranger had been a flattering, if bizarre, experience. 'It's not like I'm a movie star.'

'You're a star to me, love,' said Chase, putting a hand round her waist before casually sliding it down to grope her butt. She bumped her hip against his to push him back as a reminder that they were still in public. 'So if they made a film about our lives, who do you reckon'd play us? Shame Cary Grant's dead, he'd be perfect for me.'

Nina gave the squat, balding, broken-nosed English-man a sidelong look. 'Riiiight,' she said, running a hand through his close-cropped hair. 'You just keep on dreaming.'

While Chase returned to their apartment to finish

packing, Nina took a cab to the United Nations building on the bank of the East River. She rode the elevator up through the tall Secretariat Building and made her way to the IHA's offices.

'Dr Wilde!' said Lola Gianetti, standing up from her post at the reception desk to greet her. 'I didn't expect to see you here today. How was the White House? Did you meet the President?'

'I did.' Lola let out a muffled squeak of excitement. 'And I'm sure I made an ass of myself, but Hector told me not to worry about it, so it can't have been that bad.' She turned for her office. 'Sorry, I can't hang around – I promised Eddie I'd be quick. If we miss the flight, he'll . . .' She considered it. 'Huh. He probably wouldn't be too bothered, actually.'

'You're meeting his family in England, aren't you? Good luck with that. The first time I met my boyfriend's family, I was petrified. His mom hated me!'

'Yeah, thanks for that, Lola,' said Nina with a pained smile as she walked away.

It only took a few minutes to copy the files she wanted from her computer on to a flash drive, and a couple of phone calls reassured her that the IHA operations she was overseeing would be in safe hands for the few days she was away. Gathering up her notes, she left her office – only to encounter an unexpected face in the corridor.

'Matt!' she said. 'How are you?'

'Fine, thanks!' replied Matt Trulli, giving her a hug. The spike-haired, slightly overweight Australian submarine designer had helped Nina on her previous adventures, risking his own life to do so, and on her recommendation had decided to accept a somewhat quieter job in one of the IHA's sister agencies. Nina still wasn't used to seeing him in a suit, although he retained some vestiges of his old beach-bum look – today his shirt had three open buttons and his tie's knot was about level with his heart. 'Heard you and Eddie just got given the keys to the country. Nice one!'

'Thanks. What're you doing here? I thought you were in Australia with UNARA.' The United Nations Antarctic Research Agency was gearing up to explore the unique ecosystems of the prehistoric lakes beneath the ice sheets of the South Pole.

'Nah, got a while yet. We're waiting for winter to finish down there. I've been on a bit of a world tour, though – came up from the UNARA office to tell your sub guys about my trip to Russia. The Russians are the experts at getting subs to work under ice, so I picked up a few pointers. Handy being an Aussie – if I'd been a Yank, they probably wouldn't even have let me into the country, the way things are at the moment. Even got to go aboard one of their nuclear missile boats. Pretty cool, in a terrifying this-could-blow-up-the-world sort of way.'

'Let's hope that doesn't actually happen.'

'Too right.' Trulli looked towards Nina's office. 'Is Eddie around?'

'No, he's at home. We're flying to England later.'

'Oh, meeting his family?' Nina nodded. Trulli pursed his lips. 'Good luck with that! This girl I was once seeing? Going fine, until I met her family. They couldn't stand me!'

'Thanks for the reassurance, Matt!' said Nina in not-entirely-mock despair. 'Anyway, I'm sorry, but I've got to go. We'll catch up properly when I get back.'

'Will do,' Trulli said as she walked away. 'Oh, and don't worry about the meet-the-family thing. It'll be fine, probably!'

'Thanks again, Matt!' Nina replied through her teeth as she entered the reception area.

'Dr Wilde,' called Lola as she passed, 'I just remembered there's some mail for you. What do you want me to do with it?'

Nina paused at the door. 'Is there anything important?'

'Memos, mostly. Nothing urgent. Oh, and some stuff for the crank file.'

'Great,' Nina sighed. Since becoming the public face of the IHA, she had to her annoyance also become the locus for seemingly every crackpot on the planet with a theory about UFOs, lost civilisations, sea monsters, psychic powers . . . 'Maybe I should take something to read on the plane in case I need a laugh. Anything good?'

'The usual. Crystals and black helicopters and pyramid power – oh, and someone who says he knew your parents.'

Nina felt an unpleasant twinge in her stomach: her parents had died twelve years earlier, murdered while on their own quest to find Atlantis. If some crank was just using them to get her attention . . . 'What's his name?'

'Bernard somebody. Hold on, I've got it here . . .'

'Bernd?' Nina said, suddenly intrigued. Maybe it wasn't a crank after all. 'Bernd Rust?'

'Yes, that's right,' Lola replied, surprised, as she plucked a padded envelope from a sorting tray. 'You know him?'

'Only vaguely – but he *was* a friend of my parents.' Nina took the envelope, opening it to find a DVD-R disc in a plastic case and a single sheet of paper. She unfolded it and read the crisp handwriting.

Dear Nina,

Firstly, I hope you still remember me – it is some time since we last met, at the memorial service for Henry and Laura. Even though it has been over a decade, their loss is still felt, as they were both good friends of mine.

It is vital that we meet in person to discuss the contents of the enclosed disc. Please contact me when you receive this. It is a matter of extreme importance, and it concerns your parents.

Bernd Rust

A telephone number was written at the bottom of the page, but there was no address. Nina checked the envelope. It had been sent by airmail within the last few days, and the postmark appeared to be German.

For a moment she considered returning to her office to

examine the disc's contents on her computer, but a glance at her watch deterred her. Besides, she was taking her laptop; she could check the disc on the flight.

It concerns your parents. What had Rust found? The German was a historian, Nina remembered, and she had learned years after the fact that her parents' doomed expedition had relied upon secret Nazi documents to follow the trail to Atlantis. Had Rust been the one who provided the papers?

'Are you okay? Nina?'

She blinked at Lola's question, for a moment lost in thought. Then she hurriedly stuffed the disc and letter back into the envelope. 'Fine, thanks. Just . . . yeah, I know him, just haven't spoken to him for a long time.' The blonde receptionist still seemed concerned. 'It's fine, Lola, really. I'll have a look at it on the plane. And speaking of which,' she went on, glad of the conversational segue, 'I've got to get going. I'll see you when I get back.'

'Good luck with the family!' Lola called after her.

This time, Nina didn't react. She had something else to concern her.

Chase tilted back the seat as far as it would go, then stretched out with a contented sigh. 'Ah, *this* is more like it. But I bet if you'd worn that medal at the check-in desk, we would have been upgraded to first class.'

'I've got a gift horse here,' Nina said mockingly. 'You wanna look at its mouth?' As far as she was concerned, business class was more than a good enough free upgrade from their original economy tickets – though she had to admit that when the woman at the counter recognised her and offered to upgrade their seating, the luxuries of first class had been what sprang to mind.

'Neigh, lass. I'm just going to get some kip. I don't want to get straight into a hire car after only having two hours' sleep on a transatlantic flight.'

'Well, I'm not tired yet.' They were under half an hour into the overnight flight, and Nina was still very much on New York time. 'Can you get my bag down?'

Chase grunted. 'Great. First you demand the window seat, now you're going to make me get up and down the whole flight.' But he stood and opened the overhead locker, handing Nina her carry-on bag. She took out her MacBook Pro and the envelope containing Rust's letter and disc, then handed the bag back to Chase.

'If you wake me up five minutes after I get to sleep to go to the loo,' he grumbled as he shoved it back into the locker, 'I'm going to chuck you out of the emergency exit.'

'Wouldn't be the first time I've gone out of a plane without a parachute, would it?' They shared a smile, then Chase returned to his seat as Nina opened her laptop and inserted the disc. After a few seconds it appeared on the desktop. She copied the single file on the disc to her hard drive, then double-clicked it . . . but to her surprise was presented with a password prompt.

So what was the password?

Nina looked back at the letter. Nothing suggested itself

– except the telephone number. She typed it in and hit return. The laptop made a warning bleep, then cleared the prompt, ready for another attempt. If the password were some variation of the eleven-digit number, that meant – she quickly did the mental arithmetic to work it out – almost forty million combinations. Never mind the rest of the flight, it would take the rest of the *year* to try them all. So much for that.

She tried again, using her own name. No result. Then she moved on to her parents' names, then Rust's. Still nothing. She'd briefly met Rust's wife at the memorial service – what was her name? Sabine? Sabrina? Not that it mattered, since neither worked.

'Are you going to keep binging and bonging on that thing all night?' Chase complained.

Nina muted the speakers. 'It's encrypted, and I don't know the password.'

'Why, who's sending you encrypted files? Is it porn?'

'No, it's not porn,' Nina snapped. 'I don't know what it is, actually.'

'Then it *might* be porn! Here, let's have a look.' He sat up, Nina batting his eager hands away.

'It's from an old friend of my parents. He said he needs to talk about whatever's on the disc – and about them. See, he gave me a phone number.'

'So call it.'

'What?'

'He's obviously not going to give you the password until you talk to him.' Chase indicated the side of Nina's seat. 'There's an airphone, give him a bell. Only do it on your own credit card, 'cause it'll probably be about ten dollars a second.'

'Cheapskate,' Nina said with a smile. But it was a good idea, so she found her credit card and made the call. The phone rang several times, then:

'Hallo?' said a sleepy yet wary German voice.

'Hello,' Nina replied. 'Is this Bernd Rust?'

'Who is this?' All tiredness was suddenly gone, but the voice was now more cautious than ever.

'It's Nina, Nina Wilde. I got your letter.'

'Nina!' His relief was clear even through the echoing crackle of the satellite link. 'Yes, this is Bernd Rust, yes! Thank you for calling!'

'I got your disc as well, but I can't access it. The file on it is encrypted.'

'I know. I wanted to be sure that the wrong people could not read it.'

'So now that the *right* person's got it, what's the password?'

There was a pause. 'I . . . I can only give it to you in person. Not over the phone.'

Nina immediately became suspicious. 'Why not? What's going on?'

'Everything will make sense when I see you. But I must see you, face to face. Where are you now?'

'On a plane, actually. I'm flying to England—'

'England!' Rust exclaimed. 'That is perfect, I will take the first Eurostar this morning. Will you be in London?'

'No, no,' said Nina, trying to slow things down. 'I'll be in Bournemouth, I'm going to meet my fiancé's family—'

'Bournemouth, I see. I will meet you there, then.'

'What? No, I mean—'

Rust laughed. 'Nina, I know this must all seem rather strange.'

Nina's own laugh was rather more desperate. 'Uh, *yeah*! Kinda!'

'Do not worry. I will not take up much of your time. But I promise you, you will want to hear what I have to tell you.'

'About my parents?'

She heard nothing but static for a moment. Then: 'Yes. About your parents.'

Chase was looking decidedly quizzical by now, and Nina wanted to wrap the call up before Rust invited himself into their hotel room. 'Look, I'll give you my cell number, it'll work in Europe. Call me after nine o'clock, English time. We should be out of the airport by then.' She recited the number.

'Very good. I will call you then. Oh, and congratulations on your award. And on your engagement. Goodbye!'

'Uh, thanks,' Nina said to the click of disconnection.

'So,' said Chase, 'sounds like this bloke really wants to meet you.'

'I guess.'

'So we won't be able to meet my family? Oh, what a shame! Maybe next time, then.' He seemed quite pleased at the idea.

'No, we're still meeting them.'

'Tchah!'

'Wait, I'm the one who's nervous about it, why am *I* . . .' Nina shook her head. 'Oh, whatever. Anyway, he wants to come to Bournemouth to see me.' She stared at the icon of the mysterious disc on the laptop screen. 'Why's he being so secretive? And what's it got to do with my parents?'

'How did he know them?' Chase asked.

'He's a historian, so I suppose they met when my parents were doing archaeological research. I don't really know – I only met him a couple of times. The last time was at their memorial service.' She sat back, closing her eyes. 'Funny. I'd been thinking a lot about them recently, and now this . . .'

'How come?'

'You know, with us getting engaged. It's sad that they'll never get to meet you. They would have liked you.'

'Well, *everybody* likes me,' Chase said smugly. 'Apart from the arseholes who want to kill me, anyway.'

'At least there haven't been any of them around for a while.'

'Don't say that, you'll jinx it!' he protested. 'But yeah, everything you've told me about your mum – *mom*, I mean – and dad, they sounded like really great people.'

'They were.' Nina sighed, for a moment lost in memory. 'What about you?'

'What *about* me?'

'You never talk about your parents. I mean, you told me what happened to your mother, but—'

'Nothing to talk about. I left home to join to the army after my mum died and haven't been back since.' He shifted in his seat, turning slightly away from her.

'Why not?'

'Hmm?'

Nina knew Chase well enough to recognise the tone of his non-reply: a mock-casual *I wasn't listening* disguising a *Can we change the subject?* 'I said,' she went on, mildly needled by his attempt at evasion, 'why haven't you been back home since then?'

'Because there's nothing I want to go back for.' The tone in his voice was now irritation.

'Yeah, but why?'

He looked round at her, frowning. 'Jesus, is this a fucking interrogation? Why're you suddenly so interested in my family?'

She gave him a disbelieving look. 'Come on, Eddie! We're going to get *married*, so they're going to become *my* relatives as well. You can't claim *that* part of your past is a state secret! I just want to know what they're like, and why you don't talk about them.'

'If there was anything important to tell you, I'd tell you.'

'What, like Sophia being your ex-wife? Took you long enough to bring *that* up—'

'I don't get on with them, all right?' Chase snapped. ''Cept for my nan. To be honest, if my sister didn't live in the same town, I wouldn't have gone out of my way for you to meet her as well.'

They sat silently for several moments. 'That's a shame, Eddie,' Nina said finally.

'What is?'

'I don't have any family any more, except for some distant cousins I last saw when I was maybe twelve. You still do, but you don't want to see them? To me, that's just . . .' She let the words tail off, unspoken.

Chase turned his back to her and pulled his blanket up over his broad shoulders. 'Not every family's as close as yours. Now, any chance I can get some kip?'

Nina leaned over and kissed the back of his head. 'Good night, Eddie,' she whispered, before looking back at the mystery on the laptop screen.

2

England

'So, this Bournemouth place,' Nina asked as Chase brought their rented Ford Focus on to the M3 motorway. 'What's it like? What's there?' She'd looked at a map of southern England before leaving the States, but aside from the town's being about a hundred miles from London on the country's south coast, it hadn't revealed a great deal.

'Fuck all,' said Chase. 'There's a pier, and that's about it.'

Nina smiled. 'This isn't one of those English "north-south divide" things I've heard about, is it? I mean, I know you're big on the whole "roof, toof, Yurkshahman from oop narth" thing—'

'We've been together over two years, and that's the best Yorkshire accent you can manage?' Chase interrupted incredulously.

'Hey, it's better than your American accent. We don't *all* sound like John Wayne with severe blunt force trauma. Well, maybe in Alabama. Anyway, this place must have something going for it for your grandmother and sister to have moved there in the first place.'

'Lizzie moved 'cause she married this ponce from there,' said Chase. 'Nan moved after my granddad died because the weather's better, that's all.'

'And she wanted to be near your sister. And your niece.'

'Maybe. Whatever, the place is still dead boring.'

Any further comment of Nina's was interrupted as her phone rang. She glanced at her watch as she answered it. Not even one minute past nine. 'Hello?'

'Hello, Nina! This is Bernd Rust.'

'I thought it might be,' Nina said, giving Chase a resigned smile. 'Where are you?'

'In London. I am trying to find out how best to get to Bournemouth. Are you on your way?'

'Yeah, we're on the freeway. Motorway, I mean.'

'Excellent! I shall meet you there, then. Where are you staying?'

'The Paragon Hotel. But look, Bernd, I've got other commitments. I'm meeting my fiancé's family. I can't just drop everything to see you as soon as you arrive.'

'I understand. When *will* you be able to see me?'

'Well, we're having lunch, so . . .' Nina looked across at Chase for suggestions, but he only offered her a don't-ask-me shrug. 'Okay, how about if you meet me at the hotel at three o'clock?'

'Three o'clock, the Paragon Hotel. I shall see you there. Goodbye!'

'Couldn't you have made it *two* o'clock?' Chase grumbled. 'That way, we'd have a guaranteed escape route.'

'But you're not meeting Bernd.'

'Yeah, but they don't know that.'

'Aw, come on, Eddie,' said Nina. She realised that Chase was, for once, barely exceeding the speed limit. Clearly he was in no rush to reach their destination. 'They can't be that bad.'

'Well,' he said, voice flinty, 'we'll see.'

Nina's previous visits to England had only taken her to London, so she wasn't sure what to expect outside the capital – especially after Chase's disparaging description. But Bournemouth turned out to be a quite attractive seaside town, the pedestrianised main street an appealingly random jumble of architectural styles and eras above the standardised shop façades of the national chains.

They had arranged to meet Chase's family in the middle of town, another pedestrian zone called the Square. A park stretched away down to the beach and the pier; Nina and Chase had strolled through it to the town centre after checking into their seafront hotel, passing a large tethered balloon offering tourists an aerial view of the resort.

To Nina's delight, the Square was playing host to a

street market, stalls selling a wild and wonderful range of foods from all over Europe, everything from German sausages to exotic fruit. The air was filled with mouth-watering scents, forcefully reminding her that the only thing she'd eaten was an airline breakfast. Only the knowledge that she would soon be having lunch stopped her from sampling everything – although she was still sorely tempted.

She had an odd feeling in her stomach, but it wasn't solely from hunger. 'I'm . . . I'm a bit nervous,' she admitted to Chase.

'Why?'

'Y'know, meeting your family for the first time. It's just a weird thought, getting a whole new set of relations all of a sudden. And what if they don't like me?'

'If you're that worried, we can just leave,' Chase suggested, almost hopefully. 'Get a head start on that trip to Indonesia. I'm up for it – I'd rather be some-where exotic having an adventure than pissing about here.'

Nina smiled. 'Tempting, but you're not getting out of this that easily.'

'Arse chives. Oh, there they are,' he said unenthu-siastically. The centre of the Square was occupied by a circular café topped with a clock tower. Outside it, Nina saw three people: a small, grey-haired old lady, a girl whom she guessed to be in her mid-teens, and a woman of around forty with a rather severe haircut. The old lady and the girl waved at Chase; the woman did not. 'Well, here we go,' he said. Nina touched her pendant, wanting all the luck she could get.

They met the trio by the café's outdoor tables. 'Uncle Eddie!' cried the girl, running to him. She hugged him. 'I haven't seen you for ages!'

'Hey, Holly,' said Chase, returning the hug and smiling. His pleasure on meeting his niece again seemed completely genuine to Nina. 'I've been busy.'

'I know! And I know why!' Holly released Chase and turned to face Nina, long brown hair swishing. 'I know who you are,' she said, beaming.

'You do?' Nina asked.

'Of course! Come on! You discovered Atlantis! It was so great when it was announced, 'cause it meant my history teacher had been totally wrong about it not being real. That was fun, seeing his face when he had to admit it. I'm Holly, by the way. Holly Bennett.'

'Nina Wilde. Hi.'

'Hi! So, you're going to be my aunt! That's so cool. When's the wedding?'

'Yes, when's the wedding, Edward?' said the old lady, tottering up to Chase. 'Ooh, let me have a look at you. It's lovely to see you! My little lambchop. Come on, give your nan a kiss.' Chase, to Nina's amusement looking decidedly sheepish, bent down so his grandmother could kiss him noisily on both cheeks, then pinch them. 'It's so good to see you again!'

'Hi, Nan,' said Chase, cheeks pink, and not solely from the pinches. 'Nan, I'd like you to meet my fiancée, Nina

Wilde. *Doctor* Nina Wilde. Nina, this is my nan – my grandmother, Catherine.'

'Call me Nan: you're going to be family.' She shook Nina's hand vigorously. 'And you're a doctor! Holly tells me you're famous too. It's wonderful that Edward's getting married again. And you seem so much nicer than his first wife. I never liked her, she was very uppity. Where is she now, Edward?'

'She's in prison at Guantánamo Bay, Nan.'

'Best place for her. Oh, it's good to meet you.' She shook Nina's hand again, then turned back to Chase. Nina belatedly realised she hadn't been able to get in a single word. 'So, when *is* the wedding?'

Holly also moved back to crowd Chase. 'So why aren't you famous too, Uncle Eddie? I wanted to show my friends pictures of you finding all these amazing things, but you're never in any of them!'

'You know me, love,' he said. 'Just naturally modest.' That provoked a sarcastic snort from the third woman in the party. Chase's expression tightened. 'Oh, and Nina, this is my sister, Lizzie.'

'Elizabeth,' the woman said firmly, stepping forward to greet Nina. 'Elizabeth Chase. I changed back to my maiden name after my divorce.'

'Nice to meet you,' Nina replied, not sure how to respond to being given an answer to a question she hadn't asked. Elizabeth was clearly related to Chase in looks, but while he was only of average height and quite stocky, she was a couple of inches taller, thin and rigidly upright. Her expression was just as closed as her brother's. Whatever Chase's problem with his older sister, the feeling was apparently mutual.

'You too. So, how long have you two been engaged now?'

'Nearly a year.'

'And Eddie still hasn't committed to a date.' It was a statement, not a question. 'Well, that doesn't surprise me.'

Nina felt obliged to defend him. 'We've been busy. But now the discovery of Atlantis has been officially announced, we should have more time together, so we can decide what we want to do.'

'Speaking of deciding what to do,' said Chase, looking up at the clock, 'are we going to have lunch? They do drinks in this place, right? Lizzie, you could have some *whine*. Or maybe a pint of *bitter*.'

'Yeah, let's have lunch,' said Nina hurriedly, trying to defuse the situation by taking hold of Chase's arm and resting her head on his shoulder. 'Let's sit out in the sun, it'll be nice. *Won't* it, Eddie?'

His response was distinctly lacking in enthusiasm. 'Yeah, I suppose.'

Holly, on the other hand, was energised at the prospect. 'So you're going to tell us about all the cool places you've visited, aren't you?' she asked. 'You've been all over the world – you must have seen tons of amazing stuff. Much better than being stuck here in boring old Bournemouth.'

'Told you,' Chase said to Nina. He led the way to the café's entrance, walking slowly to let his grandmother keep pace. 'Well, when we started looking for Atlantis, the first place we went was Iran . . .'

Chase – with help from Nina, to correct the historical inaccuracies and tone down his more fanciful recountings – told Holly and Nan about the hunt for Atlantis and the discovery of the Tomb of Hercules over a leisurely lunch. Elizabeth, meanwhile, sat on the sidelines, disinterested. It wasn't until they'd finished eating and were wandering up another pedestrianised shopping street curving uphill out of the Square that she offered Chase anything more than a perfunctory response. 'I suppose I have to give you *some* credit. That's the first time lately Holly's seemed interested in anything that didn't involve text messaging.'

'Well, you know,' said Chase, 'if the subject's interesting, kids'll pay attention.'

Holly pouted. 'I'm not a kid.'

'Okay, so, what? Young lady?'

She shrieked. 'Oh, God! That's even *worse!* That sounds like you're telling me off!'

Chase shrugged helplessly. 'So what *do* you call fifteen year olds?'

'We used to call you "trouble",' offered Nan. 'Edward and Elizabeth were such rivals when they were young! Always fighting, they were.'

'Thank God that's stopped, huh?' Nina chirped, wishing she hadn't when she saw Chase's and Elizabeth's expressions.

Fortunately, Holly provided a distraction. 'So, you

know you said you broke your arm when you saved New York, Uncle Eddie?' She gestured at his left sleeve, voice dropping in part-fearful, part-gleeful anticipation. 'Was it, like, snapped in two? Or did it get sort of . . . squashed?'

'You want to see it?' asked Chase.

Holly winced, hands over her mouth. 'Oh, no, no! I don't know. Is it still gross? Not if it's gross. Is it?'

'Tell you what,' Chase said, taking off his leather jacket, 'why don't you judge for yourself?' He rolled up his sleeve and held out his left forearm. Holly recoiled, then moved back for a closer look. A crooked, X-shaped scar ran almost from wrist to elbow, smaller lines of wounded skin branching out from it.

'Does it hurt?' she asked, one hand hovering above his arm, afraid to touch it.

'It bloody did at the time!' Chase assured her. 'Smashed both the bones, had a great jagged spike three inches long sticking out right through the skin there.' He pointed, Holly making a high-pitched *Eeeeeeew!* 'They had to bolt it all back together with titanium. So I'm sort of bionic now. Freaks 'em out when I go through the scanners at airports.'

'Edward, that's terrible!' cried Nan, looking appalled. 'You poor thing! Does it still hurt? How long did it take to mend?'

'It was in a cast for nearly two months,' Nina told her.

'Yeah,' Chase added. 'When it finally came off, I had one arm bigger than the other.'

'Just like when you were fifteen and had all those

magazines under your bed,' said Elizabeth, with the air of someone who'd just scored an unbeatable point.

Chase held back a rude reply and turned instead to his grandmother. 'It still hurts a bit sometimes, but it's more or less fixed now. Had to be careful when I was training back up, though. Didn't want to overdo things and have a bolt pop out through my arm.'

Holly remained fascinated by the scar. 'So now you're okay again . . . could you beat just about anyone in a fight?'

Chase nodded. 'Why, got someone you want me to sort out?'

'No, no!' She paused, thinking. 'Although there's this absolute cow at school . . .'

'Nah, I don't hit girls,' Chase told her. 'Unless they're a really, *really* bad person. But if you ever have any bloke trouble, just let me know and I'll have words.'

'Eddie,' snapped Elizabeth, an angry warning.

'So who could you beat?' Holly asked, ignoring her. 'Could you beat . . . Jason Bourne?'

Chase laughed mockingly. 'Doddle. He's CIA, he's a spook. They're all wimps.'

'What about Jack Bauer?'

'Hmm. Tougher, but . . . yeah. No problem.'

'James Bond?'

'Which one?'

'Any of them.'

He pretended to consider it. 'All of 'em except . . . Roger Moore,' he said at last. 'He's the one I wouldn't want to mess with. That eyebrow, I just can't match it.'

Holly giggled. 'You used to be in the SAS, right? Could you beat the SBS?'

'Course I could. The SAS is the best fighting force in the world. No contest. Why?'

'Because there's a girl in my class whose big brother is in the SBS, and she says that he says that the SAS are just a bunch of gayers.'

'Holly, don't say things like that,' Elizabeth chided, although she was clearly amused by Chase's affronted expression.

'I'm just saying what she said he said!'

'Some SBS guy said that, did he?' Chase growled, irked not so much by the insult as its source.

'What's the SBS?' Nina asked.

'Special Boat Service,' Elizabeth told her. 'They're supposedly *much* tougher than the SAS.'

Chase scowled. 'Oh, fu—' His gaze flicked between his niece and his grandmother. '. . . sod the SBS.'

'Fusod?' Nina teased.

'It's . . . a military term.'

'Oh, it is, huh?'

'Well,' said Elizabeth, pointing up the hill, 'the SBS are based just up the road in Poole, so maybe you could go and challenge them to an arm-wrestling contest or something as pointlessly macho.'

'Maybe I could,' Chase replied scathingly. ' 'Cause that's all serving your country's about, being macho. I'm sure there's all kinds of other worthwhile stuff I could have done instead in the last eighteen years. Any suggestions, Lizzie? I mean, with all *your* accomplishments . . .'

Recognising that the siblings were about to reach a critical mass and explode, Nina desperately tried to change the subject. 'So, Holly, you, uh . . . like sending text messages, huh?'

To her astonishment, Holly didn't consider the question to be as hopelessly lame an attempt at distraction as Chase and Elizabeth obviously did. 'Oh, yeah! I mean, I prefer instant messaging, because who doesn't? But Mum won't let me on the computer much any more because I've got exams coming up, so I have to use texts, but my phone's *so* old and rubbish.' She held the offending item out as proof. To Nina, it looked a perfectly capable piece of technology, but she imagined someone half her age would have a very different idea of a good phone. 'I mean, it doesn't even have video! All my friends have better phones than me. It's embarrassing.'

'It's just a *phone*, Holly,' said Elizabeth, exasperated. 'It makes calls, it does texts, that's all you need. Anything else is just an expensive gimmick.'

'But gimmicks are part of the fun, right?' Chase said, winking at Holly. He pointed at a mobile phone shop up the street. 'Tell you what, seeing as I didn't bring you a present, how about I get you a new phone? Something flashy, with all the bells and whistles. Including video.'

Holly's eyes widened. 'Really?'

'Yeah, course! Wouldn't be much of an uncle if I couldn't do something cool for my niece, would I?' He led her towards the shop, looking back at Nina. 'I'll give you a call when we're done, come and find you. Shouldn't be too long, we'll just get whatever's the most expensive!'

Nan watched them go with an admiring smile. 'He always was such a nice lad. It's lovely to see him again. Don't you think, Elizabeth?'

Elizabeth's only answer was silence, but Nina didn't need to hear any words to know that she could have quite happily killed Chase at that moment – and probably his fiancée as well. 'So, ah,' she said weakly, unable to endure her future sister-in-law's thunderous glare any longer, 'what's the view like from that balloon?'

The view from five hundred feet up was actually quite impressive, Nina decided. The park below was a long finger of grass and trees with a small river running down its length, angling away to the glinting sea a quarter of a mile to the south. It was encircled by weaving, narrow roads – apparently the broad avenues and straight lines of Manhattan were anathema to English town planners. She could even see her hotel, a recently built octagon of pinkish stone overlooking the pier to the west of the park's far end. The only blot on the landscape was a hulking glass-fronted block dominating the pier approach, a disused Imax cinema which, according to Nan's ongoing and increasingly vitriolic tirade against it, had once been voted the ugliest building in England. Nina nodded and made 'Uh-huh' sounds at appropriate moments, though she had to concede that Chase's grandmother did have a point.

But even that rant was preferable to the alternative. The view had done nothing to defuse the argument between Chase and his sister. And in the confines of the balloon's gondola, there was no way to escape it.

'I am *so* mad at you right now,' Elizabeth hissed to Chase. Holly and Nan were at the opposite side of the gondola, just out of earshot, but Nina was an unwilling eavesdropper.

'For fuck's sake, Lizzie,' Chase replied irritably. 'I bought my niece a present. So fucking what?'

'Because you didn't *ask* me, and if you had *bothered* to ask me, I would have told you not to, because the last thing Holly needs right now is yet another distraction when she needs to concentrate on her schoolwork.'

'Nan said she was doing fine. So did you. Sounds like she's doing okay.'

'I don't *want* her to do "okay"! She can do so much better than "okay", Eddie! But she's a teenager, there are a million other things she'd rather be doing. It's hard enough to get her to pay attention to what's actually important without you giving her *toys*!'

'Jesus Christ, Lizzie. What is this, some kind of over-compensation thing?'

Elizabeth's eyes flashed with fury. 'No, it's an *irresponsibility* thing.'

'Eh?' Chase looked at her, confused. 'When did I say you were irresponsible?'

'I meant *you're* being irresponsible, Eddie!' She was barely able to keep her voice down. 'You have no idea how hard it is to be a parent – Holly's fifteen, for Christ's sake, so right now to her I'm like bloody *Hitler* always on her back about everything. And then you come along, being Cool Uncle Eddie the hero, running around playing bloody Indiana Jones and encouraging her to be just like you!'

Chase angrily held up his left arm, exposing part of the scar. 'Yeah, this was *playing*. Never mind that I saved thousands of lives, huh?' He pulled the sleeve back up, voice taunting. 'This isn't about me at all, is it? It's about *you* being jealous. Must be killing you, mustn't it? Your useless little brother's actually accomplished something worthwhile, but the one who got into Oxford's stuck selling insurance. Sorry, Lizzie, but that's not my fucking fault.'

'We both know *exactly* whose fault it is, Eddie,' Elizabeth said coldly.

'Well, what the fuck ever.' He turned away, walking around the gondola as the balloon began its descent, steel cables pulling it back to earth.

'Oh, same old story,' said Elizabeth, this time loudly enough for everybody to hear. 'Whenever things go bad, Eddie Chase just turns his back and *walks away*!' She flung her hands out theatrically, striding after him. 'Well, where are you going, Eddie? You're in a balloon!

Can't just walk out on me here.'

'*Mum!*' Holly through gritted teeth, cheeks bright red. Nina shared her embarrassment.

'Well, that was a lovely ride,' Nan piped up, turning away from the view to face Chase and Elizabeth. 'It's so nice to see things from a new perspective.' For a moment Nina couldn't believe she'd missed Elizabeth's rant, but the briefest of exchanged glances told her that she'd heard it perfectly – and probably not for the first time. She pinched Chase's cheek again. 'So good to see you again, my little lambchop! I wonder, could you do me a favour? You said you'd hired a car. You wouldn't mind taking me to the supermarket so I can do a big shop, would you?'

'No problem at all, Nan,' said Chase. 'The car's at the hotel – it's not far. Although Nina's meeting a friend soon, so she won't be able to come.' Nina looked at her watch, realising she'd completely forgotten about Rust – it was already after two thirty.

'Oh, that's a shame. Well, hopefully I'll see you again later, Nina – I can tell you what Edward was like when he was little. I've got photos.'

Now it was Chase's turn to look embarrassed. 'Aw, Nan!'

'"Little lambchop"?' Nina whispered to Chase as the balloon touched down. 'That's so *sweet*!'

'Yeah, yeah . . .'

'I'll show you his medals, as well,' said Nan. 'He gave them to me after he left the army, even his Victoria Cross. He got that from the Queen, you know!'

Nina looked at Chase, open-mouthed. 'Now you know where the box is,' he told her, smiling slightly. The attendants secured the gondola and opened its gate, and the passengers stepped out. 'Okay, you go and meet this bloke and I'll take Nan on her supermarket sweep.' He hugged Holly.

'Thanks for the phone, Uncle Eddie,' she said.

'Glad you like it. Just don't spend too much time on it, okay? Wouldn't want to distract you from your schoolwork.'

Holly tutted. 'God, now you sound like Mum!'

'I hope not.' Chase shot Elizabeth a cutting look, then kissed Holly on the cheek and joined Nina and Nan. 'I'll see you again before we go, okay?'

She waved. 'Bye, Uncle Eddie!'

'Bye, Holly.' Chase turned away.

'Nice to meet you *both*,' said Nina pointedly, before following Chase and his grandmother in the direction of their hotel. 'What was *that* all about?' she whispered to him.

'Family stuff.' When it became obvious he wasn't going to elaborate, all Nina could do was sigh and make the most of a pleasant stroll through the park.

3

After Chase and his grandmother left, Nina returned to the hotel room to get her laptop and the encrypted disc. Making her way back through the maze of softly lit corridors, she wondered again what secrets it held – and why Rust could only reveal them to her in person.

Rust was waiting for her in the Paragon's 'Vista Lounge', an elevated, semi-circular, glass-walled extension overlooking the seafront. Above it on the western cliff was a large brick building proclaiming itself as the Bournemouth International Centre, the beach and pier to the south. With the bright afternoon sun shimmering off the waves and holidaymakers ambling about, it was an attractive view, marred only by the looming Imax building east of the pier. Nina found herself agreeing with Nan about its being an eyesore.

So, to her surprise, was Rust. When she'd met him previously, the German had been smartly dressed, almost dapper. The dishevelled figure who stood up to greet her, on the other hand, looked as though he'd spent the night sleeping in a ditch. His jacket was crumpled, unkempt grey hair sticking up at angles as if he'd received an electric shock. With his thick-framed glasses, he looked almost like a cartoon of a mad scientist.

He still had his manners, however. 'Ah, Nina!' he said, standing and bowing as she approached. 'So good to see you again. And I am grateful you agreed to meet me.'

'Well, you didn't leave me much of an option,' she replied as she shook his hand. 'I got the feeling you would have camped out on the UN's doorstep if you had to.'

She meant it as a joke, but Rust nodded. 'Perhaps. But we are both here! Come, sit down.' He directed her to his table near the back of the room. Nina realised he had chosen to sit as far from the lounge's other occupants as possible, most of them opting for a clear view of the sea. Rust pulled out a chair for her, then regarded the other people present suspiciously before sitting himself.

She followed his darting glances: an elderly couple sharing tea and biscuits, a young man with over-gelled hair talking animatedly on his phone, a large bearded guy with an ugly scar carved into his forehead concentrating on his newspaper. Nina felt briefly sorry for him – whatever caused his disfigurement had clearly been a serious injury – before turning her attention back to Rust. 'So, what's the big secret?'

Rust leaned closer, voice dropping to a conspiratorial near-whisper. 'Nina, tell me . . . what do you know about King Arthur?'

Had Nina prepared a list of potential subjects for Rust to bring up, she doubted that would even have appeared in the top thousand. 'Er . . . in the historical sense, or as mythology?'

'Historical, of course.'

'Of course,' she said, trying to conceal her bewilderment. 'It's not really my area of expertise, but I know enough to know there's not much *to* know. He was the leader of the ancient Britons in the sixth century, he united the tribes of Britain following the withdrawal of the Romans, and fought against the Saxons and the Picts until the Saxons finally conquered England by the seventh century. Beyond that . . .' She shrugged. 'That's when legend and Monty Python take over.'

Rust nodded approvingly. 'And what of King Arthur's sword? Do you think that is just legend also?'

'I don't know. There are some historical accounts, but they're very sketchy. I mean, there isn't even agreement over whether it was one sword or two. Excalibur's the name everyone knows, but in some sources he had another one before it, although I don't remember what it was called—'

'Caliburn,' Rust cut in.

'Caliburn, right. So Excalibur might have been another name for Caliburn, or they might have been two completely different swords. If you go by the legends, then Caliburn was the sword in the stone, which only Arthur was capable of removing as proof that he was the true king of Britain, and Excalibur was forged for him by

Merlin after Caliburn was broken in battle.' She gave the German a look. 'But you know all this already, so why are you asking me?'

'Yes, I know it,' Rust admitted. 'The story of Arthur has been an . . . an *obsession*, I suppose, of mine for many years. But I wanted to be sure you were the right person to tell what I've discovered.'

Nina raised an eyebrow. 'What you've discovered? I thought this was about my parents. What's King Arthur got to do with them?'

Rust's lips pursed as if he were chewing a lump of something indigestible. 'Actually, the truth is, Nina . . . nothing.'

'What?'

'If I had told you why I really needed to see you, you might not have been interested. This was the only way to be sure. I am sorry.'

'*What?*' Nina repeated, now with anger. 'Wait, you *lied* to me? You just wanted an excuse to talk to me?'

'Please, I am sorry, I really am! But I had to talk to you. You are the only person I could turn to for help.' He glanced around the lounge again, voice a hissing whisper. 'My life is in danger!'

'Yeah, from *me*!' Nina stood, grabbing her laptop.

Rust jumped up too, hands flapping as he begged her to sit back down. 'Please, please! Your parents were great friends of mine, your father especially. We had a lot in common. Including a passion for unfashionable theories.' His look of pleading suddenly sharpened. 'Like *Atlantis*.'

'That still doesn't give you the right to use my parents as a way to get my attention.'

'Do you know why I lost my job?' Rust asked, his tone hardening. 'Because I helped your father. *I* secretly gave him the recovered Nazi documents that brought him and Laura closer to Atlantis than ever before. When what I had done was discovered, I was fired, disgraced – and in the end I lost my marriage because of it. Sabrina left me.'

'If you're looking for sympathy, you're looking in the wrong place,' Nina told him coldly. 'My parents *died* because of what you gave them.'

'Your parents were prepared to take any risk to prove that they were right,' countered Rust. 'You know this is true – you knew *them*. The search for Atlantis was their passion, their *obsession*, and it became yours too. And you would never have found Atlantis without them. Your work built on theirs.' Nina couldn't deny that; she had made extensive use of her parents' notes in her research. 'And like them, you took great risks to prove your theories. Well, I too have a theory. Nobody believes it – but nobody believed your parents either, yet they were *right*.' Having said his piece, he seemed to sag, the tension of waiting for Nina's response the only string holding him upright. 'Please,' he said quietly. 'At least hear what I have to say.'

Nina hesitated. She knew full well that Rust was playing on her emotions, and resented the manipulation as much as his deception. But he would not have given the Nazi documents to her parents without knowing the risk he was taking in helping them . . . and he had paid the price, with his career, his marriage.

'All right,' she said reluctantly, her anger still there, but subsiding. 'All right, I'll listen. But that's all.' She sat down. 'I'm not promising anything else.'

Rust returned to his own seat, relieved. 'That is all I ask.'

Arms folded, Nina regarded him through narrowed eyes. 'So. Tell me your theory.'

'My theory,' Rust began, again lowering his voice, 'concerns Arthur's sword, Excalibur. I believe it is real – and that it still exists. What is more, I know how to find it.'

'Okay, so where is it?'

'I do not know.'

Nina blew an aggravated breath out through her teeth. 'But you just said—'

'I said I knew how to *find* it; that is not the same as knowing where it is. I have always had a keen interest in the Arthurian legends, just as your parents did about Atlantis. And like them, I have devoted a great deal of time and effort to piece together every last scrap of historical fact that I could discover. The story of King Arthur stretches far outside just Britain, you know.' He looked at the sea beyond the windows. 'It goes as far as the Middle East – which is where one of the clues that will lead us to Excalibur lies.'

'There's no "us", Bernd,' Nina reminded him. 'Not unless you convince me you're right.'

Rust's eyes flicked down at the disc. 'And I will do so – all my research is there.' He looked back at her. 'You know, of course, of King Richard the First?'

'Richard the Lionheart,' said Nina, nodding.

'When Richard set out on the Third Crusade in 1190, he took with him a very special item, a gift from the monks of Glastonbury Abbey in the west of England. They gave him a sword – a sword that once belonged to Britain's greatest king.'

'Excalibur?'

Rust smiled. 'No. Richard *thought* he carried Excalibur – but the monks had given him Arthur's *first* sword, Caliburn. *This* is my theory – my unfashionable passion.'

Nina found herself starting to become intrigued, however unwillingly. 'Go on.'

'Caliburn was broken in battle by King Pellinore, according to legend. This may or may not be true, but the sword *was* broken, I have no doubt of that. The pieces were kept, and, as a weapon of great importance, attempts were made to reforge it. But a mended weapon can never have the same strength as a newly forged one – and I believe that Arthur's swords were more than mere steel. I will come to that later,' he went on, catching Nina's quizzical expression. 'So Merlin, who had made Caliburn, forged a replacement.'

'You believe Merlin was real?'

'There are too many historical references to him for me to doubt it, yes. Though he was not a wizard – at least, not in the magical sense.' Rust gave Nina a knowing smile.

58

'He created a new weapon for Arthur, a sword even stronger than Caliburn – Excalibur. Now, legend says that Arthur was buried with it in the grounds of Glastonbury Abbey. But the monks also had Caliburn in their possession, along with many of Arthur's other treasures.'

'So where does Richard the Lionheart come into it?'

'Glastonbury Abbey was one of the wealthiest monasteries in England,' Rust explained. 'Much of that wealth came from its connection to the legend of Arthur. Of course, wherever there is wealth, there will always come those demanding tribute. Richard was no exception.'

'So the monks gave him Excalibur,' said Nina, before she realised where Rust was heading. 'Or rather, they *told* him it was Excalibur – because they had no intention of giving up the real sword.'

'Precisely! Excalibur was buried in Arthur's tomb, a black stone pyramid which the monks discovered in 1191 – one year *after* Richard left on the Crusade. Though "discovered" is not the right word – they knew where it was all along.'

'They *unveiled* it,' Nina realised. 'Like opening a new attraction at a theme park.'

'Yes. The abbey had been damaged by a fire, and even that wealthy monastery's resources would have been strained by the cost of repairs. But the tomb of Arthur would bring them many visitors . . . and their money.'

'So what happened to the tomb? I know for a fact that King Arthur's bones aren't on display anywhere.'

'No, they are not. After the tomb was discovered, the bodies of Arthur and his queen, Guinevere, were moved to within the abbey itself. But when Henry the Eighth dissolved the monasteries around 1539—'

'By "dissolved" you mean "destroyed", right?' Nina cut in.

'Quite so. When the abbey was destroyed, so was the tomb, and nothing of it was ever found.'

'So the only thing left of Arthur was Caliburn?'

Rust was smiling again. 'Not quite. This is what my research has told me, this is my theory. Think about it – the monks of Glastonbury were willing to risk tricking the *king* to protect their treasure. So when they revealed – unveiled, as you say – the tomb of King Arthur to the world, I believe they had already moved the *real* contents of the tomb to another place, somewhere that fire or robbers, or kings, could not find them. Only the monks knew where this place was – and when the monastery was destroyed, the knowledge was lost. But there was one place it remained – inscribed on Caliburn!'

Nina was sceptical. 'Why would the monks do that? It'd be like giving the key to Fort Knox to Goldfinger!'

'They did not expect Richard to take the sword with him on the Crusades. And they would never have expected him to do with the sword what he did.'

'Which was?'

'On his way to the Holy Land Richard stopped in Sicily, where in the manner of kings of that time he started a small war over some trivial matter.' Rust shook his head dismissively, unruly hair waving. 'The ruler of Sicily at that time was Tancred of Lecce, and when he signed a peace treaty with Richard in 1191, Richard presented him with a token of their new friendship . . .'

'Caliburn,' Nina realised.

'Though both Tancred and Richard thought it was Excalibur.'

She was still dubious. 'I never heard *that* story before.'

'It was not exactly something Richard wanted widely publicised at home, that he had given away one of England's greatest treasures. But when Richard continued on to the Holy Land, Tancred was left with the sword, which passed down to his successors until it reached Frederick the Second.'

'Ah!' said Nina, recognising a historical figure with whom she was far more familiar. 'The Holy Roman Emperor.'

'And another Crusader – although a very different kind from Richard.'

'Making alliances with the Muslims so he could just walk into Jerusalem and claim it without a single life being lost wasn't quite what the Pope had in mind,' she said with a grin.

Rust smiled back. 'No. But it was through those alliances that the sword found its way to the Middle East. When Frederick took over Jerusalem in 1229, many Crusaders actually refused to follow him – he had been excommunicated by Pope Gregory IX, and they feared that allying themselves with him might earn them the same fate. But Frederick was able to persuade a few Crusaders to support him, including a young knight called Peter of Koroneou – though that title came later. As a reward for his loyalty, Frederick presented Peter with the sword. Then in 1231, when Gregory lifted Frederick's excommunication, it was seen as vindication for Peter's actions, and he gained considerable influence as a result. As well as territory in the Holy Land, he was also granted a castle on Koroneou, in the Greek islands.'

'So Caliburn is on Koroneou?' Nina asked. Although she still had doubts, Rust's research was definitely becoming interesting.

Rust shook his head. 'If only. Peter was killed when he returned to the Holy Land to defend his territory against the Mamelukes in 1260. His sword, the one presented to him by Frederick, was broken in battle – as I said, a reforged sword is never as strong as a new one. Peter's men returned his body to Kòroneou for burial, along with pieces of the sword. I believe I have located one of these pieces, surprisingly close to home . . . but the current owner of the castle in which it may be hidden refuses to let me search for it. Perhaps someone of your fame would be more persuasive.' He gave her a wry smile, which quickly evaporated as he spoke again, gaining urgency. 'But I know exactly where the tip of the sword, is – or rather, where it *was*, until three weeks ago. This is why I could trust only you.' He tapped the disc case. 'Why I had to destroy all my notes except this one copy – I could not risk anyone else getting hold of them.'

'Bernd, what's going on?' Nina asked. 'You said your life was in danger – why?'

'Through my research, I learned that the tip of the sword found its way back to Sicily,' Rust told her, 'to a church with a historical connection to Frederick, in the village of San Maggiori. I would have gone to see it for myself, but ever since Sabrina left me money has been a problem. I could no longer go to academic sources to fund my research, so I had to look elsewhere. I tried private sources across Europe, but nobody was interested – until I was approached by a Russian. He seemed *very* interested.' He glanced cautiously around the room again. 'Unfortunately, I told him too much – and just two days later, the priest at San Maggiori was murdered – shot – and his church burned to the ground.'

'You think this Russian tried to get the piece without you? And he killed to get it?'

'I am sure of it,' Rust insisted. 'The local police think it was the Mafia, but the timing . . . it cannot be a coincidence. That is why I went into hiding, why I could not let anyone but you see my work. This man cannot be allowed to find the rest of Caliburn, to find Excalibur. The risk to the world is too great.'

Nina was back to being sceptical. 'Why? I mean, it would be an incredible archaeological find, but Excalibur's still just a sword.'

'Excalibur is more than just a sword,' said Rust, his eyes deadly serious. 'In the ancient Welsh text called the *Mabinogion*, Arthur's sword is said to have a design of two snakes on the hilt, and when he drew it . . .' He paused to recall the exact words. '"What was seen from the mouths of the two serpents was like two flames of fire, so dreadful it was not easy for anyone to look." And in *Le Morte d'Arthur*, when Arthur drew his sword, "it was so bright in his enemies' eyes that it gave light like thirty torches". It is no ordinary blade. Everything you need to know is in my notes. Please, see for yourself.'

She opened up her laptop and double-clicked on the file she had copied from the disc. 'Okay, but I have to say this does sound a bit . . .' She wanted to say 'crazy', but instead settled for 'paranoid. So what's the password?'

'*Zum Wilden Hirsch*. All one word, no capital letters.' Nina looked at him oddly. 'It was the name of the guest house where I was staying when I encrypted the files. I needed something the Russians would never guess, even if they somehow got the disc.'

'Russians, plural?' Nina asked dubiously as she carefully typed in the letters. The computer chimed – the password had been accepted, giving her access. A folder opened, revealing dozens – no, *hundreds* – of files within. 'Wow. You've, ah, made a lot of notes.'

'Another security precaution,' said Rust. He tapped his forehead. 'The only index is in here. Without it, it will take days for anyone to sort through it all. But with my help, you will be able to see what I have found very quickly – and I hope it will convince you that I am right, that I know how to find the pieces of Caliburn . . . and that Caliburn will lead us to Excalibur.'

'Well, we'll see.' Nina looked up at Rust. 'So which file should I read—'

She froze.

An intense pinprick of pure green light had appeared on Rust's chest, unnoticed by him. It slipped across his crumpled clothing, stopping directly over his heart . . .

The high-pitched crack as a small hole was blown through the window beside Nina was drowned out by the crash as Rust flew backwards, a vivid gout of blood exploding from the bullet wound in his chest.

4

Nina leapt to her feet – partly in shock, but also in case the sniper was lining up a second shot on *her*.

But the laser spot flashed away and was gone. Nina ran to the window. A hole as wide as her finger had been punched through the glass. Beyond it, on the roof of the International Centre, she saw the sniper – a woman, hard-faced, ragged hair dyed bright orange – swing up her rifle, then duck away behind the edge of the building.

'Hey!' someone shouted from behind her. 'He's stealing your laptop!'

Nina spun to see the big man charging for the exit with her MacBook and the disc, his huge hand making the machine seem no bigger than a paperback.

Rust—

One look told her that he was dead, eyes wide and still, mouth half open as if about to speak. But he would never speak again – and whatever he had been about to share with Nina was now heading out of the door.

'Call 911!' she shouted as she started after the bearded

man. 'I mean, whatever number it is here, call the police!'

The hulking thief ran deeper into the hotel. Nina pursued him. The young guy followed, eager to prove himself a hero. But his steel faltered somewhat when he realised just how *big* his target was. 'Did you call the police?' Nina demanded, seeing the phone still in his hand. He fumbled with the keypad, slowing slightly as his attention was diverted.

Ahead, the big man reached a junction. He too slowed, looking each way, first in confusion, then frustration, before going right.

Nina rounded the corner to find herself in a clone of the corridor she'd just left. A maid was closing the door of one of the rooms, her housekeeping trolley angled across the passage. The bearded man yelled something in a foreign tongue – *Russian?* Nina thought – as he stumbled into it, scattering spray bottles of cleaning products. The maid shrieked.

The man looked back, saw Nina and her companion running after him—

And picked up the entire trolley, hoisting it almost effortlessly and flinging it down the corridor at them.

'Jesus!' Nina threw herself against a door. The slight recess gave her just enough space to dodge the angular missile – but the young man was less lucky, looking up from his phone a moment too late. The trolley smashed into him and knocked him down, its remaining contents flying everywhere.

Nina straightened, but the bearded man wasn't

finished. Now he picked up the *maid* and hurled the screaming woman at her. This time Nina had nowhere to go. Both women tumbled to the floor amongst the debris.

Their attacker let out a satisfied grunt at the chaos, then turned and ran again.

'Son of a *bitch*!' Nina gasped as she struggled upright. The maid seemed more shocked than hurt, but the young man was moaning, clutching a broken wrist. 'Are you okay?' she asked the woman, getting a confused nod in reply. She pointed at the injured man. 'Help him!'

His phone lay amongst the scattered soaps and shampoos, screen glowing. Nina snatched it up and broke into a pained run after the giant.

He reached another junction, frustration now evident as his head snapped from left to right and back again. He was lost, Nina realised – trapped by the bland conformity of the corridors, and apparently unable to read the signs directing guests through the maze.

He looked back at her and scowled, the scar on his forehead twisting the lines of his skin. Nina slowed. If he changed tactics and attacked her instead of running, she wouldn't stand a chance.

But instead he turned away, going left. *Wrong way*, she thought, reading the sign as she ran after him. If he couldn't find the exit, there was a chance he could be caught before he got away or hurt anyone else.

But she needed help, someone who could take down the overmuscled giant . . .

★

Chase was guiding the Focus through the traffic, his grandmother sitting beside him with a bag of shopping on her lap and several more lined up on the back seat, when his phone rang. He sighed and fumbled in his pocket. 'Can you answer that for me, Nan?' he asked, handing it to her. 'Don't want to get in trouble with the police on my first day back in the country.'

He expected it was Nina calling, as he doubted Holly would have got her new phone charged up so quickly, and the likelihood of Elizabeth's phoning him for a chat was extremely small. 'Ooh, hello, Nina,' Nan said, proving him right, before adding unnecessarily: 'It's Nina.'

'Thought it might be,' he replied, opting not to treat his grandmother to any of his usual sarcasm. 'What's she want?'

A procession of increasingly surprised *oohs* and *aahs* followed, Chase glancing sideways to see Nan's expression turn to one of utter disbelief. 'What?' he asked.

'She says the man she went to see was just assassinated, and she's chasing another man who stole her laptop round the hotel.'

'Oh, sh . . . oes,' blurted Chase. He shoved down the accelerator.

'You know, I didn't get the impression she was the type for practical jokes.'

'She's not,' he told Nan grimly. 'I can't bloody take her anywhere!'

★

Nina rounded another corner – to find herself facing a dead end. The bearded man lurched to a stop ahead of her, letting out another angry exclamation. He turned and glared at Nina.

'Er . . . hi,' she said, horribly aware that their roles in the chase had suddenly reversed. He took a step towards her. 'Okay, how about you *keep* the laptop? It's insured . . . I think . . .'

The man took another step. Nina fearfully backed away, passing a bright red fire extinguisher attached to the wall.

A weapon—

She yanked it from its clips, and hurled it at him with all her strength.

He brought up a hand, but too late, taking the blunt end of the extinguisher on his face with a flat metallic *blong*. He reeled back . . .

And *smiled* at her.

'*Daaaa*,' he moaned almost ecstatically through bloodied teeth. His demented grin widened, eyes fixing on Nina.

'Aw, crap . . .'

He grabbed the fire extinguisher, and flung it back at her. She dived out of its path, the end of its hose slashing across her back. The extinguisher hit the opposite wall with a bang and punched straight through it like a giant bullet, wood and plaster splintering.

Nina expected him to attack while she was down, but instead she heard a crack of breaking wood. Looking up, she saw he had kicked a door off its hinges and entered an emergency stairwell.

Wincing at the cut on her back, she went after him. The smell of food wafting up from below told her she was heading for the hotel's kitchens. There was a loud crash of doors being flung open followed by angry yelling, then a metallic cacophony of cascading pans and a shriek of pain.

Nina reached the bottom of the stairs. The doors were still swinging wildly like the entrance to a Wild West saloon. She barged through them, seeing a man in chef's whites – now spotted with red from his broken nose – sprawled on the tiled floor amongst pans from an overturned trolley. Other staff were desperately trying to get out of the bearded man's way as he ran for another set of doors at the kitchen's far end.

She jumped over the battered chef, her heel catching one of the pans and sending it clanging across the aisle. The man glanced back and saw her. Another foreign curse – and then he yanked a cleaver out of a side of beef and threw it at her.

Nina yelped and dropped to the floor as the razor-sharp slice of steel whistled over her head and buried itself two inches deep in the wall. She took a cautious look over the edge of the nearest counter, hurriedly ducking back as the hefty chunk of meat itself bounced off the metal just above her. More heavyweight culinary missiles followed – a bucket-sized can of baked beans, a whole turkey, and a glass jar that exploded on impact and showered her with pickled onions. Vinegar splashed the cut on her back, stinging.

'What is this, a goddamn *food fight*?' she cried.

More shouts came from the other end of the kitchen, followed by a colossal crash of breaking crockery. Nina risked another look over the counter, seeing the doors swinging and thousands of fragments of plates and bowls skittering over the tiles where another trolley had been overturned. The man was gone.

'Shit!' She jumped up and ran past the kitchen staff, skidding and slithering over the smashed china into the hotel's dining room. The bearded man had seemingly got his bearings, and was racing towards the exit to the reception area. She followed.

Chase powered down the hill alongside the Imax, triggering a speed camera in his haste to reach Nina. He just managed to hold in an obscenity on seeing the double flash in his mirror. Beside him, Nan clung tightly with one hand to the door handle, her other arm hugging her bag of shopping.

He swept over the elevated road above the broad pierfront esplanade and back up the hill towards the International Centre. As he braked sharply to turn into the Paragon's car park, he saw he wasn't the only one in a hurry – a gleaming black Jaguar XK convertible screeched in ahead of him from the opposite direction, a woman with punkish orange hair at its wheel.

Somehow, he *knew* she was connected with whatever trouble Nina had got herself into. If Nan hadn't been with him, he would have rammed the Focus into the Jag to stop the woman from making a getaway, but instead all he could do was watch helplessly as a huge bearded slab of a man ran out of the hotel, swatting a doorman aside with a sweep of one arm.

He had an Apple laptop in his other hand. It had to be Nina's . . .

The Jaguar skidded to a halt. The man vaulted the door and landed in the passenger seat, the car visibly tilting under his weight. The woman stamped on the accelerator, skidding the car round to head back the way it had come.

Nina charged out of the hotel and ran to the Focus. 'That's them, they killed him!' she shouted, pointing after the disappearing XK. She was about to open the front passenger door when she realised the seat was occupied. 'Oh!'

'You remember my nan, don't you?' Chase said sheepishly.

'Yeah, ah . . .' The Jaguar disappeared from view; she stared desperately after it, then pulled open the rear door and jumped in, shoving shopping aside. 'They're getting away, go go *go*!'

Chase gave her a despairing look. 'Nina, my *grandmother's* in the car!'

To their mutual surprise, Nan spoke up. 'Go after them, Edward!'

Chase's eyebrows shot up. '*What?*'

Nan shoved the bag on her lap into the footwell and gripped the door handle with both hands. 'I always wanted to see what my grandson does for a living.'

'But—'

She glowered fiercely at him. 'Edward, they're getting away! Go on, get after them!'

He revved the engine. 'This is such a fff . . . lippin' bad idea . . .'

And with that, Chase brought the Focus screaming round after the Jaguar.

5

Chase flung the Focus out of the car park into a sharp right turn. 'What's going on?' he asked Nina.

'I don't know,' Nina said tersely.

'That helps!'

'The woman shot Bernd, and the big guy stole my laptop. I think he's Russian.'

Ahead, the Jaguar slewed the wrong way through a roundabout. Another car swerved to avoid a collision and crashed on to the pavement. 'Why'd he steal your laptop?'

'That disc Bernd gave me – whatever's on it, they want it!'

Chase braked hard and skidded round the roundabout. The shopping bags in the back seat spilled their contents over Nina. 'So what's on the disc?'

'I don't know! Something to do with finding Excalibur.'

The Jaguar was pulling away up a hill. Chase wished he'd hired something more powerful than a family hatchback. 'What, King Arthur's sword?'

'No, the John Boorman movie!' she snapped sarcastically. '*Yes*, King Arthur's sword!'

'All right, Jesus Christ!' His grandmother gave him a stern look. 'Sorry, Nan. Where does this road go?'

'The top end of town,' Nan told him – but Chase was no longer listening, his attention caught by a skirl of tyres and a flash of movement in the mirror. A black Jeep Grand Cherokee swept in behind them from a side road. Someone was leaning out of the passenger-side window—

'*Get down!*' Chase screamed, left arm snapping across to shove his grandmother's head down. The rear window burst apart, glittering fragments of safety glass showering over Nina as she ducked.

Another bullet plunked through the Focus's hatchback door, cracking against the hard plastic of the seat back. Hunching low, Chase caught a glimpse of the shaven-headed gunman in the wing mirror. He was only armed with a pistol, but at such close range it was enough.

'Who the hell are *these* guys?' yelled Nina.

'More Russians!' Chase guessed. One group to carry out the hit and get the disc – and a second team to make sure nobody stopped them from escaping with their prize.

'Oh, great! I don't suppose you picked up a gun from the supermarket?'

'This is England! The only people with guns are farmers and hoodies!'

Traffic waited at a set of lights ahead, an approaching

truck filling the other lane. The Jaguar braked hard and made a sharp right turn, going the wrong way down a one-way street. Chase followed suit, slamming down through the gears into a screaming, barely controlled drift after it. Nina was thrown bodily against the left-hand door, loose bottles and boxes battering her. The Focus juddered as its tyres struggled for grip, Chase battling with the wheel to hold it on the road.

He looked ahead – and saw a bus rounding another tight corner. The Jaguar's brake lights flared as the orange-haired woman swerved and slammed it up on to the pavement to guide it into a narrow gap between the shopfronts and a line of bollards. People screamed and dived aside as the XK raced down the hill.

'Hold on!' Chase shouted as he aimed the Focus after it.

'It's too narrow!' Nina protested.

'If they can fit, so can—'

The passenger-side wing mirror clipped a signpost and flew off in a shower of glass and plastic. Nan gasped in fright.

'Okay, I should've gone a bit further over,' Chase admitted as he guided the car through the line of bollards and on to the pedestrianised area beyond. He recognised where they were – at the top of the street where he'd bought Holly her phone. Behind him, the Grand Cherokee slowed to squeeze through the gap, its bodywork scraping against the shopfronts.

Nina looked ahead in horror as Chase accelerated again and blasted a frenzied tattoo on the horn. The street was still busy, shoppers reacting in panic as the cars raced at them. 'Eddie, stop before we kill someone!'

'If we stop, *we'll* get killed!' he countered. The black SUV had cleared the bollards, the shaven-headed man raising his gun again.

The Jaguar weaved down the road, horn blaring – less out of concern for the lives of pedestrians than because hitting them would slow it down. Past the XK, Chase saw the clock tower overlooking the Square almost straight ahead, another road curving away to the left – but more bollards blocked the way, and the end of the pedestrian zone was blocked by a large metal gate—

With nowhere else to go, the orange-haired woman aimed the Jaguar to the right of the gate and speeded up. People jumped aside, but one man was too slow and bounced off the bonnet to crash through the window of a Burger King. Chase grimaced, both his passengers reacting in shock.

They cleared the gate. Chase glanced in the mirror. The Grand Cherokee was gaining, but the gap was tight even for a car, never mind an SUV – maybe too tight . . .

The Jeep suddenly fell back, braking hard. But again the gap was just wide enough for it to fit through – it would be back in the chase very quickly.

The Jaguar roared into the Square, smashing several chairs outside the café before ploughing into a cart and sending brightly coloured pashminas spinning into the air like butterflies. The market stalls formed a channel through the plaza, limiting options for escape.

Somewhere in the distance, Chase heard a siren – the police.

The woman heard it too, and started hunting for an exit route. All were clogged with people trying to flee the cars. Chase increased speed, intending to swipe the Jag's rear end and force it into a lamppost. 'Hang on!'

She saw him coming and floored the accelerator, swinging right – and sending the Jaguar headlong through a fruit stall, an explosion of colour erupting in its wake. 'Oh, fff . . . ruit!' Chase gasped as he pursued it through the demolished stall, more varieties than he could name bouncing and splattering on the windscreen. Through the mush he saw the XK turn again, clipping a bus shelter and blowing out a pane of glass before flying off the kerb on to a road.

He sent the Focus after it, the suspension bottoming out with a horrible crunch. Finding the wiper controls, Chase managed to clear his view and saw he was on the road running round the park. The Jaguar was already racing away.

The siren suddenly became much louder. A police car, a Volvo V70 emblazoned with squares of Day-Glo yellow and blue, tore round the corner ahead of them, headlights flashing. The orange-haired woman changed direction, slamming over the kerb to drive the Jaguar into the park. Chase followed, another bone-jarring impact crashing through the tortured Focus.

'The police are here!' Nina protested. 'Let them handle it!'

'You know who they'll arrest first? *Us!*' Chase shot back. The police car fell in behind them, strobe lights pulsing – and the Grand Cherokee swept through the park entrance right behind it.

The narrow path forked. The left route headed through the trees along the park's eastern side, but the Jaguar went right, towards a bridge over the river. It was barely wide enough for a car, the XK losing one of its wing mirrors to the metal railings. A man jogging across in the other direction stared in disbelief as the Jag roared at him, coming to his senses just in time to fling himself into the water.

Sparks flew up from the Focus's flank as it scraped against the bridge, the remaining wing mirror going the same way as the Jag's. The XK reached a crossroads, the path directly ahead blocked by an ice–cream van, to the right only the balloon and the way back to the crowds of the Square. It went left, towards the seafront—

Shots!

Three, four, five cracks from behind. But the shaven-headed man in the SUV wasn't aiming at Chase, but at the police, trying to get them out of his way.

Blood splattered the Volvo's windscreen as the driver was hit. The V70 veered sharply, hitting the bridge railings sidelong so hard that it folded around them, all the windows exploding. The Grand Cherokee's driver saw that his path was blocked and slammed on the brakes, but not fast enough to stop the SUV from T-boning the police car and crushing it even harder against the metal posts.

The Jeep wasn't out of the pursuit, though. Tyres smoking, broken chunks of grille and bumper trailing beneath it, it shrieked in reverse back up the hill before reaching the fork and lunging along the tree-lined path.

Chase performed a powerslide through the crossroads to follow the Jaguar. More people hurled themselves away from the cars, tumbling on to the neatly mowed grass. A crazy golf course whipped past, trees and another fork in the path ahead—

'Go right!' Nan ordered.

'What?' The Jaguar went left.

'Right, it's shorter!'

Hoping his grandmother's local knowledge was up to scratch, Chase swerved the Focus on to the right-hand path, one hand pounding on the horn. He glanced left, seeing glints of black through the bushes and trees.

And further back, the Grand Cherokee powering down a hill to a second bridge, about to rejoin the hunt.

Nan had been right – this route *was* shorter. They were gaining on the Jaguar. Ahead, Chase saw the elevated road over the pierfront esplanade, their hotel to the right. 'We're going round in bloody circles!'

Both cars raced under the raised roadway, the pier entrance directly ahead. Stalls channelled them towards the beach, but these were semi-permanent structures backed by brick and concrete, no way to simply smash through. The Jaguar's driver frantically looked for an exit as more sirens approached.

Chase's mirror suddenly filled with broken chrome teeth, the Jeep's mangled grille snarling at him. The more powerful Grand Cherokee had caught up.

A shot punched through the roof directly above his head and blew a hole in the windscreen. Nan screamed. 'Eddie!' Nina cried as he swung the car over to the driver's side of the Jeep to deny the gunman a clear shot. Cans and bottles clattered against her. 'Are you okay?'

'Yeah!' was all he had time to say. The Jaguar reached the end of the stalls, skidding round them to head up an access road beside the Imax. The Jeep's engine roared right behind the Focus. If Chase turned to follow the XK, he would put everyone in the car in the gunman's line of fire, at almost point-blank range . . .

Some mad inspiration struck Nina, and she hurled a tin out of the shattered rear window. It hit the Jeep's windscreen, crazing it. Startled, the driver instinctively swerved away.

Chase saw his chance and hauled on the wheel to bring the Focus round the stalls after the Jaguar. The Grand Cherokee went wide, tilting heavily on its suspension before coming after them again.

Nina grabbed the heaviest item she could see, a bottle of Pimm's. The amber liquid sloshing as the car juddered round to pursue the Jaguar up the hill, she prepared to throw it—

A man directly ahead jumped away – revealing a woman with a baby in a pushchair right behind him.

Chase braked, desperately swinging the Focus . . . back into the gunman's sights.

Caught unawares by the sudden braking, Nina threw the bottle. It fell short, smashing on the paving.

The gunman aimed—

The Jeep's front wheel ran over the jagged shards.

The tyre exploded. The driver lost control, sawing at the wheel as he tried to bring the two-ton-plus SUV to a stop, but it was too late.

The Grand Cherokee flipped over and barrel-rolled through the glass façade of the Imax building. It slammed into a wall – and exploded.

The raging fireball roiled through the foyer, every pane of glass shattering and raining down on to the esplanade. 'Bloody hell!' said Chase, looking back at the smoking structure.

'It's an improvement,' his grandmother said quietly.

The Jaguar made another turn, into the exit road from a small car park. On the far side, Chase realised, was the road where he'd been caught by a speed camera less than five minutes – though it felt like five hours – earlier. From there, the dual carriageway out of town was only a couple of roundabouts away.

He threw the Focus round the corner after the Jag, knowing that once the convertible was free of the twisting urban roads he would never catch it. The orange-haired woman turned right to head uphill, out of the town centre. He followed, a car coming down the hill barely missing him.

More police sirens, growing louder . . .

A roundabout ahead. The Jaguar went left – but racing straight for Chase were two more police cars, the lead one swerving the wrong way round the roundabout to block his path as the second went the other way, boxing him in—

'Fuck a duck!' Nan shrieked.

'*Nan!*' yelped Chase, shocked, as he yanked the handbrake—

The skidding Ford smashed headlong into the side of the first police car. The airbags deployed with a bang, cushioning the occupants of the front seats. Nina threw herself flat just before impact and was flung into the rear footwell, groceries ricocheting around her.

It had been a relatively low-speed collision, but Chase was still shaken. He sat up as the airbags deflated, and saw his grandmother bent over beside him. 'Nan! Are you okay?'

She slowly raised her head. 'I think . . .'

'What?'

'I think I just wee'd a little bit.'

Chase almost laughed, before remembering Nina. He looked round for her . . . and found himself staring down the barrel of an MP-5 sub-machine gun.

Not just one. Four policemen in flak jackets surrounded the car, weapons raised, fingers on triggers. An Armed Response Unit.

'Armed police!' one of them screamed. 'Put your hands up! *Now!*'

Chase carefully raised his hands, nodding for his grandmother to do the same. 'Nice one, lads. You stopped the wrong car. We're the *good* guys.'

'Shut up!' The policeman looked into the rear of the car. 'You in the back! Show me your hands, slowly! Get up!'

Nina obeyed, shaking glass out of her hair as she spoke to Chase. 'And you said Bournemouth was boring . . .'

6

'Well, well,' said a familiar voice. 'If it isn't Eddie Chase. Or should that be Mad Max?'

Chase looked up as the cell door opened. 'You took your time,' he said with a tired grin. Jim 'Mac' McCrimmon, Chase's former commanding officer in the SAS, had been the person he'd contacted with his phone call after being arrested.

'I ended up burning a lot of midnight oil at MI6.' The grey-haired Scotsman entered the cell, and Chase stood to shake his hand. Mac was dressed in a dark tailored suit, which gave away no clue that one of his legs was artificial below the knee, and carried several folded newspapers under one arm. 'You seem to have stirred up something rather large – the Yanks are very interested in it.'

'How come?'

'No idea, but Peter Alderley's giving me an update soon.'

'Alderley?' Chase groaned at the mention of the MI6 agent. 'Oh, God, you got that twat involved? He must be laughing his arse off at the thought of me spending the night in a police cell.'

'There was some amusement, yes. But he also wants to know when he's going to get his wedding invitation.'

'Why would he even want to come? He can't stand us.'

A smirk crinkled Mac's craggy face. 'Oh, he likes Nina just fine. It's *you* he can't stand. He wants to give Nina his commiserations.'

'The cheeky bastard! And after he got promoted because of us . . . Where is Nina, anyway? Is she okay?'

'She's fine.' Mac gestured at the door. 'She's waiting in reception. Along with your grandmother.'

'What, I call you and then I'm the last one you get out?'

'Ladies first, Eddie. Where are your manners?'

A policeman led them to the police station's reception area. 'Eddie!' said Nina as he entered, jumping up to embrace him. 'Are you okay?'

'Just got worked over with a rubber hose, but apart from that I'm fine,' he joked. He looked past her to see his grandmother sitting on a bench nearby. 'Nan! Are you all right?'

She nodded. 'I'm fine, Edward, thank you. I've never been arrested before, it was all very strange! Everyone was very nice, though, and they even brought me tea in my cell. It'll be quite a story to tell the other girls next time we play bridge.'

'Thank God. If anyone'd been nasty to my nan, there really *would* have been trouble.' He became aware of activity outside the glass front doors. 'What's going on?'

'Press,' Mac replied disdainfully. He handed Chase and Nina the newspapers. 'You've become big news, unfortunately. Don't worry about that lot outside, we can slap a category five DA notice on them to shut them up now the security services are involved, but it happened too late to stop this morning's papers.'

'Aah!' Nina cried in dismay, seeing her official IHA publicity photo smiling witlessly back at her from the front page of the *Guardian* under the headline 'Chaos in Bournemouth: discoverer of Atlantis arrested following murder'. 'I wasn't arrested *for* it, I *witnessed* it!'

'You think that's bad . . .' said Chase. He held up the *Sun*, the tabloid bearing the banner headline 'THE BOURNE-MOUTH IDENTITY'. Some tourist with a quick shutter finger – and a canny commercial sense – had caught the Focus as it smashed through the remains of the fruit stall, and the picture now dominated the page. Chase was just a shadow in the driving seat, and most of his grandmother's face was obscured by the windscreen pillar, but Nina was clearly visible in the back. The paper had even helpfully included an inset of her shaking hands with President Dalton.

Chase read out the opening paragraph. '"One day, she was at the White House to accept the highest honour in America from the President. The next, she was in a high-speed car chase and gun battle through a quiet seaside town. Famed archaeologist Nina Wilde, discoverer of the lost city of Atlantis, was arrested yesterday after a trail of destruction through Bournemouth left three dead and dozens injured . . ." Yeah, this isn't good.'

'Oh, *ya think*?' Nina wailed. 'And Atlantis isn't a city, it's the whole damn island! Why does everyone get that wrong?'

Chase hugged her. 'Priorities, love.'

'I know, I know. But *aaargh*!'

A fusillade of camera flashes from outside caught everyone's attention. Elizabeth Chase stormed up the steps and threw open the door, furious eyes locked on to her brother. '*You!*' she yelled. Holly scurried in behind her, worried.

'Hi, Lizzie,' said Chase with false breeziness. 'You saw today's papers, then?'

She shoved past him and crouched before her grandmother. 'Nan, are you okay?'

'I'm all right, love,' Nan assured her. 'A bit shaken up, that's all.'

'Oh, thank God.' She bowed her head in relief, then whirled to confront Chase. 'What the *hell* were you thinking? You stupid bastard! You could have *killed* her!'

'Yeah, I'm fine too, thanks,' Chase replied with chilly sarcasm.

'Actually, Elizabeth, I'm afraid this is all my fault,' said Nina.

Elizabeth snatched the newspaper from Chase's hand, jabbing a finger at the picture. 'Oh, so you were driving the car from the back seat?' She crumpled the paper into a roll and batted it angrily against Chase, prompting the policeman to politely but firmly pull her away. 'I thought you couldn't *possibly* do anything more selfish and irresponsible than you already have, but this, this . . .' She stood silently for a moment. 'God! I have never been more . . . *disgusted* with you in my entire life.'

'Elizabeth!' Nan snapped, standing up with an obvious effort. Holly hurried to help her. 'I'm all right, and so are Edward and Nina. That's all that matters.'

'No, it's *not* all that matters, Nan!' Elizabeth said. 'People were *killed*! And it's all his fault! You think he's going to explain why to their families?'

'Actually,' said Mac, raising his voice with authority, 'the two men who died while trying to kill Eddie and Nina – and your grandmother, I might add – are the reason my colleagues are so interested in what happened.'

'And who the *hell* are you?' Elizabeth demanded.

'Ma'am,' said Mac, bowing slightly. The gesture somewhat disarmed Elizabeth. 'Jim McCrimmon, at your service. I used to be in the SAS, but I'm now . . . well, let's say *associated* with Her Majesty's Secret Intelligence Service. Or MI6, if you prefer.'

'MI6?' said Holly, eyes widening. 'You're a spy?'

'Mac,' said Chase, 'this is Holly, my niece . . . and you just met my sister, Lizzie.'

'*Elizabeth!*'

Mac turned to address Holly. 'No, I'm not a spy – your uncle would probably think a lot less of me if I were. I'm more of a consultant.'

'Who saves people's lives occasionally,' Nina added.

'And my house still isn't fully repaired because of it . . .

But these two raised quite a stir at Vauxhall Cross once their identities were discovered. Not so much from us, but we share intelligence with the Americans, and they got very excited about it.' He looked through the glass doors at the reporters outside. 'But I think we should discuss this somewhere more private.'

'We can just leave?' Nina asked in surprise.

Mac smiled. 'You're free to go, for the moment. The Home Office has arranged for all charges to be dropped. It seems the American government is quite keen to talk to you about these men – and about your friend, Herr Rust.' He lowered his gaze. 'I'm sorry.'

'Thank you. But why do they want to know about Bernd?'

'I have absolutely no idea – but I'll hopefully find out soon. Is there somewhere we can go?'

'We can go to my house,' Holly suggested. Elizabeth seemed about to object, but a look from Nan silenced her.

Mac nodded. 'That sounds ideal.'

Chase gazed out of the front window of Elizabeth's house, taking in what Mac had just relayed to Nina and himself after a phone conversation. 'So this guy Yosarin and his mate the Jeep driver, if they're working as security goons for some Russian billionaire, why are they in Bournemouth shooting at my nan?' He turned to face Mac. 'Alderley doesn't know a fucking thing, does he?'

'Mac, I know this is kind of classified,' said Nina, 'but

is there any chance Catherine or Holly could sit in? Eddie's so much more polite when they're around.'

'Afraid not, but I share your sentiments,' Mac replied. 'No, I get the impression that Alderley's been shoved aside by the Americans, and he's not happy about it.'

'Yeah,' said Chase, toying with Nina's ponytail. 'I know how annoying it is taking orders from Yanks.'

'Hey!' Nina said.

Mac smiled, then sat up, seeing something outside the window. 'But I think these people might be able to provide some more illumination.'

A car had stopped outside, a large black Lincoln limousine. Chase could see its number plate, the unusual format classifying it as a diplomatic vehicle. 'Oh, 'ello, here come the Feds.' Nina got up to join him, watching as two men emerged from the car and marched up the drive. The doorbell rang; after a brief exchange, the living-room door opened and Elizabeth peered cautiously inside.

'There's some people here to see you,' she said. 'They said they're from the US embassy.'

Mac stood. 'Please, show them in, Ms Chase.'

Elizabeth led two suited men into the room. The first was in his fifties, with a thatch of thinning brown hair and a harried air. He extended a hand to Nina. 'Dr Wilde,' he said, before looking uncertainly between Chase and Mac. 'Mr . . . Chase?' Chase pointed at himself. 'Thanks.' Shaking hands with Chase, he introduced himself, his accent Bostonian. 'I'm Clarence Peach, from the

Department of Security Cooperation at the US embassy in London.'

'Peachy,' said Chase, suppressing a smirk. From Peach's weary expression, he'd endured endless jokes about his name.

The second man was younger, in his mid-thirties, and to Nina far more impressive to look at. He was a well-built six foot plus, square-jawed and handsome with intense green eyes and jet-black hair. 'Dr Wilde?' he asked, deep voice betraying a distinctive New Orleans drawl. 'I'm Jack Mitchell, from DARPA – Defense Advanced Research Projects Agency,' he clarified, seeing her puzzled look, before his voice changed to a pitch-perfect imitation of Troy McClure, the washed-up actor from *The Simpsons*. 'You may remember us from such inventions as the Internet – not just for pornography any more!'

Nina laughed. 'Hi! Good to meet you.'

'And you must be Eddie Chase.'

'Guess I must,' said Chase, not nearly as impressed as Nina by the newcomer. 'So why's DARPA interested in finding Excalibur? Thought you were just into building killbots and microwave pain beams these days.'

'There's a lot more to Bernd Rust's research than ancient relics, and I'll explain why in a moment. But unfortunately, that information is need-to-know classified.' He turned to Mac. 'I'm afraid I'm going to have to ask you to leave the room while I discuss it. Sorry, sir.'

Mac was surprised. 'I have a level five security classification.'

'I know, sir.'

Shooting Nina and Chase a look, Mac left the room. Mitchell gestured for Nina and Chase to sit down, then opened his slim metal briefcase and removed a folder. 'Do you recognise any of these people?' he asked, handing several photographs to them.

Nina immediately spotted the bearded man whom she had chased through the hotel. 'That's the guy who stole my laptop!'

Mitchell nodded. 'Oleg Maximov, AKA "the Bulldozer". Former Russian Spetsnaz special forces trooper, noted for extreme physical strength and also extremely limited intelligence – even before he got shot in the head in Chechnya.' He indicated the expansive scar on the man's forehead. 'Nobody quite knows how he survived it, but he did, and he's now got a metal plate holding half his skull together . . . and a seriously screwed-up nervous system.'

'What do you mean?'

'He suffered some sort of brain damage that affected his pleasure-pain response,' Mitchell explained. 'Basically, when he experiences pain he feels it as *pleasure*.'

'Ew!' Nina said, wincing. 'That explains why me hitting him in the face with a fire extinguisher turned him on so much, I guess.'

Chase gave her an admiring look. 'You smacked a Spetsnaz bloke with a fire extinguisher?'

'Yeah.'

'Good for you!' He pointed at one of the other photos. 'Hey, she was the getaway driver.'

Nina examined the picture. 'She was the one who shot Bernd as well – only she had orange hair.' The sullen woman in the picture, who looked about thirty, had hair that was mostly purple, with long green-dyed strands hanging down over her face.

'Her name's Dominika Romanova,' said Mitchell. 'She used to be a sniper for the FSB – the successor to the KGB – until she decided she could get more money in the private sector.' He took the photos back, shuffling through them. 'She and Maximov worked with Yosarin and Belenkov, these two charmers –' he held up two more photos, both showing unattractive and menacing-looking men – 'who got blown up in the Bournemouth Imax theatre yesterday afternoon. Fortunately, their IDs were more fireproof than they were.'

'So why did they kill Bernd?' Nina demanded. 'What was in his files that they wanted so bad?'

Mitchell took another pair of pictures from his case. 'All four of them work for this man, Aleksey Kruglov.' The picture revealed another unappealing man, older than the others, with a wide mouth and cold eyes. 'Kruglov's old-school KGB, but he now works as a "security specialist", by which I mean head thug, for *this* guy.' He gave them the last photo.

Nina frowned. The man in the picture appeared to be in his late forties, with a trim brown goatee beard and narrow rectangular wire-framed glasses. He also seemed vaguely familiar. 'I've seen him somewhere . . .'

'Probably in the news,' said Peach. 'That's Leonid Vaskovich. He's a Russian energy baron – one of the new breed of oligarchs. Personal fortune of about eight billion dollars.'

'Major player in Russian oil and gas,' Mitchell added, 'and currently working very closely with the administration in Moscow with an eye to becoming part of it. He's a hardline ultra-nationalist, who wants to make Mother Russia the number one world power, and is willing to do whatever he thinks is necessary to achieve that.' His gaze fixed on Nina. 'He's also the man your friend Rust made the mistake of trusting when he went looking for backers.'

Nina stared at the picture. 'What does finding King Arthur's sword have to do with a Russian oil baron?'

Mitchell retrieved the pictures and returned them to his case before answering. 'Dr Wilde . . . have you ever heard of something called "earth energy"?'

Nina's heart sank. Was *that* what Rust thought he'd found? 'Are you *serious*?'

'Extremely.'

'What's earth energy?' asked Chase. 'Sounds like some hippie-dippie thing.'

'It is,' Nina sighed. 'It's things like ley lines, dragon lines, feng shui – the idea that there's some kind of energy that's channelled along specific paths around the earth.' Her disappointment grew even as she spoke; she couldn't believe Rust had wasted his time on such nonsense – and that it had somehow got him killed. 'It's crap, basically. Crackpot pseudoscience.'

'Actually,' said Mitchell, 'that may not be entirely true.'

Nina regarded him in disbelief. 'What?' A lone, disgraced historian spending his time on such a theory was one thing . . . but one of the US government's most advanced scientific departments?

Mitchell leaned forward. 'Have you ever heard of HAARP?'

'Brother of Grouch, Chic and Zepp?' Chase said. Nina groaned.

'High-frequency Active Auroral Research Program,' said Mitchell, faintly amused. 'It's a US government project based in Alaska that uses a directional antenna array to selectively heat parts of the ionosphere into plasma: the idea was that we could turn the upper atmosphere into a kind of mirror for directed energy, which would let us increase the range of radio signals or radar by thousands of miles, even tens of thousands.'

'So you wouldn't be affected by line of sight limitations,' said Chase thoughtfully, interested now the subject had developed a military aspect. 'You make this mirror, then bounce signals off it so they can go over the horizon.'

'Exactly. The Russians had a similar project, called SURA. But the HAARP researchers found something unusual – for some reason, the antenna array was putting out energy ... even when it wasn't powered up. So DARPA started trying to work out why.'

'And what did you find?' Nina asked dubiously.

'Something that could only be described as "earth energy".'

'Riiight.'

He held out his open palms to her. 'It's not such a stretch, Dr Wilde, really. The entire planet is in some ways just a massive electric motor – we wouldn't be here if it wasn't, because without the field generated by the earth's core to protect us from the sun's radiation, we'd all be dead. But what we found was that there are also lines of energy at *ground* level, not just above the atmosphere. The HAARP array happened to be situated close enough to one of these lines for it to generate power through induction, much more than could be accounted for by normal telluric processes. We did tests, and found that if you built an array at a point where several of these lines converge, and you created a magnetic field that channelled and focused them, you could theoretically generate a significant amount of energy – basically for free. The earth puts out more power in a day than has been produced in the whole of human history. If we could tap into even a tiny percentage of that . . .'

'You'd put this Vaskovich bloke out of business,' Chase said. 'No wonder he wants to keep it quiet.'

Nina still wasn't convinced. 'I don't see how that connects to Excalibur.'

Mitchell's expression became more intense. 'Excalibur

isn't just connected to this theory, Dr Wilde. It's the *key*. Vaskovich has already built an earth energy generator in northern Russia, and is trying to make it work as we speak.'

'How do you know what he's doing?' Chase asked.

A half-smile. 'We've got a reliable source inside Vaskovich's organisation. We know what he's up to. But his generator . . . it's not working. Yet. Our research found that creating the magnetic fields you need to channel the earth energy requires a *lot* of power to be put in – more than the generator has managed to put out.'

'In other words,' said Nina scathingly, 'it's completely pointless.'

'The theory's sound,' Mitchell insisted. 'But to break that barrier, you need a superconducting material at the focal point – something that allows energy transfer with near as dammit one hundred per cent efficiency. With conventional technology, you create superconductors by cooling them down to near absolute zero with liquid nitrogen or helium. But to do that in an earth energy generator you'd need a massive, constant supply of coolant – so much that you'd need an entire chemical plant right there on site making the stuff. It's just not practical. So you need a superconductor that can work without coolant. And *that's* where Excalibur comes in.'

Nina raised an incredulous eyebrow. 'You're saying that Excalibur was made of a *superconductor*?'

'That's exactly what I'm saying. And it's what Rust said, too – and what he told Vaskovich. Your friend's theory was that Merlin forged Excalibur from an alloy with high-temperature superconducting properties.'

'Oh, come on!' protested Nina. 'In the sixth century?'

'Ever heard of Wootz steel?' Mitchell asked, obviously prepared for the objection. 'It's an ultra-hard form of steel that gets its strength from a matrix of carbon nanotubes within the metal. It's difficult for us to make even now – but incredibly sharp blades were being forged from it in China and India in *500 BC*. It was probably a fluke that the technique was ever discovered . . . but it *was* discovered. Whether by chance or genius, Merlin accomplished something even more incredible with King Arthur's swords. He really was a wizard – just not in the Gandalf sense.'

'Wait, *swords*, plural?' Chase cut in.

Mitchell nodded. 'Arthur's original sword, Caliburn, was the same metal, but not quite as effective. Call it Merlin's prototype for Excalibur. But Arthur had a weapon that acted as a natural channel for earth energy – and according to legend, he made use of it. Nothing could stand against Excalibur when Arthur wielded it, and it even glowed when he used it in battle.'

Nina remembered what Rust had told her at the hotel. 'Bernd said that Excalibur shone with the light of thirty torches, and lit up with flames.'

'It'd be one hell of a psychological weapon,' said Mitchell. 'Imagine having the king of the Britons charging at you with his sword on fire, cutting through everyone in his path? It'd be the sixth-century equivalent of a Spectre gunship or a daisy-cutter bomb. Once you see it coming, the last thing you'd be thinking about is fighting. You'd just want to run away like brave Sir Robin.'

Nina laughed at the Monty Python reference, then became serious again. 'You really believe this, don't you? You really think King Arthur's sword was made of this magic metal?'

'I do,' Mitchell told her firmly. 'But the problem is, so does Vaskovich.'

'Why's it a problem?' asked Chase. 'He gets the sword, his generator works, zap! Free 'leccy all round.'

'What, apart from the fact that he's murdered people to get it?' Nina said disapprovingly.

Mitchell's expression became grim. 'There's more to it than just generating electricity. Excalibur was a powerful weapon in Arthur's time . . . but today it could be used to create an even *more* powerful weapon. With the right superconductor in place, the earth energy generator becomes self-sustaining, so the external energy source you need to kickstart the process can be switched off. And the generator can then build up enormous amounts of energy – which can be released in a single burst.'

'So the thing blows itself to bits,' said Chase. 'Can't see the downside there.'

'No, it doesn't,' Mitchell said, shaking his head. 'The system uses a HAARP-style antenna array to draw in earth energy. But the array was also designed to put energy *out* – and it still can. Vaskovich could use the array to heat the ionosphere just like HAARP was designed to do – and then bounce the entire output of the generator off it in a single blast, and hit a target thousands of miles away. From the Arctic coast of Russia, he could destroy any target in the northern hemisphere.'

A chill ran through Nina. 'Just how powerful *is* this thing?'

'The force of a nuclear bomb, channelled through a lightning bolt,' Mitchell told her. 'And there's no defence against it. No warning it's coming, no way to stop it. And all Vaskovich needs to make it work is the right super-conducting metal. Which is why I'm here.' He straightened. 'This is a matter of national security – not just for the United States, but for every country in the world. Dr Wilde, we want you to find Excalibur – before Vaskovich does.'

'Me?' said Nina, shocked. 'Why do you think *I* can find it?'

'You were the last person to speak to Rust. You said in your police statement that he told you where to find the pieces of Caliburn, which contain the location of Excalibur.'

'He didn't exactly give me map references,' she protested. 'He just told me he *thought* he knew where they were – and then he got shot!'

'It's all we've got. Now Vaskovich's people have got Rust's research, you're the only person who stands a chance of beating them to the sword. After all,' he said, with an encouraging flick of his eyebrows, 'you've got some experience in this kind of thing.'

'But what if Bernd was wrong?'

'Then Vaskovich has nothing. But the United States can't take the chance that he was *right*. If Vaskovich can make his weapon work, it'll be the most destabilising threat to the world since the Cold War. Russia's already rattling its sabre over the Arctic; this would give them the power to back up their threats by force.' He stood. 'I'd like you to come back to the embassy in London to work out a plan of action.'

'Wait a minute,' said Chase. 'We work for the IHA, not DARPA.'

Again, Mitchell had clearly anticipated the objection. 'The IHA has already agreed to co-operate with DARPA on this mission.'

Nina was surprised. 'It has? But the IHA's a civilian United Nations agency, not part of the US military.'

'The IHA was set up to ensure historical artefacts didn't fall into the wrong hands,' Peach piped up. 'I think this qualifies.'

'It'll officially be an IHA operation,' said Mitchell. 'But the United States, specifically DARPA, will be backing it. The director of the IHA has already authorised it.'

'I'd like to discuss this with Hector myself,' said Nina, tight-lipped.

'I thought you would. That's why he's on his way to England right now – he might even be at the embassy already. You can talk to him in person.'

'Bloody hell,' muttered Chase. 'Bit quick off the mark, aren't you?'

'Vaskovich's people will be ready to move as soon as they figure out where the sword pieces are,' Mitchell said. 'So we need to move faster.'

'Huh,' said Nina. 'I guess we're going to London, then.'

Chase stood and looked out of the window at the limo. 'We'd better take your car – ours is a bit knackered. Good job we took out the damage insurance . . .'

The American embassy dominated one end of London's leafy Grosvenor Square. It was, Nina thought as the limo rounded the anti-terrorist security blockades to pull into a guarded side gate, a singularly unattractive structure: a brutalist block of concrete and glass, completely at odds with the elegant Victorian and Georgian townhouses nearby. But for all that, the sight of the Stars and Stripes flying outside gave her a momentary swell of pride. A piece of home away from home.

Their departure from Elizabeth's home had been hurried, with Holly and Nan surprised and sorry to see them leave, and Elizabeth saying very little, frustrated at being unable to vent her remaining anger at Chase. Mac had also been surprised; though Mitchell's reiteration of the classified nature of the mission meant Chase couldn't tell him anything, the brief exchange of glances between the two former SAS men reassured Chase that Mac would use his own contacts to help if he could.

Now, Peach brought them to an office overlooking Grosvenor Square, where Amoros was waiting for them. 'Hector,' said Nina. 'My God, you look exhausted!'

'I've had a hectic twenty-four hours,' he said grumpily. 'It's not every day that my Director of Operations – and her Special Assistant,' he added, glaring at Chase, 'get arrested for destroying half a town. Then, as if dealing with the press wasn't enough, suddenly I'm told it's now a national security issue and I get hustled on to a State Department jet and flown to England without even being given time to pack a toothbrush!'

'Sorry about that, Admiral,' said Mitchell, stepping forward to shake Amoros's hand. 'Jack Mitchell, DARPA. We spoke on the phone.'

Amoros regarded Mitchell as if he wasn't what he'd expected before turning back to Nina. 'They've filled me in about the situation. I imagine you're not entirely happy about it.'

'Hardly,' Nina snorted. 'Hector, I appreciate that yes, if what Mr Mitchell says is true then there are national security issues. But if that's the case, surely this is now a job for the CIA, not the IHA. If we're seen to be taking sides or actively working for one particular government, it could make it a lot harder to get co-operation from other countries in the future.'

'I hear what you're saying, and to a certain extent I agree. But this situation is different.'

'Yeah? How come?'

Amoros was not pleased to be challenged. 'Because, Nina, the chickens have come home to roost. The IHA might have been set up under the flag of the UN, but it was the NATO nations, and especially the United States, that funded it. The US has put a lot of money and resources into the IHA – and over seventy lives, I'm sure I don't need to remind you. So now Uncle Sam is asking the IHA to do something in return.' On seeing Nina's disapproving expression, he went on: 'Jesus, Nina! This is exactly why the IHA was created in the first place, you know that! If this Vaskovich gets Excalibur, we could have another Atlantis on our hands – and not that sanitised fairytale version we put out to the public, but the *real* story, the one that almost ended with millions of people dead!'

'But we've got almost nothing to go on!' Nina objected. 'Bernd told me that the priest at that church in Sicily was murdered by the Russians, but the local police said they suspected the Mafia. And maybe they were right, maybe the death was just a coincidence.'

'And if this thing *was* there,' Chase added, 'wouldn't that mean Vaskovich has got what he needs already?'

'The murder was three weeks ago. If he'd been able to use it to get his system working, we'd know about it by now,' said Mitchell. 'It's possible the piece was too small to be useful – or that Caliburn isn't an effective enough superconductor.'

'Or,' Nina countered, 'Bernd could have been wrong about the whole thing.'

'But he might not,' said Mitchell. 'Which is why we have to make sure – and why we're asking you to help us, Dr Wilde. After everything you've accomplished in the past few years, you're clearly the best person for the job.'

He nodded at the picture of President Dalton on the office wall. 'We need you. Your *country* needs you.'

'This has all come from higher up,' Amoros said, glancing at Mitchell. 'The IHA is committed to helping DARPA find these artefacts before this Russian can.'

'I'm convinced your friend was right about Excalibur – that it exists, and that he was on the right path to finding it,' Mitchell said to Nina. 'If Vaskovich uses his research to find Excalibur before we can, then he'll have died for nothing . . . and a lot of other people might die as well.'

For the second time in two days, Nina knew she was being emotionally blackmailed – but she also knew there was no way she could say no. Not when the security of the country – of the *world* – was at stake.

And if Excalibur *did* exist, if the Arthurian legends were actually true, then she would be the one to prove it. Another great accomplishment, turning thirty be damned . . .

She turned to Chase. 'What do you think, Eddie?'

'Me?' he said, shrugging. 'Sounds like fun. Get some action and save the world at the same time – I'm up for that.'

Nina was silent, weighing her options. 'All right,' she said finally, 'I'll do it. But it's going to be an IHA operation. Not some kind of split jurisdiction affair where somebody's second-guessing everything I do, and *definitely* not a military mission. If I'm doing it, then I'm in charge.'

'That was actually going to be the plan anyway,'

Mitchell told her, 'so we took care of that without any problems! There are just two provisos – only little ones,' he said with a perfect white grin as Nina opened her mouth to protest. 'The first is that when we find Excalibur, DARPA gets to analyse it so we can figure out exactly how Merlin made a high-temperature super-conductor about fifteen hundred years early. It'll go back to the IHA as soon as we're done.'

Nina nodded. 'And the second?'

'The second . . . is that I'll be going with you.'

'Oh, you will, eh?' Chase said, raising an eyebrow.

'I'll be DARPA's representative – but it'll still be an IHA operation,' Mitchell assured Nina, before snapping her a sharp salute. 'At your service, ma'am.'

'That was a proper salute,' Chase realised. 'You didn't mention you were in the forces.'

'Commander, United States Navy,' Mitchell said proudly. 'Before I transferred to DARPA.'

Nina was impressed; Chase rather less so. 'A matelot, huh?' he said.

'Nuclear submarines – USS *Jimmy Carter*.'

Chase made a face. 'You wouldn't get me on a nuclear sub. Not without a lead codpiece.'

'They're not that bad. Well, ours aren't – I don't know about the Russians'. But what we need to do now is figure out where to go next. Dr Wilde, I need you to tell me absolutely everything you can remember about what Rust told you.'

'Nina.'

'Excuse me?'

'If we're working together, I think it should be on a first-name basis. So call me Nina.'

Mitchell smiled again. 'That suits me fine, Nina.'

'Okay . . . Jack.' They smiled at each other.

Chase rolled his eyes. 'So where are we going?'

'I don't know,' said Nina, shaking her head. 'The only place Bernd actually gave me a name for was Koroneou, in the Greek islands . . . but he said the sword pieces *weren't* there.' She thought for a moment. 'But there must have been something there that led him to where he thought they were. And he said one of them was "close to home" – I think he lived in southern Germany, near Munich.'

'That doesn't exactly narrow it down,' Chase said wryly.

'It's better than nothing,' said Mitchell. 'I'll arrange us priority transport to Koroneou, then – it's the only lead we've got.'

Chase grinned. 'So, I guess Greece is the word.'

7

Greece

'Priority transport' turned out to be a brand-new US State Department Gulfstream G550 jet. Although the aircraft was fitted out to accommodate sixteen people in luxury that put even first class on most airliners to shame, Nina, Chase and Mitchell were the only passengers – which made Nina feel slightly guilty that the three of them were waited on by an equal number of cabin staff during the flight as she used the plane's satellite link to research Arthurian legend. From the way the crew hovered obsequiously, it was clear they were used to attending to considerably more demanding and self-important fliers, like politicians and bureaucrats.

But she soon forgot about the extravagant use of her taxes once they arrived at their destination. Surrounded by the glittering blue of the Aegean Sea, the small rocky island of Koroneou possessed a rugged beauty, greenery clinging to every surface able to support it.

The natural attractions of the island weren't what concerned her, however. She was far more interested in Koroneou's man-made delights – in particular, the one that greeted her when Mitchell drove their black SUV round a corner of the road along the island's southern coast to reveal a headland beyond. A village was strung out along the narrow tongue of land, white-painted buildings shining like beads under the sun, but it was the much larger building at its tip that commanded her attention.

Though its crenellated outer walls and some of the outlying structures had fallen into ruin, the castle of Peter of Koroneou was still intact, a block of pale stone flanked by a pair of taller cylindrical towers. Given the idyllic surroundings, Nina couldn't help thinking the place had a certain fairytale quality to it.

Mitchell had the same thought. 'Funny, we're trying to find the sword of King Arthur, and the first place we visit looks like Camelot.'

'Camelot?' said Nina with a smile. 'You know, I've heard . . .' She put on an English accent, 'that it's a very silly place.'

Mitchell grinned back at her. 'The kind of place you might find . . . a *shrubbery*!'

Chase buried his head in his hands. 'Oh, for fuck's sake. Bloody Monty Python quotes? It's like I'm trapped in a car with a bunch of students!'

'Jack, help me, I'm being oppressed!' Nina trilled. 'What's wrong with Monty Python? It's classic British comedy, I thought you'd love it!'

'It's all right, but not when everyone thinks they're being so bloody clever by reciting bits over and over again. And how come you're both so big on Monty Python anyway? You're Yanks!'

'Come on, Eddie,' she said. 'Python 101 is practically compulsory at American colleges. Well, among certain types of students, anyway.'

'You mean nerds?'

'I was *not* a nerd!' Nina protested. 'I was just . . . very focused on my studies.'

'Well, *I* sure as hell wasn't a nerd, and I watched it too,' said Mitchell. 'Matter of fact, *Monty Python and the Holy Grail* was the first movie I saw with the girl I ended up marrying.'

'Thank you, Jack.' Nina stuck out her tongue at Chase, prompting him to roll his eyes again.

Mitchell gave her an amused look before regarding the view ahead once more. 'You think this castle might be the one Rust mentioned?'

'I don't think so. It's owned by the Greek government, but Bernd implied that the one he was talking about was privately owned. Besides, this isn't exactly close to his home.'

'Good point.'

Mitchell had made arrangements in advance; after passing through the village, the SUV was met at the castle gates by a representative of the Greek Ministry of Culture, a tall, hook-nosed man in his fifties with skin that practically matched the island in its weather-beaten ruggedness. When his visitors emerged from their vehicle, he briefly greeted Mitchell before turning his attention with rather more enthusiasm to Nina. 'Dr Wilde! A great honour to meet you, a great honour!' He clasped her right hand in both of his and squeezed it forcefully.

'Thanks,' she replied, wondering if she would get her hand back before he cut off her circulation. 'Nice to meet you – and I'm glad you agreed to help us.'

'I would hardly turn down a chance to meet the discoverer of Atlantis! You have already done wonders for our tourist industry – anything to do with Plato or Hercules is now very popular!' He finally released her, then shook hands with Chase. 'Petros Georgiades. Good to meet you all.' He gestured in the direction of the castle. 'So, what would you like to know about Peter of Koroneou?'

Surprisingly little of the castle's interior was accessible to tourists, several sections being blocked off by scaffolding. 'Restoration work,' Georgiades explained as he led his visitors past a cordon and deeper into the building. 'Until about ten years ago, parts of the castle were in the same condition as the fortifications outside. The walls have mostly been repaired, but there are still unsafe areas. It is a slow process.'

Chase glanced up at the ceiling. 'It's not going to collapse on us, is it?'

'I hope not! But try not to bang your head on anything, eh?' He chuckled, then stopped at a low arched doorway. 'This is Peter's tomb. Please, go inside.'

Nina ducked through the entrance, finding herself inside a cool, musty chamber. A pair of lamps on metal stands provided illumination, the only natural light coming from three small stained-glass windows high on the south wall. At the centre of the room was what was unmistakably a stone coffin. 'Is his body still here?' she asked as the others entered.

Georgiades shook his head. 'The castle has been occupied and robbed many times.' He indicated the lid of the coffin; a jagged diagonal split showed where it had been smashed open in the past. 'Even though the people of the village sometimes managed to hide the most valuable relics, eventually almost everything was taken.'

Nina was about to ask another question, but Mitchell got in first. 'Was he buried with a sword?'

'Oh, yes – the sword presented to him by the Holy Roman Emperor.' Nina, Chase and Mitchell traded looks; at least part of Rust's research had apparently been accurate. Georgiades noticed the exchange. 'The sword is why you are here?'

'It's one of the reasons,' Mitchell said smoothly. 'Do you know what happened to it?'

'It is part of local legend. Look.' The Greek indicated the central window. Nina craned to get a better look at the mottled glass, making out the figure of a man in armour bearing a red Crusader cross on his chest, a sword raised in his right hand.

'Is that Peter?' she asked. Georgiades answered in the affirmative. She looked more closely. 'Is this an original window?'

'Yes – the one on the left was broken and has been restored, but the others are both thirteenth or fourteenth century, as far as we know.' Georgiades had a slight smile, as if waiting for her to spot something.

'The sword . . .' she said, frowning at the image, before glancing at the coffin. 'Is it okay if I climb up for a better look?'

'Peter is long gone. He will not mind.' Nina nodded, then carefully climbed on to the end of the coffin.

Closer up, the window revealed more, though the poor condition of the glass made resolving the finer details difficult. There seemed to be small symbols on the sword's blade, ornate circular patterns, but it was the weapon as a whole that had caused Nina's puzzlement – and attracted her interest. 'Why's his sword on fire?' she asked.

That was clearly why Georgiades had been smiling. '*That* is the legend!' he crowed as Nina used her digital camera to photograph the window. 'It was said that on dark nights here at the castle, when Peter held the sword a fire could be seen running through its blade. Supposedly, this was the source of his strength in battle – his sword was said never to go blunt.'

'Until it broke, anyway,' said Nina. Chase was about to help her down, but Mitchell moved in first. 'Thanks.'

Chase gave Mitchell a look of mild annoyance before turning his attention back to the window. 'So what happened to the sword after it broke? Was he buried with it here?'

'Only part of it,' explained Georgiades, moving to the coffin. 'Peter was buried here with the hilt. The tip was returned to Sicily in honour of Frederick.'

'What about the rest of it?' Chase asked, raising an eyebrow. 'You've got the hilt, you've got the tip . . . what about the blade?'

Mitchell looked back at the stained glass. 'Wait, so it broke into *three* pieces? Rust never told you that.'

'He *was* kind of interrupted,' Nina reminded him.

'The blade stayed in the Holy Land,' said Georgiades. 'In fact, Peter was killed with it. He had returned to the Holy Land to defend the territory under the control of his order from the Mamelukes.'

'In 1260,' said Nina, remembering what Rust had told her.

'Yes. After the Mamelukes drove back the Mongols invading Syria, they turned their attention to the lands occupied by the Christians. The region under Peter's control was small and quite isolated, along what is now the border of Syria and Jordan, so it was an easy target. Peter had no choice but to travel to the Holy Land to defend it. The story goes that he fought bravely against great odds until he faced the Muslim leader, a man called

Muhammad Yawar. When they fought, Peter had the upper hand – until Yawar struck a lucky blow that broke *both* their swords. Yawar took Peter's broken blade and used it to kill him, then kept it as a trophy.'

Nina couldn't help but feel a twinge of excitement; despite her misgivings, the long shot of their visit to Koroneou was already producing results, as well as vindicating Rust's research. 'Do you know where the blade is?'

'No,' said Georgiades, shaking his head. 'Somewhere in Jordan or Syria, perhaps. A historian there might know more about Yawar, but our knowledge here all comes from Peter's surviving men. Nobody is even sure exactly where the battle took place – as you know, the maps of the time are not very accurate.'

'I see.' Her excitement was quickly deflated . . . but they had still learned something, not least that there were *two* pieces of Caliburn they needed to find before the Russians. And if the picture within the stained-glass window were an accurate representation of Peter's sword, she would recognise the blade when she saw it.

If she saw it.

'So, what do you think?' Mitchell asked. They had thanked Georgiades for his help and left the castle, and were now sitting outside a small café in the village square to reflect upon what they'd learned. 'Convinced that Rust just might have been right yet?'

Nina grinned at the joking challenge. 'Okay, I admit

that what he told me about the trail the sword took seems to be panning out. So far. But it'll take a lot more to convince me that it had some sort of magical power.'

'It's only magic in the sense of Clarke's Law.'

She smiled again. 'So you're saying DARPA's developed technology that's indistinguishable from magic?'

'I'm not at liberty to discuss that,' said Mitchell, a hint of humour behind his poker face.

'What's Clarke's Law?' Chase asked distractedly, looking away from a monument across the square.

'"Any sufficiently advanced technology is indistinguishable from magic,"' Nina quoted. Chase gave her a blank look. 'Arthur C. Clarke? Famous author and scientist? Wrote *2001: A Space Odyssey*? Invented the communications satellite?'

'Oh, hang on, I know who you mean,' Chase said. 'He used to present this TV show when I was a kid, about crystal skulls and the paranormal and all that. He was always walking along a beach under a golf umbrella saying it was actually a load of bollocks.'

Nina sighed exaggeratedly and turned to Mitchell. 'I guess it's true what they say about Britain and America. Two nations separated by a common language. And weird TV shows.'

'But the Brits came up with Monty Python, so they can't be all bad,' Mitchell replied. This time it was Chase's turn to make a sarcastic noise. 'But getting back to why we're here, you saw the picture in the window. I'd say a flaming sword counts as something out of the ordinary. And it matches what you said Rust told you about Excalibur lighting on fire when Arthur held it.'

'But why would Peter be able to make it light up and not anyone else?' said Nina. 'You'd think Richard the Lionheart or the Holy Roman Emperor would be attributed with that kind of power, not some obscure knight.'

'Something to do with the lines of earth energy, maybe?' Mitchell wondered, almost to himself. 'Maybe there was one near here . . . But,' he continued, 'none of that matters if we can't find the thing. So, what have we got?'

'Well, the blade's somewhere in the Middle East, and . . . that's about it,' said Nina. 'I think we'll have to go there and speak to someone with local historical knowledge, like Petros suggested.'

'We shouldn't have any trouble getting what we need in Jordan,' said Mitchell. 'Syria might be more of a problem, though. They're not exactly our biggest fans.'

'But we'd be going as an IHA mission, not American,' Chase reminded him.

'I don't think it'll make much difference,' Nina replied ruefully. 'Syria and the UN have had disagreements recently – an archaeological team had its permission to enter the country revoked just a couple of weeks ago.'

'Let's hope the sword's in Jordan, then,' Chase said. 'But if it isn't, and knowing our luck it won't be, I can get us into Syria some other way.'

'You know people there, I suppose,' said Nina.

Chase looked smugly secretive. 'Might do.'

'Attractive women, I bet.'

Now he was just smug. 'Could be.'

'What, one beautiful woman isn't enough for you?' Mitchell asked, indicating Nina. 'Man, that's just greedy!' Before Chase could respond, he continued, 'So, if we can find the life story of this Muhammad Yawar there's a chance we can find one piece of the sword. But what about the other piece, the hilt? Once the Russians make sense of Rust's notes they'll have a clear run at it, while we've got nothing.'

'There must be *something*, though,' said Nina. 'Bernd said he'd spoken to whoever owns the place where he thought it was. Somewhere "close to home" – close to Munich, I suppose. So there has to be a link between Koroneou and Germany.' She realised that Chase had leaned back in his chair, grinning smugly once more. 'What?'

'*I* know what the link is,' he said.

'What is it?'

'First you've got to tell me how great I am.'

'Eddie!'

'Come on, would it kill you? At least say how fantastic I am in bed.'

'*Eddie!*' She swatted at his arm before giving Mitchell a sheepish look.

'Oh, all right,' Chase grumbled, standing and pointing across the square. 'See that monument?'

Nina saw a modest slab of dusty black stone inscribed

with Greek lettering, a Star of David at its top. 'Looks like a Jewish memorial.'

'Yeah, it is. Come on.' He crossed the square, Nina and Mitchell following. As she approached, Nina saw that the memorial bore a list of about a dozen names as well as a date: 1944. 'I might not have a degree in it, but I know some history too – military history, anyway.' They stopped before the black stone. 'The Greek islands were occupied by the Nazis in the war, and they treated the Jews there the same as they did anywhere else . . . by shipping them off to places like Auschwitz. But people weren't all they shipped – a lot of places, they nicked everything valuable they could get their hands on before the Allies kicked them out. There's your link.'

'You think the *Nazis* took the sword?' Mitchell asked.

'Why not? It fits with what Nina's friend told her.'

'It used to be part of Bernd's work as a historian,' Nina realised. 'Of course! He would already have the information he needed. The Nazis kept paperwork on everything. The German government'll still have those records – hell, they've probably been computerised by now! We just need to find anything concerning the castle –' she glanced in the direction of the fort beyond the village – 'and follow the trail from there, see what comes up around southern Germany.'

Mitchell looked thoughtful. 'We'll be able to get access to the German records via the State Department. We can use the satellite link on the plane.'

Nina regarded the memorial again, then looked at

121

Chase, impressed. 'Go on, you can say it,' he said, grinning broadly.

'Okay, I admit it – you're pretty great. Sometimes . . .'

The computer aboard the Gulfstream revealed the information Nina was after even more quickly than she had hoped. The German government database was clearly extremely efficient.

'Well, whaddya know?' she said, reading her discoveries off the screen to Chase and Mitchell. 'Peter's castle was actually used as the local SS headquarters during the war. That's why it needed rebuilding – the Allies and the local partisans shelled it during the assault on the island. But the SS commandant had already cleared out, and it seems he left with a lot more stuff than he arrived with. Maybe he took the sword with him as well.'

'Where did he go?' Mitchell asked.

'Austria. It looks like a lot of looted treasure from the Mediterranean and the Aegean went through there on its way back to Berlin. The commandant took over another SS regional headquarters. A place called Staumberg Castle.'

'A castle, eh?' said Chase. 'Just like your friend said.'

'Right. And get this – it's less than sixty miles from Munich. I'd call that "surprisingly close to home" from Bernd's perspective. Worth checking out?'

'Definitely,' said Mitchell. 'But where do we go first – there, or the Middle East?'

Nina rested her chin on her hands, thinking. 'We've got

nothing to go on in the Holy Land apart from the name of the man who killed Peter of Koroneou. The longer we leave it before we go there, the more time it'll take us to find anything out – and the Russians might already have got the location from Bernd's notes.'

'So we go to Jordan first,' Mitchell decided. 'I'll make the arrangements.'

'What about the castle?' asked Chase. 'What if the Russians go *there* first?'

'They won't know what to look for,' realised Nina. 'Bernd said the owner refused to let him search the place.'

'Yeah, but even if they don't know, *we* don't know where to look either.' Chase looked thoughtful. 'Unless we get somebody to do some research while we're in Jordan.'

'Let me guess,' said Nina. 'You know an attractive woman in Austria who can help us.'

'Actually, no.'

'Really? I'm surprised.'

He grinned. 'But I know one in Switzerland.'

Nina sighed. 'I'm *not* surprised.'

Mitchell regarded him dubiously. 'This whole operation's classified, remember. I'd prefer not to get anyone else involved if I can avoid it – especially not civilians.'

'Don't worry, you can trust her. Besides, we don't have to tell her anything about this earth energy business.'

'But you'll need to warn her about the Russians,' Nina said. 'What if they turn up while she's there?'

'Don't worry!' Chase repeated. 'All she needs to do is check the place out and see if she can persuade the owner to see us, then wait for us to get back from Jordan. There's no way I'm going to ask her to do anything dangerous.' He frowned slightly. 'Although knowing Mitzi, she'll probably want to do it anyway.'

8

Switzerland

After the State Department jet landed at Zürich airport the following morning, rather than heading for the city itself Mitchell drove another waiting SUV up into the surrounding mountains, guided by its satellite navigation system to where Chase's friend Mitzi Fontana had agreed to meet them. Surprisingly, it turned out to be nothing but a steep alpine pasture ... which was playing host to a very unusual sporting event.

'What the hell are they doing?' Nina asked, regarding the scene in amazement – and not a little worry for the health of the participants.

Chase let out a disbelieving chuckle. 'I told you she'd want to do something dangerous. But bloody hell, this is something new.'

Stretched across the bottom of the pasture was a high

net, a white paper tape running between two poles a few metres in front of it. Beyond that, a rough path of flattened grass wound about a hundred metres up the bumpy hill to a relatively level area where the competitors were waiting. It was a racecourse, but those taking part were neither on foot nor in any kind of vehicle. Instead, they were strapped inside giant inflatable spheres resembling transparent golf balls.

Chase couldn't see Mitzi among the spectators, so wasn't the least bit surprised when he saw that one of the first two contestants had long blond hair. 'Oh, Christ,' he moaned as a man yelled out a countdown from three in German.

'She's in a ball?' Nina asked nervously.

'She's in a ball.'

'*Go!*' the man shouted. The plastic bubbles began to roll down the hill, picking up speed with alarming rapidity. As far as Chase could tell the occupants had absolutely no control – they were just along for the ride, whirling around like clothes in a tumble dryer as the balls bounced off bumps, boulders and even each other.

It was over in about fifteen seconds, Mitzi's sphere breaking the paper tape just ahead of the other ball and careering onwards into the net, rolling up into the air before dropping back to earth and coming to a stop. People hurried over to hold the spheres steady as the occupants unstrapped themselves and slithered out. The defeated racer, a scrawny young man with a goatee beard, immediately slumped to the grass, while Mitzi managed to stand, if rather unsteadily. She spotted Chase and the others standing nearby and waved excitedly, only to wobble and almost fall backwards before someone supported her.

'I'll give your friend this,' said Mitchell, 'she makes one hell of an entrance.'

They walked over to her. Nina realised that the curvaceous and pretty blonde was somewhat younger than any of Chase's other international 'girlfriends', only in her early twenties. 'Eddie!' Mitzi cried, beaming broadly as they approached and hurrying, still a little off balance, to embrace him.

'Hi, Mitzi!' Chase replied enthusiastically. 'Steady on,' he added as she kissed him full on the lips. 'Don't want to make my fiancée jealous.'

Still hugging Chase, Mitzi looked round at Nina. 'Hello. You're engaged to Eddie? Congratulations! And congratulations on discovering Atlantis, too. I read the article about you in *Time*.' She released Chase, then regarded him questioningly. 'You were hardly even mentioned! What happened?'

'Ah, I'm not bothered – fame's not really my thing,' said Chase with a dismissive shrug. 'Now *fortune*, I wouldn't mind that!' Mitzi giggled.

Introductions were made, then Chase glanced at the inflatable spheres, which were being lifted on to large hoop-shaped trolleys to be winched back up the hill. 'So what's all this?'

'It's called Zorbing,' Mitzi told him. 'It's a lot of fun.'

Chase grunted. 'Looks like a load of balls to me.'

Mitzi giggled again. 'So what brings you to Switzerland? You know I'll always do anything to help you. Even though you're now off the market.' She smiled at Nina. 'You're very lucky.'

'Yeah, sometimes I think so,' said Nina, noting with amusement that Chase actually seemed faintly embarrassed by the younger woman's attention. 'How do you two know each other? Did you work together?'

'No, nothing like that,' Mitzi answered. She squeezed Chase's arm. 'Eddie rescued me. And my mother, too, about four years ago.'

'Just doing my job,' Chase said modestly.

'It was much more than that. You changed my life – I mean, as well as saving it! I used to be rather quiet,' she said to Nina, 'a stay-at-home sort of girl. Kind of a geek.'

Mitchell nudged Nina. 'Nothing wrong with that, huh?' She smiled.

'But after meeting Eddie,' Mitzi continued, 'I realised that life is there to be *lived*, that there was so much out there to experience. I wanted to do *everything* – just like him.'

'I haven't done *everything*,' said Chase. He looked up the slope, where the spheres were being unloaded from the trolleys. 'I've never rolled down a hill inside a big plastic ball, for a start.'

'Maybe you should,' Nina suggested mischievously.

Mitzi's face lit up. 'Yes, you should! Come on, you can race me.' She grabbed his hand and tried to pull him up the pasture.

Chase stayed put. 'Don't be daft!'

'It won't take long. I'm friends with the organisers, I can get you in the next race.' She tugged at his arm again, more insistently. Chase looked helplessly at Nina, who grinned and gave him a go-on nod. With a sigh, Chase acquiesced and allowed Mitzi to lead him up the slope.

'So how long have you and Nina been engaged?' she asked.

'About a year. Not long after I last saw you, actually.'

She let out a comically exaggerated sigh. 'So I missed my chance.'

'Nah, you deserve better than an ugly old sod like me.'

'I don't know. All the men I meet who are my own age? They're such . . . *boys!*'

Chase laughed. 'I still owe you the money for that parachute, by the way.'

'Don't worry,' Mitzi insisted. 'Although Mama was not very happy when I told her about it.' She huffed, the universal sound of exasperation with parents. 'You should come and see her while you're here. I know she'd love to see you again.'

'Well, we're in a bit of a rush, but . . . yeah, we can pop in.'

'Where are you going next?'

'Jordan.'

'Jordan!' Mitzi said excitedly. 'I'm going there later in the year, to see the ruins at Petra. Why are you going?'

'Can't say much, I'm afraid – top secret. But you'll be

doing us a huge favour if you can help us out with something in Austria.'

'Top secret? It all sounds very mysterious. Is it something like finding Atlantis?'

'Something like that. I'll tell you all about it after we're done.'

She smiled. 'I can't wait.'

They reached the level area of pasture where the spheres were waiting. Mitzi spoke in German to one of the organisers, who agreed to let her and Chase go next, then used her smile – and low-cut top – to disarm the two young men whose places they had usurped. That done, they began their preparations.

'A neck brace?' said Chase as he was handed a stiff padded black collar with Velcro fastenings. 'Most sports don't need these until *after* you've fucked yourself up. You sure this is safe?'

'Of course!' Mitzi said as she fastened her own collar. 'Don't tell me you're nervous.'

'I've just got a thing about modes of transport with nobody in control. I've been in 'em a couple of times, and it usually ends with an explosion.'

Mitzi grinned, then clambered into her sphere. Grimacing, Chase entered his own, squeezing through a narrow tube into a second, smaller sphere within held in place by hundreds of taut nylon cords attached to the outer skin. Lying against the inner wall, he fastened a harness round his chest, then gripped a pair of straps above his head. Spread-eagled, he looked across at

Mitzi, who smiled back at him. 'Ready?' she called.

'Nope.'

'*Er ist bereit!*' she said to the organiser, who immediately began the countdown.

Chase scowled at her. 'Buggeration and *fuckaagh*!' he yelled as his sphere was shoved over the edge of the slope.

The world suddenly became nothing more than a dizzying whirl of sky and grass and sky flashing through his vision, faster and faster. Plastic creaked and nylon twanged as he hit a bump, then for a moment he was airborne before the sphere bounced back down to earth and continued its descent, now barrelling him along on his side rather than head over heels. Another noise, a squeal of plastic on plastic as he collided with the pale blur of Mitzi's sphere, then suddenly he felt himself rising sharply into the air, only to roll back down the net at the bottom of the field. The sphere was grabbed and pulled to a standstill, but to Chase the spinning sensation showed little sign of stopping. He blearily unfastened his harness and slithered out through the tube, seeing Nina and Mitchell seeming to zigzag towards him as the world spun.

'You lost,' said Mitchell. 'Tough luck.'

'How was the ride?' Nina asked.

Chase just about managed to stand upright, the ground still swaying under his feet. 'Jesus, I've done parachute drops in thunderstorms that were smoother than that.'

'Maybe you're getting old,' Mitchell suggested. Chase glared at him.

A beaming Mitzi reeled over to Chase and supported

herself on his arm. 'Woo! Didn't I tell you it would be fun?'

Chase made a non-committal noise. 'You know, if you want a *real* adrenalin rush, you should join the army. None of this extreme sports bollocks.'

'You're just saying that because I won,' she said, pouting. 'Besides, people might shoot at me!'

'You don't have to be in the army for that to happen,' Nina told her ruefully.

'So will you help us?' Mitchell asked.

'Of course! Just tell me what you want me to do,' Mitzi said. 'We can talk about it at my parents' apartment.'

An impatient look crossed Mitchell's face. 'We need to get moving.'

'It's okay,' said Chase. 'It's more or less on the way back to the airport anyway.' He rubbed his head again and groaned. 'And I could do with a nice long sit-down . . .'

Zürich gleamed in the morning sun, the crisp light shimmering off the lake to the south of the city. A line of clean white snow capped the surrounding peaks in postcard-perfect fashion, evergreen forests sweeping down to the red-roofed urban fringes. The view was quite beautiful, Nina thought – and all the more impressive because she was seeing it from the heart of the city itself.

The penthouse's rooftop terrace was larger than Nina and Chase's entire New York apartment. Considering where they were, she guessed its owner was extremely high up in the financial world – which turned out to be the case.

'I'm sorry my husband couldn't be here,' said Brigitte Fontana, handing her a cup of steaming *café crème*. She was practically a more toned and tanned version of her daughter, though her clothing was decidedly less revealing. 'He's in China at a financial conference, in Shanghai.'

'Shanghai?' said Chase. 'I was there last year.'

'On business or pleasure?'

'Business.'

'Ah.' Brigitte gave him a knowing look. 'It went well, I hope?'

Chase made a pained face. 'It was . . . mixed.'

'So when's the wedding day, Eddie?' asked Mitzi, handing two more cups to Chase and Mitchell. 'I hope we're all invited.'

'Course you are! We just haven't settled on a date yet.' Chase squeezed Nina's hand. 'It's been kind of a busy year.'

'But it obviously worked out well for both of you,' said Brigitte. 'Congratulations!'

'Thank you. So,' Nina asked, 'how did you meet Eddie? Mitzi said he rescued you?'

'That's right. He—'

'We were kidnapped!' interrupted Mitzi with surprising enthusiasm.

'Mitzi,' Brigitte warned, pained by the memory.

Her daughter ignored her. 'A gang took us hostage to

133

force Papa to give them access to his bank's computers. But he hired Eddie and his friend Hugo to rescue us instead. And they did.' She gazed admiringly at Chase as she sat.

'What happened to the kidnappers?' asked Mitchell.

'Oh, Eddie kil—'

'They didn't hurt anyone again,' said Brigitte quickly. 'But Eddie and Hugo saved our lives.' She looked across at Chase. 'I was so sorry to hear what happened to Hugo. I didn't even know he had died until I read about the discovery of Atlantis.'

'Thanks,' said Chase uncomfortably. The official story concocted by the IHA had his partner Hugo Castille dying in a diving accident at Atlantis; while that was technically true, it omitted the very much premeditated chain of events leading to it.

'Poor Hugo,' added Mitzi sadly. 'He was so nice.'

Brigitte nodded, then sipped her drink. 'So Eddie, Mitzi said you have a favour to ask; you know we will always be happy to give you anything you need.'

'It's not so much a thing as a person,' Chase answered. 'I'd like to borrow Mitzi for a while. Don't worry, I'll bring her back in good nick.'

Mitzi giggled, but Brigitte's mouth tightened into a hard line. 'Oh. Actually, that's something I'm *not* happy about. Not after what happened last year.'

'Last year?' Nina asked Chase. During their search for the Tomb of Hercules he had gone to Switzerland to find his ex-wife, but Sophia's involvement had made it a part of the adventure about which she had not enquired too deeply.

'I asked Mitzi to help me with some stuff,' he explained. 'She got me some gear, and gave me a lift.'

'She got you guns and explosives, and then you jumped off a bridge from the roof of her car at a hundred kilometres an hour!' Brigitte snapped.

'I had a parachute . . .'

She regarded him disapprovingly. 'Ever since you rescued us – and I *am* grateful for that, and always will be – Mitzi has turned into an adrenalin junkie. Skydiving, or waterskiing, or – or bungee-jumping, even. She can't enjoy herself without risking her life!'

'Oh, Mama!' cried Mitzi, exasperated. 'I'm a grown woman, I can take care of myself. I'm just having fun!'

'Don't worry, she won't be doing any of that,' Chase assured Brigitte. 'Not unless it's the world's most extreme library.'

'Library?' asked Mitzi, crestfallen.

'Yeah. We need someone to do some research for us, about some castle in Austria.'

'Oh.' She sounded hugely disappointed. 'Well, of course I'll help you, but . . . are you sure that's all you want me to do? You don't need me to help you climb a mountain or anything?'

'Nah, just check out this castle and persuade the bloke who owns it to talk to us. Are you up for that?' He looked at Brigitte, who still didn't seem happy. 'And you?'

Brigitte sighed. 'As she says, she's a grown woman.'

'Because if it bothers you, we can do it ourselves,' Chase offered. 'I mean, I wouldn't want to make you mad at me or anything.'

She managed a faint smile. 'After everything you've done for us, I think that would be hard.'

'Of course I'll do it, Eddie,' Mitzi insisted. 'It might not be as exciting as the last time I helped you, but who knows? Maybe I'll discover something that surprises you.'

Chase smiled at her. 'Knowing you, you'll have found what we're looking for before we even get back. And don't you worry, Brigitte. She'll be fine, I promise.'

Mitchell opened his case and handed a sheaf of papers to Mitzi. 'These are what we have on the castle and its owner, and what we'd like you to find out for us, if you can.'

'I'll have everything you need by the time you get back,' she told him confidently.

'Great stuff,' said Chase. He finished his drink and put down the cup. 'Well, sorry to have to rush off, but we're kind of working against the clock.'

'Exactly what *are* you looking for?' Brigitte asked.

'I'm afraid we can't tell you at the moment,' said Mitchell, 'but it's very important to the IHA and the United Nations.'

'We really appreciate you helping us out,' Nina added. 'Thank you. Both of you.'

Brigitte nodded. 'I wish you a safe journey, then. And I hope you find whatever it is.'

'Good luck!' Mitzi chimed.

Chase stood and kissed her cheek, then did the same to Brigitte. 'We'll be back in a couple of days, no problem. See you then.' He waited as Nina and Mitchell shook hands with the two women, then swept an arm theatrically towards the horizon beyond the lake. 'Okay. Jordan, here we come!'

9

Jordan

Where Zürich had been clean, neat and above all orderly, the Jordanian capital of Amman was by contrast a living monument to organised chaos. One of the oldest continuously inhabited cities in the world, each new stage of civilisation had been built around – or sometimes on top of – that which went before, resulting in a gloriously jumbled mix of ancient and modern, centuries-old structures separated from brand new apartment blocks by no more than the span of a man's arms. The metropolis rippled under the baking sun of the Arabian peninsula, tinted a soft orange by sunlight, sand and smog.

Nina would have loved to explore the city, but she had work to do. Mitchell had arranged for her to meet the curator of the University of Jordan's Center for

Documents and Manuscripts, the bureaucratic name only hinting at its true purpose: to act as a vast archive, cataloguing the history of a large part of the Middle East. She wanted to delve into the wealth of ancient texts even more than the city, but for now she forced herself to concentrate on one very specific slice of the past.

'Muhammad Yawar,' said their host thoughtfully. Adeeb al-Jafri was a middle-aged man with oversized glasses and a neat black moustache; although he was Jordanian, his clipped accent was still very much that of the English university where he had studied. 'Yes, I remember the name.'

'You remember him?' Nina asked. 'Why, has someone else been asking about him?'

'Yes, about six months ago, by phone. I think he was German. He asked if we had any material in the archives concerning him, and we told him that we did, but matters never progressed any further than that.'

'It must have been Bernd,' Nina said, with a look at Chase and Mitchell. 'But nobody else?' Al-Jafri shook his head.

'At least they haven't figured out his notes yet,' said Mitchell.

Al-Jafri's eyebrows rose quizzically over the thick frames of his glasses. '*They?*'

'The man who contacted you was murdered,' Nina told him. 'To stop him from telling the IHA how to find what he was searching for.'

'Really?' He sounded more intrigued than shocked, as

139

if hearing about a plot twist in a detective novel. 'And for what was he searching?'

'That's classified, I'm afraid,' Mitchell said. 'But it's for safety reasons, trust me. The people who killed him won't hesitate to kill again.'

Curiosity was replaced by concern on al-Jafri's face. 'Ah. I see.'

'That's why we need to find what he was looking for first, so nobody else gets hurt,' said Nina. 'And to do that, we need to find out everything we can about Muhammad Yawar.'

'He's not really a terribly important figure, historically speaking. Are you sure he is the right person?'

'He's all we've got to go on,' she admitted. 'He supposedly killed a Crusader called Peter of Koroneou in AD1260 – what we want to know is where that happened.'

'Peter of Koroneou . . .' said al-Jafri, brow knitting as he consulted his memory. 'Ah, yes. He occupied an area of land close to what is now the Jordanian-Syrian border.'

'Which side of the border?' Chase asked.

'The Syrian side.'

'I bloody *knew* it!'

'Will your archives have the exact location?' asked Nina.

'Perhaps,' said al-Jafri, 'but as I said, Muhammad Yawar is a very minor figure – I doubt he rated much more than a footnote.'

'Anything that you have will help us enormously,' she assured him.

Al-Jafri nodded. 'In that case, if you'll follow me to the archives, I'll show you what I can.'

'Tell you what,' said Chase to Nina, 'while you're doing your reading, I'll go and sort out everything we need.'

'The US embassy can take care of all that,' Mitchell told him.

Chase was unimpressed. 'They've got a local guide who can get us across the border, have they?' He turned back to Nina. 'Give me a call when you're done. I'll come and meet you.' To Nina's surprise, he pulled her close and gave her a rather more intense kiss than she'd expected before releasing her. 'See you later.'

'Uh, bye,' she said as he left, taken aback. Al-Jafri looked bemused, while Mitchell veiled a smile. She felt her cheeks flush as she turned back to the curator. 'Okay, well, so . . .'

'The archives?'

'Please!'

'Here we are,' said al-Jafri. Wearing a pair of white cotton gloves to protect the ancient pages, he pointed at a particular piece of Arabic text within the book he had taken from one of the Center's climate-controlled underground vaults. Although the tome itself dated from the fifteenth century, it described events from two centuries earlier, collated from other accounts of the many wars that raged across the Holy Land during that period. 'This is the first mention of Muhammad Yawar.'

Nina's knowledge of Arabic was limited. 'What does it say?'

'Not much,' said Mitchell, peering over her shoulder.

'You know Arabic?'

'Enough to get by.' He grinned. 'But Dr al-Jafri's right – Yawar wasn't important enough to rate more than a few lines.'

'Those few lines may have what you're looking for, though,' said al-Jafri, carefully running the tip of his finger across the time-browned page. 'It says, "The barbarian leader himself came forth to challenge Muhammad, his sword shining bright. But like the Prophet whose name he bore, Muhammad was brave and righteous and a true servant of Allah, and with a blow broke his sword into pieces. With the longest of these, he slew the infidel. Their leader dead, the other invaders retreated in fear."'

'Barbarians?' said Mitchell, puzzled. 'Is this the wrong battle? Sounds like they're talking about the Mongols.'

Al-Jafri suppressed a mocking chuckle. 'No, it's the right one,' Nina explained. 'The Muslim perspective on the Crusades is ... well, kinda different from the Christian one. They saw the Christians as brutal invaders, there to murder the followers of Islam and plunder their lands.'

'*Plus ça change* ...' al-Jafri said quietly. Mitchell shot him a cutting look. 'But there is one more line about Yawar here. "Muhammad returned home to Kafashta and gave the blade to the imam of the town, to show that the servants of Allah will always be triumphant.'''

'Kafashta?' asked Nina.

'It's a small town in southern Syria. Well, it was considered a town in Yawar's time – it probably barely qualifies as a village now. I can find it on a map for you, if you'd like.'

'That's okay, thanks,' Mitchell told him, straightening. 'That's what we needed to know. We've got to go to Kafashta.'

'In Syria,' Nina reminded him. 'What was it you said? Something about them not exactly being big fans of Americans . . .'

Chase met Nina and Mitchell outside the US embassy a couple of hours later, accompanied by his local contact, a Jordanian woman named Karima Farran. As Nina had come to expect, she was extremely attractive, her long dark hair wafting in the breeze.

Karima's Land Rover looked almost as ancient as Amman itself, the military green paint so sand-scoured that it looked like patches of mould on the bare aluminium. After greeting the new arrivals and helping them load the gear Mitchell had requisitioned into the rear of the 4x4, she tied her hair back and wrapped it in a dark headscarf before handing another one to Nina. 'You'll need this.'

Nina took it reluctantly. 'I, er . . . I thought hijabs weren't compulsory for women in Jordan?'

'They're not,' Karima replied, sharing a look of amusement with Chase. 'I just don't like getting sand in my hair.' She gestured at the Land Rover's decidedly tattered canvas roof. Nina got her point and quickly followed suit.

They headed northeast along a highway, quickly leaving the city behind and entering a parched landscape of pale sand and rocks. 'So, Eddie,' said Karima to Chase, who was beside her in the front passenger seat, 'when is the wedding?'

Chase half laughed. 'You know, so many people keep asking us that, I think we might actually have to come up with an answer sometime.'

'Are you married, Karima?' Nina asked. The Arab woman was wearing several ornate rings, but Nina wasn't sure whether they had any significance or were simply jewellery.

'No, I'm not,' she replied, glancing back, 'but there is someone. The problem is getting him to make a commitment.'

'I know that feeling,' said Nina. Chase snorted.

They drove for over two hours, Nina using the time to continue the crash course in Arthurian mythology she had begun during the flights. Karima eventually turned off the highway and guided them along a succession of increasingly bumpy back roads. Finally, they bounced to a stop in a village so tiny Nina suspected the handful of tumbledown houses wouldn't even rate a dot on a map. Around it, the desert stretched off forebodingly in all directions. The sun was a bloated red ball shimmering above the western horizon.

'This is as far as we drive,' said Karima, climbing out. The others followed, stretching and working the kinks out of their rattled spines. 'The border is about eight kilometres north of here.'

Nina stared into the distance, seeing nothing but rocks and the occasional scrubby bush poking above the sand. 'We're walking?'

'No, no! But the Syrians watch out for vehicles that cross the border away from the official checkpoints. So we need another kind of transport.' She led them round one of the buildings.

'What kind of transport . . .' Nina began to ask, tailing off as she saw the answer. 'Oh.'

Waiting for them were four camels.

An Arab man in dusty robes stood with them, beaming when he saw Karima. They exchanged greetings, then she turned back to the group. 'This is Attayak – he's from one of the local Bedouin tribes.' Nina noticed that in addition to a gun and a knife, he had a walkie-talkie and a GPS handset on his belt: clearly the Bedouin had no problem with incorporating modern technology into their traditional lifestyle. 'There aren't many nomad tribes left, but the ones that are cross the border all the time – they have lived here for thousands of years, and don't care about lines on a map. Most of the time, the Syrians ignore them. Which is very useful if you want to enter the country undetected. As Eddie knows.'

Chase looked innocent. 'Can't comment on military operations I may or may not have carried out in a hostile sovereign state . . . but, yeah, I do know how to ride a camel.'

Mitchell nodded. 'Funnily enough, so do I.'

'Er, hello, hi,' Nina said. 'I *don't*.'

'It's a doddle,' Chase assured her. 'Just as easy as riding a horse.'

'Which I don't know how to do either!'

Chase went to the nearest kneeling camel and stroked its forehead. It eyed him, then shook its head lazily and made a noise somewhere between a grunt and a yawn. 'Good lad,' said Chase, moving back and swinging a leg over the broad padded saddle behind the camel's single hump. He gathered up the leather reins, then gently tugged on them, calling, 'Heya, heya!' The camel shook its head again, then obediently unfolded its legs and rose to its full height.

Nina had seen camels in zoos, but only now fully realised just how large they were. Standing, the animal was considerably taller than her, and Chase's head was at least eleven feet off the ground. 'Okay, that's . . . that's quite big.'

Under Chase's guidance, the camel trotted towards her, bowing its head for a closer look. She leaned back nervously. 'Does Attayak speak English?' she asked Karima, who replied in the negative. 'Oh, good. Because this really, really *smells*. It smells *bad*.'

'Oh, you'll hardly notice it after a few hours,' Chase

said cheerfully. He backed the camel away, then with another command and flick of the reins prompted it to kneel so he could dismount. He and Mitchell retrieved the group's belongings from the back of the Land Rover and loaded them into the animals' saddlebags.

'Here,' said Mitchell, handing Chase a pistol. 'Thought you'd find this useful.'

Chase nodded approvingly. 'Ruger P95,' he said, quickly and expertly checking the weapon before loading it. Mitchell did the same with his own Ruger. 'Not bad. I still miss my Wildey, though.'

'You had a Wildey?'

'Yeah, a .45 Winchester Magnum. Until some bastard used it to assassinate a government minister and put the blame on me. It's probably still in an evidence locker in Botswana somewhere. Good gun. You ever used one?'

'God, no,' said Mitchell, shaking his head vehemently. 'Bulky, heavy, limited ammo capacity, insane amounts of recoil? I'll stick with something that's actually practical. And you know,' he went on, a teasing glint in his eye, 'I'm sure you could draw some psychological inference from a man using a gun with an eight-inch-long barrel.'

'Well, I wouldn't expect a navy man to know anything about proper guns,' Chase replied with a scowl. 'The recoil's no problem if you're not limp-wristed . . .'

'Now, now, boys,' said Nina, stepping between them. 'Enough with the inter-service rivalry.'

'Yeah, I suppose,' Chase said grudgingly. He looked at

Mitchell. 'At least you weren't in the air force!' Both men laughed at that.

'We should get moving,' said Karima, tipping her head towards the setting sun. 'We'll cross the border before nightfall, and then we'll set up camp.'

The camels loaded, Karima said her farewells to Attayak before mounting one. Nina regarded her own slobbering beast with trepidation. Though the smallest of the four, it was still almost eye to eye with her even while kneeling. 'Y'know, maybe I'll just jog alongside it.'

'Ah, get on there,' said Chase. 'You'll be fine. All you've got to do is not fall off.'

'Don't worry, Nina,' Mitchell assured her. 'Camels really are very easy to ride. You'll get the hang of it in fifteen minutes.'

'And how many times will I fall off in those fifteen minutes?' she asked.

'You won't fall off. Here, let me help you get on.'

He held out a hand, but Chase hurriedly interposed himself. 'Nah, I've got her. Just get your leg over.' He cackled at the double entendre. Nina tsked and warily hoisted herself over the saddle, gripping it tightly as the animal shifted position beneath her. 'You sorted?'

'If I say no, can I get off?' The saddle was actually more padded than Nina had expected, but its width forced her legs uncomfortably wide. Chase gave her the reins; she took them in one hand while keeping the other firmly clenched round the raised front of the saddle. 'So what do I do now – *aaah!*' she cried as Chase barked a command

and slapped the camel's rump, and she found herself being pitched back and forth as it clambered to its feet. 'Whoa, I'm slipping!'

'Squeeze your legs tighter,' Mitchell suggested.

'I can't, they're open so wide it feels like I'm being split in half – and don't you even *think* about coming out with some horrible innuendo!' she warned Chase.

'Would I?' said Chase, clapping a hand to his chest in feigned offence as he walked back to his own waiting camel. 'She says that every night,' he added in a stage whisper as he hopped on to the saddle.

'Eddie, I am *so* going to kill you!'

'You'll have to catch me first! Heya!' He tugged the reins, and his camel set off at a trot. Nina's animal followed suit, bouncing her on the saddle with every step.

'*Eddie-ee-ee-ee-ee!*'

The last faint red glow on the western skyline had faded, the diamond shimmering of starlight taking its place overhead. The four camels were kneeling again, lined up near the small campfire opposite a pair of collapsible tents, grunting and mumbling to each other in contented camelese as Karima fed them.

Mitchell, sitting beside Nina at the fire, glanced over at Karima. 'So, Eddie, just how many women do you have stashed away around the world ready to help you out? First Mitzi, now Karima . . .'

Chase, on Nina's other side, shrugged. 'A few.'

'More than a few,' said Nina. She began counting on

her fingers. 'Let's see, there's Shala, Maria, TD, Mitzi, Karima . . . and those are just the ones I've met!'

Chase shrugged again, smirking. 'What can I say? Women can't resist me.' He put an arm round Nina's shoulders and pulled her to him. 'And that's *before* they experience the thrill of the Chase. If you know what I mean.' He leered at her.

'*Everyone* knows what you mean, Eddie,' Nina chided, pushing him away. 'All the time.'

'Tchah!'

'Yeah, subtlety and the army never really mix, whatever country you're from. No offence,' Mitchell added with a grin as Chase glowered at him. He turned to Nina. 'So what about you? You got dozens of hunks all over the world waiting for your call?'

She shook her head. 'Afraid not.'

'Good,' Mitchell said quietly, smiling again. 'But you're not jealous of Eddie's ladyfriends, I take it.'

'No, I'm used to it by now. I know that Eddie's got a past – even if he never tells me about any of it,' she said pointedly. Chase grunted. 'But after everything we've been through, I know I can trust him.'

'You've been through quite a lot, from what I've heard. Saving New York, finding the Tomb of Hercules, discovering Atlantis . . .'

'I know! I'm sometimes amazed we're both still alive. But it's how we met.'

'Ah,' said Mitchell, nodding knowingly.

Chase regarded him suspiciously. '"Ah"? "Ah" what?'

'Just that, well, considering how different you are, I wondered how you'd got together. But I guess that sharing a really intense experience is one way to break the ice, huh?'

'You could say that,' Nina answered. 'Although your approach of bonding over a Monty Python movie was definitely more like how I'd *expected* to meet someone. You said you met your wife at college?'

'Ex-wife.' Mitchell indicated his empty ring finger.

'Oh, I'm sorry.'

'It's okay.' He looked away, at the crackling fire. 'It was one of those two-careers-on-different-paths things – it happens. And we didn't have a huge amount in common. You and Eddie aren't the only ones with very different backgrounds. So . . .' A shrug. 'There weren't really any bad feelings, it just didn't work out. We've both moved on.'

'Still, I'm sorry,' Nina said again. She turned to Chase, to see that he was already looking at her. 'What?'

'Nothing,' he said after a moment.

'Things turned out okay in the end,' Mitchell said, noting the exchange but not remarking on it. 'She went into law, and I got my doctorate.'

'You're a PhD?' Nina asked, surprised and impressed. 'What field?'

'High-energy physics. Thought I might as well put my experience on a nuke boat to good use. And it eventually brought me into DARPA's earth energy experiments.'

Nina was still highly dubious about the entire concept,

but decided not to voice her doubts again. 'I gotta admit, *Doctor* Mitchell,' she said instead, 'you're a lot more dashing than the average physicist.'

Mitchell beamed, a megawatt movie-star smile. 'Dashing, huh? I like that. And I have to say, *Doctor* Wilde, you're definitely in my top three favourite archaeologists.'

'And who are the other two?'

'Indiana Jones and Lara Croft, of course!'

'And am I above or below Lara?'

He smiled again. 'Definitely above.'

'A-*hem*!' Chase fake-coughed loudly enough to attract even the attention of the camels. 'So, Jack, get us the map, will you? I want to check where we're going tomorrow.' With a playful look at Nina, Mitchell stood and went to one of the tents. The moment he was out of earshot, Chase poked Nina in the side. 'Oi!'

'What?'

'Pack that in!'

'Pack what in?'

'Bloody flirting!'

Nina couldn't really deny it. Instead, she grinned. 'What's the matter, Eddie? Jealous?'

Chase didn't return the smile. 'What, of *him*? Don't be daft. It's just that he's a bit of a pretty boy.'

'Oh, you think so too? I'll tell him you said that.'

'No you bloody won't!'

Mitchell returned with the map. 'We're about here,' he said, indicating a point on the southern Syrian border. 'Kafashta is . . . here.'

Chase looked more closely. 'Maybe eighteen or nineteen miles north. If we set off at dawn, it should only take us about three hours to get there.' He studied the map for a little longer, then sat up. 'In that case, we should grab a bite and then get some kip.' He faced Nina, eyeing her suggestively. 'See if you can do anything new now that camel's stretched your legs.'

Nina wasn't impressed. 'Aren't you forgetting something?'

'Like what?'

'There are only two tents.'

'Two tents, four people, two to a tent. Seems fine to me.' The others regarded him silently, waiting for the penny to drop. 'What?'

'Two men, two women, only *one* couple,' Nina reminded him. 'I'll be sharing with Karima.'

'Wait, you mean I've got to share with *'im*?' cried Chase, pointing at Mitchell.

'I'm also thrilled,' Mitchell sighed.

'Buggeration and fuckery!' Chase paused, realising what he'd just said. 'And no, that's *not* a suggestion!'

10

Syria

Though the desert landscape was indistinguishable from that of Jordan, it somehow seemed indefinably more hostile, menacing, now they had crossed into Syria. Nina surveyed the horizons as best she could from her rocking mount as the group headed northwards, fearing the appearance of a patrol.

But nobody approached over the stony dunes. They were truly in the wastelands, the nearest town of any size many miles away. The camels padded on through the sands for an hour, two, nothing breaking the monotony of their surroundings, until . . .

'That's it,' Mitchell announced, pointing at the unassuming blocky structures rising from the shimmering haze ahead. 'Kafashta.'

'Doesn't look like much,' Nina observed. If not for the

presence of a mosque, easily identifiable by its single minaret standing tall above everything around it, she could easily have imagined it as something from a Western, missing only a nameless gunslinger in a poncho.

'So what's the plan?' said Chase. The village was barely more than a couple of streets intersecting at a square, run-down houses hunched around it. The mosque was by far the largest and best-maintained building, but even it was fighting a losing battle against time and weather, sporting a rickety platform of scaffolding round the top of the minaret where a wall was being repaired.

'I'll speak to the imam,' said Karima. 'You'll need his permission to go into the mosque, but there are over two hours before the next call to prayer, so hopefully he'll allow it.'

They dismounted and tethered the camels, then walked along the short street to the mosque. Karima went through the gates. Nina looked round. The village was so quiet it almost felt abandoned. Remove the telephone poles, she thought, and Kafashta would look little different from how it had in the time of the Crusades.

The sound of raised voices within the mosque caught her attention. 'Ay up,' said Chase, opening his leather jacket wider for quicker access to his gun. 'Trouble.'

Karima reappeared, looking angry, followed by a young man with a rather feeble attempt at a beard. He yelled at her in Arabic, robes flapping as he gesticulated. His outrage grew when he saw the three Westerners.

'A slight problem,' Karima informed them thinly. 'The

imam doesn't want anyone from "the Great Satan" – his exact words – in his mosque.'

'*This* is the imam?' said Nina, surprised. The young man, still ranting, seemed to be barely twenty.

'No, he is not the imam,' said a new voice. A much older man, probably sixty but with the sun-hardened wrinkles of his face adding a good decade more to his appearance, padded towards them across the mosque's inner courtyard. He drew heavily on the stub of a cigarette before flicking it out on to the street. The younger man glared at him in disgust. 'He would like to be, he thinks he is, but he is not. Not yet. I am the imam of this *magnificent* place of worship,' he said, sarcasm clear in his voice. 'My name is Mahmoud al-Sabban, and this *boy*,' he jerked a dismissive thumb, 'is Rami Hanif, recently arrived from Damascus to drive me to an early grave with his maddening book-learned piety so he can have my job!'

'Your English is very good, sir,' Nina said politely.

Al-Sabban smiled crookedly. 'Thank you. I taught myself, Berlitz tapes. I have been here for over thirty years, and I already know every word of the holy Koran – I needed new ways to fill the time.' He regarded his visitors with amusement. 'So, you are from the Great Satan?'

'*I'm* not from the Great Satan,' Chase objected. 'I'm from the *Little* Satan.'

Al-Sabban examined him more closely. 'You do not look Israeli.'

'Israeli? No, I'm British.'

'*Israel* is the Little Satan, my friend,' al-Sabban told him with a mocking laugh. 'Britain is, hah, an imp at most.' Ignoring Chase's peeved expression, he waved them inside. 'But that does not matter. Come in, come in.'

Hanif shouted at the imam, but al-Sabban dismissively waved him away. Lips quivering, the younger man whirled and stalked across the courtyard into the depths of the mosque. 'Children!' al-Sabban spat. 'No respect. And a poor scholar too – the Koran tells us to welcome all strangers as friends. Even strangers from the Great Satan.' He chuckled. 'So, what brings you to my mosque?'

The imam had a private room, an office-cum-study with a copy of the Koran open on a desk, at the rear of the mosque. The low-ceilinged space smelled strongly of coffee and nicotine, the narrow windows tinged with yellow. Used to the smoke-free establishments of New York, Nina couldn't help coughing as al-Sabban lit up his third cigarette in a row. 'I thought the Koran was against smoking,' she said hopefully.

'There is some dispute among scholars,' al-Sabban replied, taking a long draw before carefully blowing out a smoke ring. 'And as a scholar myself, I say . . . it is fine.' He leaned back in his threadbare chair. 'Yes, I know the item you have told me about. I will let you see it. For a . . .' He reached over to close the Koran as if shielding it from what he was about to say. '*Donation.*'

'We're willing to pay, of course,' said Mitchell. 'Will dollars be okay?'

'I would have preferred euros, as dollars have been devalued recently – every refugee from Iraq comes with an armful of dollars! But they will do, I suppose. For a good price.'

Mitchell nodded. 'We were hoping to do more than just look at the piece, sir – we actually came here to buy it.'

'Then the price will have to be excellent!' He carefully stubbed out the cigarette, balancing it on the side of his ashtray for later, and stood. 'Come with me.'

Al-Sabban led them through the mosque to its central prayer hall. 'Parts of this building are over eight hundred years old,' he said. 'Unfortunately, it shows.' He indicated the base of the minaret at the corner of the hall. A pile of loose bricks lay at the bottom of a ladder, beside a wooden pallet attached to a dangling rope. 'At least there is one good thing about having Rami here. I can make *him* climb the ladder to call for prayers!'

'It's impressive,' Nina told him. Although the mosque as a whole was shabby, the decorations on the prayer hall's ceiling were mostly intact, needing only proper cleaning to restore their beauty.

'You think?' said al-Sabban, shooting her a look of incredulity. 'If I could, I would flatten the whole place and build something that was not falling apart!' He came to a stop at the prayer hall's southern end. An ornately decorated arched recess was set into the wall: the *mihrab*, indicating the direction of Mecca, towards which the faithful would pray. Beside it was a small flight of wooden steps leading up to a pulpit – the *minbar*, from which the imam delivered his sermon.

The sides of the steps were panelled, but al-Sabban crouched and fiddled with what at first seemed to be a piece of painted ornamentation, before it moved with a click. He swung open a small door, shifting round so the others could see inside. 'Down here,' he said, tapping on a flagstone, 'is where the relics are kept.' He straightened, stroking his beard thoughtfully. 'We need tools to open it. I will get them, and bring lights. Wait here. Although, Mr Mitchell, this would be a good time for you to fetch your donation!'

'Well, that was easy,' Chase observed once the imam had left.

'At least we know the Russians didn't beat us to it,' said Nina. 'How much money do you think he'll want?'

'Unless he's insanely greedy, I've got enough to cover it,' Mitchell said.

Karima wasn't happy. 'I can't believe an imam would openly take a bribe like that. No wonder they want to replace him, if that's how he behaves.' She narrowed her dark eyes. 'Allah will judge him.'

Mitchell shrugged, turning to go back to the camels. 'The important thing is that he's willing to help us.'

He returned with a messenger bag a few minutes later. Al-Sabban reappeared soon after, carrying a rusty crowbar, a lantern and a pocket torch. 'Here,' the imam said, pointing to a spot on one side of the flagstone, where a small gap was visible. 'One of you, open it.'

Everyone looked at Chase. 'Oh, like that, is it?' he complained, taking the crowbar. 'Eddie the packhorse.'

'I was thinking more Eddie the strongman,' Nina reassured him, patting his arm. Chase slid the end of the crowbar into the gap and pulled it back. The flagstone rose a couple of inches with a dry rasp, enough for Mitchell to get his fingers underneath to lift it. The two men quickly moved the stone aside.

Al-Sabban pointed his torch down the hole, revealing a low cellar beneath the floor. 'I keep the few treasures of the mosque down there,' he said. 'They may not be much, but being here for over thirty years has taught me that there are always men who want to steal them. Dr Wilde, you come down with me. The rest of you, wait here.'

Chase's reluctance to let Nina go without him was clear, but he stood by as first al-Sabban, then Nina, lowered themselves into the cellar. 'Watch yourself,' he told her.

'I'll be fine,' said Nina. 'See you soon.' She switched on the lantern and ducked into the low passage.

The cellar was more extensive than she had expected, a central corridor with chambers on each side. The ceiling was barely five feet high, the arched entrances to each side room lower still. Al-Sabban hunched down ahead of her, kicking up dust with each step as the circle of his torch beam swept back and forth. 'Down here.'

She followed him to a chamber near the cellar's far end. It was occupied by battered cardboard boxes and old wooden planks stacked haphazardly against one wall. Al-Sabban carefully lifted the planks aside to reveal another box behind them, a metal chest that from the faded stencilling on its side Nina guessed had once been used to hold ammunition. He blew cobwebs from the handle, then opened it.

'This is the blade that Muhammad Yawar used to kill the leader of the infidels,' he said, reaching into the box. Whatever the mosque's other treasures were, they were apparently hidden elsewhere in the cellar, as the metal case was empty except for the length of steel he carefully withdrew.

Nina brought the lantern closer. It was definitely part of a sword, almost three feet long, but jagged and broken at each end, missing both the tip and the hilt. Although grubby, the metal still appeared in good condition.

It was not plain, though: patterns had been inscribed along its length, just as she had seen on the stained-glass window in Peter's tomb. Could they really hold the clues that Rust had believed would lead to Excalibur?

'May I hold it?' she asked.

Al-Sabban nodded. Nina put down the lantern, then he handed it to her. Turning it to pick out the inscriptions in the lantern's glow, Nina saw a faint line of text in Latin: ARTURUS REX. 'King Arthur . . .' she whispered.

In any other circumstances, that would have

immediately convinced her the sword was a fake: it was extremely unlikely that Arthur would have inscribed a nametag on his own sword. But in this case, she was actually searching for a fake, created by the monks of Glastonbury Abbey to convince their king that he had been given the real thing. The nobility of the twelfth century were far more wealthy and ostentatious than their counterparts from six hundred years earlier, and would have expected their symbols of power to be just as showy. 'Pimp my sword . . .'

'What?' asked al-Sabban.

'Sorry, just thinking out loud.' Her gaze moved on to the other markings scored into the metal. Most seemed to be purely decorative, florid loops and curls, but there was also a repeated symbol: a labyrinth, a tightly wound path contained within a circle. Unlike a maze, there was only one route from the outside to the centre. Along the path were dots marking particular points. The number and position of the dots varied on each symbol, but there was no readily apparent pattern.

Nina turned the sword over, finding more of the same markings. She associated the symbol of the labyrinth with Greek mythology, the legend of Theseus and the Minotaur, but it also appeared in other cultures, the particular form of this one nagging at her memory. It had appeared somewhere amongst her cram studies of Arthurian legend . . .

Sudden shouting broke her reverie and she looked round, startled. 'Rami!' cried al-Sabban, annoyed. The commotion was coming from the prayer hall. 'Wait here, I will deal with him.'

Above, Chase and Mitchell stood helplessly as Hanif, more angry than ever, screeched at them in Arabic. Karima tried to speak, but barely got a few words out before being shouted down. 'Guess we *really* pissed him off this time,' Chase muttered.

Al-Sabban's head popped up through the hole like a gopher. 'Rami!' he snapped, beginning a vocal exchange with the younger imam. He finally managed to shout Hanif into silence, then clambered out of the cellar entrance. 'He is angry because you two are in the prayer hall,' he told Chase and Mitchell, 'and also because you are with her.' He indicated a curtain at the other end of the room that could be drawn to divide the prayer hall into two sections. 'Men and women are kept apart during prayer. He thinks you are insulting Islam by being here like this.'

Hanif began shouting again, and al-Sabban listened before irritably conceding some point. 'It seems I will only be able to shut him up if you wait in the court-yard.'

'What about Nina?' Chase asked.

'She is fine. She is *engrossed*,' said the imam. He shook his head, then started for the door. 'Come, wait outside. Mr Mitchell, this may be a good time to talk about your donation.' He eyed Mitchell's bag.

Hanif followed the group, waiting in the prayer hall's doorway like a guard dog as al-Sabban led Chase,

Mitchell and Karima to a small pool in the courtyard. Chase blinked in the sunlight; the cool of the mosque's interior made returning to the desert heat all the more jarring. Over the gurgle of water from the fountain he heard a car coming along the street outside, the first sign of life in the village.

'So how big a donation were you thinking, Mr al-Sabban?' Mitchell asked.

Al-Sabban made a show of considering the question. 'I was thinking of . . . something in the region of . . . ten thousand dollars?'

'Done,' said Mitchell, holding out his hand. Somewhat startled, al-Sabban hesitantly shook it. Mitchell then opened the bag and laid out several bundles of banknotes on a low wall before the imam. Karima looked on disapprovingly, but Chase simply smirked. Al-Sabban had clearly expected to haggle, thinking ten grand was an amount well out of reach, whereas Mitchell had been willing to pay more – probably a lot more.

Karima wasn't the only person who didn't approve. Hanif scurried over as al-Sabban counted the money. Chase's knowledge of Arabic was modest, but he didn't need a translator to know Hanif was demanding to know what the hell was going on.

Al-Sabban's answer left the young imam open-mouthed in dismay. He jabbed a finger at the banknotes, then pointed to Mitchell. 'No! Take back! Take money back!'

'Well, at least he's not so angry at *us* any more,' said

Karima as Hanif continued his impassioned rant in Arabic.

Al-Sabban just smiled. 'The young, they do not understand. But I have been over thirty years in this horrible place!' He swept his arms wide to take in the run-down surroundings. 'Peasants, simpletons, ugh! Now I can finally get away from them, and retire in comfort!'

'But you're doing it by selling a holy relic,' Karima objected.

'Holy relic?' al-Sabban scoffed. 'It has been in a box for years, nobody cared about it until today. It is junk! Who will miss it?'

'He might,' said Chase as Hanif returned to the prayer hall in disgust.

'After *he* has been here for thirty years, he will feel the same way!' The imam continued talking, thanking Mitchell, but Chase suddenly stopped listening.

There was engine noise outside the walls of the mosque – not the light vehicle he'd heard before, but a truck.

And a second car—

He pulled out his gun. 'I think we've got a problem,' he said, hurrying to the gate. After the total inactivity of Kasfashta when they arrived, three vehicles at once was practically a parade.

'What are you doing?' al-Sabban protested. 'This is a place of worship, you cannot bring guns in here!'

Chase ignored him, inching open one of the wooden doors to peer out at the street. 'Oh, fuck.' A jeep was pulling up on the other side of the dirt road – a jeep painted in the dull green of the Syrian army, three soldiers inside. 'Company's com—'

Company was already there.

The other door burst open as someone slammed against it, knocking Chase backwards. Momentarily dazed, he stumbled before recovering his footing. He brought up his gun—

Too late.

Syrian troops poured into the courtyard, rifles aimed at them.

11

Wondering what was keeping al-Sabban, Nina returned to the cellar entrance with the sword. She climbed out, surprised that nobody was waiting. Hanif was lurking at the doors, his back to her, peering out into the courtyard.

His stance was odd, as if he were frozen in shock . . .

Something was wrong.

Hanif turned to face her, his expression no longer angry, but fearful. Noises reached her from outside. Boots on the paving, the clanks and thumps of men laden with equipment.

The Syrians. Somehow they had discovered they were here.

Hanif was the obvious suspect, but as he ran to her she saw something in his eyes that instantly convinced her otherwise. He was as horrified by the arrival of the soldiers as she was. 'Quick, quick!' he said, his accent so thick the words were barely understandable. 'You, hide!'

'What's going on?'

'Mahmoud – bad man! He, he . . .' He shook his hands in frustration, unable to find the right words, before miming holding a telephone receiver to his ear.

'Phone?'

'Yes, yes! He phone army! Sell you!'

'He sold us out?' Hanif nodded frantically. 'Son of a *bitch*!'

'You hide! I stop them!' He raced back to the door, robes flapping.

'Shit,' Nina gasped. The young imam may not have approved of their presence in the mosque – but he clearly approved of al-Sabban betraying them for money in a house of worship even less. She could only assume that al-Sabban's plan had been to take Mitchell's money in exchange for the sword and then tell the Syrians they'd stolen it, allowing him to keep both the sword *and* the money after they were arrested.

She hunted for an escape route. The cellar was out – it had no other exits, and nowhere she could hide that would not be discovered almost immediately. Nothing she had seen going to and from al-Sabban's office suggested that there were any exits that way either.

That left the minaret.

Most of the mosque was a single storey, but the tower was over twice as high as the rest of the building. Maybe there was a way on to the roof . . .

She ran to the ladder and looked up. Daylight was visible at the top. There had been a staircase running round the interior of the narrow tower at one time, but little now remained, just stumps poking from the walls. The rope tied to the sturdy wooden pallet ran up to a pulley attached to the ceiling. Several electrical flexes dangled loosely from the upper floor, but she had no idea what they were for.

No time to wonder, either. She heard yells from the courtyard, Hanif's protests shouted down by deeper voices.

Climb—

She raced up the rungs. Below, the doors flew open. She looked back. Hanif had his arms spread wide, trying unsuccessfully to stop three soldiers from coming in. They saw her.

One of them raised his gun—

Hanif slapped it down. The soldier, an officer, raised an angry hand as if about to hit him, but held back the blow. He may have been young, but he was still an imam.

One of the soldiers, skinny and rat-faced, barely more than a boy, ran to the ladder and leered up at Nina. His rifle was slung over his shoulder, but he had a long and unpleasant-looking knife in one hand.

Nina tried to climb faster, the broken blade impeding her. The ladder shook as the young soldier scurried after her. 'Shit shit *shit!*'

The ladder led to a wooden platform. The power cables turned out to be connected to a tape deck and a large loudspeaker, used to sound the *adhan*, the Muslim call to prayer, across the village, but Nina ignored them as she searched for a way to stop her pursuer. Maybe she could kick down the ladder . . .

No use. It was tied to the platform.

She hurried to the half-repaired wall, seeing Chase and the others being forced at gunpoint into the back of a truck behind the mosque. But there was no way down, the scaffolding only extending a few feet below the level of the platform, just enough to give the builders a foothold.

The rope around the pulley – could she use it to climb down the outside of the minaret?

She grabbed the hanging length of rope, a knot stopping it from falling back through the pulley, but already knew the plan would fail. At 116 pounds she was hardly a heavyweight, but the pallet used to lift bricks to the top of the tower probably weighed less than a quarter as much. As a counterweight, it would barely slow her.

But it was too late anyway. The soldier had reached the top of the ladder, the knife ready in one hand.

Still holding the rope, Nina backed away. The soldier grinned mercilessly, seeing she was trapped as he clambered on to the platform beside the loudspeaker—

She hit the tape deck's 'play' button.

The *adhan* boomed from the speaker. It almost deafened Nina – but it was like a physical blow to the soldier. He slapped his hands to his ears with an inaudible scream, staggering, and stumbled over the rope.

Nina pulled with all her might. The rope snapped tight around his ankle. She pulled again . . . and the soldier toppled over the edge of the platform.

The rope shot through the pulley as the man plunged to the ground. Nina stopped the tape, the *adhan* still ringing in her ears as she looked down. Screaming and flailing, the soldier fell – pulling the pallet towards her at the same speed.

She threw herself back as it slammed into the pulley, shards of wood scattering everywhere. The rope pulled taut with a *thwack*. The scrawny soldier's fall had been caught just above the ground, where he was dangling by one leg, screeching and flapping as his two comrades ran to help him.

Their faces turned upwards, guns rising—

Nina grabbed the pallet, flinging herself over the broken wall and into the open air beyond.

She had her counterweight.

The soldier was whisked back up the minaret as Nina dropped down its exterior. She kicked at the wall, trying to abseil down – but was falling too fast, her feet slipping and spinning her out of control. The sword piece fell from under her arm. With a panicked shriek, she swung towards the ground, the military truck rushing up at her . . .

A soldier started to emerge from the back of the truck to investigate the noise – and Nina smashed into him feet first, propelling him inside again. He collided with a second soldier, both of them collapsing at the feet of their prisoners.

Nina landed in a heap on the ground and let go of the rope, which instantly whipped away back up the minaret, the luckless soldier on its other end plunging back down the tower to crash on to the two other men. Winded, she looked up. Chase, Mitchell and Karima stared down at her from the back of the truck. 'And I thought *Mitzi* made a good entrance,' said Mitchell.

Chase grabbed an AK-74 assault rifle from one of the fallen guards. 'Let's truck off!' He jumped down from the vehicle, quickly checking for other soldiers before pulling Nina to her feet and kissing her on the cheek. 'Oh, and thanks.'

'Any time,' she replied, shaken but managing a smile. Mitchell took the other soldier's AK, and Karima yanked a pistol from his holster before they too jumped down to the ground.

'How many of them are there?' Nina asked.

Chase glanced round one side of the truck to check the way was clear, Mitchell doing the same on the other. 'About ten. Two jeeps and this truck.' Five down . . . but five still remaining, all armed.

'Where's the sword?' Mitchell demanded.

Nina looked round. 'Shit, I dropped it – no, there!' She pointed; the broken blade was sticking out of the sandy ground.

'Come on.' He ran with Nina to retrieve it. 'Time to leave.'

Nina heard more shouting from the mosque's courtyard as she picked up the sword. 'You do remember that we're twenty miles from the border, right?'

'Then we'd better get started!' Chase called. 'Karima,

get back to the camels. Nina, go with her.'

'We can't outrun them on camels!' Nina protested. 'They've got jeeps!'

Chase grinned. 'Not for long.' He waited until she had started after Karima before firing a single shot to blow out one of the truck's front tyres. Then he signalled for Mitchell to follow him round the side of the mosque to the street.

The sound of the shot would have told the soldiers where they were – which was exactly what Chase wanted, as it would draw them away from the two women. He and Mitchell jogged down the alley, AKs raised.

A Syrian soldier ran round the corner – and skidded almost comically to a stop in a cloud of dust, getting off a single wild shot purely on reflex before flinging himself back into cover as Chase and Mitchell fired. Stone chipped and splintered where the bullets hit.

Chase knew where the two jeeps were parked, having memorised their positions while he was being taken to the truck. The rest of the soldiers would be just round the corner by now, some of them moving across the street to cover the alley while the others prepared to spring out from behind the mosque and blast anyone in sight.

Chase didn't give them the chance. Instead he ran to the far side of the alley, the first jeep coming into view across the street. Three of the Syrians were using it as cover, lying in wait – but they hadn't expected him to sprint right into the open, needing a moment to react—

The moment was all he needed, flicking the AK to full

auto and unleashing a thudding burst of bullets – not at the soldiers, but at their jeep. They ducked as its rear wing cratered, hot lead ripping through the metal . . .

Into the fuel tank.

A line of fire spurting on to the dusty road gave the soldiers all the warning they needed that they should run, *now*. Chase was already racing back to take cover against the mosque as the petrol vapour inside the punctured fuel tank ignited—

The jeep blew up like a small bomb. The fleeing soldiers were thrown to the ground by the blast as the blazing vehicle cartwheeled across the road, flaming fuel spewing out behind it. The two soldiers round the corner desperately hurled themselves out of its path as it smashed into the mosque wall, then bounced back to land upside down in the middle of the street.

One of the soldiers sprawled at the end of the alley looked up, saw Chase pressed against the wall, raised his rifle – and took the butt of Mitchell's AK to his temple. Chase dropped his now empty gun and picked up the unconscious Syrian's weapon to replace it. 'Thanks.'

Mitchell peered round the corner. 'Did you get 'em all?'

'We'll see in a sec,' said Chase. Two men at his feet, one already out cold: he sent the other to join him by kicking him in the back of the head. It would hurt when he woke up – but at least he *would* wake up. He had no love for the Syrian military, but nor did he have any personal grievance against these conscripts, most of whom were probably still in their teens.

Of the three men by the jeep, one had been thrown against a wall by the explosion and didn't look as though he would be moving for a while; another rolled in panic on the ground, his sleeve on fire. The third staggered to his feet, AK in hand, but hurriedly dropped the rifle when he saw Chase and Mitchell coming towards him, weapons raised. Chase pointed between two of the houses across the street at the open desert beyond. The soldier gulped, then with his hands raised high turned and ran for the empty sands.

'You could have just shot him,' Mitchell said.

'We're not at war with 'em. Hey, your arm!' Mitchell's left sleeve was torn, a small patch of dark red slowly spreading through the material. The first Syrian's lone shot had clipped his bicep.

'Damn,' the American muttered, regarding the wound with surprise. 'Didn't even feel it!'

Chase quickly assessed the injury as minor, nothing a simple bandage couldn't fix. Mitchell had been lucky. 'You'll live, tough guy. Okay, let's move.' He fired a couple of rounds to blow out a rear tyre of the second jeep, then rapidly surveyed the scene. Movement in the mosque – al-Sabban, peering fearfully round the gate. Chase glared at him. The imam hurriedly tossed the bundles of dollars out into the street, then slammed the wooden doors.

Satisfied that nobody would be in a position to challenge them before they reached Nina and Karima, Chase moved to pick up the money, but Mitchell shook his head. 'Leave it. We got what we came for.'

'You're just going to chuck away ten grand?' said Chase, reluctantly following him at a jog towards the edge of the village.

'Uncle Sam's paying for it.'

'You mean me and Nina are paying for it. That's come out of our taxes!'

Mitchell made an amused noise, and they continued along the road until they reached the camels. Karima and Nina had already mounted their animals, the sword blade protruding from one of Nina's saddlebags. The other camels were standing, spooked by the gunfire.

The two men clambered on to their saddles. 'Okay,' Chase yelled to Nina, 'we're going to have to hoof it! Just grab on as tight as you can!'

Mitchell brought his camel round to head south. 'Come on, move!' he shouted, flicking the reins. His camel grunted and broke into a run, Karima right behind him.

'I don't wanna do this . . .' Nina muttered through clenched teeth. But she followed Mitchell's example and snapped the reins, clinging as tightly as she could to the saddle. The camel reared up, almost throwing her off its back, then started running. 'Ow – ow – ow – son of a – *ow*!'

Chase set off, staying behind her so he could help if she got into trouble. But she was holding on well enough despite her staccato complaints. He looked back at the receding village. Some of the soldiers were recovering, the officer in charge limping out of the mosque and taking in the burning jeep with dismay before spotting his erstwhile prisoners disappearing into the desert.

'Come on, shift your arses!' Chase yelled to the others as thumping AK fire echoed off the buildings. Little geysers of sand burst up around them, shots smacking into the ground. But they were already beyond the AK-74's effective range: the Russian weapon was valued more for its qualities as a near-indestructible bullet hose than its accuracy.

They kept riding, the ungainly gallop of the camels belying their impressive pace through the soft sand. Kafashta dropped away into the heat haze, the soldiers swallowed with it.

Nina was finally getting some degree of control over her charging camel, drawing alongside Mitchell. 'Oh, my God, you're hurt!' she cried, seeing his bloodied arm.

'It's just a scratch,' he said with a smile. 'A flesh wound.' Nina smiled back.

'Oh, for fuck's sake,' Chase groaned from behind them. 'More bloody Python.'

They kept up their pace until it became clear that there was no immediate sign of pursuit. Still keeping a watchful eye out for Syrian helicopters, they slowed the camels to a brisk trot as they continued south towards the border.

Chase drew level with Mitchell. 'Got to admit,' he said, slightly grudgingly, 'you did all right back there. For a sailor.'

Mitchell gave him a thin smile. 'I did more in my military career than just sit inside a steel tube.'

'Oh? Like what?' Nina asked.

The smile broadened. 'Can't say. Classified.'

She rolled her eyes. 'Great, another guy full of secrets. You're as bad as Eddie!'

An hour and a half later, they crossed the border, Mitchell taking a GPS handset from a saddlebag to confirm they were safely back in Jordan. They had made it.

And they had the first piece of Caliburn. The first clue to the location of Excalibur.

12

Austria

The contrast could hardly be any more stark: from the stifling, parched desolation of the Arabian desert to the cool, clean air of the Tyrolean Alps. The view from the picture windows of the coffee house in the village of Rasbrücke was spectacular, looking up the valley at the towering peaks to the south. The valley floor was carpeted in forests so vividly green that they almost seemed fake, while above them rose the pristine white slopes of the little ski resort. Even the chill edge in the high-altitude air was a relief after the inescapable heat of Syria.

After returning the camels to Attayak, Karima drove Nina, Chase and Mitchell back to Amman and the State Department jet. Now, a day later, they were waiting to find out if Mitzi Fontana had discovered anything that might help them locate the second piece of the sword.

'Here she is,' said Chase as a bright red Porsche Cayenne pulled up outside. Mitzi, wrapped in a puffy skiing jacket that matched the colour of her SUV and carrying a satchel, climbed out and waved at him before entering the coffee house.

'Hi!' she said brightly, greeting Nina and Mitchell before sitting next to Chase and kissing his cheek. 'How was Syria?'

Chase shrugged. 'Kind of boring, actually.'

'Oh,' she said, disappointed. 'Did you find what you were looking for?'

'Yes,' Mitchell told her in a clipped tone that made it clear he wanted that line of discussion to end as quickly as possible. 'But what about you, Mitzi? Did you have any luck?'

She smiled and opened her satchel, taking out several large sheets of paper. 'I did, actually! It took a little while, but I persuaded someone in the local records office to help me.'

'A man, by any chance?' Chase asked casually, looking at a point several inches below Mitzi's face. Her jacket was only half fastened, revealing her scoop-necked sweater – and her cleavage within it.

'Actually, yes. How did you know?'

He shrugged. 'Oh, just a hunch.'

'What did you find?' Nina asked Mitzi, jabbing Chase with her elbow.

She unfolded the papers, revealing them as photocopies

of old architectural plans, all the text written in a heavy Gothic script. 'These are plans of Staumberg Castle from their archives. I was hoping to find older ones, but these were all they had. They were made in 1946, when the castle was returned to the Staumberg family after the war.'

'These are great,' Nina assured her. From the plans, the castle appeared to be T-shaped, the foot extending into a courtyard surrounded by high walls. Three floors above ground, and what looked like two levels of cellars . . .

'So what exactly are we looking for?' Chase asked.

'That's something I did find out about,' said Mitzi excitedly. 'There's a story that when the Germans shipped stolen treasure back through southern Europe, some of it ended up at the castle. The commandant was supposed to have secretly hidden it. But nobody ever found it after the war, and now the owner refuses to let anyone else look.'

'Maybe he wants to look for it himself,' mused Mitchell.

'Or maybe he just doesn't want treasure hunters smashing up his home,' Chase countered. He put on a German accent. '"You vant to tear ze place apart looking for Nazi gold? *Ja*, go ahead!" I don't think so.'

'Did you manage to contact the owner, Mitzi?' asked Nina.

'I spoke to him, yes. Briefly. I talked mostly to his butler.'

'He actually has a *butler*?' Chase laughed. 'I bet he's got a monocle too.'

'His name's Roland Staumberg, and he's one of the owners of this resort. The castle's been his family's home for generations. He seemed very nice – he just didn't want any visitors.'

Nina picked up another page of the plans. 'Did you find out anything about him?'

'A little. He's well liked around here, but the man at the records office said he is very private. He's apparently quite a sportsman, though. Skiing, of course, but he also goes snowmobiling, scuba-dives, races yachts—'

'Diving?' Nina asked.

'Yes. Is that helpful?'

'Maybe. He might at least talk to us, if we're lucky. But that won't get us anywhere unless we can convince him we know exactly what we're looking for.' She examined the plans again, turning the sheet in her hands so that it was aligned along the castle's long axis. The layout of the rooms was a perfect mirror image . . .

'Ay up,' said Chase, noticing her thoughtful expression. 'She's got something.'

Nina pushed everybody's cups aside to clear more space on the table, laying out the pages so they were all oriented the same way. 'Look how symmetrical it is. But if there really *is* a hidden room, it won't be on these plans, because they were made after the war. We need to look for anything that's not mirrored.'

She carefully scanned the pages, the others shifting round the table to look for themselves. 'This isn't the same,' said Chase after a short while, indicating a door that only appeared on one side of the castle's second floor.

'There's a spiral staircase that isn't mirrored here,' Mitchell added, tapping a finger on another sheet.

'But they're not rooms, they're just alterations,' Nina said. 'We need to see if there's a difference in the actual physical layout of the building . . .'

'Like this?' Mitzi asked. 'The lowest level of the cellars, there are two long rooms on each side of this passage.'

'Probably wine cellars,' said Nina, looking more closely.

'Yes, but look!' Mitzi used her phone as a makeshift ruler, lining it up across the end of one of the rooms. 'The one on the right is shorter than the one on the left.'

She was right, Nina saw. The difference was not much, no more than a few feet on the scale of the plans . . . but it was definitely there. 'My God, it is!'

Chase gave Mitzi an admiring look. 'Bloody hell, love, I think you've got it! Nice work!'

She beamed proudly back. 'Thank you!'

'I guess your mum was wrong – it's a good job we asked you to help. Come here.' He leaned over to hug her. She returned the gesture enthusiastically. 'So now what?'

'Now?' said Nina, scrutinising the slight asymmetry of the plans, 'I think it's time I talked to this Roland Staumberg.'

'Dr Wilde,' said Roland Staumberg, bowing to Nina before taking her hand. 'An honour. It is a thrill to meet the discoverer of Atlantis!'

Leaving Mitzi – to her disappointment – waiting in the

village, Nina, Chase and Mitchell had driven further up the valley to Staumberg Castle. As Nina hoped, her current celebrity status had piqued his interest. Though a little surprised that she was already in Rasbrücke, he nevertheless agreed to meet her.

The castle was an imposing, starkly beautiful structure perched atop a ridge protruding from the mountainside. It overlooked the resort's ski slopes and forests from the end of a steep zig-zagging road that despite having been ploughed was still coated with snow. Mitchell's four-wheel-drive Chevrolet Suburban SUV, another vehicle laid on by the US government, was much appreciated.

When the castle's outer gates whirred open, they entered the courtyard and parked near a pair of snowmobiles, to be met by a tall, whip-thin man in dark clothes who introduced himself as Kurt, Staumberg's butler. Staumberg himself, waiting at the castle's door, was in his forties, sand-blond and barrel-chested, with an air of refined intellect. To Chase's barely contained glee, he was indeed wearing a monocle.

'It's good to meet you too, Herr Staumberg,' Nina replied. She introduced Chase and Mitchell, then took in the large hall they had entered. Just as the plans had suggested, it was symmetrical, stone stairways rising up on each side to a balcony that ran round the side and rear walls, stained glass windows lining it. Chandeliers hung from the high ceiling, and large and heavy tapestries reached almost to floor level, suits of armour standing stiffly between them. The whole room was panelled in dark wood, its varnish so thick and warm that it almost seemed like a coating of amber. 'This is . . . wow, this is very impressive.'

'Thank you,' said Staumberg, 'but it costs so much to heat!' Everyone laughed politely at the ice-breaking joke. 'Please, follow me. There is a warmer room upstairs.'

He led them up one of the flights of stairs and along the balcony, where more suits of polished armour were on display. At the end was a wrought-iron spiral staircase leading down, one of the asymmetrical elements they had seen on the plans. The butler opened a door beside it and ushered them into the room beyond.

It was a study, a log fire snapping in a stone fireplace. A tall window looked down the valley towards the village, although the arrangement of the leather armchairs made it clear that Staumberg spent more time looking at the rather incongruous plasma TV than the stunning view outside.

'For the football,' he explained as he gestured for the others to sit before taking his own seat. 'Would you like something to drink? Coffee, tea, schnapps?'

Deciding it was a little early to start drinking, Nina politely accepted coffee, Mitchell and Chase doing the same. Kurt bowed and exited.

'Thank you for seeing us, Herr Staumberg,' Nina said.

'Oh, it is my pleasure! I was reading about you just the other day.' He riffled through a small stack of magazines, pulling out a diving title. 'Here, you see?' He opened the magazine; Nina's IHA publicity portrait grinned from the page beside a larger photo of a minisub over one of the Atlantis excavation sites. 'I enjoy wreck-diving – exploring sunken ships. But what you have done is much more exciting! So what can I do for you, Dr Wilde? Much as I would love to hear about your discovery of Atlantis, I do not think that is why you have come to see me, no?'

'I'm afraid not. Although we are looking for something else, another ancient legend.' She glanced at Mitchell. 'I don't know how much I can tell you about it . . .'

'Let me guess,' sighed Staumberg, skin folding around the rim of his monocle as he frowned. 'You are looking for Excalibur.'

Nina blinked in surprise. 'How did you know?'

'I was pestered by a man about it some months ago. He had a mad theory that part of it was hidden here in a Nazi treasure-trove. But I have lived here all my life, and there is no such hidden treasure. I explored every centimetre of the castle as a child, so I would know! But this man, what was his name, Rust?'

'Bernd Rust.'

'You know him?'

'I *knew* him,' said Nina. 'He was murdered.'

Staumberg was shocked. 'Murdered? I am sorry. I did not like the man, he was annoying, but I did not wish him harm.'

'The thing is,' Nina continued, 'he was murdered because of his search for Excalibur. I didn't believe him at first either, but since then . . . well, we think he may have been right. That's why the IHA is looking for the other pieces, so we can find them before his killers do.'

The Austrian was now decidedly uncomfortable. 'And you think one of these pieces is here.'

'Yes.'

'Which means his killers may *also* think it is here.'

'That's a distinct possibility,' said Mitchell. 'Which is why we'd like your permission to search for it.'

'But search where?' Staumberg asked. 'I cannot think of anywhere it could be hidden that would not already have been found.'

'What about the cellars?' Nina asked. She unfolded the plan of the castle's lowest level. 'Here, you see? The castle is perfectly symmetrical, except for this one room that's slightly shorter than the other.'

Staumberg took the plan and examined it with interest – then blanched. 'Oh. The wine cellar.'

Kurt entered at that moment bearing a tray of steaming coffee mugs. He caught Staumberg's expression and asked him a question in German, getting a somewhat agitated response. Nina picked up enough to know they were discussing the cellar. 'Is something wrong?'

'I would . . . ah, prefer not to show you that room,' Staumberg answered.

'Thought you said there wasn't anything hidden here,' said Chase.

'There is not, that I know of, but . . .' He rubbed the back of his neck. 'It is just . . . I would rather not have visitors in that room. But Kurt and I, we can search it again and see if we find anything, *ja*?'

'You could,' said Mitchell, 'but the thing is, the people who murdered Rust also stole his research. The same research that brought him here in the first place,' he added pointedly. 'If they've got it, they'll probably pay you a visit, just like us. But they won't *ask* to search the castle.'

'We can keep them out,' said Staumberg unconvincingly.

'If they want to get in here, they will,' Chase said. 'They've already killed people looking for this thing – and tried to kill us, too.'

'If this piece of the sword really is here, we *have* to keep it out of their hands,' Nina pleaded. 'It's very important that the IHA get it first – it could lead to a discovery as important as Atlantis.'

Staumberg stared out of the window for a long moment before responding, his shoulders visibly slumping. 'Very well, I will let you see the cellar. But before I do . . . I must insist on your complete discretion.'

'You have it,' Nina assured him. 'Everything will be absolutely confidential.'

'Very well.' Still reluctant, Staumberg spoke in German to Kurt, who nodded and opened the study door to show them out.

They descended the spiral staircase and went through double doors at the back of the great hall, passing along a corridor before descending two flights of stairs to the lowest floor. Kurt switched on the lights, dim bulbs illuminating a low stone passage. 'This way,' said Staumberg, going to a heavy oak door on the right. He swung it open, revealing the room beyond. It was a wine cellar, as Nina had expected – but on a grand scale, wooden racks holding literally thousands of bottles lining both sides of the room.

'So his big secret's alcoholism?' Chase whispered to Nina.

Kurt led the way to the far end of the long room, Staumberg behind him. He looked back at Nina. 'The reason I ask for secrecy is . . . well, my reputation, both as a member of the Staumberg family and as a businessman. Only a few of my most trusted friends have seen what is in here.'

'As I said, this will be confidential,' she said, now intrigued.

'Good. Good.' They reached the end of the room, where there was a door. For a moment Nina wondered if what lay beyond was the hidden room on the plans, but that made no sense. The back wall was made from wooden planks, not stone; no attempt had been made to disguise it, and it seemed relatively recently built.

Kurt took a key ring from his pocket and flicked through it, finally selecting a particular key and unlocking the door. He opened it, revealing nothing beyond but darkness. Nina sniffed the air as an odd mix of scents emerged from the mysterious room. Wood, leather, some sort of polish, the faint tang of old candle smoke . . .

Staumberg took a long breath as Kurt entered the room. 'Well . . . come in.' He stepped aside for the others to enter as the butler switched on the light.

Nina, first in, stopped abruptly as she took in the contents of the room. 'Oh . . . my,' she muttered, struggling for words.

Chase, on the other hand, could barely contain his laughter. 'Bloody hell.'

They had entered a dungeon.

But not some medieval torture chamber; this was a thoroughly modern affair, blood-red walls and a floor of glossy black tile, full-length mirrors strategically placed so the occupants could always see themselves reflected. A wooden bench, padded with red leather and fitted with numerous thick restraining straps, dominated the centre of the room. A long rack by the door held dozens of whips and paddles, and on a table near the back wall was a row of what Nina at first took to be oversized black candles before realising they were in fact quite terrifyingly large dildos.

Chase couldn't hold it in any more. 'Oh, Christ!' he cackled. 'Your own personal S&M dungeon? No wonder you wanted to keep it quiet!'

Staumberg's face flushed with embarrassment and anger. 'You promised you will not tell anyone about this!'

'I won't, I won't! Don't worry, I'm good at keeping secrets. But Jesus, this is a pretty impressive set-up.'

'Not *quite* the word I would have used,' said Nina through her fixed grin.

'Hey, come on, every man's got a hobby. Some blokes play footie, some've got model trains, and some . . . well, it takes all sorts.' He glanced at Kurt, who was standing silently by the door. 'So, Kurt, are you the master or the servant in here?'

'Eddie!' Nina cried. But the tiniest hint of a smile on the butler's otherwise impassive face made it perfectly clear there was one room of the castle where the roles were reversed.

'This is all very . . . *personal*,' said Mitchell impatiently. 'But can we get back to why we're here?' He strode past the bench to the back of the room. 'If there really is a hidden chamber, it's behind this wall.'

Avoiding Chase's amused gaze, Staumberg joined him, putting a hand on the red paint. 'This is stone, as far as I know. I never noticed anything different about it.'

'We'll need to knock through it.'

'With your permission, of course,' Nina quickly added to Staumberg.

He considered it, then gave a resigned grunt. 'Very well, *ja* . . . But you will repair it after?'

'Send the IHA a bill,' Chase advised as he and Nina walked to the wall. He bumped a clenched fist against the painted stone. 'Seems solid.'

'Do you have any tools?' Mitchell asked. 'Hammers, or pickaxes?'

'Yes,' Staumberg replied. 'Kurt can get them.'

'Or we could just whack it with this,' said Chase, pointing at the largest of the dildos. 'One hit with that'd knock anything down. Christ, it must be three inches thick.' He smirked at Nina. 'Nearly as big as mine, eh?'

'Widthways or lengthways?' she replied, deadpan.

'All bloody right,' scowled Chase, one-upped, as Mitchell laughed. Even Staumberg briefly smiled. 'Let's see what's on the other side, then.'

Kurt brought a long-handled rubber mallet and a pickaxe. Chase delivered the first blow, slamming the mallet against the wall. Staumberg winced, but the damage immediately revealed that Mitzi's theory had been correct – there was indeed a space behind the wall, the stones caving backwards. Another blow, and one fell away into the blackness beyond with a crunch.

Chase waited for the dust to settle, then shone a torch through the hole. 'It's not that deep; I can see the back wall. Less than three feet.' He shifted position, angling the beam downwards. 'And there's something in here! Looks like boxes under a tarp.' He moved back. 'Jack, give me a hand.'

Mitchell obliged, hooking the pick behind more of the stones and pulling them out until the hole was just large enough for Chase to edge his upper body through. Torch in one hand, he carefully lifted a corner of the dusty tarpaulin.

Grubby wooden crates rested underneath. The stencilled symbol of a swastika immediately told him the local legends had been true all along.

'I think what we've got here is ... *Nazi gold*,' he announced as he slid back out.

Staumberg appeared to be stricken by a sudden migraine, and Nina understood why. There were international laws relating to the discovery of Nazi materials – especially those which had been stolen from other countries. 'We'll have to tell the Austrian government about this. I'm sorry.'

'I know, I know.' Staumberg rubbed his forehead. 'But can you please give us time to move our, ah, equipment to another room before you do?'

'I think that would be fair, considering how helpful you've been.'

He smiled in faint relief. Meanwhile, Chase and Mitchell expanded the hole, pulling out more stones to reveal six crates in all. Chase removed the tarpaulin, finding a leather-bound ledger hidden beneath. A brief flick through the pages revealed an itemised list, all in German. 'What do you reckon this is?'

Staumberg examined it. 'It is a list – a list of everything in the crates!'

'German efficiency,' Chase joked.

Staumberg's eyes widened as he read further. 'It really is treasure – there is gold, silver, jewellery, religious relics . . .'

'What about the sword?' Mitchell demanded. 'Does it mention a sword?'

The Austrian kept reading. 'Yes, here! "Jewelled sword hilt with gold and silver decorations, blade broken.

Obtained Koroneou, claimed to be of historic significance." There is also an estimated value in marks, and – and it even says which crate it is in.' He looked through the hole as Chase directed the torch beam over the stencilled numbers on each box. 'That one!'

Mitchell and Chase quickly removed the crate and placed it on the floor, using the pickaxe as an impromptu crowbar to prise it open. Inside were several objects wrapped in waxed paper.

'It's got to be this,' said Chase, taking out the largest. He unwrapped it . . .

'Wow,' whispered Nina.

It was indeed the hilt of a sword, gemstones set into the steel, lines of gold and silver twined around them. But they weren't what caught Nina's eye: instead, she looked at the broken stub of the blade, sheared off some five inches below the ornate guard. Inscribed in the metal was a symbol.

A labyrinth. Just like the ones on the piece they had recovered from Syria.

She took the sword from Chase, holding it up to the light. 'I think we have a match,' she announced.

'Awesome,' said Mitchell. 'Now we need to—'

The door was kicked open with a bang.

A rangy, hollow-cheeked man with hair shaved down to a black stubble stood outside, a pistol aimed into the room. Everyone froze. The man entered, momentary surprise at his surroundings quickly vanishing as he focused on his objective. He pointed at Nina. 'You,' he said, accent thickly Russian, 'give me sword.'

Mitchell moved in front of her, hands raised. 'Stay calm,' he ordered. He took another step, passing Chase. The Russian regarded him suspiciously. 'We already have the blade, and without it your boss will never find Excalibur.' He added something in Russian.

The man replied in kind. Nina had no idea what he said, but he was certainly vehement about it. 'Worth a try,' Mitchell sighed, backing away. 'Nina, give him the sword.'

'You just want to hand it over?' Chase said.

'It's that or get shot. Nina, go on.'

Hesitantly, Nina stepped forward. The Russian nodded: *Come here*. She advanced again. 'You want the sword?' she asked. '*Catch!*'

She tossed the hilt at his face.

He instinctively snapped up his own hands to catch it, the gun clanging against the ancient metal. But it only took a moment for him to recover, anger flaring as he brought the gun back down—

Whock!

The Russian abruptly spun through ninety degrees, wobbled, and slumped face first on to the black tiles. Chase looked down at him with satisfaction . . . then gave a startled 'Ugh!' and dropped his makeshift cosh – the largest of the dildos – as it occurred to him what he was holding and where it had probably been.

He picked up the unconscious man's gun. 'Bloody hell. I've done a lot of weird stuff in my life, but I never, *ever* thought I'd break a man's jaw with a foot-long rubber cock.'

'We need to get out of here and call the police,' said Mitchell. He took out his phone. 'Shit. No signal.'

'We *are* in a cellar,' Nina reminded him as she retrieved the sword hilt. She turned to Staumberg and Kurt. 'They're after us and the sword, not you. Is there anywhere down here you can hide?' Staumberg nodded.

'Go there and wait for the police,' Chase told him. He checked the gun, a Steyr M9 – fifteen 9mm rounds, fully loaded – and moved to the door. Nobody else in the wine cellar, and no sounds of movement. 'Nina, Jack, come on.'

They hurried back through the cellar. 'How the hell did they find us?' Nina asked. 'They couldn't have gone through Bernd's notes this quickly!'

'Guess they weren't as hard to decipher as he thought,' said Mitchell. 'No point worrying about it now, though.'

Chase stopped at the door to check ahead. Still no one. The Englishman taking point, they headed for the stairs.

Halfway up, they heard a door slam. 'Wait,' Chase whispered, creeping upwards until he could see the main passageway on the upper cellar level. Nobody there, though he could hear activity off to one side. He warily peered round the corner and saw an open door, lights on beyond it and the bangs and rattles of somebody looking through cupboards. Presumably Rust's notes hadn't offered any specific suggestions about where the Nazi hoard might be hidden. 'Okay, come on.' Nina and

Mitchell advanced as quietly as they could, Chase keeping the gun trained on the open door as they passed him and ascended the next flight of stairs.

'What's the plan?' Nina asked as he followed them.

'Get to the car and get out of the Schloss Adler here. Soon as we're clear, we call the cops. We just need to stay ahead of them until we can get help.'

'Maybe, but we still have to reach the SUV,' said Mitchell as they reached the top of the stairs. Chase made sure the way was clear, then they ran to the double doors of the great hall.

He eased them open and looked through. He couldn't see anyone in the hall, but his view of the balcony above was limited, and the main doors at the far end were open. There could be intruders in the courtyard.

Mitchell looked over his shoulder. 'Is it clear?'

'Have to chance it.' He darted through the doors, whipping the gun from side to side. 'Okay, come on.'

They ran down the hall towards the exit—

Someone shouted in Russian.

'Shit!' Chase yelped, whirling to bring up his gun. Another man was on the balcony to his left, a sinister little Czech 'Skorpion' machine pistol in his hand. Chase unleashed four rapid shots, splintering the wooden railing and forcing the Russian to dive to the floor. He shouted again, this time for help.

'Get into cover!' ordered Chase – but Mitchell had already done so, pulling Nina between the hanging tapestries and suits of armour into the area beneath the damaged balcony, the spiral staircase at its rear. Chase quickly backed across to the opposite side of the hall, gun at the ready. The moment his opponent showed his head, he was going to lose a chunk of it . . .

More shouts, but now from the far end of the hall. Three people ran in through the front doors.

All armed.

'Oh, *fuck*!' Chase gasped, hurling himself behind one of the thick oak pillars supporting the balcony as a spray of sub-machine gun bullets ripped into it.

13

'Shit! What do we do?' Nina cried, looking across at Chase. He was in the cover of the pillar, but it would only take a few seconds for the new arrivals to reach a position where they could either shoot directly at him, or force him into the line of fire of the man above them.

'There's nothing we *can* do!' Mitchell told her. He pulled her towards the metal spiral staircase. 'Come on!'

Chase saw them move. On the stairs, they'd be visible to the bad guys at the other end of the hall, easy targets as they climbed . . .

He leaned round the ravaged pillar and let off three shots, as much to distract as to kill. As he'd hoped, the Russians ran for cover.

The Skorpion's high-pitched clatter echoed from the balcony, another burst of bullets tearing chunks out of the oak. Chase shielded his face as splinters flew around him. He had to find better cover.

Nina scrambled up the stairs, Mitchell right behind her. She looked down the hall as Chase fired another two shots. 'Jesus! It's her!' One of the trio running towards the stone staircase at the end of the balcony opposite was the female sniper she'd seen in Bournemouth, her hair now dyed a vivid red.

'Dominika Romanova,' said Mitchell.

'She killed Bernd—'

'I know. Keep going!'

Chase blasted two more suppressive shots up at the balcony. Metal clanged as one hit a suit of armour. The Skorpion stopped firing as the Russian ducked again.

Move—

He sprinted for the pair of broader wooden columns supporting the corner of the balcony at the hall's rear. More bullets flew after him, setting the tapestries flapping and causing one of the suits of armour to crash in pieces to the floor. He dived, rolling behind the rectangular base of the two pillars. From here he was shielded from the balcony *and* the far end of the hall, and had a better firing angle at both.

Though with only four bullets left, he'd have to make each of them count.

The man above saw that he had lost his target. He ran for the stone stairs at the end of the balcony to join his comrades.

Nina reached the top of the spiral staircase. A chill of fear hit her as she saw the gunman on the balcony – but his back was to her as he descended the stairs.

The door leading to Staumberg's study was only a few feet away. 'Come on!' she said. 'Through here—'

The door opened.

Nina found herself face to face with yet another of Vaskovich's thugs, a squat man with his hair tied in a topknot. They both flinched at the unexpected close encounter – then the Russian smiled malevolently as he brought up his gun—

Mitchell swept Nina aside, whipping round with shocking speed to deliver a roundhouse kick. The gun flew from the Russian's hand and spun over the railing. Before the startled man could react, Mitchell kicked him again, driving a heel into his stomach and sending him flying back through the door. There was a nasty crack as his head hit a wall, and he collapsed.

Dominika heard the commotion and shouted an order. The man descending the stairs reversed course, heading back to the balcony. One of her companions fired a burst at Chase to pin him down, then sprinted up the stairs after his comrade, long black coat swirling like a cape.

Chase looked up – and saw Nina and Mitchell, unable to see what was happening on the staircase, running along the balcony towards the Russians. 'No, go back!' he shouted – but was drowned out as Dominika and the other man opened fire with their MP-5Ks. Chunks of the pillars protecting him blew apart under the onslaught. 'Jesus!'

Nina reached the stairs – and stopped as she saw the Russian running back up, another man a few steps behind. Both men were armed, and the only weapon she and Mitchell had between them was a broken sword.

If they couldn't attack, they had to *defend* . . .

A suit of armour stood guard at the top of the stairs, empty arms crossed over its chest above a broad shield. Nina shoved the whole display over. The armour tumbled down the stairs, exploding into a cascade of gleaming metal pieces. The steel wave swept the first Russian back down the steps with a pained cry.

The second man leapt over him – and *kept* leaping, propelling himself off the wall across to the banister, then back to the wall and finally into a somersault that brought him to a perfect landing in front of Nina. His overcoat swirled around him with a dramatic *fwumph*.

'Ah . . . 'kay,' said Nina, startled by the gravity-defying display. 'Jack, what now?'

Mitchell pushed past her, hands raised in a martial arts form. 'I'll take care of him.'

'He has a *gun*!'

'It's not his style. Is it, Zakhar? Think you can take me?' To Nina's surprise, Mitchell was right, the slick-haired young man slipping his compact sub-machine gun into his coat. The two men sized each other up – then both moved at once, fists snapping out and feet slicing in a flurry of strikes and blocks. They seemed evenly matched . . . but then Mitchell started to be driven back along the balcony.

Chase saw the whirling brawl from below. What the hell was Mitchell *doing*? But he had no time to think about it as he came under fire again. The oak columns now resembled well-gnawed apple cores, his cover being eaten away. He snapped off two shots, firing practically blind. Only two bullets left now—

One of the double doors in the rear wall flew off its hinges with a crash and landed several feet away. The gunfire ceased. Chase whirled to take in the new threat. The giant scar-faced Russian who had stolen Nina's laptop – Maximov, 'the Bulldozer' – leered through the gap at him.

'Oh, fuck off, Zangief,' said Chase, pulling the trigger.

Maximov jerked back, but not fast enough. The bullet ripped into his thick bicep, splattering the remaining door with blood. Chase heard a groan from the corridor.

An almost *orgasmic* groan.

He suddenly remembered what Mitchell had told them about Maximov's scrambled nervous system. 'Buggeration . . .'

The heavy door swung back – and vanished into the corridor, wrenched from its frame. A moment later it reappeared, a huge hand clamped round each edge as the Russian held it in front of him like a shield.

Chase fired his last shot at the centre of the door, where Maximov's chest would be. The giant jerked and came to a standstill – but only for a second. The bullet had been slowed so much by two inches of dense old oak that it lacked the power to penetrate his ribcage. Instead, the impact only seemed to spur him on. 'I come for you, little *maaaaaan*!'

He rushed at Chase, swinging the door like a colossal

fly-swatter and sending the Englishman flying, demolishing another suit of armour. Pieces scattered cacophonously around him, the blade of the long-handled halberd it had held thunking an inch deep into the floorboards.

Groaning, Chase looked up. Dominika and her comrade had advanced – but though their MP-5Ks were still raised, their fingers were off the triggers. Both were smiling. They wanted to watch the show.

The man laughed and nudged Dominika, saying something mocking in Russian. Chase sat up, one hand falling on a piece of curved metal – and he hurled the armour's high steel collar at the snickering man like a Frisbee. Its edge slammed into his face, crushing his nose with a splintering wet crunch. He shrieked and staggered backwards, blood spurting from both nostrils.

Dominika snapped up her gun – but Maximov had now reached Chase. She held fire, waiting for a clear shot.

Blood seeping down his chest where the bullet had struck, Maximov effortlessly lifted Chase so they were practically face to face, grinning at him with yellow teeth—

Chase head-butted him.

And wished he hadn't. 'Ow, fuck!' he gasped as coloured starbursts flared in his vision. The bastard really *did* have a metal plate in his skull! Maximov's demented grin widened, a rumbling laugh escaping his throat as he tossed Chase back down into the pile of debris.

Chase yelled as the spike sticking up from the back of

the halberd's axe-head stabbed into his arm. He jerked away, leaving blood on the steel.

Maximov advanced again, plate-sized hands reaching out for him. Chase seized the halberd just beneath the axe-head and tugged it free, bounding to his feet. Dominika raised her gun, Maximov's proximity making her hesitate . . .

Chase cracked the end of the halberd's shaft against her kneecap. She stumbled. Before she could recover, he swept it up and caught the woman a vicious blow under her chin. She fell against one of the hanging tapestries.

'Dominika!' yelled Maximov, his concern rapidly turning to rage as his mad eyes locked on to her attacker.

Chase swung the halberd again.

Maximov raised a tree-like arm to block it, the handle snapping in two to leave Chase clutching just a stump of wood with a blade attached. He hurriedly flipped what was left of the weapon over to wield it like a hatchet, but unless he took Maximov's entire head off with a single swipe he didn't fancy his chances.

He didn't try. Instead, he grabbed the rope holding up the tapestry with one hand – and slashed the axe-head through it with the other.

Chase was no featherweight, but the weight of over a hundred square feet of thick, richly embroidered cloth on a sturdy wooden hanger was more than enough to whisk him upwards as the tapestry fell. It knocked Dominika to the floor beneath its folds.

Chase grabbed the balcony railing. He pulled himself

over and took in the scene below. The man with the broken nose was still blindly reeling as he tried to staunch the blood gushing down his face. Dominika was engulfed by the tapestry, while Maximov scowled impotently up at him, the idea of retrieving one of the guns apparently too complex for his brain to accommodate.

Nina—

She was on the opposite side of the balcony, watching as Mitchell fought the Russian in the long coat.

One of Zakhar's kicks finally broke through the American's defences, a heel smashing into Mitchell's shin. He lurched, face twisting with pain. He knew another blow would be coming and tried to raise his arms to intercept it – but not quickly enough. Zakhar ploughed his knuckles into Mitchell's throat. He collapsed, choking.

'Jack!' Nina cried, but the Russian stepped over him, one hand smoothing his long hair. He looked down at the broken weapon she was clutching.

'Hello, sexy lady,' he said. 'Give me sword, please.'

Nina backed away. 'I'd rather not.'

He pouted theatrically, running his hand through his hair once more. 'Okay, I ask again.' He pulled out his gun and pointed it at her. '*Now* give me sword. Please.'

Nina hesitated, and heard a sudden clash of metal – from *above*.

She looked round, as did Zakhar – who was abruptly swept off his feet as Chase, swinging from a chandelier, scooped him up between his legs and sent him flying through one of the stained glass windows. He screamed as he fell, the shriek abruptly truncated by a breathless 'Oof !' as he slammed down on the roof of an outbuilding in the courtyard.

Chase had problems of his own. He was already spinning back out over the hall – and a sharp crack from above warned him that the chandelier was about to pull loose from the ceiling.

He flung himself at the other balcony . . .

And fell short.

Chase grabbed desperately at a tapestry as the chandelier tore free and smashed to the ground. One hand caught the edge of the thick cloth. Flailing for another handhold, he dangled from the tapestry some fifteen feet in the air . . .

Rrrrrrip.

'Oh, shit.' The cloth was tearing away from the beam on which it was hung. Even as he watched, the ragged gap raced across the width of the tapestry. 'Oh, *shit!*'

Chase swung wildly as the tapestry tore. He was heading right at Maximov, whose arms were eagerly raised to grab and crush him—

He slammed his outstretched legs into Maximov's chest.

There was a thud of impact, then Chase fell painfully to the floor. His kick had only knocked Maximov back, not down. The Russian was a bearded Terminator, seemingly invincible.

Nina ran over the shards of broken glass to help Mitchell. 'Are you okay?'

'Won't be singing in the choir for a while,' he wheezed, rubbing his bruised throat. 'Where's the sword?'

Nina held it up. 'Right here.'

'Eddie?'

'Oh, Christ.' Chase was scrambling on his back along the floor below, Maximov stomping after him. 'Come on!' She vaulted Mitchell and ran down the stairs as the Russian grabbed Chase and yanked him up like a child.

The armour she had knocked over was scattered all around, the man it had hit on all fours, just recovering. The Skorpion was inches from his hand. He looked up as he heard Nina's footsteps—

She swung the knight's shield at his head. There was a ringing thud of metal against bone, and he dropped to the floor. Another of Vaskovich's mercenaries stood nearby, both hands clamped over his bloodied face; another swing, another clang, and he too went down.

Nina threw away the dented shield and picked up the gun. Across the hall, Maximov was busy slamming Chase repeatedly against a pillar. 'Hey!' she shouted.

Maximov turned his head, saw the gun – and threw Chase at her like a balding missile.

She tried to dodge, but he hit her shoulder, sending them both to the ground. The gun went off as she fell. The bullet ricocheted off something with a high-pitched twang.

Nina opened her eyes to see Maximov looking up cross-eyed at his own forehead. For a moment, a dull sheen of metal was visible behind the torn skin before blood flowed over it, dripping on to his nose. The huge Russian's knees trembled and he slumped on to his backside with a thump. A vacant grin spread across his face.

It dawned on Nina that – for the moment – they had taken down all their opponents. But the buzz of a helicopter outside the broken window told her how the Russians had entered the castle – and that there were still others. 'Come on, Eddie,' she said, pulling him up, 'gotta go, gotta go!'

Mitchell reached the bottom of the stairs, regarding the two fallen men with surprise. '*You* did that?' he asked her, voice hoarse.

'I'm a real bitch when anyone messes with my man,' she said, grinning.

They ran outside and crossed the courtyard, seeing that the castle's gates were now open. Two more trucks were parked near their SUV.

'That was some pretty fancy martial arts back there,' Nina said to Mitchell as they reached the Suburban. 'Eddie usually just punches people.'

Mitchell rubbed his throat again. 'Not fancy enough.' He got into the driving seat, Nina helping her battered fiancé into the back before running round the truck and hopping in the passenger seat. 'Call the cops,' Mitchell told her, tossing her his phone.

A shadow swept over them, the roar of the helicopter echoing round the courtyard as the Suburban set off. Chase tracked the aircraft as the SUV passed through the gates. 'Chopper's coming around.'

Nina looked up. 'You think they've got guns?'

A snowbank at the roadside suddenly burst apart as a line of small explosions stitched through it. The helicopter buzzed overhead before pulling up sharply to turn for another pass. 'Never mind!' She shoved the sword hilt inside her jacket, fastened her seat belt and raised the phone. 'What's the emergency number in Austria?'

'One three three,' Mitchell told her, braking hard as the SUV approached the first hairpin turn. Even with four-wheel drive, the big vehicle still fishtailed on the snow.

'Jesus, watch it!' Chase warned. 'You don't want to roll us over—'

Bullet holes punched through the SUV's bonnet with a *plunk-plunk-plunk* of cratered metal, followed a fraction of a second later by a bang as one of the front tyres blew out. The shredded wheel bit into the road surface, spinning the entire truck round and slamming it broadside-on into a bank of ploughed snow. The Suburban flipped over on to its roof, slithering to a halt at the very brink of a steep, snow-covered slope.

'Told you,' said Chase after a moment of silence.

He and Mitchell were both now on the cabin's erstwhile ceiling. Nina awkwardly hung suspended by her seat belt, ponytail swishing back and forth against the roof beneath her. Through the cracked windscreen, all she could see were the dizzyingly inverted mountains across the valley and a blank white expanse dropping away to a thin line of trees – and what looked like a cliff edge just beyond them.

Chase, surrounded by the scattered items that had fallen from the SUV's now open emergency compartment, peered out of the rear window. As well as the helicopter, he could hear another sound, a harsh rasp.

Rapidly growing louder.

'Snowmobiles,' he said. 'They're coming after us.'

Mitchell looked outside. 'Where did the chopper go?'

'Dunno, but it sounds like it's coming back.'

'Then we'd better get out of this thing,' said Nina. She put one hand against the ceiling to support herself as best she could and raised the other to the seat-belt release—

Chase realised what she was about to do. 'Nina, *wait!*'

Too late.

The buckle popped free, and Nina dropped heavily on to the roof . . .

The SUV shifted.

'Oh, *bollocks*,' Chase said as the overturned 4x4 tipped over the edge of the slope.

14

Nina stared in horror as the landscape through the windscreen tilted sharply – and started moving past her.

'Nice one!' Chase shouted sarcastically.

'Don't start! I didn't know that would happen!'

Mitchell grappled with his door handle. 'It's jammed. The frame's bent.'

Nina tried her door, but with the same lack of result. Snow slid past the window as they picked up speed. Behind her, Chase crawled towards the rear door. 'I'll open the tailgate. Jack! Find the bonnet release!'

'What?'

'The *hood*, the hood release! It'll drop down and act like a brake!'

Mitchell hunted for the lever as Chase batted aside the coiled tow-cable dangling from the emergency compartment. The roof shuddered beneath him as the SUV bumped over the snow.

'Got it!' Mitchell shouted. He pulled the lever and the

bonnet slammed down in front of the windscreen, its broad front edge digging into the snow. The Suburban slowed, but didn't stop. Snow sprayed up from each side of the bonnet, gravity and three tons of upside-down truck continuing to drag them down the mountainside.

'Shit, we're spinning!' Nina shouted. The bonnet was scooping up snow unevenly, slewing the SUV round. The trees further down the slope drifted into view through her side window.

An idea flashed through her mind. She squeezed under her seat's headrest, straining to reach the handle of the door behind her.

Chase reached the rear door and tugged the handle. The tailgate popped open; he braced himself and pushed it down like a drawbridge.

A sound reached him over the thumps of the truck's descent – engines, rasping and raw. Snowmobiles.

And the helicopter, swooping down to pass them . . .

Nina pulled the handle. The rear door opened slightly. She forced it wider. Snow spat into the cabin, biting at her eyes. Wincing, she pushed harder as the Suburban continued to turn sideways, picking up speed . . .

It swung back, the door acting as a rudder. They straightened out, slowing again as the bonnet gouged into the snow—

The open door hit something under the snow and the window burst apart. Nina shrieked and jumped back. But her idea had worked, and the Chevrolet was back in a straight line – for now.

A large bump threw Nina and Mitchell against the seats, loose items bouncing around them as the slope steepened. Even with their makeshift brake, they were still gaining speed. She looked back – and saw Chase clambering on to the open tailgate. She thought he was going to jump off, but instead he leaned forward, reaching for something on the SUV's underside. 'Eddie! What're you *doing*? Jump, get off!'

Squinting into the spraying snow, Chase had no intention of jumping, however. Instead he bent over the rear bumper for the spare wheel mounted under the cargo bed, all the while aware that the top of the cliff was rapidly getting closer.

The helicopter moved into a hover past the cliff edge, wanting a grandstand view of their deaths. And from behind, Chase heard the rattle of automatic weapons fire, the snowmobilers trying to bring them about even sooner—

The Suburban hit a rock hidden beneath the snow, throwing the entire vehicle into the air. It crashed down nose first, ripping the bonnet loose. The windscreen shattered. The SUV immediately picked up speed on its hellish sledge run down the mountain.

Nina fought her way up the cabin as snow flew all around her. Chase had somehow managed to keep hold, silhouetted in the open tailgate. 'Eddie!' she yelled. 'Save yourself, jump!'

He crouched. 'Not without you!' Another side window exploded as the truck smashed over a rock. 'Give me that line!'

Nina used the headrests to pull herself along. The tow-cable hanging from the emergency compartment twitched crazily at every bump, just out of reach. She stretched for it . . .

Bullets clanked against the Suburban's flank, one of them piercing the thin steel and hitting the seat above her with a *whump*. She flinched, then grabbed for the cable as it continued its mocking dance. This time, she caught it.

She used it to pull herself closer, then untangled it. Chase leaned into the cabin, arm outstretched. Nina reached out for him . . .

'Oh shit,' said Mitchell in a voice of imminent doom. Chase looked ahead. The line of trees was coming up fast – as was the cliff edge just beyond. 'Whatever you're doing, do it now!'

Chase's gaze met Nina's.

With a final effort, she lunged forward. Chase snatched the cable from her hand and straightened, the wind slashing at his face as he leaned over the rear bumper. He had already freed the spare wheel from its recess; now, he rapidly uncoiled the cable and threaded one end between the alloy spokes before knotting it.

Another window shattered, snow and glass showering around his legs. He ignored it, tying the other end of the cable around the SUV's towhook. The treeline was only seconds away—

He hurled the spare wheel.

It spun off to one side, the cable snaking behind it.

Snow sprayed into the air as it bounced down the slope parallel to the Suburban.

The snowmobiles closed in. Chase ducked, gripping the towhook tightly as another bullet blew out a light cluster just inches from him. The whining chatter of the helicopter rose ahead, chainsaw snarl of the snowmobile engines behind as the Chevy hurtled towards the cliff.

The spare wheel bounced past a tree – on the opposite side from the Suburban.

The cable snapped taut, whipping the spare wheel round the trunk once, twice, before it smashed into the bark. The SUV suddenly jerked round, sweeping across the clifftop at the end of the line, so close to the edge that there was nothing below the frame of the broken windscreen but empty space. Nina screamed as centrifugal force tore loose her grip and threw her towards the hole—

Mitchell's hand clamped round her wrist.

The Suburban continued along its arc, swinging back *up* the slope. One of the snowmobilers had swerved to avoid the trees – now he found three tons of battered steel whooshing straight at him like a giant's hammer.

The two vehicles collided, the sheer momentum of the SUV swatting the lightweight snowmobile backwards. The rider was flung skywards as its rear end flipped up. He somersaulted over the Suburban, over the cliff . . .

And into the blades of the hovering helicopter.

The man instantly became nothing but a red haze spraying out from the whirling rotor. The helicopter reeled from the impact. Its nose dipped sharply, pulling the aircraft into a steep descent despite the pilot's desperate attempts to level out.

Rotor blades slashed against the sheer rocks, shattered—

The helicopter ploughed into the cliff, smashing the cabin and its occupants flat before the rest of the fuselage tumbled down the wall and exploded.

Chase finally lost his hold, thrown from the tailgate into the snow as the SUV swung round the tree. It hit a rock broadside-on, the roof caving in and rolling the Suburban back on to its side. Its wheels dug into the snow, flipping it upright and bouncing it into the air—

The second snowmobiler had stopped his stolen vehicle short of the cliff – only to be smacked from his seat as the Suburban tumbled over it at chest height. He hit the ground – and the SUV landed on top of him. Roof crushed, chassis bent, it finally slid to a stop, upside down once again.

Chase shakily stood and picked his way across the steep slope. He passed the idling snowmobile and reached the wreckage of the Suburban, a long red smear marking where the rider had been scraped along beneath it. 'Nina! *Nina!* Are you okay?'

No reply. He crouched and looked inside.

The flattened interior was filled with snow and dirt. He peered round the seats. *'Nina!'*

Movement from the front. 'Eddie?' grunted Mitchell, dazed.

'Jack! Where's Nina?'

'I dunno. I . . . I couldn't keep hold of her.'

A cold stone formed in the pit of Chase's stomach. 'Are you okay?' he asked, forcing himself to check on the closest person first when every part of his mind was screaming at him to search for Nina.

'Think so . . . banged up, but I don't think anything's broken . . .'

'Good. I'll be right back.' Chase stood, looking for any sign of his fiancée.

He stumbled round the wreck, eyes hunting desperately for anything that wasn't white or brown or green. 'Nina!' He turned, and kept turning, the mountainous landscape around him becoming a blur—

Red.

Not blood, but the subtler shade of her hair poking above a snowdrift a few yards away.

He ran to it, snow crumping under his feet. Nina was sprawled on the cold ground, thrown out of the SUV as it flipped over. She lay face down, not moving.

Chase reached her and dropped to his knees, feeling for signs of life – or death. It was impossible to pick out a heartbeat through her thick jacket, and he couldn't even tell if she was breathing. His hands moved to her neck, brushing her ponytail aside as he pressed his fingertips under her chin. She was still warm to the touch, but he didn't feel a pulse.

His own heart racing, he tried a different spot.

A pulse.

He waited, holding his breath.

Another, and another. Steady. Gasping in relief, Chase carefully supported her head and turned her on to her back. Her face was cut in several places, red lines running down her cheek and chin.

He quickly unzipped her jacket. The sword hilt weighed down one side as he opened it, but he ignored the hunk of metal as he hunted for signs of other injuries. No blood, no spikes of broken bones as he ran his hands over her chest—

'There's . . . a time and a place for that, Eddie,' she whispered.

Chase realised both his hands were on her breasts. Her eyes flickered open, and she managed a weak smile.

'Hah!' gasped Chase, the exhalation somewhere between relief and annoyance. 'Very fucking funny!' He withdrew his hands. 'Are you hurt anywhere?'

'I'm hurt *everywhere* . . . but I think I'm okay.' She tried to raise herself. 'Ow, ow.' Chase helped her to sit up. She caught sight of the mangled Suburban nearby. 'Oh, my God! Where's Jack? Is he all right?'

An arm waved from the open tailgate in reply. Mitchell wormed his way between the seats of the overturned SUV into the cargo space. 'I'm fine,' he called. 'The sword! Have you still got the sword?'

Nina pawed at her open jacket. 'Shit, it was right—'

'It's here,' Chase told her, holding it up. 'We've got it, don't worry.'

Mitchell crawled from the Suburban. He looked at the

nearby cliff edge, and the swathe of snow the truck had scraped from it. 'Jesus! That was close.'

'We're not done yet,' said Chase, as he looked back up the mountainside and saw reflected sunlight flash from one of the Russians' SUVs as it rounded the first hairpin. 'Got to keep moving.'

Nina eyed the snowmobile. 'You're not thinking . . .'

''Fraid I am, love.' Chase pointed down the valley: the sheer cliff gradually shallowed, becoming a steep but traversable slope down to the valley floor – and the road leading through it. 'We can get down that way, and we'll do it a lot faster than those Russian twats. Did you call the police?'

'I lost the phone,' Nina admitted.

Chase looked back at the path of their wild ride down the mountain. 'Suppose I can let you off, considering.' Unzipping a pocket, he took out his own phone and gave it to her. 'Call the cops. As long as we can stay ahead of those arseholes until they arrive, we'll be okay.'

Mitchell joined them as Chase lifted Nina to her feet. 'Three people on a snowmobile? We should split up. You two go on ahead – I'll take the sword into those trees over here and call the embassy, get them to send a chopper.'

'Do a lot of alpine survival training in the navy, did you?' Chase asked. Mitchell looked irked.

'We should stick together,' Nina insisted as she dialled the Austrian emergency number. On getting through, she explained the situation as best she could in fractured German while Chase checked the snowmobile for damage. 'Okay, the cops are on the way,' she said, finishing the call. 'They don't know how long it'll take to get here, though.'

Chase climbed aboard the snowmobile. 'Call Mitzi, the number's in the memory. If she picks us up we can drive back and meet 'em halfway. Okay, let's go.' He revved the engine. Nina clambered on behind him, Mitchell sandwiching her. 'Hold tight!'

He set off in a spray of snow, pointing the snowmobile's nose uphill at an angle for maximum traction on the treacherous surface. Nina glanced nervously up the mountainside. The Russian SUVs were still descending, but Chase was right: the snowmobile would reach the road below long before they could negotiate the winding route.

Mitzi answered the phone. 'Hello?'

'Mitzi, it's Nina! Sorry, this is an emergency – we're coming back from the castle and we need you to pick us up.'

The young Swiss woman's voice filled with concern. 'Are you okay? What's happening? Is Eddie okay?'

'Mitzi, sorry, there's no time to explain right now – please, just meet us on the main road as quick as you can!'

'I'll be there in five minutes, less!'

'Okay, thanks. See you soon.' Nina rang off. 'She's on her way,' she told Chase.

'Great! Told you she was a top lass, didn't I?'

It took them only a few minutes to reach the valley floor through the thickening stands of snow-laden evergreens. Nina looked uphill again as they crossed the road to the castle. The Russians were well behind.

'There's Mitzi!' Chase cried. Ahead on the main road was her red SUV, flashing its headlights as it approached. He skidded to a stop beside the churned line of snow thrown up by the ploughs. 'Everybody off!'

The Cayenne halted a short distance away. Mitzi jumped out. 'What's going on?'

'Tell you on the way,' said Chase as Mitchell and Nina hopped off the snowmobile. 'The police are coming. We need to meet 'em, fast!'

Mitzi saw the cuts on Nina's face. 'You're hurt!'

'I'll live,' she replied as Mitchell opened the rear door for her.

Chase jumped over the snow bank and ran to the SUV's passenger side. 'Come on, Mitzi, let's go!'

'Okay, okay!' She turned to climb back into the Porsche.

Nina was about to slide across the seat to let Mitchell in when she realised he wasn't following her, instead looking back up the mountain. She followed his gaze. One of the Russian SUVs had stopped, a figure with hair of unnatural red standing beside it.

A flash of pure green light . . .

There was a flat, wet thump. Something drummed against the Cayenne's windscreen like thick rain.

But it wasn't water.

Mitzi fell against her open door, slamming it shut as she dropped to the ground. On the other side of the

Porsche, Chase was frozen, staring in shock at the empty space where a second before there had been a beautiful young woman, then an explosive cloud of grey and red—

The crack of Dominika's sniper rifle reached them, trailing behind the supersonic bullet.

Nina screamed and scrambled out of the back seat in terror and revulsion at the spray of blood and brain and bone and hair across the windscreen. She stumbled away from the Porsche, collapsing to her knees and spewing acid vomit into the snow.

Chase broke free of his paralysis, training and experience automatically kicking in as he dropped behind the cover of the Cayenne to avoid the next shot.

It didn't come. Instead, the distant flame-haired figure leapt back into her SUV, which roared down the road after its twin.

The Russians were still coming after them. Chase knew he should take the wheel of the Cayenne and get Nina and Mitchell to safety, but instead he ran round the Porsche to Mitzi. Mitchell was crouching as if to lift her up—

'*Don't touch her!*' Chase roared. Mitchell jumped back. Chase knelt beside her and checked for a pulse.

But he already knew he would find none. The entry wound was a scorched black circle just behind Mitzi's temple, no wider than a pencil. He didn't need to look to know that the exit wound on the opposite side of her skull would be far bigger, the size of his clenched fist. The nauseating splatter across the Cayenne's windscreen confirmed his worst fears.

'Jesus,' he whispered. 'No, shit, no, *no* . . . I promised, I fucking *promised* . . .'

In the distance he heard the echoing wail of a siren. The police.

The Russians reached the junction with the main road . . . and sped away up the valley, leaving behind the red Cayenne and the three figures next to it.

A smaller figure lay at their feet, unmoving.

The journey back to Zürich in the State Department jet was a sombre one, Chase barely saying a word the entire time. Mitchell took the sword hilt to the security of the US embassy, while Chase and Nina went on to the penthouse apartment of Erwin and Brigitte Fontana.

Nina watched from the door of the rooftop terrace as Chase spoke to Mitzi's parents. She had wanted to stand with him, to share the blame, but despite her pleas he had refused, insisting he talk to them alone.

Mitzi's father, a tall, stern man, had returned from Shanghai. He stood upright and silent with his hands on the back of Brigitte's chair, knuckles slowly tightening. Brigitte too remained still, at first. Then her hands began to shake as she spoke. Nina was too far away to hear what she was saying, but her expression of disbelief, then anguish, spoke as clearly as any words. She stood, quivering hands to her mouth as Chase said something else. Erwin flinched, scraping the back legs of the chair against the balcony floor.

Brigitte let out a keening wail – then lashed out at Chase, slapping his face with a crack that echoed across the terrace. He stood there unmoving as she hit him again and again, screaming in German before staggering back and slumping on to the chair, weeping. Erwin placed his hands on her shoulders and said something to Chase through tight lips.

Wordlessly, Chase turned and walked stiffly from the terrace. He passed Nina without speaking, unable even to look at her as a tear rolled down his cheek.

15

London

'So, we've got two pieces of Caliburn,' said Mitchell, gazing at the hilt and broken blade laid out on a table in the US embassy. He indicated the missing tip. 'And Vaskovich has the third. Question is, is that enough to let him find Excalibur – and is what *we* have enough for *us* to find it?'

'I know where we'll need to look,' Nina told him. She and Mitchell were alone in the room; Chase had stayed at their hotel. She had wanted to comfort Chase on the flight back to London, to assure him she was there to help in any way she could . . . but he had said nothing. Nothing at all.

She had never seen Chase act that way before, but knew him well enough to realise that Mitzi's death – and the blame her parents had placed on him, and that he had accepted – had wounded him deeply. But she also knew trying to force him to respond to her would only make things worse. All she could do was wait.

Wait, and return to her research of Arthurian legend. And it had borne fruit. Nina knew she'd seen the symbol of the labyrinth inscribed on the sword before, and it hadn't taken long to discover where.

'Glastonbury,' she continued, opening one of the books and placing it by the sword. The page showed the same labyrinth – distorted, stretched diagonally, but the winding line following exactly the same turns. 'It's a representation of the path to the summit of Glastonbury Tor in Somerset.' Another book provided a colour photo of a small hill rising almost unnaturally from the surrounding flat English landscape, a stone tower at its peak. The hill had an unusual stepped appearance, a rounded grassy ziggurat. 'These terraces run all round it, but if you follow the path up from the foot of the hill, it leads to the top along exactly the same route as the one on the sword.'

Mitchell examined the photo. 'That doesn't even look real. Is it man-made?'

'The Tor's natural, but the terraces have been shaped by man over millennia. The site's been populated since the neolithic era, over six thousand years.'

'What about the tower? Is that part of the Arthurian legend?'

She shook her head. 'No, it's a lot more recent – it's what's left of a medieval chapel called St Michael's. But the Tor itself has definite links to Arthurian mythology.'

Mitchell tapped one of the symbols on the sword. 'So you think these are some kind of clue to finding Arthur's tomb, and Excalibur? A map?'

'Of some sort, yes. I don't know exactly how it works or what the dots on the labyrinth represent, but I'm sure I'll be able to figure it out on site.'

'You want to go to Glastonbury?'

'Absolutely,' said Nina. 'Today, if we can.'

'Better let the Brits know what's going on, I suppose – if we're going to dig up one of their country's greatest legends, they'll probably have something to say about it.'

'What happens if we *do* find Excalibur? The Tor's part of the National Trust, like a national monument. Anything we find there technically belongs to the British people.'

'I think we can persuade the government to bend the rules,' Mitchell said with a smile. 'I'll get them to find a local expert for us as well; it'll be useful to have somebody who knows the place. You really want to go today?'

'The sooner we go, the more chance we have of finding Excalibur before Vaskovich's people.'

Mitchell nodded. 'I'll make the arrangements. Where's Eddie?'

'At the hotel.'

'How's he doing?'

'I don't know,' Nina admitted truthfully.

'I'll phone you once I've arranged everything,' Mitchell told her. He carefully placed the pieces of the sword inside a padded metal case. 'You go see Eddie, check he's okay.'

'I will,' said Nina as he picked up the case and left the room.

But she couldn't help thinking that Chase *wasn't* okay – and that nothing she said would improve matters.

'Eddie? Are you in here?'

'Yeah,' came the flat reply.

At least he was talking, Nina thought as she closed the hotel room's door. She found him lying on the bed, staring up at the ceiling. 'What've you been doing?'

'Nothing. Just . . . thinking.'

She knew what was on his mind, but didn't want to bring it up yet, worried about his reaction. Instead she sat next to him and held his hand, stroking it softly. 'Can I get you anything?'

'No, I'm fine. Where've you been? The embassy?'

She nodded. 'I think we figured out where Excalibur is.'

'We? You and Jack?'

She picked up a new edge in his voice at the mention of Mitchell, but chose to ignore it. 'It's at Glastonbury. Probably somewhere under the Tor. We're going to go and check it out.'

'You and Jack.'

'No, all of us,' she insisted. 'You and me.'

He looked directly at her for the first time since she entered the room. 'No. I'm not going.'

'What?'

'I'm not going. And you're not either.'

Nina stared at him. 'Excuse me, *what*?'

'I said, you're not going. All of this, it's over.'

'What do you mean, "this"?'

'I mean,' said Chase, sitting up sharply, 'all this running around the world, treasure-hunting, looking for bits of worthless old *crap*! Let this fucking Russian have his sword, who gives a shit?'

'You know we can't do that,' said Nina, trying to keep down her own anger. 'It's a national security issue.'

'I *don't* know that! You said yourself, you thought this business about earth energy and ley lines and all the rest of it was bullshit!'

'I'm not sure any more. Whether it is or not, Vaskovich obviously believes it – which is why we've got to find Excalibur before he does!'

He pulled his hand away and got off the bed. 'Even if it means dying for it?' he said, voice bitter.

'Eddie, what happened to Mitzi wasn't your fault,' Nina protested.

'Then whose fault *was* it? I *promised* Brigitte I'd look after her, that I'd take care of her, and now she's *dead*! If I hadn't got her into all of this, she'd still be alive! For fuck's sake!' His voice cracked. 'She was just a *kid*! She wasn't a professional, it wasn't like when Hugo got killed – he was doing a job, he knew the risks. But it wasn't *her* job to take risks, she didn't even know there were going to *be* any risks! She just wanted to help me out – and it got her killed! *I* got her killed!'

'You *didn't*!' cried Nina. 'It was that bleach-haired bitch who shot Bernd who killed her! You – you are *not* to blame here, Eddie! You are not responsible for this!'

'Yes I am. I was responsible for Mitzi, and I'm responsible for you. The whole thing's got too dangerous. So you're not going. And that's that.'

Nina stood and faced him, almost toe to toe. 'You don't tell me what I can and can't do, Eddie,' she said, the coldness in her voice barely masking a trembling rage. 'If that's the way you think, then maybe it's a good thing we hadn't set a date yet.'

Chase regarded her silently, then his stone face returned. He snatched up his leather jacket and went to the door.

'Where are you going?' Nina demanded.

'Out.'

'Eddie, wait—' But the door had swung shut behind him with a decisive clack.

Nina stared at the blank wood for a long moment, unsure what to do. Then, reluctantly, she backed away and returned to the bed. She perched on its edge, struggling to untangle her conflicted emotions.

'Fancy meeting you here,' said a warm Scottish voice over the lunchtime bustle of the pub.

Chase looked up to see Mac standing by his table, a glass of Scotch in his hand and a faint smile on his face. Chase didn't return it. 'If Nina sent you, she's wasted your time.'

'I spoke to Nina a couple of hours ago, yes,' said Mac, taking a seat opposite him and putting down his glass, 'but she didn't ask me to do anything. She just wanted to know if I'd seen you. I told her I hadn't – but I had a feeling you might have come here.' He surveyed the surroundings. The Jug of Ale was a fairly generic central London pub, lined with fake olde-worlde wooden beams and shelves of faux-antique bric-a-brac bought by the yard, but it held meaning for Chase. 'This always used to be your bolt-hole when Sophia was being difficult at home. I see old habits die hard. It's been a while since we had a drink together here, though. Five years?'

'Something like that.'

'It looks quite different since the smoking ban. I can actually see the back wall.' He raised an eyebrow and turned back to Chase. 'Good God, was the wallpaper always that hideous?' Chase's expression didn't alter. 'Hrmm. Not even a hint of a smile – things must be worse than I thought.'

'Any particular reason you're here, Mac?' Chase asked impatiently.

'Actually, yes. The first one is that I wanted to offer my condolences about Mitzi. I'm sorry. I only met her the once, but she seemed a very nice girl.'

Chase looked down at his drink. 'She was,' he said leadenly, taking another mouthful.

Mac regarded the half-empty glass. 'Not like you to drink during the day. How many have you had?'

Another swig. 'This is the fourth.'

'So you're drunk?'

'What, on only four pints?' Mac stared at him unblinkingly. 'Yeah, a bit,' Chase finally admitted.

'Now I *know* something's wrong,' said Mac, his tone somewhere between amusement and mild concern. 'You would never have owned up to feeling drunk so soon when you were in the Regiment.'

'Things change,' Chase told him dismissively, shaking his head. 'I'm getting old.'

Mac picked up his drink and downed it in a single gulp. 'I'll join you in the ongoing march of the ageing process, then.'

'Not really sure I want any company right now, Mac.'

'Well, you're going to have some anyway. You see, the second reason I wanted to talk to you is that Nina sounded rather upset when she called me.'

Chase's jaw muscles tightened. 'Not so upset that it's stopped her from wanting to carry on fucking tomb-raiding.'

'You don't think she'll be safe?' Mac asked. Chase shook his head again. 'She knows the risks.'

'I don't think they're worth it.'

'She does.'

'Doesn't mean she's right.'

'If you're so worried, why don't you go with her?'

Chase took another mouthful, then put the glass down with a bang. 'Because I don't want her to go *at all*. But she still wants to anyway.' He scowled. 'With Jack Mitchell. We had a big fight about it.'

'The man I met at your sister's?'

'Yeah, that's him. The tall, dark and handsome one.' Chase slumped back in his chair, letting out a long and unhappy breath of frustration.

Mac leaned forward, his voice taking on a forceful edge as he addressed the younger man. 'Jack Mitchell's not the problem, though, is he? He's not why you're sitting in a crappy pub getting pissed at one in the afternoon.'

Chase was silent for a moment. 'No, not really,' he said finally.

Mac's expression suggested that he already knew the answer, but he asked the obvious question anyway. 'Then what?'

Another pause. 'It's Mitzi. I never . . . I never lost someone I was looking after before. It's not just that she died, I've seen friends die before, but . . . not like that. It shouldn't have happened. It *wouldn't* have happened if I hadn't got her involved.'

'So you blame yourself?'

'Who else is there?'

'The person who pulled the trigger,' said Mac. 'The person who sent out that person in the first place. They're the ones you should be looking to hurt. Not yourself.'

Chase raised his eyebrows. 'You're saying I should go for some revenge? Not very professional.'

'If you still think Nina's in danger, then your mission isn't over yet. These people are *hostiles*, Eddie. They've proved that. Eliminating a known threat to a mission is entirely justified, in my opinion.'

Chase let out a bitter laugh. 'My *mission*? It's Nina's mission, not mine. I was just along for the ride – and she doesn't even want me there any more.'

'You don't believe that,' Mac said sternly. 'She loves you. And I know you love her.'

'And that's the problem! Losing Mitzi was fucking horrible enough, but what if I lose *Nina*?' His voice caught. 'I do love her. I love her so much I'm scared of losing her. I'm actually *scared* of it. I don't know what I'd do.'

He lowered his head. Mac watched in silence, then reached across and put his hand on Chase's arm. 'I'm not the person you should be saying this to.'

'I know, but I . . . I don't know what to say to her. I don't want her to see me in this state.'

'In what state? Drunk?'

Chase looked up. 'No, Christ, she's seen me drunk before. No, I mean . . . you know.' His voice fell to little more than a whisper, the admission struggling to be heard over the noise of the room. 'Weak.'

Mac leaned closer, fixing Chase with an intense gaze. 'Eddie, you're going to get *married*. She's going to see you in *every* state, whether you like it or not. "For better or for worse", I remember. And you were married to *Sophia*, for God's sake – you know there are always going to be fights in a marriage. There's nowhere to hide – you either have to face any problems head-on, or walk away from them. And you've never struck me as the kind to walk away from anything. As I said in the Regiment, "Fight to the end." And you always did.'

'Not always,' Chase said, another quiet confession. 'Not until you taught me. There was one fight before I met you that I . . . that I walked away from. And I shouldn't have done.' He sat up, contemplative. 'Nina was right.'

'About what?'

'About family. She said it was a shame I didn't get on with mine. And it didn't have to be like that.' He straightened. 'Yeah, I need to talk to Nina, and I will. But there's someone else I need to talk to first.'

'Who?'

'My sister. All this's made me realise I need to tell her something. Face to face.' He glanced at his glass. 'I'll have to take the train, though. Might have a problem hiring a car if I turn up pissed – assuming anyone'll even let me after what happened to the last one.'

16

Warm late afternoon sun, a perfect clear blue sky, and dazzlingly verdant surroundings . . . yet they were just the icing on the cake for Nina as she took in the ruins at the heart of the parkland. 'This is beautiful!'

'Bit of a fixer-upper, though,' Mitchell joked.

They stood within the grounds of Glastonbury Abbey, an oasis of tranquillity surrounded beyond its walls by Glastonbury itself. The village, about 120 miles west of London, was an odd mix of the everyday and the exotic, ordinary shops and businesses sharing streets with outposts of New Age expression and outright tourist traps, jugglers and street musicians and hippies mingling with residents carrying their groceries, who ignored the colourful strangeness around them with traditional British reserve.

But the abbey, or what remained of it, had an atmosphere of nothing but calm, the grey stone walls so weathered by time they felt almost a natural part of the landscape, as integral as a rock or a river. 'It's quite something, isn't it?' said their companion. Dr Chloe Lamb was a rosy-cheeked, broad-hipped woman slightly older than Nina, straw-coloured hair tied back almost in a copy of Nina's own ponytail. 'So tragic that it was destroyed. Henry the Eighth may have been one of England's most important monarchs, but he was a disaster for monastic architecture!'

'It's still pretty incredible,' Nina said, pausing to take a photo as they passed between the remains of two still-towering pillars into the abbey's former vaulted choir. Where there had once been stone flags was now just grass, a neatly mown lawn leading to the broken stubs of the eastern walls.

'But it hardly compares to some of the other places you've been,' said Chloe. 'I mean, Atlantis! You turned the studies of history and archaeology on their heads overnight – and then you did it again when you discovered the Tomb of Hercules!' Her already pink cheeks flushed a little more. 'To be honest, I was surprised the IHA asked for my help. I have to admit that I feel a little intimidated by you.'

'Oh, God, please don't be!' Nina said, laughing. 'When it comes to Arthurian legend, I'm only really a step above anyone who's watched *Monty Python and the Holy Grail*.' That was false modesty, considering her recent immersion in the subject, but she decided the self-conscious academic would benefit from an ego boost. 'We needed help from someone who specialised in that area – particularly with regard to Glastonbury.'

Chloe smiled. 'Well, hopefully I can provide it. And this is the ideal place to start.' She indicated a sign at the head of a stone rectangle marked in the grass.

'"Site of King Arthur's tomb",' Mitchell read. '"In the year 1191 the bodies of King Arthur and his queen were said to have been found on the south side of the Lady Chapel . . ." Only "said" to have been found?'

'Unfortunately, there's an awful lot "said" about King Arthur here at Glastonbury. The abbey monks were . . . well, *notorious*,' Chloe said conspiratorially, as if concerned they would somehow overhear her. 'They were extremely good at turning legend into gold. For example, the Holy Grail is now intimately entwined with Arthurian myth – but the two weren't even remotely connected until the twelfth century, when Robert de Boron wrote *Joseph d'Arimathie*.'

'Not *the* Joseph, surely?' Mitchell asked. 'As in Mary and Joseph?'

Nina shook her head. 'Joseph of Arimathea was the man who donated his own intended tomb to bury Jesus after the crucifixion. He was sent the Grail by a vision of Christ and brought it to Britain as a pilgrim.'

Chloe nodded. 'Since the abbey was already connected with Joseph because of the story of the Holy Thorn,' she glanced towards the part of the abbey grounds where a hawthorn tree was said to have been planted by the pilgrim, 'the monks took advantage of that to join two entirely separate legends, both of which conveniently happened to cross paths right here, into one.'

'So they got a twofer,' Mitchell realised. 'The Christians come in the footsteps of Joseph, the Brits want to pay respect to their legendary king – and both groups give generously to the abbey.'

'Absolutely. Glastonbury was second only to Westminster Abbey in terms of wealth.' Chloe looked at the sign again. 'And now the legends are inseparable. But so much of what we now think of as Arthurian legend is just the same – either merged with material from other sources, or simply made up by the twelfth-century romantic writers.'

'Things like Lancelot,' Nina said.

'Lancelot wasn't real?' asked Mitchell.

'I'm afraid not,' said Chloe. 'He first appeared in a poem by Chrétien de Troyes in the 1160s – no mention of him anywhere before then.'

'Huh.' He sounded disappointed. 'So much for the legends. Next you'll be telling me the Round Table wasn't real either.' Both women looked at him apologetically. 'Aw, come on!'

'It didn't appear until 1155, in Robert Wace's *Roman de Brut*,' said Chloe.

'And the knights didn't eat ham and jam and Spam a lot?'

'Sorry,' Nina replied with a grin. She turned back to Chloe. 'But as for the aspects of the legends that *do* have a historical basis . . . how does Glastonbury Tor tie in with the story of King Arthur?'

'Ah!' said Chloe. She led them out of the ruined abbey,

strolling across the rolling parkland. 'Now Glastonbury Tor really does have an interesting part to play in the mythos.' She swept a hand towards the flat, lush English countryside to the south. 'You see, this whole region is a flood plain. Until the marshes were drained for farmland, it would only need a small rise in the water level for it to disappear under water.'

'How deep?' Mitchell asked.

'Not much, maybe as little as a couple of feet. But it would make almost the entire area inaccessible for a good part of the year. Glastonbury, and the abbey, were high enough to escape most of the floods.'

Nina tried to picture her idyllic surroundings as they would have looked over a thousand years earlier. 'So where we are right now, it would have been an island?'

'Yes. Although sometimes even this might have been at risk from flooding. But there's one place the water could *never* reach.' She stopped, pointing east. Their walk had taken them past a line of trees, giving them a clear view of . . . 'Glastonbury Tor.'

Seen for real rather than framed within a photograph, the hill seemed to Nina even more out of place, rising up with the unexpectedness of a child's lone sandcastle on an otherwise flat beach. The lowering sun gave its terraces an even more exaggeratedly unnatural look, the hillside striped in alternating shades of green. The isolated tower on its peak only increased the almost fairytale feel of the landmark.

'It's been associated with English folklore since even before the time of King Arthur,' Chloe explained. 'A lot of magical mumbo-jumbo as well. I'm sure you saw plenty of it in the village. Fairies, ley lines, UFOs and all that.'

'Some of it might not be mumbo-jumbo after all,' said Mitchell.

Chloe gave him an odd look, as if expecting a punchline and being surprised at his sincerity. 'Well, anyway. According to legend, after Arthur was mortally wounded at the battle of Camlann, he was brought to a place called the Isle of Avalon, which is where he died and was buried. "Avalon" is one of the earlier names of Glastonbury – and since the surrounding marshes were often flooded . . .'

'. . . there's your isle,' Nina finished, indicating the Tor.

'Precisely.' They all stared up at the strange hill before Chloe turned to address the others. 'Would you like a closer look?'

Holly opened the front door, reacting with pleased surprise when she saw who was standing there. 'Uncle Eddie!'

'Hi, Holly,' said Chase, managing something that was more or less a smile.

'I thought you'd gone abroad?'

'I did. Now I'm back. Is your mum in?'

'Yes, in the kitchen.' She ushered him inside and led him through the house. 'How was your trip? Did you have a good time?'

'Had better,' he said stiffly.

They entered the kitchen, and found Elizabeth loading the washing machine. 'Eddie?' she said, surprised and far from thrilled to see him. 'What're you doing here? Come back to destroy the rest of town, maybe?'

'Hi, Lizzie. How's Nan?'

'She's all right – no thanks to you. But I'm sure she'll appreciate your belated concern.' She slammed the washer's door. 'What do you want?'

'Can I talk to you? In private.' Holly looked peeved, but exited the room.

Elizabeth leaned against the counter, arms folded. 'Well?'

Chase took a long, slow breath. 'I wanted to tell you that . . .' He paused. 'That you were right all along. About me.'

She was confused for a moment; then a triumphant, almost gloating expression spread across her face. 'Well, I never thought I'd hear you say *that*! Eddie Chase finally admitting that he's wrong, that he's not perfect! I should get Dad on the phone. I'm sure he'd love to hear you own up—'

'Elizabeth.' The hardness of Chase's voice as much as his use of her full name stopped her mid-sentence. 'Someone's *died*.'

'What?' The triumph faded, her eyes widening in shock. 'Oh, my God! Not – not Nina?'

'No,' said Chase, feeling a deep shame and guilt for the relief the single word brought him. 'Not Nina. But somebody else I cared about, and . . . and she's dead because of me.'

'How?'

'Doesn't matter. But she'd still be alive if I hadn't got her involved. And it made me realise you were right – about me walking away rather than . . . rather than facing up to losing someone,' he said, the admission almost physically painful. 'But I couldn't walk away this time. I had to go to two people I knew, friends – and I had to tell them their daughter was dead. And that – that it was my fault.'

'My God,' Elizabeth said softly. 'I'm sorry.'

'No need for *you* to be – you were right all along. I *did* just walk away when Mum died. But I was never able to admit it before. And . . . *fuck*!' He turned away, banging his hands down on the worktop. 'I just walked straight out after the funeral and joined the army without even looking back, and left you to deal with everything else, with Dad, fucked up your degree . . . Christ, no wonder you hate me.'

'I don't *hate* you, Eddie,' Elizabeth said, crossing the room to join him. She hesitantly extended a hand, then placed it on his arm. 'You're my brother. That doesn't mean I don't still have some very strong feelings about the things you've done . . . but I never hated you.'

'Yeah, but it still messed things up for you, didn't it? You were the smart one, had all the big plans for after university, and if you hadn't had to quit to sort things out at home—'

'If things had turned out differently,' said Elizabeth firmly, 'I wouldn't have had Holly. And I wouldn't change that for anything.' She squeezed his wrist. 'I'm sorry about your friend, Eddie, really. And I know you feel guilty about it – but it's normal to feel guilt when someone you love dies. I did when Mum died, even though there was absolutely nothing I could have done to change things. It was cancer, what was I going to do?'

'But I *didn't* feel guilty,' Chase protested. 'I just left and joined the army because with Mum gone I didn't see any reason to stay in that house a minute longer. I was too busy with training to feel guilty. I *hid* from it. But this time, I couldn't hide. I had to face it.'

'And it hurts.'

He let out a bitter laugh. 'Yeah. It really fucking hurts.'

'Eddie,' she said softly, 'there's nothing wrong with that. I know you've been this tough, fearless super-soldier for all these years . . . but you're also a human being, you're still my little brother. You *had* all these feelings, all the time – you just kept them hidden. But the time to be worried would be if there was nothing *to* hide, if you really *didn't* care. And I know you're not like that.'

He had no real answer to that. Instead he stood silently, contemplating her words.

'Have you talked to Nina about this?' Elizabeth asked.

'No.' Chase sighed. 'I don't . . . I wouldn't know what to say.'

'Say what you feel. She deserves to know. You're going

to be marrying her – she should know what her husband's really like.'

'But what if I lose her, too?' Chase said. 'What if I can't protect her either? I couldn't handle that, I wouldn't be able to cope!'

She moved her hand over his and gripped it. 'Eddie, whatever you think, it's not your job to protect everyone.'

'It *is*, though,' he insisted. 'It's what I do.'

'You're going to be Nina's *husband*. Not her bodyguard. You know you've got to tell *her* all of this.'

'I know, I know,' Chase admitted wearily. 'It's just tough. I'm not exactly good at this sort of thing.'

'You did okay.' A hint of humour, the no-limits commentary of siblings. 'You know, considering it was the first time you've ever talked about your feelings.'

'Always have to get in a jab, don't you?' Chase warned, but there was a glimmer of lightness in his voice too.

'It's still progress. Maybe you *should* call Dad.'

'Now *that's* not funny.'

'Yeah, somehow I thought that wasn't going to happen.' She let go of his hand. 'But you definitely need to talk to Nina.'

'I will,' he said. 'I will. Just need a bit of time to think through what I want to say to her.'

'Well, in that case, you might as well at least be comfortable. Go on, go and sit down.' She nodded at the door. 'I'll get you some tea.'

Chase finally managed a small but genuine smile. 'Thanks . . . Elizabeth.'

★

A brisk twenty-minute walk brought Nina, Mitchell and Chloe to the foot of the Tor. Even though the route they were about to take to the summit was the easiest, Nina realised it was still deceptively steep. The even steeper alternative path on the northern slope was probably less suited to humans than to goats.

Or cows. She was surprised to see several black and white Friesians making their languid way around the terraces, munching on the grass. 'A lot simpler than mowing it,' Chloe told her. 'You just have to watch out for the – oops!'

'Eurgh!' wailed Nina, extracting her right foot from a recently laid cowpat.

'For the poo,' Chloe concluded. 'Sorry. Although it's supposed to be good luck.'

Nina scraped her foot through the grass. 'Funny, I don't *feel* lucky.'

The shoe as clean as it was going to get, they continued up the hill. 'Is this the path of the labyrinth?' Nina asked.

Chloe shook her head and pointed at one of the terraces to their side. 'No, but you can still see where it was – most of it, anyway. Some parts have been eroded to the point where they're barely climbable. And if you did follow it, it'd take you over four hours to reach the top.' She looked sidelong at Nina. 'The Glastonbury labyrinth doesn't have any connection to King Arthur – at least, not that I know of. Are you just asking out of curiosity, or . . .'

Nina stopped walking. 'There might be a link, but

we're not sure. Which is why we needed the opinion of an expert.' She took out several photographs. 'What do you make of these?'

Chloe examined the first photo, a close-up of one of the symbols of the labyrinth inscribed on the blade they had found in Syria. 'It looks like the same basic path . . .' She checked the next image. 'So does this. And – what *is* this?' she asked, reaching a picture showing the whole blade.

Nina took a breath. 'We think that's Caliburn.'

'You're joking,' Chloe gasped. She waited for a response, and got none. 'You're not joking? Oh, my God, you're *not* joking!'

'We're not joking,' Nina assured her.

Chloe hurriedly flicked through the rest of the photos. 'If it were anyone else but you, I wouldn't believe them. But – you really think this is Caliburn?'

'As far as we can tell. But the reason we're here is that . . .' She paused and looked round. Although there were other people on the Tor, none of them were within earshot. 'We think these symbols are a clue to something hidden here.'

Chloe eyed her. 'Some*thing*?'

'Or some*one*. King Arthur.' Chloe let out a little excited squeak. 'There's a chance Arthur's tomb could be here, under the Tor. Problem is, we don't know where.'

'But you're the Director of the International Heritage Agency, you could get whatever equipment you want!' said Chloe, her eyes lighting up at the thought. 'A complete ground-penetrating radar survey, or even a gravimetric—'

'Unfortunately, there's a time factor involved,' Mitchell cut in. 'I can't go into details for security reasons, but if the tomb *is* here, both our governments have agreed we need to locate it as soon as possible.'

'We think you're the best person to help us find it,' Nina said to Chloe. 'Do you think you can?'

'Well – well, I'm flattered,' Chloe stammered, blushing again. 'But I don't know. I mean, I know the Tor very well, but . . .' She examined the pictures again. 'Unless you've got something specific to work from, I don't know how much help I can be. This is the pattern of the Glastonbury labyrinth, yes, but – how did you find this? How does finding Caliburn lead you to Arthur's tomb?'

'It's . . . complicated,' said Nina. 'And that's the understatement of the year. But long story short: we think those symbols were inscribed on Caliburn by the Glastonbury monks as a way to find Arthur's tomb – his *real* tomb, not the one they dug up for show in 1191. It's where they hid Arthur and Guinevere, to keep them safe . . . and it's also where they hid Excalibur.'

'Excalibur?' Chloe's mouth hung open for a moment. 'Blimey. That would be a hell of a find.' She suddenly looked worried. 'If you find it, you will . . . you *will* mention that I helped, won't you?'

Nina gave her a reassuring smile. 'You'll get full credit, believe me. But the main thing is actually finding it in the first place.' She pointed at one of the symbols in the topmost photo. 'We assume it's got something to do with these dots marked on the labyrinth, but we don't know what they represent.'

Chloe scrutinised the picture, brow furrowing. 'If you account for the real labyrinth being distorted by the shape of the Tor,' she said, 'then the nearest of the dots would be . . . on the third terrace. Over here!' She picked her way along the narrow, scrubby terrace to one side, Nina and Mitchell following, then came to a sudden stop. 'Of course!'

'What is it?' Nina asked, catching up.

'It's a marker stone!' At Chloe's feet was an unassuming lump of rock, half buried in the ground. 'They were used so people walking the labyrinth could tell how far they still had to go. Most of them are missing now, but there are still a few in place.'

'So the tomb's under one of the markers?' said Mitchell.

'Maybe,' Nina said, 'but which one? Each of the symbols has different stones marked. And we're missing the symbol on the sword's tip.' She took the pictures back from Chloe, fanning them out like a hand of cards. 'How many of these marker stones were there originally?'

'Nobody's sure,' Chloe replied, 'but probably about thirty.'

The number of stones marked on the various symbols of the labyrinth seemed to confirm that. Nina looked back and forth between the photos. Each symbol countained a different number of stones, in different positions, but there was definitely a crossover between them. Some stones appeared on more than one labyrinth, and of those some showed up more frequently than others . . .

'I need a pen and paper,' she said, an idea taking form.

Chloe rummaged through her little rucksack. 'I always come prepared,' she said, taking out first a Thermos flask, then a large ham and egg salad sandwich wrapped in plastic, before finally producing a dog-eared notebook and a biro. 'Here.'

Nina took the pen and notebook. 'What're you thinking?' Mitchell asked.

'That we can narrow down where to look even if we don't have enough information to find it exactly.' She drew a large copy of the labyrinth on a clean page, then added the positions of the marker stones from the symbol in the first photograph. 'Okay, that's the first one. Now, let's add the second . . .'

From each picture in turn, she marked the stones on her drawing of the labyrinth. It took several minutes, but gradually the clues hidden by the monks became clear. Only three stones appeared on all of the labyrinths.

Nina regarded the final result – not merely a drawing, now a *map*. 'I bet the symbol on the missing piece of the sword would only have one of those three marked on it,' she said, circling them. 'That's where the tomb is, that's how to find the entrance. It just looks like a decoration, but if you know what it means, it leads you right to the door!'

Chloe took a closer look. 'I know how to find those points, but none of them have marker stones any more. And if there really is an entrance, it won't be easy to find – thousands of people follow the labyrinth every year, but nobody's ever discovered anything this major.'

'But they didn't know where to look, did they?' said Mitchell. 'Where's the nearest one?'

Nina gave the notebook to Chloe. She turned it to match the orientation of the crude map with the Tor. 'The fifth terrace, west side. This way.' She led them back to the path uphill.

Once they reached the terrace, Chloe guided them round the Tor's flank. 'Somewhere around here,' she said finally, coming to a stop. The hillside was steep, only the very top of St Michael's tower visible above. But there was nothing unusual about the spot, just rough grass and rabbit holes.

'I don't see anything,' complained Mitchell.

'If anything's here, it'll be buried. Here, give these a try.' Chloe opened her rucksack again, taking out a handful of thin steel tent pegs, eight inches long with hooked ends, and handing one each to him and Nina. 'Have a poke.'

Nina bent and shoved the spike into the earth. It was quite dense, offering resistance, but she kept pushing until it was as deep as it could go. 'Well, nothing there,' she said, pulling it back out and trying a different spot a few feet away. Mitchell got the idea and joined in, as did Chloe.

But nearly half an hour of probing discovered nothing

but stones: certainly nothing that might conceal an entrance. 'So much for that,' Mitchell said.

'There're still two more sites,' Nina reminded him.

The next was on the sixth terrace, looking northwest. Now within sight of both the summit and the steep zigzag path up the Tor's north side, the group attracted some curious looks from tourists as they jabbed at the ground. But again they found nothing.

'Third time lucky,' Chloe said hopefully as she checked the map once more. 'Okay, the last one is . . . first terrace, on the southeastern side. All the way back down and around, I'm afraid.'

Nina eyed the sun, which was steadily dropping towards the western horizon. 'Will we still have time to get there?'

'We should, although we won't have a huge amount of time to look around before it gets too dark. Where are you staying, by the way?'

'London,' Mitchell told her.

She looked horrified. 'You're going to drive all the way back to London? Oh, don't be silly, it'll be the middle of the night before you get there! I live in Shepton Mallet, it's only about ten miles away. You can stay with me tonight, I have a spare room. And a sofa,' she added to Mitchell. He appeared less than impressed at the prospect.

'Are you sure?' Nina asked.

'Oh, it's no problem. And how often do I have the discoverer of Atlantis at my house? It'll be an honour.'

'In that case, we accept. Don't we, Jack?' He grunted non-committally.

'Brilliant! Okay, we'd better get going.'

Shadowed from the sun, the southeastern face of the Tor was colder, more ominous. The steepness of the hill meant the tower above was now completely out of sight, and even Glastonbury itself was blocked from view, adding to the feeling of isolation. The chatter of sightseers was gone; apart from the croaks of distant birds, the only sign of life was a lone cow in the field below, completely oblivious of the visitors.

'This is where the marker stone must have been,' said Chloe, looking at the map again.

Nina examined the hillside. It seemed no different from the two other spots they had already searched. 'If the tomb's here at all, it's got to be near.' She took her steel peg and stuck it into the earth. The others followed her example.

They searched for ten minutes, twenty, finding nothing out of the ordinary. The sky beyond the Tor gradually took on a salmon-pink shade, slipping to a vivid orange as the sun neared the horizon. Another five minutes. Still nothing.

Then—

Nina's probe stopped abruptly, only four inches beneath the surface.

To begin with, she didn't react. It wasn't the first rock she'd found. Instead, she withdrew the peg and tried again, six inches away. If it were just a stone, a small change of position would be enough to miss it.

But the peg stopped again. Four inches deep.

She moved again, tried again. Four inches. Pushing harder, she heard a faint clink of metal on stone through the soil. 'Hey, guys,' she said, feeling a growing sense of excitement, 'over here.'

'What?' Mitchell asked as he and Chloe joined her.

'Something quite big. Could just be a rock, but it seems very flat. Help me see how big it is.'

They stabbed the pegs into the Tor, moving further apart. Every attempt stopped four inches deep, until they had covered a width of over four feet. Checking perpendicularly, whatever lay under the soil was just as tall.

A square.

'There's no way that's natural,' muttered Nina, seeing the pattern of holes marking the object's edges.

Chloe took a trowel from her pack. 'Here, let me.' She knelt and scooped out several clumps of soil from the centre of the square, working more carefully as she got deeper. The tip of the trowel scraped against stone. She exchanged a look with Nina, then widened the hole, brushing loose soil away with her hand.

What lay beneath the ground was clearly man-made, smooth and flat. But that wasn't what set Nina's heart racing. Instead, it was a word, inscribed in the stone.

MERLIN.

Chloe sat back, stunned. 'Blimey.'

Nina brushed more of the soil away, revealing additional words in Latin. '"The wrath of Merlin"?' she translated incredulously. She snatched the trowel from Chloe's hand and hacked at the hole to widen it. 'No, wait. It's part of a sentence. "... the wrath of Merlin, which strikes –"' More frantic digging. '"– which strikes only those who see his face. Those who know the truth may find ..."' She fell silent, amazed.

'What?' Mitchell demanded. 'What does it say?'

Nina looked up at him, awed. '"Those who know the truth may find the tomb of Arthur."' She placed her hands on the ancient stone slab, barely able to believe what she had discovered. 'It's real. It's actually *real*.'

Nina held up her hands. 'No, really, I couldn't eat another thing.'

'Are you sure?' Chloe asked. She pushed a plate towards her guest. 'Another slice of cake?'

'No thanks, really.'

'Some ice cream? After Eights? Cheesy nibbles?'

'No, thanks!' Forced to abandon further excavation by lack of light, they had covered the exposed stone with soil once more and driven to Chloe's house with the intention of returning to the Tor the following morning. Nina looked round at the door of Chloe's dining room, through which she could hear Mitchell talking. He had told the two women that he needed to make a phone call, though Nina suspected he was really trying to escape Chloe's constant offers of more and more rich, fatty food.

Chloe regarded the last piece of cake hopefully. 'You don't mind if I . . .'

'Help yourself!'

Mitchell came back into the room as Chloe slid the cake on to her plate. 'Oh, all finished? Shame.'

'You can have this slice if you'd like,' Chloe offered. 'Or some ice cream? Cheesy nibbles?'

'That's okay, thanks!'

'Who were you calling?' Nina asked, just as her own phone rang. 'Oh, excuse me.' She took it from her pocket, seeing Chase's name on the screen. So he'd finally deigned to speak to her, had he? 'Eddie?'

'Hi, love.' He still sounded glum, but at least he was no longer angry. 'You okay?'

'Yeah, I'm fine. What about you?'

'Better than I was. Listen, there's something I need to tell you, but I want to do it in person. I'm about to get a train back to London.'

'Back? Wait, where are you now?'

'In Bournemouth. There was something I had to tell Lizzie as well. Are you still at the hotel?'

'No, I'm, ah . . . in Somerset.'

A pause. 'What?'

'I came to Glastonbury.'

'*What?*'

'No, listen, we found something! There's something underneath Glastonbury Tor. We think it's King Arthur's tomb – we found the entrance!'

Another, longer pause. Then: 'For fuck's sake, Nina!'

The verbal explosion was loud enough for her companions to hear. 'I told you not to go!'

'Yes, and *I* told *you* you don't tell me what to do, Eddie! We've got a job to do, remember – finding Excalibur? Well, that's what we've been doing.'

'We? Is Jack there?'

'Yes, Jack's here,' Nina snapped. She glanced at the others. Chloe, embarrassed, was regarding a clock with intense feigned interest, while Mitchell had a questioning expression. 'For God's sake, Eddie. Is that why you've been so territorial with me when he's around? You might as well have been cocking your leg.'

He fumed silently for a few moments. 'Look, just get back to London, all right? I still want to talk to you.'

'It'll have to wait until tomorrow. I'm staying here overnight.'

'With Jack?'

Nina ground her teeth in frustration. '*Yes*, Eddie, with Jack.'

'That's it, I'm coming up there. Lizzie, I need to borrow your car.' In the background, Nina heard Elizabeth tell him in no uncertain terms that he couldn't have it. 'All right, I'll get a bloody taxi! Where are you?'

'Eddie, you're being completely ridiculous – look, I don't even want to carry on with this conversation until you stop acting like a damn child! Okay? I'll talk to you tomorrow when you've got a grip on yourself.' She stabbed at the button to switch off the phone before Chase could say anything else. 'Aargh!'

'I'll, er, put these plates in the dishwasher,' said Chloe, hurriedly clearing the table. She bustled into the kitchen, leaving Nina and Mitchell alone.

'God *damn* it!' Nina was about to bang her phone down on the table before remembering she was a guest and settling for smacking it against her thigh instead. 'I'd forgotten how *mad* he can make me. I sometimes wonder what the hell I see in him.'

'Must be that whole opposites attract deal, I guess,' suggested Mitchell. He reached across and patted her upper arm.

'Yeah, well, sometimes he's a bit *too* opposite, y'know? I mean, I'm engaged to the guy, but we're hardly anything alike. Sometimes I worry that . . .' She tailed off.

'What?'

'I shouldn't really be talking about this. It's my problem, not yours. You probably don't even want to hear it.'

He gave her a sympathetic look. 'Maybe I can help.'

Nina scrunched up her face, confused. 'I don't know, it's just . . . I'm just worried we might be *too* different!' she blurted, the admission filling her with a mixture of catharsis and guilt.

'You think that if you get married, it might not work out?'

'Exactly! Eddie's already been married once, and . . . Well, maybe that's an extreme example of things going bad, but at least he and Sophia were from the same country. They had that much in common.'

'Have you talked about this with him?'

'Yeah, right,' Nina scoffed. 'It takes a near-death experience before Eddie'll discuss his feelings without making some stupid joke out of everything.' She let out a frustrated growl. 'Oh, what do I *do*? Did you go through anything like this before you got married?'

'Afraid not,' said Mitchell. 'We thought we were a perfect match. Naivety of youth, I guess.'

'Great, I really needed to be reminded that I'm not officially young any more.' But there was a hint of humour behind her words. 'God, he *infuriates* me sometimes. Why can't he be a bit more, more . . .'

'Like you?'

'Exactly! Well, not *exactly*, that'd just be weird and narcissistic.' Mitchell laughed; after a few seconds, Nina managed to join in. 'Heh. But yeah, there have definitely been times when I've wished he could be less . . . Eddie-y.'

Mitchell moved his chair slightly towards her, looking into her eyes. 'And more . . . PhD-y?'

Nina laughed again, giving him a knowing grin. 'Eddie was right about you, you know. You *do* flirt.'

'You got me,' said Mitchell, putting a hand to his heart in mock contrition. 'It's a grave personality flaw, I admit. But the only thing that matters is: do I flirt *well*?'

She smiled, enjoying the attention. 'I'd have to say . . . not bad.'

'Room for improvement?'

'Mmm . . . maybe.'

'Then I guess I'll have to keep practising.' He smiled back, leaning a little closer to her . . .

Chloe entered the dining room, doing a slight double take when she saw her guests sitting much closer together than during the meal. The moment broken, Nina blinked and pulled back. 'Well, the dishwasher's loaded!' Chloe said, a little too loudly. 'I'll go and sort out some bedclothes for you.'

'Thanks,' said Nina. 'And get Jack an extra blanket – we don't want him getting cold on the *couch*.'

'Ah, well,' Mitchell sighed, 'practice makes perfect.'

17

Early morning sunshine lit up the southeastern side of Glastonbury Tor. Of the hole in the ground and the stone slab beneath, there was no trace except for some disturbed earth – and the hooked end of a steel peg poking from the soil. 'Here we are,' said Chloe, pointing at it. She laid down the rest of her equipment on the terrace.

Mitchell looked on dubiously as she marked out a cordon round the dig site with wooden poles, then tied a length of red and white striped plastic tape between them. 'Are you sure that'll make any difference?'

'This is England,' Chloe told him with a smile. 'Never underestimate the power of a simple piece of stripy tape to keep people away. Besides . . .' She held up a fluorescent yellow safety jacket. 'Nothing makes a person more invisible than a workman's coat!'

Mitchell didn't seem convinced, but kept quiet. Instead, he put down his black holdall. 'I got the embassy to deliver some gear of my own,' he remarked as he unzipped it and showed Nina two heavy-duty flashlights and a pair of walkie-talkies.

'Oh, so that's who you called last night,' said Nina.

'Yeah, I wanted to be prepared. We don't know what's inside there.'

'If there *is* anything inside there.' Nina's initial enthusiasm had faded overnight, her fight with Chase still dwelling on her mind.

With the shovels Chloe had brought, it didn't take long to expose the whole of the stone slab. Nina used a brush to clean the soil from the chiselled letters. The entire inscription was in Latin, several lines long.

'"Know you that behind this stone lies the one true tomb of Arthur, king of the Britons, and his second queen, Guinevere,"' Nina read. '"Only those who know the history of Arthur and the legend of Arthur shall be worthy to reach his presence and pay respect. The one shall see you through the labyrinth to face the trial of Nivienne . . ." Nivienne?' she asked Chloe.

'One of the possible names of the Lady of the Lake,' she replied.

'Right. ". . . the trial of Nivienne, who shall hold the unworthy in the place where she dwells, and the wrath of Merlin, which strikes only those who see his face. Those who know the truth may find the tomb of Arthur; those who do not . . ." Oh boy.'

'What?' Mitchell asked.

' ". . . shall never leave." Yeah, this isn't good. Sounds like the monks left a couple of booby traps.'

'But the tomb's hundreds of years old,' Mitchell objected. 'The traps wouldn't still be working after all that time.'

'You'd *think,* wouldn'cha?' said Nina with sarcasm born of painful experience.

'That might explain one old legend,' Chloe said. 'There's a story that a group of thirty monks once entered tunnels they found beneath the Tor, and only three came out alive.'

Nina winced. 'Oh, I don't like those odds.' But she still took a spade and began to dig.

Once the soil around the stone slab had been cleared away, Nina and Mitchell carefully inched its upper end clear of the deeper-set stones on which it was resting, then tilted it back to reveal . . .

'Oh, my God,' said Nina. 'Would you look at that.'

It was a tunnel, narrow but passable, descending into the Tor. More Latin text was inscribed on one of the stone supports framing the entrance. Nina immediately converted the Roman numerals. '1191,' she said. 'The same year the Glastonbury monks said they found Arthur's tomb in the grounds of the abbey. But this was the real tomb . . . the real treasure.'

Mitchell shone a light into the passage. 'These props look kinda iffy.' While the entrance was stone, inside the tunnel support was provided by wooden beams set into the clay and sandstone walls, and they had succumbed to rot from the damp earth over the centuries.

Nina picked up another torch and checked for herself. 'They lasted this long,' she said, hoping she wasn't cursing herself by speaking. She quickly touched her pendant to be safe. 'As long as nobody kicks them out, they should be okay.'

'I'm not so sure,' Chloe said nervously. 'I think I'd prefer to wait out here, hold the fort. If that's all right with you?'

Nina gave her a reassuring smile as she picked up a yellow hard hat from Chloe's gear. 'You've probably got absolutely the right idea. But we've got to check it out as soon as we can, so . . .'

Mitchell donned a second helmet, then switched on one of the walkie-talkies and handed it to Chloe. 'You know how to use one of these?' She nodded. 'Great. We'll tell you what's down there, step by step.'

'Good luck,' Chloe offered as Nina and Mitchell gathered up their gear and ducked through the entrance.

'Thanks – just hope we don't need it!' Nina replied.

The first thing that struck her as she edged down the steep slope was the smell, a damp, all-pervading stench of rotting vegetation. Chloe had said the surrounding countryside used to be marshland, and it certainly smelled that way. The second was that while the tunnel was extremely confined, it hadn't been made in a hurry. It had been carefully and diligently dug from the Tor, the walls smooth, the wooden props regularly spaced. Even though it had been intended to remain hidden, the monks still wanted it to be a tomb fit for a king.

Behind her, hunched low, Mitchell raised the walkie-talkie. 'Okay, radio check. Dr Lamb, can you hear me?'

'Loud and clear,' came the reply. 'How is it so far?'

'In a word? Stinky.'

Nina smiled at his unscientific description, then focused on the tunnel ahead as she reached the foot of the slope. 'Okay, it's flattening out.' She stopped, seeing that the path ahead branched. 'Oh, great.'

'What?' said Mitchell.

'It's not a labyrinth, it's a maze.' Above the path to the left was a small carved slab embedded in the clay. 'Give me the radio.' Mitchell complied. 'Chloe? I think we need your expert opinion here. There are two routes – the left one's marked with a plaque that reads "Morgain".'

'More commonly known as Morgan le Fay,' Chloe replied over the walkie-talkie. 'Arthur's sister, according to legend. What does the other route say?'

'Nothing, and it doesn't look like it ever did – there's no hole where another plaque might have fallen out. What do you think?'

'I'm not sure,' said Chloe. 'It doesn't mean much on its own.'

Nina shone her light down both passages. They seemed identical, curving away sharply after a few paces. 'Guess we'll just have to see where they lead, then.' She looked back at Mitchell. 'Morgain, or not-Morgain?'

He shrugged. 'Don't ask me. This is your line of work!'

'Yeah, I was afraid you'd lay it on me. Okay . . . Morgain,' she decided, starting down the left tunnel.

Water had pooled on the thick red clay of the floor. Nina splashed through it and rounded the first corner. Not far ahead, the passage twisted again, leading out of sight. The ground here was drier, though the walls and wooden props had the same damp sheen as the rest of the tunnel. She slowed, something about that niggling. Why were there no puddles?

Mitchell pressed up behind her. 'Something wrong?'

'Not sure, just . . .' She shook her head. 'Let's see where this goes.'

She stepped forward – and the floor collapsed beneath her foot.

She shrieked as she pitched over, her wildly spinning torch revealing a deep, dark hole below as it fell away—

Mitchell grabbed her, yanking her to a painful halt just before she plunged into the hole. Straining, he pulled her back up.

'*Shit!*' she gasped, heart kicking inside her chest as she hugged Mitchell for support. 'Oh, Jesus, those son-of-a-bitch monks.'

'Are you okay?'

Nina took several long breaths, trying to calm herself. 'Yeah, I think. Shit!' She cautiously looked into the hole, and saw how she'd been tricked. A flimsy wooden square had been precariously balanced over the top of the pit, then a thin layer of clay smeared over it to blend it into the floor. Only a single footstep had been needed for it to break free – and drop into a waterlogged hole with several long and sharp wooden spikes poking up from its base.

'Nasty,' Mitchell noted with considerable understatement.

'Help me across it,' Nina said, her composure returning.

'You sure? If there's another . . .'

'We've got to see where this passage goes.' The gap was some four feet wide, the crossing made more awkward by the low ceiling, but with Mitchell's aid Nina was able to traverse it. He tossed the remaining torch across to her, and she looked round the corner. 'Okay, I hope whichever asshole monk came up with this is having a good laugh! It's a dead end.'

Mitchell helped her back over the pit. 'So what does that mean?'

'It means,' said Nina, bringing up the walkie-talkie, 'we need somebody who knows the difference between Arthurian history and legend.' She thumbed the talk button. 'Hello, Chloe?'

'Hi, Nina,' said Chloe cheerfully, oblivious of what had just happened underground. 'Have you found something?'

'You could say that. Listen, I think I know what the inscription on the stone meant, the part about history and legend, and the one seeing you through to the tomb. The route marked with Morgain . . . well, it didn't turn out so good. My guess is that at each junction, we're going to find the name of someone or something connected to Arthur. The ones which are based in historical fact are the proper route, and the ones which are myth . . . we don't want to go down them, put it that way.'

'I'll do what I can, but the line between Arthurian history and myth is very blurred.'

'Just give us your best guess.'

'Think you're right?' said Mitchell.

'If I'm not, you're gonna have to pull me out of a lot of pits.'

They returned to the first junction and took the unmarked passage, Nina warily testing the floor with each step. It remained firm. Nevertheless, she advanced cautiously along the winding tunnel until a second junction eventually presented itself.

'Okay, Chloe,' she said. 'I was right, there's another plaque.'

'What does it say?'

Nina brought the torch closer to read the text on the flat stone above the left passage. ' "Bedivere." '

'Oh, Sir Bedivere is absolutely genuine,' Chloe announced. Her voice was now more distorted, interference worsening the deeper they went into the Tor. 'If anything, he appears in more historical accounts than Arthur himself. He was called Bedwyr in the earliest Welsh references, and . . .'

'I guess we go left,' Nina told Mitchell as Chloe rambled on. They entered the new tunnel. Nina started paying attention to the walls and ceiling as well as the floor. Experience had taught her that trap builders rarely used the same trick twice.

But her theory seemed to be holding out as they wound deeper underground to reach yet another junction. This time, the sign was above the right-hand exit. 'Chloe, you're up again. This one says "Badon".'

'The Battle of Badon,' Chloe replied immediately. 'Arthur's greatest victory over the Saxons. Either late fifth century or early sixth – the dates given to it vary, but it was definitely a historic event.'

'Then Badon it is,' said Nina, going right.

They continued cautiously through the maze, stopping at each successive fork in the path for Chloe's advice. The distortion of her voice grew steadily worse, the hiss of static at times almost swallowing it. But they could still make out her answers: Llacheu, Arthur's son, was considered a person of historical truth by the Glastonbury monks, while Arthur's knight Sir Karados and Bron, the Fisher King, were consigned to the status of myth. Nina and Mitchell pressed on, the air growing more foul the deeper they went. Then:

'Aah!' Nina gasped, flinching back in surprise as she rounded a corner – and came face to face with what she thought for a moment was a woman. As her shock faded, she saw it was actually a statue, a slender, graceful figure standing at the edge of a pool of water, the iron-rich soil turning it a muddy reddish-brown. The chamber beyond was considerably larger than the tunnels, the pool filling its entire width.

'It must be Nivienne – the Lady of the Lake,' Nina said. She took out her camera and snapped several pictures; even if they couldn't progress any further, she would still have something to study when they returned to the surface.

'Not much of a lake.' Mitchell rolled up a sleeve and dipped his arm experimentally into the murky water. It was clear that it was deep. He shook off the water, then directed his light at the far side of the pool. 'Check this out.'

In the reflected torchlight, Nina saw the tops of two tunnel entrances just barely rising above the water, another stone plaque over the opening on the left. But that wasn't what Mitchell meant. Instead, he was shining the beam at the water itself. Small bubbles rose and popped intermittently on the surface. 'Fish?' she asked hopefully.

'Gas,' Mitchell answered. 'That's why the damn place stinks so bad – it's got swamp gas bubbling up through it!'

'We must be near the level of the water table,' Nina realised. The Somerset marshes might have been drained on the surface, but the earth beneath was still sodden, the build-up of decomposing vegetation producing a repellent by-product: methane. Had the monks known this, or was it a coincidence?

She told Mitchell to illuminate the statue. Nivienne had one arm held out, inviting them to step into the water, but Nina was in no rush to do so. 'This must be the trial of Nivienne. But what's the trial?'

'I think we're gonna have to get wet,' Mitchell grumbled, pointing at the two tunnels across the pool.

'What does the stone say?' Nina squinted to read the small text across the pool. 'Looks like . . . "Anna".' She used the radio to describe the chamber and the plaque to Chloe; the reception was now so bad that her reply was barely audible.

'Anna was Arthur's sister,' Nina made out through the crackling distortion. 'But I'm not sure how strong a historical basis she has. She's generally considered to be the mother of Sir Gawain, but in the early Welsh accounts – the ones that included Bedivere – a woman called Gwyar is Gawain's mother. Anna could be another name for the same person, but . . .'

'So you don't know if she was real or myth?' Nina asked.

'I'm afraid not.'

Nina took her thumb off the transmit key, muttered 'Perfect!' then pushed it again. 'Which is more likely, though? *Could* she have been real?'

'Possibly. There are other references to her, but they date from later.'

'After 1191?'

'No, but some of them are from earlier in the twelfth century, including Geoffrey of Monmouth – and in terms of historical veracity I'd put Geoffrey about on a par with Monty Python!'

Nina and Mitchell shared a quick smile at the reference. 'Does finding the tomb add any extra weight to either option? There's obviously *some* truth to the Arthurian mythology.'

Chloe considered this. 'I suppose it does make it a bit more likely that Anna really was Arthur's sister, but it's still hard to be sure. The Glastonbury monks were willing to lie about aspects of the legend for their own benefit, so we can't entirely rely on any of their accounts.'

'They were willing to kill, as well,' Nina said. 'Chloe, I'm getting the feeling that the trial of Nivienne is kind of a life-or-death deal. Pick the wrong tunnel and you don't get to the other end before you run out of air.'

'Maybe you should come back out,' Chloe suggested. 'Wait until you can get some diving gear.'

'We can't wait,' Mitchell insisted. 'If Excalibur's here, we have to get it as soon as possible – the longer we wait, the more chance there is of Vaskovich's people using Rust's research to find the tomb.'

Nina sighed. 'Yeah, I thought you might say that.' She spoke to Chloe again. 'Can you give us *anything*?'

'You'll have to decide for yourself, I'm afraid. Sorry.'

'Okay, thanks.' Nina glumly broke contact. 'So, what do you think? The first of Arthur's sisters we met was a myth – you think this one was real?'

'Don't ask me, you're the historian,' Mitchell said. 'It's your choice.'

'Why does everything have to end up as my decision?' Nina moaned.

Mitchell pursed his lips. 'I seem to recall a woman with red hair demanding to be in charge of the operation . . .'

'Y'know, I was kinda hoping you wouldn't remember that.' Nina frowned at the plaque. 'Okay, so either Anna was King Arthur's sister, or she wasn't. No pressure.' She closed her eyes, running through every scrap of information she could remember on the subject. 'I say that she . . . *was.*'

'Educated guess?'

'Just the second word,' she admitted. 'So, how are we going to do this?'

'Take off anything that'll get waterlogged,' Mitchell said, already slipping out of his jacket. 'Your coat, shoes, that sweater.'

Nina baulked. 'Um . . . there's not a lot else under the sweater.'

'Wait, you're not wearing a bra?'

'*Yes*, I'm wearing a bra! But it's a bit, y'know, thin.'

Mitchell stripped off his shirt, standing naked to the waist. He handed the garment to her. 'What?'

'Nothing,' Nina said hurriedly, trying not to look too impressed by his bare – and muscular – torso.

He smirked. 'Different from Eddie?'

'He's more . . . densely packed, I guess you could say. And kind of hairy. Oh, God, I'm going to shut up now.'

Mitchell chuckled and turned away as she took off her sweater and donned his shirt in its place. 'Leave anything valuable here as well – wallet, phone, whatever. The flashlight'll be fine underwater. Is your camera waterproof?'

Nina nodded as she removed her shoes, then hesitantly dipped her toes in the water. 'Oh, crap, it's cold.'

'This is nothing,' proclaimed Mitchell as he stepped into the pool, holding the torch. 'I've been in the Atlantic in the middle of winter. Now *that's* cold! Come on, I'll help you in.'

'Oh . . .' With great reluctance, Nina took his hand and entered the water. It was as frigid as she had feared. 'Son of a . . .'

'It'll feel better in a minute.' He kicked away from the bank and swam to the tunnel entrance. 'So, Anna. You're sure about this?'

'Nope.' She joined him. The pool was deeper than she could feel with her feet, which was a concern. What if the tunnels went even lower?

'You could wait here while I go through and check it out,' Mitchell suggested. 'If it's the right tunnel, it can't be all that long. The monks would have had to swim through it, and I'm guessing they weren't exactly at the peak of physical fitness.'

'But if it's the wrong tunnel, you might need help to get out. We should stay together.' Nina paused, then frowned. 'Hmm. Did I really just volunteer to swim through a dark tunnel that might be a dead end?'

'I'll look after you,' Mitchell assured her. He handed her the torch. 'You hang on to this, and hold my belt. I'll pull you through. Trust me,' he added, seeing her look. 'You don't get far in the navy if you're not a good swimmer.'

'So basically I'm going to be grabbing your ass?'

He grinned. 'I can live with that. You ready?'

'No.' But she gripped his belt anyway.

'Okay, now get as much oxygen into your system as you can.' He took several deep breaths, Nina following suit. 'Ready?'

She shook her head, saying 'Nuh-uh' through closed lips. Mitchell smiled again . . .

And dived.

Nina was pulled after him as he swam into the tunnel. Eyes closed, all she could hear was the rhythmic *whoosh* of each of his powerful strokes as he advanced through the opaque water. He had been telling the truth about his skill as a swimmer; even though she was kicking as strongly as she could to keep up, she was still being hauled along like baggage.

Mitchell changed direction, going left and slightly downwards. Her flashlight brushed against a wall as the tunnel turned. Another few strokes, and he paused before turning again, feeling for the way ahead.

The pressure in Nina's chest began to rise. Thirty seconds had passed since they entered the tunnel, she estimated. She wasn't sure how long she could hold her breath; she had once lasted for over a minute, but that had been a long time ago, when she was still a kid . . .

Mitchell seemed to be slowing, the force of the water over her face lessening. Another turn, still going down. Not good. She wanted to go *up*. Close to a minute by now, surely. A burning sensation was spreading through her lungs . . .

Mitchell stopped suddenly, Nina drifting into him from behind. She held out an arm to steady herself and touched a wall. She could feel him twisting in the water, searching for the turn in the passage.

Shit! What if she'd made the wrong choice, if this were the dead end meant to trap and drown those who didn't know myth from history?

A gulp of air tried to escape from her throat; she choked it back, her body twitching. Mitchell felt it. He swam to the right, then the left, still groping blindly for the way forward.

A hissing sound, not in the water but in her ears as her heart beat faster, struggling to extract what little oxygen remained in her lungs. She bumped against Mitchell again. Well over a minute, and she could barely hold out as it was, never mind swim all the way back through the darkness.

He moved. Not upwards, or back to the entrance, but *down*, deeper into the murky water. Nina wanted to protest, but all she could do was hang on as the hissing rose to a roar . . .

Mitchell changed direction again – and went up.

His strokes became harder, less precise, more frantic. Nina felt the tunnel narrowing as it rose, her limbs brushing the walls as they ascended towards either a fatal dead end or—

Air!

Mitchell broke the surface, immediately grabbing Nina's arm and pulling her up beside him. She whooped for breath, water streaming down her face as she filled her lungs.

And coughed. The air was anything but pure.

The chamber they had emerged in was full of gas.

18

Chase was in a very irritable mood by the time he reached Glastonbury Tor. Still unable to persuade Elizabeth to lend him her car, he had been forced to take the train from Bournemouth, a tedious journey requiring two changes en route – and Glastonbury was almost ten miles from the nearest station, requiring an expensive taxi ride for the final leg.

Adding to his annoyance, he realised on arriving that he didn't know where Nina was. Somewhere under the Tor, presumably, but seen in person the hill was considerably larger than it had appeared in Elizabeth's road atlas. Picking his way through the squishy mine-field left by the wandering cows, he strode round the base of the strangely terraced hill until he spotted something on the next level up. He climbed past another couple of cows to find a plump blonde woman sitting inside a cordon of stripy tape. She stopped eating her sandwich and regarded him uncertainly as he approached.

'Hi,' said Chase. 'You haven't seen an American archaeologist round here, have you? About yea high, red hair, pain in the arse?'

The woman stood. 'Would you be . . . Eddie, by any chance?'

'I would,' Chase replied. No sign of Nina or Mitchell – but the hole the woman was guarding gave him a pretty good idea where they were. His displeasure returned. Nina had completely ignored him. Again.

'Hi. I'm Chloe, Chloe Lamb. Dr Chloe Lamb.' She extended her hand.

Chase shook it. 'Eddie Chase,' he said curtly, glancing at the hole. 'So, she's in there, is she?'

'Yes, with Jack.'

'Oh, with *Jack*. Great.'

Chloe shifted uncomfortably, wanting to stay out of any personal disputes. 'Yes, they've made some very interesting discoveries. But I haven't spoken to them for a bit. They've been out of contact.' She held up a walkie-talkie.

'How come?'

'Well, she said they'd reached a flooded tunnel and were going to swim through it.'

'It's *flooded* down there? Oh, for fuck's sake!' Chloe was taken aback at his swearing, but he ignored her reaction. He noticed a torch amongst the pile of equipment beside the hole, and picked it up. 'Really can't bloody take her anywhere.'

'Um, Eddie? Mr Chase?' said Chloe nervously as he

moved to the hole. 'You'll need to be careful too. There are traps down there.'

'Traps?'

'Yes, apparently they were designed to catch people who took the wrong route to the trial of Nivienne—'

'Wait, what?' Chase spluttered. 'The place is full of *traps*, there's some kind of *trial*, and you haven't heard from them for ages? Jesus! They could be dead already!'

'I'm sorry, I'm sorry!' wailed Chloe. 'I didn't realise, Nina just seemed to know what she was doing!'

'Yeah, she usually does – until stuff starts exploding!'

'I'm sorry, really,' Chloe repeated.

Chase took a breath. 'That's okay, it's not your fault.' He shone the torch into the hole. 'Just tell me how to catch up with them.'

Hacking in the foul air, Mitchell climbed out of the water and hauled Nina up after him. The ground was soft and muddy, squishing revoltingly.

The flashlight was still lit, having survived its submersion. The beam revealed another chamber, smaller than the one at the other end of the passage – with a huge stone face set in the rear wall.

'Merlin,' Nina realised.

The wrath of Merlin, which strikes only those who see his face . . .

But she *had* seen his face, which was curled into a mocking sneer. And so far, nothing had happened.

Still coughing, she staggered towards the carving, feet

sinking inches deep into the mud. The stench of methane grew worse, gas belching out from the decomposing muck with each step.

'Man, this smells like a sub after the mess serves beans,' Mitchell wheezed, squelching up behind her. 'I guess this is Merlin, huh? So where's his wrath?'

'I'm not sure.' Nina used the torch to survey the chamber. At one side was a stone door, firmly closed.

And there was something on the floor, half buried in the oozing mud . . .

'Is that a *skull*?' said Mitchell, spotting the discoloured object.

'Wait here, don't move,' Nina ordered. She carefully crossed the room, trying to disturb the disgusting sludge underfoot as little as possible. The object was indeed a skull, blackened with soot, all but a few lumps of charred flesh long since rotted away. Other bones poked through the mud around it.

Including a hand, clutching something. A piece of wood.

She turned back to Mitchell. 'I know what the wrath of Merlin was. And it's kind of ingenious, in a sadistic sort of way.'

Mitchell eyed the chamber. 'Are we safe?'

'We should be. But if we'd come in here a couple of centuries ago, we'd be dead by now.' She held up the torch. 'This whole room's one big trap. If you don't have a sealed electric light, any torches you're carrying are going to go out during the swim, right?'

'I guess.'

'So let's say you're smart enough to have planned ahead, and wrapped up another torch to keep it dry. What's the first thing you do when you come out of the water in here?'

'You light it . . .' said Mitchell, realising.

'Exactly. You light it – and create a flame. In a room filled with methane gas. *Whoomph!*' She threw out her hands to mimic an explosion. 'The last thing they saw before they got toasted was Merlin's face, just as it said on the stone at the entrance.'

'Those cunning little monks,' Mitchell said, almost admiringly. He went to the door and pointed at the base of one of the stone pillars framing it. A slot had been carved in it, a wooden wedge poking out. Nina checked the other pillar to find an identical arrangement. 'Pull 'em out, you think?'

'Just a sec. Let's make sure Merlin doesn't have a double helping of wrath.' She scrutinised the wedges to make sure they hadn't been booby-trapped with flints. 'Okay, let's give it a shot.'

Mitchell gripped the first wedge and pulled, straining against the weight of the door pressing down on it. Nothing happened for a few seconds, then with a sudden groan of wet wood it slid free. The door lowered slightly on that side. Nina took a deep breath, wished she hadn't, then tugged at the second wedge. It took longer, but it too finally came loose.

The door dropped into the floor, displacing a rush of

mud and turgid water. They jumped back as it washed around their legs.

A loud rumble filled the chamber. 'Shit!' Mitchell cried. 'It's gonna blow!'

'No, wait!' Nina aimed the torch at the hole through which they'd entered. 'It's draining!' Frothing and churning, the water was indeed falling as they watched. A draught blew past them through the newly opened door. The air was still rancid with the stench of marsh gas, but not quite as strong. 'The gas is escaping as well. Guess they decided that if you knew the secret of getting in, they might as well make it easier for you to get out again.'

Mitchell looked suspiciously through the doorway. 'So the tomb's just through there? *Excalibur's* through there?'

'Soon find out.' Nina took out the camera to take a picture of the carving of Merlin.

'Whoa, whoa!' said Mitchell. 'Flash, spark, remember?'

'The camera's waterproof, so the flash must be a sealed unit as well. It'll be fine.' She pressed the shutter to prove her point – although with a momentary pang of concern.

'Wait – oh, Jesus.' Mitchell flinched as the flash fired, but the chamber stayed free of flames. 'Okay, how about you don't do that again? That was a pretty damn stupid risk to take.'

'Oh, don't you start,' Nina said as she stepped over the lowered door into the passage beyond. 'You really *are* as bad as Eddie!'

★

Waiting anxiously at the entrance, Chloe looked round as a group of people approached, walking briskly along the terrace towards her cordon. Something about their appearance – their clothing, haircuts, even their complexions – instantly told her that they were foreigners. Eastern Europeans, maybe? Russians?

Wherever they were from, there were quite a lot of them. She counted nine in all: eight men, and one woman whose ragged hair was dyed a bright punkish green.

They stopped at the edge of the tape barrier. 'Hello,' Chloe said politely. Presumably they thought from her jacket that she was some kind of guide. 'Can I help you?'

One of the men, the oldest, took a step forward, drawing the tape taut round his waist. His broad mouth reminded Chloe of a frog. 'Yes, I hope you can,' he said, his accent strong. Russian, almost certainly. 'We are looking for Excalibur.'

Chloe felt a stab of concern. Mitchell had made it very clear that the search for Excalibur was somehow connected with national security – and therefore a secret. She put on a polite smile. 'Oh, I'm afraid you've come to the wrong place. King Arthur's tomb was supposedly found at the abbey, in the village. If Excalibur existed, it would have been there.' She gestured in the direction of Glastonbury, out of sight on the far side of the Tor.

The man stepped forward again, the tape pulling tighter . . . and snapping. 'No,' he said quietly. Chloe's concern turned to fear as she realised the man's companions had moved to surround the cordon, blocking her in. He continued his advance, glancing at the tunnel before his cold eyes fixed on Chloe once more. 'I am *certain* this is the right place.'

Nina rounded one last turn in the passage . . . and found herself at the entrance to the tomb of King Arthur.

Unlike the earth and wood of the tunnels, the walls here were stone, the ceiling vaulted to support the weight of the Tor above the rectangular chamber. The resemblance to the architecture of Glastonbury Abbey was unmistakable, a product of the same era, even the same hands. The walls were inscribed with Latin texts, a cursory reading showing her they were all dedicated to the history of Arthur, a monument to the legendary king of the Britons.

Legendary no more, she thought. Rust had been vindicated; Arthur was real.

But if this was Arthur's tomb, then . . .

'So where's the man himself?' Mitchell wondered aloud, completing her thought. There were no coffins or grave markers, the chamber a hollow space. 'Shit, did someone beat us to it?'

'No,' said Nina, moving to the centre of the room. Although it was empty, there was something on the floor. A painted shape, a circle divided into segments, coin-sized holes at the outer edge of each one. And at the centre, a coat of arms . . .

'No way,' said Mitchell. 'I thought Chloe said the Round Table didn't exist?'

There were thirteen segments in all – and the hole in the one farthest from the entrance was filled by a bronze figurine about six inches high, protruding from the floor like a peg. Nina shone the torch over it. A regal figure bearing sword and shield, text running round the base beneath its feet.

ARTURUS.

'It's King Arthur,' she whispered. The purpose of the other, empty holes was revealed when she directed the torch beam into one corner of the chamber. A small alcove contained stone shelves, more figures standing on them. She went to it. Each figure was revealed as a Knight of the Round Table, familiar names at their feet. Bedivere, Lancelot, Gawain, Galahad, Tristan, Bors . . . Twelve knights in all, one for each of the remaining holes in the floor.

Mitchell examined the chamber's end wall, which closely resembled the stone door that had blocked the exit from the gas-filled chamber. 'This looks like it might open. Maybe there's another room through here.'

'It's a puzzle,' Nina realised. She carefully lifted the figure of Lancelot from its position, finding that it too was resting in a hole: extending beneath the base was a metal shaft with a square protrusion at its end. 'A key. I think we're supposed to put the knights in their correct positions at the Round Table.'

'Sounds like Chloe's area of expertise.'

'Maybe not.' Nina moved to stand at the centre of the circle, trying to recall all the Arthurian background she had immersed herself in over the past days. 'Lancelot was literally Arthur's right-hand man; he always sat immediately to his right.' She indicated the appropriate hole. 'And the seat to Arthur's left was called the Siege Perilous. It was kept empty, reserved for the knight who found the Holy Grail – which was eventually Galahad.'

'So two down, ten to go. But what about the others?'

'We'll have to work them out,' said Nina, gazing at the waiting knights.

She crossed the chamber and knelt in the circle. Though the Round Table was meant to be egalitarian, with no physical 'head' as found on a rectangular one, in practice Arthur himself would have fulfilled that role wherever he sat. There would also have been a pecking order amongst the knights, Bedivere and Lancelot traditionally being considered the king's closest comrades.

But that knowledge didn't really help her. If Lancelot were on Arthur's immediate right, would Bedivere then sit on *his* right, or to the left of the Siege Perilous? And what of all the other knights? Even knowing Lancelot and Galahad's positions, there were still – she paused to work it out, the answer coming easily – 3,628,800 possible combinations of the remaining ten. Considering her experiences with the rest of the tomb, however, she suspected she would only have one attempt to open the door.

And there was something else, the fact that Chloe had said the Round Table was merely an invention of the twelfth-century romantic writers. Maybe she was wrong, maybe the idea had been developed from a kernel of truth in earlier accounts . . . but the inconsistency gnawed at her. 'Those who do not shall never leave,' she whispered, remembering the words on the stone at the entrance.

'Something wrong?' Mitchell asked.

'Yeah. There are over three million possible combinations, but I'm guessing we'll only get one try.'

'Maybe not.' Mitchell walked into the circle, holding the figures of Lancelot and Galahad. He showed the keys to her. 'See? I checked the others, and they're all the same. No way a bunch of twelfth-century monks would be able to make precision locks. It won't even matter what holes they're in if all the keys are identical – they just need to be in them.'

Nina was dubious. 'Sure you want to take that risk?'

'You're bloody one to talk about risk,' growled a familiar voice from behind them.

'Eddie!' Nina cried, jumping to her feet. Chase had just entered the chamber, his jeans wet and mud-spattered.

Chase in turn eyed her clothes, particularly Mitchell's oversized, damp shirt, before shooting a deeply suspicious glare at the bare-chested DARPA agent. 'What's all this?'

'We're trying to unlock the tomb—'

'No, I mean why've you both got your kit off? Looks like I got here just in time!'

'For Christ's sake, Eddie,' Nina said, exasperated. 'You seriously think that I'd go through trap-filled tunnels into the long-lost tomb of King Arthur just to find somewhere private to . . .' She lowered her voice, even though there was no way Mitchell could fail to overhear. 'To get laid? Jesus, Eddie, you know me better than that.'

'Yeah, I know you. And I knew you'd come down here, even though I told you not to!'

Nina nodded disdainfully. 'Uh-huh, yep. I thought that'd be what this little mood of yours was *really* about.' Behind her, Mitchell examined the holes in the floor, then carefully inserted the two figures on either side of Arthur before returning to the alcove to collect the rest of the ornate keys.

Chase crossed his arms. 'And what would that be?'

'That you think you're losing control of things.'

'Oh, really?' Chase sneered.

'Yes, really. Eddie, I don't know how many times I have to say this, but what happened to Mitzi was *not* your fault, no matter how much you try to put the blame on yourself. And overcompensating by trying to take control of everything I do isn't the way to deal with it!'

'I'm not trying to *control* you,' Chase protested. 'I'm

trying to *protect* you! For fuck's sake, you could've been killed getting here!'

'But I wasn't, was I?' She reached out and clasped one of his hands. 'Look, I love you, and I want to spend my life with you, I really do. But you can't be with me every minute of every day – you're not my bodyguard any more. I shouldn't need to get your permission to do what I do. It doesn't work like that. It *won't* work like that.'

'If I *hadn't* been with you, you'd be dead about twenty times over,' Chase reminded her sharply. 'You're not Indiana Jones, you're not Lara Croft, you're a real-life person who can get hurt. Or *killed*. And I do *not* want that to happen – especially not for some fucking dusty old legend!' he concluded with a dismissive flick of the head at the chamber around them.

'It's not a legend,' Nina said angrily, 'it's *real*, it's actual history—' She stopped abruptly, eyes widening as it struck her exactly why the discrepancy between what Chloe had told her and what the tomb itself had revealed was bothering her so much.

And she also fully registered the clink and scrape of metal against stone behind her—

She whirled. Mitchell had inserted the remaining knights into the empty holes, and was reaching for the figure of Arthur . . .

'*Don't!*' she screamed. Mitchell froze, hand hovering over the key. Nina pushed him back and yanked the figure out of the hole.

'Okay, what was that?' he asked, worried yet mystified.

'This isn't just the entrance to the tomb,' Nina said, waving the figurine at him. 'It's the last trap! Chloe was right, the Round Table *didn't* exist. But it had already been incorporated into Arthurian legend by 1191 – and the monks took advantage of that! It's the final test of your knowledge of the difference between history and myth. If the Round Table didn't exist, then *none* of Arthur's knights could have sat at it. And nor could Arthur!' She held the bronze figure in front of his face. The key beneath the king's feet was noticeably shorter than the others. 'This is the key – but you have to take it *out*. The real lock's somewhere else.'

Mitchell let out a worried breath. 'So what happens if you try the fake lock?'

'Exactly what the monks said. "Those who know the truth may find the tomb of Arthur; those who do not shall never leave."' She raised the torch, turning to examine the ceiling above the entrance. Set above the opening was a thick stone slab, a door primed to drop like a guillotine blade to block the way out of the chamber. 'Screw up the puzzle, and that falls and seals you in.'

Mitchell regarded it dismissively. 'Might have been a big problem nine hundred years back, but we've got jackhammers and explosives now.'

'You got gills?' Chase asked sarcastically. Nina turned to see him examining a section of wall. The stone was discoloured, lines of muddy brown and algae green running down it from the ceiling, where a rectangular hole revealed only blackness above. She realised as she scanned the rest of the chamber that the same stains were present on other parts of the walls.

'Jesus,' she said. 'You don't just get shut in. You get shut in . . . and then the chamber floods. There must be a cistern above the ceiling – those stains are from when it's overflowed in the past.'

Mitchell's expression now revealed considerably more respect for the tomb's builders. 'So where's the real lock?'

'Over here.' Nina went to the alcove, shining the light down into the holes where the figurines had been slotted. The one which had been home to Lancelot revealed a recess within – just deeper than a finger could reach, but matching the length of the Arthur key. She inserted it into the hole.

'You sure about that?' Chase asked warily.

She smiled at him. 'It's a risk . . . but a calculated one.' With that, she gripped the key – and turned it.

There was a metallic clink from within the shelf, but nothing else happened. 'It didn't work,' Mitchell said, disappointed.

'I'm not done yet. Bring all the other knights back here – all of them except Lancelot and Galahad. Eddie, give him a hand.'

'And she says *I'm* controlling,' said Chase. But he still went to help Mitchell retrieve the figures.

'Why not Lancelot and Galahad?' Mitchell asked as he brought the first set back to the alcove.

'Because all the others have at least some historical basis. But Lancelot was a fictional creation, and since

Galahad was Lancelot's son, he can't have existed either.'

The other figures now back in place, Nina lowered the Arthur key into the hole in the shelf once more. Hoping she was at least as smart as the Glastonbury monks, she turned it again.

Another faint clink.

This time, the entire alcove trembled slightly, as if some unseen pressure had been relieved. Exchanging cautious looks with the two men, Nina warily pushed against the stone. It moved fractionally at one side. She pushed harder. It hinged open by a couple of inches, which rapidly widened as Chase and Mitchell applied their weight. The alcove ground back, revealing a doorway into another chamber.

The final chamber, Nina knew. They had passed all the tests, proved themselves worthy. This was their destination – the resting place of King Arthur.

She brought up the torch and stepped inside. Chase and Mitchell followed.

The room was small and surprisingly plain, devoid of the inscriptions adorning the chamber outside. But the objects inside were more ornate. Two large coffins of black stone stood raised above the floor on slabs, carvings of angels along their sides picked out in silver and gold. Set into the top of each coffin was a golden cross, Latin text written upon them to confirm who lay within.

Arthur, king of the Britons, and Guinevere, his queen.

They were real. And they were here, buried beneath Glastonbury Tor.

But despite that, Nina couldn't look away from the object that sat between the two coffins. A block of solid granite, roughly hewn into a cube close to three feet high.

Protruding from it, its blade buried deep within the stone, was a sword.

They had found Excalibur.

19

'Well, bugger me,' said Chase. 'Is that what I think it is?'

'It is,' said Nina, amazed. Unlike the elaborately decorated Caliburn, this sword was plain, almost stark in its design, the only ornamentation being intertwined twin snakes inscribed into the hilt – just as Rust had described. Yet it was evident a great deal of time and work had been put into its creation, the metal of the blade having an almost mercury-like reflective sheen, the hilt perfectly moulded to the grip of one particular man. 'Oh, God, poor Bernd. He spent all those years trying to work out how to find it, and he was right . . . but he couldn't be here to see it.'

Mitchell stepped forward, brushing past Nina to stand between the two coffins. 'The important thing is that *we* found it – and before the Russians.' He knelt, waving for Nina to bring the torch closer. Slightly irked, she did so. 'Look at the finish of the metal, how smooth it is. We were right, it's more than just steel.'

He reached out one hand to take the hilt.

'Ahem,' Nina said. 'Before you get your muddy hands over everything, can I at least document what we've found?' She held up the camera.

'Of course. Sorry.' Mitchell backed out so Nina could photograph the room and its contents.

'So,' said Chase, his anger fading to be replaced by a surprising eagerness, 'which of us gets to be the next king of England, then?' Nina looked at him questioningly. 'Oh, come on! It's the sword in the bloody stone! It's got to be done.'

'Caliburn was the sword in the stone,' she pointed out, 'not Excalibur.'

'Whatever, it's still King Arthur's sword. Even I know about the whole "once and future king" business.' He stepped up to the stone. 'At least take a picture. Come on, something to show the grandkids.'

'Where the hell did *grandkids* come from? We haven't even set a wedding date yet!'

'Just take the picture.' He struck a pose beside the stone, hand poised over the hilt. Nina rolled her eyes and reluctantly nodded. 'Oh, yeah,' said Chase with a huge grin, gripping the sword. 'I'm the king of the world!'

Nina took a picture as he grunted and strained to pull the weapon free. 'God, what a face.'

'Yeah, that's what all the lasses say,' Chase declared, releasing the hilt. The sword hadn't moved in the slightest. 'Guess I'm not king material. Mind you, I kind of suspected that already.'

'What about you, Jack?' Nina asked. 'Fancy taking a shot at the throne?'

'I'm more interested in getting this thing out of here to somewhere secure,' Mitchell told her. Nevertheless, he reached for the sword as Chase stepped aside. 'Still, you never know . . .' Nina took another picture as he too strained to raise the sword – with the same result. 'Looks like we'll have to take the stone with it.'

'Think we'll need some help,' said Chase. 'It's what, nearly a yard to a side? Must weigh well over a ton.' He looked at Nina. 'You not having a go?'

'Yeah, right. If you can't move it, I'm hardly going to be able to.' Nina returned the camera to her pocket and crouched by the granite block, holding the torch beside the blade. 'You're right about the metal though. It's definitely not ordinary steel.' She leaned closer, examining tiny details. 'It's been used as a weapon; there are scratches and chips in the blade – but they're very small. It must be extremely strong.' She straightened, holding Excalibur's hilt to pull herself up—

The whole weapon lit up with an eerie blue glow. Nina jumped in shock – and pulled the sword cleanly out of the stone. She yelped, letting go. The glow instantly vanished, Excalibur clanging to the stone floor.

'What the hell was that?' Chase demanded. The only light now coming from the sword was the reflected torch beam.

'That glow,' said Mitchell, cautiously raising a hand towards Excalibur as if feeling for heat, 'almost looked like Cherenkov radiation.'

Nina backed away. 'You mean it's *radioactive*?'

'So much for the grandkids,' Chase muttered.

'I don't see how,' said Mitchell. 'But there was definitely some kind of high-energy reaction.' He leaned forward to touch the sword.

'What, are you crazy?' Nina asked. But nothing happened.

He withdrew his hand. 'You try.'

'I'd really rather not!'

'You'll be okay. I have a theory.' Her frown deepened, but Mitchell gave her a reassuring smile. 'Trust me.'

Nina dubiously touched the sword with the tip of her forefinger. It lit up again as if she had switched on a light, glowing from end to end. When she flinched away, the effect immediately disappeared.

She touched it again, more firmly. The glow returned, the metal itself somehow emitting light. Examining it more closely, she realised the glow was not uniform; instead, it had an almost rippling quality, subtly yet constantly shifting. She slid her finger down the flat of the blade. 'It's not even warm.'

Chase stepped forward and put his fingers on the hilt. The glow didn't alter. But when Nina drew her hand back, the light vanished once more.

She looked at Mitchell. 'Okay, Jack. What's this theory of yours?'

'We were right,' said Mitchell, gazing at the sword. 'It really is a superconductor, and it really can channel earth energy.' He raised his hands, indicating the chamber's ceiling. 'This whole place, Glastonbury Tor – it must be a convergence point for that energy. And for some reason, when you hold the sword, you're *focusing* the energy.'

'Why? How? And, er . . . *what*?' Nina pressed her fingers to her temples in pained confusion. 'What the hell are you talking about? How can I be making it do anything?'

'I don't know. But there's obviously something about you that makes it react that way. And whatever it is, King Arthur had it too. Remember the legends of Excalibur lighting up when he wielded it? Shining with the light of thirty torches, something like that? Maybe your body has a specific kind of bioelectric field, the same as his, I don't know. We might be able to check with Kirlian photography.'

'Kirlian photography?' hooted Nina. 'Okay, now we're getting into auras and chakras and crystals.'

He pointed at Excalibur. 'You explain it, then.'

Nina picked up the weapon, which flashed into life again. 'I can't, can I? But you seem to be coming up with stuff very quickly.' She raised it for a closer look at the blade.

'DARPA's been researching the potential of earth energy for some time. But this is . . . well, an unexpected development. It fits in with our theories, though.' He regarded her thoughtfully. 'An earth energy generator would need a superconductor to work. Excalibur *is* a superconductor, it must be. But for whatever reason, when you hold it, it enhances its abilities. You're making it channel earth energy directly, without needing an antenna array.'

'But how? It's just a piece of metal.' Nina lowered the blade and clanged it against a corner of the granite block to illustrate her point . . . and the sword sliced through the stone as if it were no harder than butter. A fist-sized chunk fell heavily to the floor.

'Aah!' Nina jumped back. 'What the *hell*?'

'Push it back in the stone,' Mitchell suggested. Nina did so, the weapon sliding easily several inches deep into the granite. She let go of the hilt; the glow vanished, leaving the sword sticking out of the block at an angle.

Chase tried to pull it loose. Metal crunched against stone, but he couldn't actually remove it. 'Okay, you just chopped through solid stone.'

'But . . .' Nina took hold of the hilt, and the blue glow returned. It took almost no effort for her to slip Excalibur back out of the granite.

She rounded on Mitchell as Chase knelt to take a closer look at the damage she had done to the stone. 'Okay, if you have a new theory, I really, *really* want to hear it!'

'Actually, I do – but it can wait. Give me the sword.' Taking great care to hold the blade away from him, she passed it to Mitchell. The glow vanished when she let go. 'This is what we came for. The rest of the site, you can get a full archaeological team to survey it, but we need to get the sword to DARPA for analysis as soon as possible.' Mitchell carefully ran a finger along the blade, then whistled admiringly. 'We did it. *You* did it, Nina. You found Excalibur. Congratulations!'

'Thanks,' Nina replied. She walked towards the door to the main chamber. 'But for now, how about we get out of here and put on some dry clothes, huh?'

'Yes, something *sexy*,' said a Russian-accented voice from outside.

Nina froze. Standing in the chamber was the long-haired man Chase had thrown out of the window of Staumberg Castle, Zakhar. Beside him was a broad-shouldered, shaven-headed thug with an ugly scar running across his throat practically from ear to ear. Both were armed, the bald man with a pistol, Zakhar with a compact MP-5K sub-machine gun.

'Hello again, sexy lady,' said Zakhar with a crooked smile, running his free hand through his hair. 'Come out here. And you, Jack.' He looked past Nina, gesturing with the gun for Mitchell to follow her.

Nina risked a glance back as she left the tomb chamber. Chase had moved as soon as he heard the new arrivals, and was now crouching in the cover of Arthur's coffin. But it wouldn't take much for the Russians to spot him.

Fortunately, they were more interested in what Mitchell was holding. 'Ah!' said Zakhar. 'Good, you have sword.'

Mitchell raised it, as if preparing to enter battle. 'Care for a rematch, Zakhar?'

Zakhar smiled again and shook his head. 'I do not think so. Besides, I already beat you once. Now, put down sword and move over there.' He nodded in the direction of the back wall.

Mitchell reluctantly placed Excalibur on the floor before following Nina across the room. She looked back at the tomb again. Chase was nowhere in sight – and the two Russians apparently thought only she and Mitchell were there.

'There's more here than just the sword,' she said to Zakhar, indicating the opening. 'That room's the tomb of King Arthur – and it's full of treasure. If you let us go, you can have it. You can have it all.'

'Treasure?' said Zakhar. He looked at the door, seeming disappointed by what he saw beyond. 'I see no treasure.'

'It's in the coffins. All of King Arthur's royal gold and jewels.'

The two Russians exchanged glances. 'Stand by wall,' said Zakhar, directing Nina and Mitchell back with his gun. He nodded to the other man. 'Orlovsky?'

The bald man grunted and moved to the tomb entrance, peering inside and seeing the two stone coffins. He glanced back at Zakhar, then stepped through—

Chase's hand whipped round from the other side of the opening and smashed the chunk of cut stone into Orlovsky's face, sending teeth showering out in a cascade of ivory. The Russian let out a gurgling scream and fell backwards, spitting blood from his ruined mouth. His gun bounced from his hand and skittered across the stone floor.

Zakhar gasped in surprise, then whirled and fired his

MP-5K at the doorway as Chase lunged back into cover. In the confined space the gunfire was almost deafening. Nina yelled and pressed her hands to her ears as Mitchell dived at Zakhar. He saw him coming and brought the gun back round, still firing. Chips of stone exploded from the walls as the bullets hit. Nina ducked, the line of holes stitching just over her head.

Mitchell grabbed Zakhar's gun hand, stopping the weapon short just before it reached his face. Zakhar snarled and fired again anyway. The muzzle flame scorched Mitchell's temple, the American screwing up his face in pain. Zakhar wrenched the gun from his grip, taking aim at Mitchell's head—

Nothing came from the MP-5K but a dry metal click. The magazine was empty.

Chase heard the sound and ran into the chamber, vaulting over the fallen Russian. 'Nina, go!'

'What about Jack?' she cried, seeing Mitchell struggling with Zakhar. The empty gun clattered to the floor beside the protruding figures of Lancelot and Galahad.

'Just *go!*' He shoved her towards the exit, then turned to join the fight in the centre of the room.

One eye still squeezed closed, Mitchell was unable to react fast enough to block Zakhar as he twisted round and slammed his elbow into his temple. Mitchell staggered back, and Zakhar immediately took advantage, delivering a crunching kick into his stomach. Mitchell crashed against the side wall and dropped to the floor, winded.

Zahkar smiled in triumph, then turned to face Chase.

Who had snatched up the sword and was swinging it at his head, about to cleave it in two—

The Russian's hands flashed up with shocking speed, palms clapping together to arrest the blade's swipe just above his forehead. A drop of blood fell from the edge of the sword. For a moment, the two men stared at each other, eye to eye.

Then Zakhar moved.

Chase knew the kick was coming, but despite his best efforts wasn't quite fast enough to avoid it as Zakhar spun and lashed out a foot, cutting his legs out from under him. Chase stumbled, landing hard in the centre of the painted Round Table. He lost his grip on Excalibur as he fell – and realised to his shock that Zakhar had kept hold of it, bloodied hands still squeezing the blade.

Zakhar flipped the sword over and caught it by the hilt, hands raised high over his head. He looked at Chase, ready to plunge it down like a stake into the Englishman's stomach—

A bloody hole burst open in his left shoulder.

The chamber rang to the echoing boom of Orlovsky's gun – now in Nina's hands. Zakhar lurched round, Excalibur flying from his grip to land at the side of the room. Clutching at the wound, he staggered backward . . . and tripped over the figure of Lancelot.

The key turned.

A harsh scrape of metal came from beneath the floor as some ancient mechanism, held in check since the twelfth century, was finally released.

'Oh, *bollocks*,' muttered Chase.

Nina looked up as a rush of wind came from the nearest of the holes in the ceiling – air being driven ahead of the deluge that was about to come. But there was another, more menacing sound just behind her as the huge slab above the main entrance began its grinding descent. *'Come on!'* she yelled. Mitchell was getting to his feet, Excalibur not far from him, Chase still on his back in the centre of the chamber . . .

Dirty brown water erupted from the holes above with punishing force, hard enough to sweep up Orlovsky and slam him against the wall. Zakhar fell, landing with a splash and a screech of pain. The chilly torrent hit Chase from all sides at once, making him splutter and choke as he tried to sit up. Only Mitchell, bracing himself against the side wall, was able to pull himself upright. He fumbled for Excalibur, pulling the dripping sword from the muddy froth.

The churning flow surged around Nina's legs, knocking her back against the edge of the door and jarring the gun from her hand. It vanished into the flood. The slab was still dropping, five feet above the floor, less . . . She ducked under it into the passage outside. 'Eddie! Jack!'

Mitchell kept moving around the edge of the room as the water rose. 'Nina, get out of here!'

'Not without Eddie!'

Battered by the plunging columns of water, half blinded by spray, Chase rolled on to all fours to raise his head above the water. But it wasn't by much – the room was filling with frightening speed.

And it would fill much faster once the door finally closed . . .

Mitchell reached the exit. Three feet and falling. He dropped to a crouch and leapt through.

'*Eddie!*'

The panic in Nina's voice drove a surge of adrenalin through Chase's body, punching through the numbing effects of the cold onslaught. He got his bearings, saw the gap reducing to just two feet, eighteen inches, almost touching the surface of the water . . .

Last chance—

Chase sprang upright – then immediately dived forward, landing on his stomach a few feet short of the door and being carried along by the rush of water through the rapidly shrinking gap. The bottom edge of the stone scraped against his heels as he shot through. Over the thunder of the deluge he heard a last terrified scream from Zakhar – then both sounds were abruptly cut off by a ground-shaking bang as the stone slab slammed closed.

The rush of water immediately died down to a trickle, the torrent which had already escaped the chamber sluicing away down the passage. Chase sat up, gasping for breath as filthy water streamed off him.

'Eddie, are you okay?' Nina asked, helping him stand.

'Jesus!' he spluttered, wiping his face. 'What *is* it with you and places full of death traps? Nice shooting, though.

He would've killed me if you hadn't tapped him in the shoulder.'

'I was aiming for his head.'

Chase raised an eyebrow. 'Really?'

'Well . . . no,' she admitted. 'I just thought that would sound cool. I kind of fired in his general direction.' He smiled and squeezed her shoulders.

Mitchell leaned against the wall, panting. 'Damn, that was close.' He straightened, then picked up Excalibur.

'Thanks for your help, by the way,' said Chase with unconcealed sarcasm.

'This isn't the time, Eddie,' Nina said, moving to stand between the two men. 'How the hell did they find us, anyway?' That thought instantly led to another. 'Oh, my God. Chloe. What if there're more of them outside?'

'We'd better get moving,' said Chase, shaking as much water from his sodden clothes as he could and giving Mitchell another glare before they hurried back through the tunnels. Most of the water had drained from the trial of Nivienne, but the revolting stench of flammable gas from the chamber housing the carving of Merlin now permeated the entire system, spreading outwards once the tomb was open to the outside air.

They retrieved their belongings from the edge of the pool. Nina removed Mitchell's shirt and put on her clothes, then picked up the walkie-talkie. 'Chloe, are you there?' Silence. 'Chloe, can you hear me?' Still no response. 'Shit!'

They continued towards the entrance, Mitchell taking the lead with the sword. The smell of gas finally started to fade as they reached the foot of the slope. Daylight glared down from above. Nina peered round Mitchell in the hope of seeing Chloe, but all that was visible was sky. She was about to call out Chloe's name, but Chase put a hand on her arm in silent warning.

'I'll go check it out,' whispered Mitchell as he clambered up the incline. 'Wait here.'

Nina and Chase watched as he dropped to a crouch, cautiously looking over the lip of the entrance. He paused, apparently seeing nothing, then advanced another step, leaning forward to check each side—

Suddenly, he was seized by a pair of huge hands and yanked out of the tunnel to be thrown to the ground. Maximov loomed over him, a white Band-Aid across the centre of his forehead. Another man stepped up beside him.

Nina knew the face from the photos Mitchell had shown them. It was Vaskovich's right-hand man, Kruglov. 'Jack Mitchell,' he said with distaste, adding something in Russian. Mitchell began to reply, but Kruglov kicked him in the side, silencing him. The Russian looked down the hole. 'Dr Wilde! I know you are down there, so show yourself.'

Nina had moved back into the darkness, pressing against Chase. 'Shit!' she whispered. 'What do we do?'

'Dr Wilde!' Kruglov repeated impatiently. 'Show yourself *now*, or I will kill your friends.'

'Oh, God,' said Nina, fear rising. 'He's got Chloe as well.'

'Gimme your camera. Quick!' Chase ordered. Confused, Nina pulled it from her pocket and passed it back to him. 'Go on.'

'*What?*'

He fiddled with the camera's controls. 'I'll be right behind you, just buy me a few seconds. Go!'

Reluctantly, Nina stepped into the light. Kruglov's wide mouth spread into a smug smirk. 'Good. Thank you for finding Excalibur for us.' He gestured for her to climb the slope.

'Where's Chloe?' Nina demanded as she slowly ascended. Like Zakhar, Kruglov clearly had no idea that Chase was in the tomb.

'She is here. Yorgi, bring her.' Kruglov signalled to someone; a moment later, Chloe appeared, shoved into view by the man with the topknot whom Mitchell had knocked out at the castle. He stood behind her, gripping her arm.

'Chloe,' Nina said, stopping a few feet short of the entrance. 'Are you okay?' Chloe didn't reply, only managing a terrified nod. 'Let her go. You don't need her any more.'

'No, we don't,' Kruglov agreed. 'Yorgi.'

Yorgi grinned – and Chloe convulsed, throwing her head back and gasping. He released her arm . . . and she dropped face first to the ground, an ugly knife protruding from her back.

'No!' Nina screamed. 'No, you *bastards*! You didn't have to kill her, she didn't do anything!'

Maximov seemed to share her feelings, obviously objecting in Russian. His boss cut him off with a dismissive wave of one hand. 'Come out of the hole,' Kruglov ordered, taking out a gun. 'Now!'

Nausea rose in Nina's throat as she advanced, to see Chloe on the ground, red running down the yellow of her jacket. 'Oh, God,' she whispered as she emerged into daylight, seeing the Russians surrounding the entrance. Maximov, Dominika, Chloe's killer, three others she didn't recognise. Mitchell was sprawled on the ground at Kruglov's feet, Excalibur beside him.

No way to escape.

Unless Chase could do something.

Forcing back his shock at what had just happened outside, Chase found what he'd been looking for – a sharp stone protruding from the sloping tunnel wall. He stepped out of cover and smacked the camera against it, breaking the glass covering the flash. Kruglov heard the sound, snapping round to find its source.

Chase pushed the shutter, and tossed the camera back down the tunnel behind him. He began a mental countdown. Ten, nine . . .

'You! Out!' Kruglov yelled, raising his gun.

'All right, I'm coming,' said Chase, raising his hands and quickly climbing to the entrance. He saw Mitchell on the ground, Nina kneeling beside the unmoving Chloe – and Kruglov's people clustered round their leader. He gave

Nina a look, his eyes momentarily flicking downwards. Understanding crossed her face. 'But do you know what goes "quack"?'

Kruglov stared at him, puzzled. 'What?'

'A *duck*!' He dived to the ground, Nina also dropping flat.

At the bottom of the tunnel, the camera's timer reached zero.

It clicked, the cracked flash firing . . .

And the electric spark ignited the methane in the air.

20

The concentration of gas was barely high enough for it to catch fire – but it did, within an instant the thin flame leaping through the tunnels to the much denser pockets of methane deeper inside the Tor. They erupted, a chain reaction blasting the shockwave of expanding fires back towards the entrance—

A hot wind burst from the tunnel, showering Kruglov and his thugs with dirt and sending them reeling – followed a moment later by a fireball that exploded into the open air like the breath of an enraged dragon. Kruglov managed to dive away, shielding his face, but one man fell screaming as his clothes and hair were set aflame.

Chase jumped up into the hot air of the dissipating fire, slamming a punch into Yorgi's face and knocking him backwards down the steep hillside. Mitchell snatched up Excalibur and rolled to swing it at Dominika, smacking her gun hand with the flat of the blade and knocking the pistol into the grass. He grabbed it and sprang to his feet.

Nina was also up, seizing a shovel and swinging it like an axe into the groin of another goon. He let out a choked scream and stumbled over the edge of the terrace. She was about to brain Kruglov with the spade when Mitchell ran past and pulled her away. 'Come on! We gotta go! *Now!*' She flung the spade at another Russian, knocking him down.

Chase realised that Kruglov had dropped his gun and was about to dive for it when he saw Mitchell practically dragging Nina away along the terrace. 'Eddie, move it!' the American yelled.

Chase hesitated, then ran after them. 'You have a *gun!*' he shouted at Mitchell as he caught up. 'Shoot them!'

'There's too many of them! We've got to get out of here!'

Chase didn't agree – they had the advantage of numbers, but Kruglov's people had been thrown into confusion, and were only now starting to recover. But since Mitchell had the gun, Chase had no choice now but to go along with his decision.

They raced along the terrace, heading towards the steep northern face of the Tor. Despite the terrain, several cows stood on the hillside ahead of them, startled by the noise. Chase looked back as they skirted the nervous animals. Kruglov was on his feet, bellowing orders. His subordinates gave chase. 'Jack, shoot!'

'You want to shoot the *cows?*'

'No! Shoot *over* them, scare them!'

Mitchell pointed the gun back and fired three rapid

shots into the air. The cows immediately panicked, breaking into clumsy gallops away from the noise . . .

Straight at the Russians.

Kruglov saw the approaching stampede and without hesitation leapt from the terrace, rolling down the hill. The others were slower to react, Dominika after a moment following Kruglov's example and flinging herself down the slope. Maximov stumbled to a stop as if unable to believe his eyes, while another two men hurriedly reversed direction and ran back along the terrace.

They didn't get far.

Not even someone of Maximov's size and strength could stop a charging cow – though that didn't prevent him from trying to grab the leader of the herd as it ran blindly at him. He was swept off his feet, clinging to the cow for a couple of seconds before being flung clear and hitting one of the fleeing men. They both cartwheeled downhill to end up in a dazed heap.

The cows thundered on. The other Russian looked back and had just enough time to begin a scream before two of the animals slammed into him, one on each side, crushing the life from his body.

'They should've *moo*ved,' said Chase with a grim smile.

Nina made a disgusted noise at the pun. 'Where are we going?'

Mitchell pointed ahead as they rounded the Tor. A path led away from the hill across the field. A gate was visible at its edge, a road beyond it. A few sightseers stood in confusion on the path, unsure how to respond to the unfamiliar sound of gunfire. 'If we can find a car, we can get clear and call for backup. I'll make an emergency call to the embassy, and they'll tell the Brits – we'll have armed units, choppers, whatever we need in twenty minutes!'

They ran across the field. Nina glanced back. The remaining Russians were in pursuit again. 'That's if we can *last* twenty minutes!'

'We're gonna have to!' The sword still in one hand, Mitchell used the other to vault effortlessly over the gate. Chase waited until Nina had climbed it, then scrambled over the obstacle himself.

'Okay, a car,' said Nina, looking round. They had emerged from the field in a lay-by at the side of a narrow country lane. A pair of identical black 7 Series BMWs were parked at one end; almost certainly the Russians' vehicles. 'Can you hot-wire them?'

Mitchell shook his head. 'Not in time.' The only other vehicle in sight was an old sky-blue Volkswagen camper van. They exchanged unimpressed looks. 'Not what I would've picked . . .'

No choice. Kruglov and the others were still coming.

They ran to the van. The passenger door was open, smoke drifting lazily from within. Chase flung open the driver's door. A young couple looked at him in marijuana-fuddled surprise. 'Hello, hi,' said Nina. 'We need to borrow your van.'

'Sorry, but you can't have it,' said the man languidly, his

posh accent suggesting that his choice of vehicle was less out of financial necessity than as a fashion statement. 'You see, there's this concept known as personal property, and—'

Mitchell snapped up the gun. '*Get outta the damn Microbus!*'

The young woman shrieked and leapt from the VW, the man raising his hands and stumbling out after her. 'Okay, take it, I don't really like it that much, just don't hurt me!'

'Get rid of this shit,' Chase growled at him, plucking a joint from the camper's ashtray and flicking it on to the road in a flurry of burning embers. He climbed into the driving seat, finding the keys in the ignition. 'All aboard!'

Nina hopped into the front passenger seat as Mitchell slid open the back door and climbed inside. The van's rear was set out like a tiny apartment, with a bed, a small table and even a gas camping stove. He dropped Excalibur on the bed and readied his gun.

Chase turned the key. The starter whined for a moment before the distinctive puttering rattle of the Volkswagen's air-cooled engine kicked in. He revved hard and slammed the long gear lever into first with a crunch, then let out the clutch. The VW didn't so much spring away as lurch, but at least they were moving.

A glance in the mirror—

'*Down!*' he yelled, hunching in the seat as he swerved the van on to the narrow lane. Nina bent double in her seat, Mitchell dropping flat on the floor behind her as the rear window shattered. Shots cracked from the lay-by as the Russians opened fire. The rear-mounted engine took several hits, bullets clanging off the cylinder block as they ripped through the bodywork. Cushions and pillows exploded in clouds of feathers.

Still sitting low, Chase kept driving. The winding road was so narrow the van almost filled it, hedges blurring past little over a foot from each door. If anyone came the other way, they would be trapped.

The shooting stopped. Chase raised his head high enough to check the mirror. The Russians were running for the BMWs. Then the road curved, and they disappeared from view.

Nina cautiously sat up. 'Are we okay?'

Mitchell rose to his knees behind her, brushing away feathers. 'Yeah, but they're gonna catch up real quick.'

She rolled her eyes. 'In their BMWs? Ya think?'

'I'll call the embassy.' He took out his phone.

'What about you?' Chase asked Nina. 'You okay?'

'Yeah, but . . .' The full impact of what had just happened finally hit her. 'Oh, my God. Chloe. They just killed her, they *murdered* her, right in front of us. For nothing!'

'Kruglov's a psychopath,' said Mitchell, looking up from his call. 'But he's also a smart one – he didn't want to leave any witnesses.'

'Seemed like he knew you,' Chase noted, rounding a bend to bring the van towards the outskirts of Glastonbury.

'Our paths have crossed. Unfortunately.' Chase was

about to ask him more, but then his call continued. 'Peach? Mitchell. We have a situation here – I need you to get on to the Brits, right now, and get us as much support as they can. Yeah, this is an emergency. We've taken fire and the bad guys are going to catch up fast. We're not exactly in a muscle car here.'

'Tell him to send the police to Glastonbury Tor as well,' Nina said, turning in her seat. 'There's been a murder.'

Mitchell nodded and relayed the information, then listened to Peach for several seconds before replying. 'Okay. We'll just have to stay ahead of them for as long as we can. We're in a blue VW Microbus, heading for the north end of Glastonbury village, going west.' He listened again, then said, 'Okay,' and ended the call.

'How long?' Chase asked.

'Depends how on the ball your guys are. Twenty minutes, maybe fifteen.'

Nina saw a flash of gleaming black metal behind them. 'Too long!' Both BMWs were powering along the winding lane after them.

Mitchell used his gun to knock out the broken glass in the rear windscreen, then crouched. The first 7 Series roared closer, Kruglov leaning from the front passenger window, taking aim—

Mitchell fired first – but not at Kruglov. Instead he unleashed six rapid shots at his driver. The windscreen crazed as if hit by a shotgun blast, an almost opaque white speckled with red.

The BMW swerved. Kruglov ducked back inside and

grabbed the steering wheel, but too late. The car rode up on to the steep grassy verge, tearing through bushes before clipping a tree and rolling on to its roof. The other windows blew out.

Nina caught a glimpse of green hair as Dominika struggled through one of the rear windows. The second BMW braked hard to avoid a collision. The overturned car, its front end still buried in the bushes, had partially blocked the road. For a moment she thought the chase was over, but then Kruglov crawled from the wreck, angrily waving the other car on. The 7 Series mounted the opposite verge, its bumper shoving the inverted car deeper into the bushes, before dropping back on to the tarmac and pursuing again.

'This might be a bad time,' said Mitchell, 'but I've only got two bullets left.'

Nina remembered how the Grand Cherokee's pursuit had come to a sudden end in Bournemouth. 'Are there any bottles back there? We could throw them in the road, blow out their tyres!'

Mitchell pulled open the little cupboards beneath the table and under the bed. 'Plastic, plastic, metal,' he said as he tossed items aside. 'No glass, dammit!' He yanked the covers from the bed, more feathers flying. 'Nothing!'

Chase now had greater concerns. 'Shit,' he gasped, seeing a T-junction coming up fast. 'Hang on!'

'To *what?*' Nina demanded. 'This whole thing is just one big crumple zone!'

Chase had no choice but to brake, the corner too tight.

The VW rolled like a ship in heavy waters as they screeched through the junction. Branches thwacked the van's side as it skidded on to the verge before Chase managed to straighten out. Ahead, he saw a car – no, a line of cars, crawling along behind something out of sight round a long bend.

No traffic coming the other way – yet. He crashed down through the gears, foot to the floor. The camper van's engine buzzed like furious wasps in a tin can. Forty miles an hour, fifty, the speedometer needle rising agonisingly slowly as they caught up with the dawdling traffic.

'Here they come!' Mitchell warned, raising his gun again. The BMW slid round the corner, tyres smoking.

The cars ahead were doing less than thirty. Chase pulled out to pass them, sounding the horn. The VW was at fifty-five, and struggling to go any faster. The 7 Series was already catching up.

The curve straightened out – to reveal an oncoming car rushing straight at them.

The BMW pulled out as well, trapping them—

Still sounding the horn, Chase desperately swerved the VW to the left, slicing into the line of traffic and side-swiping a Renault Mégane with a crunch of metal. Nina shrieked as the passenger window broke with the impact, showering her with glass. The oncoming Fiat missed by barely an inch, the force of the car's slipstream rocking the Volkswagen.

Chase grimaced, foot still pressed hard on the

accelerator as he turned back into the right-hand lane. The Mégane braked hard – and the car behind smashed into it.

The Fiat skidded as its driver panicked, blocking the road and leaving the BMW with nowhere to go except into the suddenly braking traffic.

It body-slammed another car, sending it crashing through a hedge. The Fiat clipped the 7 Series and tore off its rear bumper. The Russians spun out, coming to rest almost sideways-on to the traffic.

'Jesus!' Nina gasped. At the relatively low speed at which the line of cars had been travelling she doubted anyone would have been seriously hurt, but there would still be several badly shaken people.

Mitchell didn't share her concern, however. 'Got 'em!' he whooped.

'Yeah, but for how long?' Chase asked. Unless the BMW had been crippled by the collisions, its driver would be able to restart and straighten out in ten seconds, twenty at most.

He looked ahead. The front of the line was coming up fast, the cars held up behind a trundling Vauxhall Vectra, its elderly driver hunched over the wheel resolutely denying the existence of anything beyond his narrow cone of vision. Despite not wanting to involve innocent bystanders, Chase still swept the van back into the left-hand lane just inches in front of the Vauxhall, hoping to shock the old man into checking his mirrors once in a while.

The road ahead was clear and straight – and had no exits, being hemmed in by fences and trees on both sides.

The camper van was still stuck at fifty-five. The BMW was moving again and gaining rapidly, a black panther about to pounce. The man who had been burned at the Tor leaned out, aiming—

Mitchell fired a shot. The bullet hit the BMW's windscreen, cracking the glass, but missing the men inside. The Russian returned fire. Mitchell dropped flat on the bed as more holes ripped through the van.

The firing stopped. Chase checked the mirror. The gunman withdrew into the 7 Series, reloading.

And the car itself grew larger, leaping forward to ram them—

The VW's occupants were jolted by the impact. The van swerved towards a fence, Chase barely managing to straighten out before being hit again – the 7 Series was pushing them from behind.

The speedometer needle whipped past sixty, rapidly heading into unknown territory as the snarl of the BMW's engine filled the cabin. The steering wheel shuddered in Chase's hands, the vehicle starting to snake. He fought to keep it in line. If he lost control, the van would flip over.

He looked ahead – and saw the end of the road approaching rapidly, the brick wall of a farm building on the other side of a T-junction directly ahead. 'Shit!'

Only the roof of the 7 Series was now visible in the mirror, the driver still barging them along like a locomotive—

'Jack!' Nina yelled. 'Do something!'

'I've only got one bullet left!' Mitchell protested. But he still got to his knees, and was about to shoot at the driver when a burst of gunfire from the other Russian forced him back down. 'Dammit!'

They were running out of road. Nina glanced back and saw the camping stove lying on its side. 'The stove, throw the stove!'

Mitchell was lost. 'What?'

'Throw it – and shoot it!'

Realisation flashed across Mitchell's face. He snatched up the fallen stove and hurled it through the rear window.

The gunman was about to shoot him when the gas cylinder slammed into the bullet-damaged windscreen, hanging partway through the cracked glass like a fat blue fly in a spider's web. His eyes instinctively flicked towards it—

Mitchell fired.

The last bullet punched through one side of the cylinder and out of the other as it drove the cylinder through the windscreen, hot lead igniting the gas in its wake.

It exploded directly between the two men, shrapnel ripping their flesh like a shotgun blast before they were incinerated. The car swerved sharply before hitting a tree and flipping over, bowling along the narrow lane in a shower of flaming debris.

Chase slammed on the brakes. The tyres screamed, as did the occupants of the Volkswagen as it hurtled towards the farm wall, smoke belching from its wheels—

They hit.

But at barely five miles per hour. There was a muffled crunch as the camper van's bowed nose was flattened against the unyielding brickwork, then it rolled backwards and came to a stop.

Chase found himself bent over the steering wheel, one foot still jammed on the brake. He looked across to see Nina blinking at him from the passenger footwell. 'So . . . we *are* still alive, right?'

Mitchell was flattened against the back of Nina's seat. 'More or less,' he said, coughing as acrid tyre smoke wafted through the broken windows. He sat upright and looked back. The burning hulk of the 7 Series lay on its side about fifty feet away, blocking the road. 'Don't think they are, though.'

'Great.' The engine had stalled, but to Chase's surprise it restarted when he turned the key. 'Okay, now what?'

Mitchell searched for his phone. 'First thing, clear the area, in case Kruglov's found another car. I'll call the embassy again, guide a chopper to us.' He located his phone, but kept looking round, growing worried. 'Shit! Where's the sword?'

'Here,' said Nina, pulling herself back on to her seat. Excalibur had slid under it into the footwell. She picked it up. 'Hey, it's not glowing any more.'

'Maybe we're not on a ley line here,' Mitchell suggested as he pushed the redial button. 'Earth energy seems to follow natural lines of flux; we might be too far away from one to channel any.'

'Well, whatever,' said Nina, too exhausted by the chase to care about his theories. 'We got it.'

Chase put the Volkswagen into reverse. The legendary sword of King Arthur in Nina's hands, they drove away down the country lane.

21

'Well,' said Mitchell, 'you did it.'

'*We* did it,' Nina corrected.

Excalibur lay on a velvet cloth, carefully cleaned of dirt and gleaming under the lights in the office at the US embassy. The pieces of Caliburn sat beside it in their open metal case; a similar container had been prepared for the intact sword.

'Yeah, we did,' said Chase curtly. He stood away from the other two, leaning against a wall. 'Cost us enough, though.'

'It would have cost a lot more if Vaskovich had gotten his hands on it,' said Mitchell. Ignoring Chase's dark expression, he leaned closer to examine the blade, then gave Nina an admiring look. 'You stuck this thing right through *stone*.'

'Yeah, what was the deal with that?' Nina asked, wanting to avert another dispute between the two men. 'You said you had a theory – what is it?'

Mitchell almost reverently lifted Excalibur from the

cloth. 'It's something else DARPA's been working on – but I didn't expect to see it here.'

'So DARPA's building lightsabers, are they?'

Mitchell smiled. 'Not quite – but we *are* making monomolecular blades. Or at least trying to.' Seeing her questioning expression, he continued, 'If you can create a cutting edge that's made up of one long, single molecule, then in theory it should be able to cut through almost anything. We've had some success by using carbon nanotubes, but only on a micro scale. Nothing with practical applications yet. But this . . .' He eyed the sword. 'Remember what I told you about Wootz steel, how it incorporated carbon nanotubes to give it incredible sharpness in 500 BC? So does this – but somehow, whatever it is about your body's bioelectric field that's causing the sword to channel earth energy is also aligning the nanotubes into a monomolecular edge. As soon as you let go, they lose their charge and go back to their original alignment – which is why I couldn't pull the sword from the stone. But you could.'

Nina's eyebrows rose. 'That's a hell of a theory.'

'I know. But it fits the facts.'

'So if the right person was holding it, they could cut through *anything*?'

'Maybe not anything, but definitely a lot of things. No wonder Arthur was unstoppable in battle.'

'So why me? How come I could make it glow and you couldn't?'

'You got me there,' said Mitchell, handing the sword to

her. 'Who knows, maybe you're descended from King Arthur!' He laughed, but Nina did not. He crossed the room and switched off the lights; the metal gave off a faint shimmering glow against the twilight beyond the embassy windows.

Chase raised an eyebrow. 'Christ, you're a Jedi.'

'Try it with Caliburn,' Mitchell suggested. Nina returned Excalibur to the cloth and picked up the piece of broken blade. It seemed to remain completely inert until she lowered it into the shadows below the table, whereupon the slightest glimmer of blue became discernible. 'Looks like it reacts to you too, just not so much,' he said as he turned the lights back on. 'I guess Merlin must've needed another try to get the formula right.'

'I guess so,' she said, 'but I still don't understand how. And why's it lighting up here? We're in the middle of a city!' She put the piece of Caliburn back in its case.

Mitchell looked thoughtful. 'Maybe all the highways leading through the countryside and converging on London disrupt the lines of earth energy, even redirect them. We know we can use an antenna array to gather earth energy, so there could be other ways to affect it as well. But that's something we can figure out now that we've got it.' He carefully folded the velvet around Excalibur, then placed it in its case and closed it.

'So what happens now?' asked Chase.

'Now? Both the swords go to DARPA for analysis. Then after we're done, Excalibur comes back to England

and I'd guess takes pride of place in the British Museum or Buckingham Palace or wherever. And meanwhile, Vaskovich gets jack shit.' Mitchell smiled. 'Which suits me just fine.'

'And what about us?' said Nina.

'You go back to the IHA with yet another string to your bow. Atlantis, the Tomb of Hercules, and now King Arthur and Excalibur – that's a pretty goddamn impressive résumé! You should be proud.' He picked up the two cases. 'As for me, well, back to the States with these babies so we can figure out how the hell Merlin made them in the first place. Once we do, we can create our own superconductors – and Uncle Sam gets the world's first fully functioning earth energy generator.'

Nina nodded. 'I'm going to have to be more open-minded in future, I guess. I thought this whole thing about earth energy was just pseudoscientific nonsense, but Bernd was right about that too. I bet he never imagined that I'd actually be physically able to prove it, though.'

'But you did,' Mitchell said. He paused, then put down one of the cases. 'I owe you a hell of a lot. We would never have found the swords without you, Nina . . . and you, Eddie.' He kissed Nina on the cheek, then extended his hand to Chase. 'Seriously, man – you did a great job.'

'You weren't too shabby yourself,' said Chase flatly. After a moment, he shook Mitchell's hand.

'Okay, then,' said Mitchell, picking up the aluminium case again, 'I guess this is it for now. You're still booked into the hotel for tonight, compliments of DARPA so you'll finally be able to put on some clean clothes. And enjoy the rest of your vacation – sorry it got interrupted.'

'Actually, I didn't mind that part so much,' Chase muttered. Mitchell smiled, then left the room, taking the cases with him.

Nina waited until the door closed before speaking. 'I think I *do* know why the sword reacted to me and nobody else,' she said. 'I just didn't want to bring it up in front of Jack – I don't know how much he knows about the Atlantean genome. After we discovered Atlantis, Kristian Frost told me his research found that about one per cent of the world's population possessed the same genome as the ancient Atlanteans – that they were directly descended from them. I'm one of that one per cent. Some of the more fanciful Atlantis legends said the Atlanteans had unusual powers; I never believed them because they sounded like pure fantasy, but who knows?' She looked at her hands. 'Causing a sword to light up just by touching it would definitely qualify as unusual. Maybe the Atlanteans knew how to make a superconducting metal, even if they had no idea what that meant. Merlin might just have been trying to recreate the same thing.'

She waited for a response from Chase. Nothing seemed forthcoming. 'Eddie? Did you hear me?'

'Course I heard you, I'm not deaf,' he replied, frowning. 'I just didn't *care*.' He stepped towards her. 'For fuck's sake, Nina! I told you not to go, and look what happened! You almost got killed. And I don't know what . . .' He took a breath. 'I don't know what I'd do if I lost you.'

'To *Jack*?' Nina exclaimed, incredulous.

'What?' Chase was briefly confused before realising she had completely misunderstood him. 'No, that's not what I—'

'For God's sake!' Nina snapped. 'I cannot believe you are actually *jealous* of Jack! What, you think that first he took your job and now he's going to take your woman?'

'What do you mean, my job?'

'You think your job is to look after me, don't you?' said Nina. 'I just run around getting into trouble so that you can save me. But Jack comes along and can do the same thing, *and* he's an American, like me, *and* he's a PhD, like me, and you feel threatened!'

Chase crossed his arms angrily. 'That's the most fucking ridiculous thing I've ever heard.'

'Is it?' She turned away to look out across Grosvenor Square, its trees and buildings silhouetted against the dusk sky. On the street below, she saw Mitchell descend the steps outside the embassy's front entrance and climb into a waiting black cab. For some reason, he was only carrying one of the two cases. 'You're the one who's being paranoid about Jack and behaving like a . . .' She tailed off.

A *taxi* . . .

'It's got nothing to do with Jack!' Chase protested behind her – but Nina was no longer listening.

She stared at the taxi in growing horror, colour draining from her face as realisation hit. 'Oh, my God.'

'What?'

'Oh, my God!' she repeated, whirling to face him. 'It's Jack – he's not taking Excalibur to the States. He's taking it to *Vaskovich*!' She ran to the door. 'Come on!'

Chase stared at her, anger turning to bewilderment. 'What're you talking about?'

'He's *stealing* it, he's stealing my goddamn sword! Come on!'

She ran for the stairs, Chase following in confusion. 'How do you know?'

'Because he just got into a taxi!'

Sarcasm filled his voice. 'Oh no, a *taxi*! That *proves* he's evil! *Now* who's being paranoid?'

They clattered down the stairs, a couple of embassy workers jumping out of their way. 'Since when does Jack use taxis? Every time he's gone *anywhere*, he's had an official US government vehicle – car, plane, whatever! But now he's carrying something incredibly valuable – and he decides to take it to the airport in a *cab*?'

They reached the lobby. Nina spotted Peach talking to a tall, granite-faced man with a close-cropped brush of pure white hair – who was holding the other metal case. 'Mr Peach! Hey!'

Peach looked round in surprise. 'Dr Wilde! What's the matter?'

She jabbed a finger at the case. 'Did Jack Mitchell just give you that?' she asked the white-haired man.

Peach spoke for him. 'Yes. We're putting it into secure storage until it can be transferred to DARPA.'

'Uh-huh. And what about the *other* case?'

'What other case?'

'The case he's about to give to the Russians! Eddie, come on!' Nina rushed for the exit, Chase shrugging helplessly at Peach before following her. One of the Marines stationed at the metal detectors inside the doors moved to block them, but Peach shouted for him to let them through. They ran down the steps and into Grosvenor Square.

Nina hunted for the taxi. 'Where'd he go? Where'd he go?'

'Over there.' Chase pointed to the left; the road round the square was a one-way system, circulating clockwise. The traffic was light, the only cab in sight heading east along the long side of the gardens towards the heart of London.

Nina spotted a black cab outside the Marriott hotel to their right. They ran to it, the driver looking up expectantly. 'Follow that cab!'

'Are you taking the piss?' the driver hooted.

'No, no! That cab, over there!' She pointed to the opposite corner of the park. 'We need to be wherever he's going, fast!'

The driver regarded her as if she were an escaped mental patient. Chase sighed and took out several banknotes. 'Fifty quid do you?'

'That's the ticket,' said the driver with a broad smile. 'Hop in!'

The taxi set off with a determined diesel rasp. Nina

peered ahead as they drove past the embassy and turned to head east. 'There! There he is!'

The driver accelerated. 'Saw you both come out of the embassy,' he said. 'So this geezer we're after – terrorist, is he? Spy?'

'A thief,' Nina told him. The driver didn't seem impressed, but continued the pursuit regardless.

'You *think*,' said Chase.

Nina addressed the driver. 'If you were going to Heathrow from the embassy, would you go the way he's going?'

'God, no!' the driver said, laughing. 'Completely the other direction, miss.'

'Told you,' she said to Chase. 'That's why he didn't take an official vehicle – he doesn't want anyone from the embassy to know where he's going.'

'I still don't get what you're thinking,' he complained. 'If he was going to give the sword to Vaskovich anyway, why didn't he just hand it over at Glastonbury?'

'Maybe he didn't want to blow his cover. Not in front of us.'

'Okay, so if he's really working for Vaskovich, he could have had Kruglov kill us and then make up whatever story he wanted. Why would he care about keeping us alive once he's got the sword?'

'I don't know,' said Nina, shaking her head. 'But Jack knew Kruglov and the rest . . . and they knew *him*.'

'If they're so matey, why were they trying to kill him?'

Nina didn't have an answer for that. Instead, she sat

335

back and watched as they caught up with Mitchell's taxi, their driver keeping a couple of cars between the two black cabs. They turned south, eventually emerging on Regent Street and passing through the neon blaze of Piccadilly Circus before heading east again.

'Looks like he's going to Leicester Square,' the cabbie said. Traffic had slowed considerably even by London's sluggish standards, people crowding the pavements ahead.

'What's going on?' Nina asked.

'Film premiere at the Empire, miss. I dropped some girls off there earlier – they wanted to see that American bloke starring in it, wossname, that guy with teeth. Grant Thorn, that's the one. My missus likes him, but I reckon he's just another one of those plastic Americans. No offence, miss.'

'Uh-huh. Hey, he's stopping,' Nina said, seeing the other taxi pull over.

'Stop here,' Chase told the driver. The taxi squealed to a halt a few car-lengths behind its quarry as Mitchell climbed out. Chase paid the driver. 'Keep the change.'

'Thanks, mate,' the driver replied. Nina opened the door as Mitchell headed into the crowd. 'Hope you catch your thief!'

'Do you know your way around here?' she asked Chase as they hurried after Mitchell, battling to keep sight of him through the throng.

'More or less. I lived in London when I was with Sophia.'

'You did? Huh. You never told me.'

'Can we not fucking start all that again?' They followed Mitchell into Leicester Square itself. Its northern end had been cordoned off to form a roadway leading to the Empire cinema, flanked by a crush of onlookers. Cameras flashed and people yelled in excitement as a limo pulled up at the red carpet, only for their enthusiasm to disappear as its occupants emerged, apparently not famous enough to earn a cheer.

Nina glanced at the cinema. A huge billboard proclaimed the movie as *Gale Force*, the face of Hollywood flavour-of-the-moment Grant Thorn dominating an image of stormy seas, an exploding helicopter and a voluptuous young woman in a bikini. 'Looks like your kind of movie,' she quipped. The crowd then caught her attention: more specifically, the number of yellow-jacketed police officers and security personnel in and around the cordon.

Chase had the same thought. 'If he really *is* going to give the sword to Vaskovich's people, he's picked a good place to do it. Lot of people around, lots of cops – less chance of them just killing him and taking it.'

Mitchell was now heading south down the side of the garden at the square's centre. Though much less crowded than the area in front of the Empire, it was still busy, Leicester Square being home to several other cinemas as well as restaurants and bars. He reached the southwestern corner of the garden, stopping beside a bust of Sir Isaac Newton at its entrance.

'Shit,' Chase muttered. 'We can't keep going this way, he'll see us. Go back, go into the park.'

'What if we lose him?'

'Doesn't look like he's planning on moving. Come on.'

They doubled back, entering the gate at the garden's northwestern corner and hurrying down the diagonal path towards its centre, passing a Union Jack-emblazoned stall selling London-themed tourist tat. To Nina's relief she quickly sighted Mitchell again, still waiting by the statue. Then she froze, grabbing Chase's arm as she recognised someone else. 'Eddie, Eddie!'

'Whoa, shit,' said Chase, making a rapid half-turn away from Maximov, who was crossing the square not far ahead. 'Did he see us?'

Nina cautiously peered round him. 'No, he's still heading for Jack. Oh, God, that punk bitch is there too.'

Chase followed her gaze and saw Dominika emerge from behind the ticket office at the garden's south end, her green hair standing out like a flare under the streetlights. She too was making for Mitchell. He realised they were dangerously exposed – if any of the Russians took their eyes off Mitchell . . . 'Come on, get behind that tree.'

They moved into the limited cover of a tree at the edge of the grass and hunched behind it, less than twenty feet from Mitchell as the two Russians slowly closed in on him. Mitchell had seen Dominika and Maximov approaching, but stood his ground.

'Can you see any more of 'em?' Chase asked.

He suddenly felt Nina tense behind him. 'Oh, yeah,' she said nervously. 'Eddie, kiss me! Now!'

Chase turned – and Nina locked her lips against his, quickly spinning him round. Kruglov was barely five feet away, on the other side of the garden's perimeter railings. He strode past, eyes flicking to her – and continued towards Mitchell, having seen only the back of Chase's head in the evening light.

Nina turned Chase all the way round before releasing him. 'You're a good kisser when you're scared,' he said quietly. She batted his arm before they both returned their attention to the Russians.

'Hello, Jack,' said Kruglov as he stepped round the corner to stand before Mitchell. Dominika and Maximov waited nearby, eyes fixed coldly upon the American.

'Aleksey,' Mitchell replied. 'You mind telling me what the hell you were doing today?'

'I could ask you the same.' Kruglov slowly circled Mitchell, glancing at the case in his hand. 'After what happened in Austria, I had my doubts about your loyalty. So I decided to take charge personally.'

'I *told* Leonid I'd bring him the sword,' Mitchell snapped. 'He trusted me – why couldn't you?'

'Jesus,' a shocked Nina whispered to Chase, her fears confirmed.

'Because it's my job not to trust people,' said Kruglov. 'Especially people who are trying to . . . what is the phrase? Take us for a ride.' He narrowed his eyes. 'We had the German's notes; you could have just given us the broken sword in Austria. We would have found Excalibur ourselves, and the IHA woman would have nothing. Instead, you kept it, and now some of my people are dead. We even lost a helicopter! They are not cheap.'

'I had to keep my cover,' Mitchell insisted. 'I would have given your guy the sword right there at the castle if he hadn't been completely incompetent and let Chase take him out.'

'You should have let us kill Chase and the woman,' Dominika said angrily. A passing couple gave her odd looks.

Kruglov spoke in Russian, a command to keep her voice down. 'But she has a point,' he went on to Mitchell. 'Once you had Excalibur, there was no need to keep Wilde alive.'

'Like I said,' Mitchell began, exasperated, 'I had to maintain my cover. I'd be no use to Leonid if DARPA even suspected I was feeding him information. They'd cut me off, put me under a full investigation. But doing everything I could to keep her alive puts me above suspicion.'

Kruglov frowned, considering his argument. Eventually, he nodded. 'And what now?' he asked, regarding the case again. 'Are you prepared to give us the sword?'

'That's why I'm here. As far as DARPA's concerned, they're going to take delivery of *a* sword – but not the one they think. I've taken care of all the paperwork. Officially, this sword,' he held up the case, 'no longer exists. So I'm ready to take it to Leonid.'

'What're we gonna do?' Nina hissed. 'We can't let them take it!'

Chase glanced back to where they had entered the garden. 'I'll be right back.'

'What? Where're you – *Eddie!*' She watched in disbelief as he hurried away, then turned back to the scene playing out before her.

Kruglov's wide mouth twisted into an expression suggesting he had just sucked dry an entire lemon. '*You* want to take it to Leonid?'

'That was the deal,' Mitchell insisted. 'I said I would *personally* take it to Leonid, and he agreed.'

'I don't trust you.'

'I don't give a rat's ass whether you do or not. The point is, *Leonid* trusts me. I told him I'd bring him Excalibur. Well, I've got Excalibur right here, and I'm ready to take it to him. He's waiting for it, Aleksey. And you know he doesn't like to be kept waiting.'

A cheer rose from the other end of Leicester Square; somebody famous on the red carpet. Nina looked round to see Chase hurrying back, crouched low to stay hidden from the Russians behind the tree. He had something in one hand. 'Er, *what?*'

'Big Ben was the best I could manage,' said Chase, holding up a rather poor gilded miniature of the world-famous clock tower, bought from the nearby stall. 'Wait here.'

'What're you *doing?*'

'Nina, just stay back here. *Please*, don't argue,' he added as she began to protest. 'I'll handle this.'

Lowering his head, he stepped out from behind the tree, casually walking through the other people on the path towards the group. Kruglov's back was to him, while Dominika and Maximov were both focusing their attention on Mitchell.

Kruglov finally nodded. 'Okay. We will bring Leonid the sword . . . *together*.'

'I can live with that,' said Mitchell. He smiled. 'So, let's—'

Chase stepped up behind Kruglov and thrust the ornament into his back, hoping its shape and hardness would convince the Russian he had a gun. 'Ay up. How's things?'

'Eddie!' Mitchell exclaimed.

'Planning a trip, were you? Keep still,' he warned Dominika as she reached into her coat. 'Try anything and Toadface here has a nine-millimetre heart attack.' She lowered her hand.

'You would shoot me in the back?' said Kruglov calmly. 'With all these policemen around?'

'I'd shoot you in the fucking *face* for what happened to Mitzi,' Chase growled. 'Jack, put down the case. I can't fucking *believe* that after everything we went through, you were working for these bastards all along.'

Mitchell put the long metal case on the ground. 'Eddie, if you've got any of the sense you finally convinced me you had, you'd walk away right now.'

Chase pushed Kruglov forward. 'Guess you were wrong. Okay, everyone back up.' Still advancing, he watched as Mitchell, Maximov and Dominika warily retreated. He prodded Kruglov in the back with his 'gun'. 'All right, shithead. Pick up the case. Very slowly.'

'So, you are Chase?' Kruglov asked, voice still not betraying the slightest concern, as he bent and took the case by its handle. 'You're as brave – and as stupid – as I'd heard.'

'Maybe, but I'm not the one with a gun in my back, am I?'

'No, but Nina is,' said Mitchell.

Chase grinned mirthlessly. 'Nice try.'

But the look of malevolent pleasure spreading across Dominika's face warned him Mitchell might not be bluffing. He risked a brief glance over his shoulder—

And saw the last of Kruglov's henchmen, the man with the topknot, standing behind the terrified Nina.

It wasn't a gun he was holding to her back. It was a knife – the one he had used to kill Chloe Lamb.

22

Nobody moved, the group forming a strange tableau amidst the bustle of Leicester Square.

Nina was the first to speak. 'I'm sorry, Eddie. I didn't see him coming.'

'Put down the gun, Chase,' said Kruglov. 'Or she dies.'

Chase jammed the point of the ornament into his back. Kruglov grunted. 'If he even twitches, I'll kill you.'

'He won't do it, Aleksey,' said Mitchell. 'He loves her too much.'

'You shut up, you fucking two-faced—'

'He already blames himself for the death of a friend,' Mitchell continued. 'He won't let anything happen to Nina as well. Even if that means letting you go. Eddie, I'm giving you both a chance here. Just walk away.'

Chase angrily jolted the case with his knee. 'People have died for this fucking thing. You seriously think I'm going to let you hand it over to this bunch of twats?'

'You don't have a choice,' Kruglov said. 'Yorgi, when I count to three, kill her. One.'

'Eddie, he'll do it!' Mitchell said. 'Just –'

'Two.'

'– walk away, right now!'

Chase stepped back and dropped the metal souvenir, which clanged to the ground between Kruglov's feet.

The Russian looked at it and chuckled, then turned to face Chase, smiling his frog-like smile. 'Three.'

'*No!*' Chase screamed. Behind Nina, Yorgi moved, about to thrust the knife into her back—

His face blew apart.

Mitchell had whipped out a silenced handgun and fired it almost directly at Nina, the bullet passing so close to her face that it singed her hair. The dead Russian fell backwards, chunks of ragged flesh flapping from the shattered bones of his skull.

'Get out of here!' Mitchell shouted—

Maximov slammed him back against the bust of Newton. The gun flew from his hand. Chase spun to face Kruglov, but the Russian smashed the case into his stomach, knocking him to the ground. Kruglov yelled an order, then sprinted into the garden.

A bystander saw the mangled corpse and screamed, panic quickly spreading across the square.

Nina snapped out of her shock as Kruglov ran past her, the case in his hand. She saw Chase struggle to his knees, winded but unharmed. She paused, caught between conflicting impulses ... then ran after the Russian. If he got away with Excalibur, everything she had been through, all the deaths she had witnessed, would have been for nothing.

Chase stood, and realised Nina was no longer there. 'Shit!' He was about to follow her when a metallic sound reached him, clear as a musical note even through the yells of the crowd. Dominika had drawn and cocked her gun, aiming it at him—

Shouting from his right: two policemen running towards them. Dominika's eyes flicked towards the noise, then she looked back and fired – but Chase had already rolled away, the bullet chipping the pavement. She turned and ran.

The policemen went after her – and were sent flying back as Maximov swung Mitchell at them like a human baseball bat. The three men tumbled to the ground as the Russian bellowed in triumph before lumbering away across Leicester Square, swiping pedestrians out of his path.

Chase was about to run after Nina when another gunshot made him whirl. Somebody had tried to be a hero and attempted to tackle Dominika – and had received a bullet in the gut. The green-haired assassin was sprinting south out of the square. More screams erupted in her wake. Chase snatched up Mitchell's gun. He wanted to find Nina and Kruglov – but Dominika was the more immediately dangerous target. She had to be stopped before she hurt anyone else.

There was another thought in his mind. He had a score to settle with Dominika.

Kruglov reached the north side of the garden, barging people aside. Nina was gaining, the Russian slowed by the awkward case. Another cheer rose from the crowd outside the Empire, cameras flashing as a limo disgorged its celebrity cargo.

Nina saw Kruglov looking for an escape route. The cordon ran the full width of Leicester Square, completely cutting off the northern end, and all the other streets leading away were jammed with people. He glanced back, to see her running after him. His free hand moved inside his coat, emerging with—

'*Gun!*' Nina screamed, hoping the police – and the pedestrians in the line of fire – would hear and respond. 'He's got a gun!'

Kruglov fired at her. Nina dived on to the grass behind a bench, bystanders scattering like frightened pigeons.

The crowd outside the cinema was still cheering, oblivious of the events behind it. Kruglov saw police officers closing from both sides and charged into the crush, battering people with the case and his gun as he clawed his way towards the barrier. Nina jumped up and raced after him.

Dominika ran down a road out of the square. Chase followed, a momentary glance at a sign telling him he was on St Martin's Street. He knew he was heading in the general direction of Trafalgar Square, but there was no direct route, Dominika's path blocked by buildings.

Fewer people here. He raised the gun, a silenced Ruger

SR9, and risked a shot at the fleeing woman's legs. It missed, cracking off the road surface just past her. Dominika returned fire over her shoulder. She had almost no chance of hitting him, but the two shots still forced Chase to duck and swerve, slowing him.

She reached a crossroads and went left. Chase pounded round the corner after her, seeing her heading for the glass doors at the rear of the large building to the south.

The National Gallery.

Dominika fired another shot just before she reached the doors, preventing Chase from taking aim as she went through. Not that he would have: he could see people inside, a group of children – she had just entered the gallery's Education Centre. For one terrible moment he thought she was going to take them hostage, but when he reached the doors he saw her haring up a flight of stairs.

He kicked the doors open and pointed his gun after her, but she had already rounded a corner. Some of the children had seen Dominika's gun, and his arrival only made matters worse. 'Everyone get down!' Chase yelled over the high-pitched screams as he ran to the stairs. He looked up. Dominika was aiming at him—

Chase threw himself backwards as three shots echoed through the room, blasting craters in the wall beside him. He landed flat on his back, sending four rapid shots back at Dominika. She dived for cover as the banister splintered, then scrambled to her feet and ran to the top of the stairs.

'Clear the building!' Chase yelled at the gallery staff as they tried to help the terrified children. 'Get everyone out!' He raced up the stairs, gun at the ready. As he reached the top he saw Dominika dart down a corridor to the left.

What the hell was she doing? She seemed to be fleeing at random, in a panic – but Chase couldn't believe Kruglov and his people would have agreed to meet Mitchell in a crowded public place without having an escape plan.

Something was wrong.

He rounded the corner and followed her into the galleries.

Kruglov reached the edge of the cordon, thrashing at the crowd with increasing fury. An enraged man tried to grab him; he smashed the butt of the gun into his face, breaking his jaw. As the man fell back, spitting blood, Kruglov flung himself over the barrier. A nearby security guard saw the commotion and ran to deal with the intruder—

Kruglov shot him. A hole burst open in his chest, showering the crowd with blood. People screamed, the fun turning to fear. All order broke down as they trampled each other in their desperation to get away. Nina threw up her arms to shield her face as she ran into the mob, flailing elbows and feet swiping at her from all directions.

Another gunshot. Through the chaos she saw a yellow-jacketed figure tumble to the ground: a policeman shot in the shoulder.

Nina fought her way forward, and suddenly burst free of the retreating crowd, crashing against the railing. Kruglov was running for the nearest limo, gun raised. Despite the threat cameras were still flashing, paparazzi and public alike capturing the deadly spectacle, a real-life action scene playing out at the premiere of a Hollywood version. The Russian lowered his head in a futile attempt to avoid being photographed as he pointed his gun at the limo driver, screaming at him. The driver didn't need to know any Russian to understand his orders, and scrambled frantically from his vehicle.

Nina jumped over the railing and ran for the limousine. Kruglov kicked the driver away and leapt into the limo, tossing the case and the gun on to the passenger seat. He rammed the car into drive, looking up as he stepped on the accelerator—

He saw Nina running towards him.

The stretch limo surged forward, ripping up a section of the red carpet and smashing a photographer aside with its open door as Kruglov swerved the three-ton vehicle straight at her.

No way to dodge—

Nina dived forward, landing on the limo's long bonnet on her stomach and sliding to hit the windscreen as the car accelerated. It clipped the barrier, scything one of the metal sections into the crowd, before Kruglov regained control.

She grabbed one of the windscreen wipers and looked into the limo, to see Kruglov glaring back at her. He fumbled for his gun as she leapt to her feet—

Bullets blew out chunks of the windscreen beneath Nina as she hurled herself on to the limo's roof. Slithering across the slick surface, she flung out one hand, just catching the chrome trim along one side of the roof before she fell off the other.

Lying flat, she tried to get a grip with her other hand—

Holes exploded between her outstretched arms, flecks of paint spraying into her face as Kruglov fired through the roof. Each new eruption of jagged steel was closer to her head, closer . . .

The firing stopped. The Russian was out of ammo. Nina could smell the smoke from the last hole, barely a hand's width from her face.

The limo picked up speed, charging towards the end of the cordon. A movable barrier had been placed across it to let vehicles exit while keeping pedestrians out.

But nobody was going to move it aside this time, everybody throwing themselves out of the limo's path—

Nina's free hand closed round the other side of the roof just as the vehicle smashed through the barrier and skidded into Charing Cross Road. Traffic had already been stopped by people fleeing into the street, but the limo's front wing still clipped a car as Kruglov swerved hard to the right, turning south towards Trafalgar Square.

Nina swung across the roof, legs dangling over the side as she fought to keep her grip. The limo wallowed, a hubcap flying off and clanging across the pavement. The chrome strip began to tear loose beneath her fingertips . . .

With a squeal from the tyres, the limo lurched and straightened out. Nina was jolted back across the roof. The engine surged, and she felt her hair whipping in the wind as Kruglov accelerated through the streets of London.

Paintings lined the high rooms, but Chase couldn't spare so much as a moment to look at the treasures of the National Gallery as Dominika weaved through the interconnected chambers and corridors ahead of him. Startled visitors jumped out of their path, evening viewings unexpectedly disrupted.

Fire bells burst to clamorous life, the staff in the Education Centre having finally raised the alarm. At least that would get the tourists out of the way. But he still had to deal with Dominika – and whatever she was planning. She was definitely heading for somewhere specific.

She reached another junction, rounding a corner and throwing down a litter bin in his path. Chase hurdled it, barely breaking stride. He didn't want to use the gun if there were any civilians nearby, but all he needed was a clear line of fire . . .

He saw a large banner ahead, and realised where she was going.

The gallery was holding an exhibition of works by Rembrandt. Art was hardly Chase's field, but even he had heard of the Dutch painter, knew his works were worth millions . . . and Dominika was about to run through the exhibition with a gun in her hand.

She wasn't going to hold people to ransom to bargain for her escape. She was going to hold *national treasures* to ransom.

Chase felt a moment of cold triumph. Dominika's plan might have worked with Nina, but he was still a self-declared Philistine despite his fiancée's best efforts. If Mitzi's killer thought threatening to put a bullet hole in some priceless work of art would save her, she was dead wrong.

Emphasis on the *dead*.

The Russian ran through the exhibition gallery's arched entrance, people scattering as they saw her gun. Chase rushed after her. 'Get down!' he yelled.

Dominika stopped near the archway at the far side of the gallery. She snapped up her gun to aim at one of the paintings, a scene of the crucifixion. Chase didn't care. He lined up his own weapon on her—

She fired. But not at the painting.

Instead, she hit its frame. The ornately carved wood splintered, the whole painting shaking.

A siren screamed over the fire bells, alerting everyone in the building that somebody was tampering with one of the most valuable artworks. The piercing screech, intended to disorient would-be thieves, hit Chase hard enough to make him flinch, distracting him for the merest fraction of a second . . .

That was all Dominika needed to escape.

She dived through the archway as a security gate dropped down with the speed of a guillotine blade. The portcullis-like barrier clashed against the floor just behind her.

Chase recovered and fired, but his shot clanged uselessly against the gate. Dominika threw herself into cover. He ran to the exit; the barrier was a heavier-duty version of the kind used to protect shopfronts, horizontal slats linked by chains. He tried to lift it, but it was locked in place. More barriers had already rolled down to block the other exits.

'*Fuck!*' He peered through the gaps between the slats, but Dominika was no longer there.

She'd had an escape plan all along. And he'd fallen for it, ending up trapped while she got away.

He turned, seeing the gallery visitors also locked in the room regarding him with faces of absolute terror. He grinned sheepishly. 'She's . . . a modern artist, you can tell by the hair. Really doesn't like old-fashioned paintings.'

His attempt at levity didn't change any expressions. Sighing, Chase slumped against the archway, hoping Nina was all right.

She was anything but.

'Oh, *shit!*' she screamed as the limo accelerated towards a crawling double-decker bus, swerving at the last moment to squeeze between it and the cars going the other way.

Sparks sprayed up as the limo's left side screeched against the bus. Nina lost her grip, the thin chrome strip snapping in her hand. Kruglov hauled the limo back round the bus. She swung helplessly across the roof, about to slide off into oncoming traffic . . .

Her forefinger hooked into one of the bullet holes.

Gasping as the torn metal cut into her flesh, Nina pulled herself back on to the roof.

Sirens ahead. She saw flashing lights at the edge of Trafalgar Square, a police car followed by a van moving to block the road ahead. The limousine had already passed the only side street, to the left—

Kruglov went *right*, throwing the limo into a skidding turn on to the paved plaza in front of the National Gallery. People dived out of its way, a couple of luckless tourists sent flying with bone-breaking cracks.

Nina clung to the roof, appalled by the carnage but unable to stop it. All she could do was hang on and hope the police intercepted Kruglov at the other side of the square.

The Russian swerved again – and sent the limo hurtling down a broad flight of marble steps into Trafalgar Square itself.

The car was airborne for a moment before crunching down nose first, the chassis buckling. Nina was thrown loose and tumbled on to the bonnet. The engine roared, Kruglov keeping the pedal to the floor. She saw one of the square's fountains rushing at her—

The limo slammed into the fountain's thick basin,

catapulting Nina forward. She landed in the pool, the water only partly cushioning the impact as she hit the bottom and bounced across it in a stinging spray. The far wall arrived all too quickly; she thumped against it shoulder first, head cracking against the stone rim.

Dazed, pained, she lay unmoving, completely soaked by the cold water. The spotlit pillar of Nelson's column loomed above her, a spear jabbing into the dark sky. Someone grabbed her arm and she looked round in fear, thinking it was Kruglov coming to finish her off. But it was just a bystander trying to help.

Kruglov—

Nina struggled upright, legs wobbling as water streamed from her clothes. The limo was crumpled against the other side of the fountain, the driver's door open.

No sign of the Russian. Or the metal case.

He had Excalibur.

'Where'd he go?' she slurred, staggering out of the pool. The man helping her looked bewildered, as if she were speaking in tongues. She pushed him away, groggily searching for Kruglov, and spotted a running figure shoving through the crowd, a flash of aluminium in his hand.

She tried to run after him, but dropped to her knees as her legs refused to co-operate. Pain overcame the brief numbing effect of the cold water, flooding in from all over her body. 'Okay,' she said, plaintively, 'guess I'm not going anywhere.'

Shouting from behind her. She turned to see several policemen running at her.

'Bad guy went that way,' she tried to tell them, pointing after Kruglov – only to be thrown face first to the ground and rapidly handcuffed. One of the policemen shouted something, but the throbbing pain in her head reduced it to an incoherent garble. She was roughly hauled to her feet.

'Oh, jeez, not again,' she muttered as she was carried away.

'Well, this isn't entirely unexpected,' said Peter Alderley, barely able to suppress his laughter. 'You ending up in jail. Again!'

'What the hell are you doing here, Alderley?' Chase growled as the policeman brought him out of his cell. After being arrested, he had been taken first to Agar Street police station a quarter of a mile away, before later in the night being transferred to New Scotland Yard. Having only had a couple of hours' sleep he was already irritable, and Alderley's smugness did nothing to improve his mood. 'I called *Mac*, not some tosser from MI6.'

'There's gratitude for you,' Alderley replied, a smirk visible beneath his drooping moustache. 'I'm here as a favour for Mac. C wanted him for a little chat about why someone he vouched for keeps ending up in the nick.'

'It wouldn't be a problem if the bloody woodentops

ever arrested the right people,' snapped Chase, shooting the policeman an annoyed look. 'For fuck's sake, how hard is it to spot a woman with green hair?'

'Well, you're out now. Personally, I would have left you there, but that would have been unfair to Nina, since you seem to come as a pair.'

'Where is she?' Chase demanded. 'Is she all right?'

'She's fine. A bit bruised, I think, but nothing too bad.'

Alderley led him to a reception area. Chase saw Nina waiting on a bench and hurried to her, doing a double take when he got a proper look.

'Don't even start,' she said, raising a warning finger. Her hair had been left unwashed overnight, and had dried into a crinkled frizz. Her clothes were also stained from the strong chemicals in the fountain.

'I'm just glad you're okay,' Chase said, embracing her. He sniffed her hair. 'Been swimming?'

'I *told* you not to start!'

'Well, this is all very romantic,' said Alderley with a disparaging sigh, 'but you have an appointment at the American embassy. Whatever this absolute balls-up is about, the Yanks want to talk to you about it.'

'Yeah, well, I want to talk to *them*,' said Chase. 'About the fact that the bloke they put in charge of the operation was a fucking traitor!'

'I still can't believe it,' Nina said, shaking her head. 'He was working for Vaskovich the whole time? How did DARPA miss that?'

'He'd just better hope that they find him before I do,'

Chase rumbled, clenching his fists. 'Because I want to have words . . .'

Alderley took them to the embassy, driving through the building's side gate to be met by Peach. 'Well, so long,' said the MI6 agent cheerily. 'If you need SIS to do anything else for you in future, please . . . don't. By the way, have you set a wedding date, Nina? I'm still waiting for my invitation.'

'Goodbye, Peter,' said Nina firmly, climbing out of the car. 'Mr Peach, hi.'

'Good morning, Dr Wilde.' Peach looked more flustered than ever. 'Mr Chase. I'm glad you're both okay.'

'Yeah, us too. What's going on?'

'Please, follow me.'

They headed through the embassy to the office overlooking Grosvenor Square. Nina's heart sank: the first thing she saw after Peach opened the door was a line of newspapers on the table. 'Not again!' For the second time in a week she was front-page news, in one picture jumping on to the limo's hood, in another clinging to the roof as it surged away from the Empire.

Several suited men were waiting for them, Hector Amoros stepping forward to greet her. 'Nina! God, I'm glad you're all right. You too, Eddie.'

'I thought you'd gone back to the States?' said Nina, surprised to see him.

'I did. And then I came right back – I've been called to

appear before a parliamentary committee to answer questions about everything that happened yesterday. Which could take some time. This operation didn't turn out quite as we'd hoped.'

'Understatement of the year,' Nina said – then froze when she saw who was standing amongst the group of men.

Mitchell.

Face bruised, a bandage on his cheek . . . but not a prisoner.

'What the *fuck* is he doing here?' she shouted.

Chase's reaction was more physical. He charged at Mitchell. It took three of the men to hold him back. 'Oi! Twat! I'll fucking kill you!'

'Yeah, I kinda thought you'd react that way,' said Mitchell irritably. 'Hector?'

Amoros cleared his throat. 'Nina, Eddie, there's something you need to know. Eddie, cut that out.' A commanding military tone entered his normally pleasant voice. Chase reluctantly stopped struggling and shrugged himself free of the men. 'Yes, Jack was going to give Excalibur to Vaskovich . . . but DARPA knew all about it.'

'DARPA *approved* it,' Mitchell added. 'Vaskovich thought I was a double agent. I'm not. I'm a *triple* agent – I was working for DARPA the whole time. Who did you think the "reliable source" inside Vaskovich's organisation was? It was *me!*'

'You mean this whole thing was a set-up?' Nina gasped.

'Yes. My mission was to put Vaskovich's weapon out of

commission. I would've taken Excalibur to Russia, used that as proof of my loyalty so he'd take me to his earth energy facility, and *boom*.' He glanced at the newspapers. 'Only now, you two have screwed everything up in about the most public way possible – Vaskovich has Excalibur, and I had to blow my cover to keep you alive!'

Nina's own anger began to rise. 'And why the hell didn't you tell us this in the first place? People have died because of this plan of yours!'

'If you'd known, there was a risk you would have given me away. Not that it made any goddamn difference, as it turned out!'

'So why didn't you just let them find the sword on their own?' Chase demanded. 'Nobody would have got hurt.'

'You sure about that? They killed a priest in Sicily to get the first piece of Caliburn, they killed Bernd Rust, they would probably have killed Staumberg and his butler in Austria as well. These people aren't boy scouts. And I had to be involved, because Kruglov didn't trust me – if I didn't personally give Excalibur to Vaskovich, there's no way he would have taken me to the facility. Which meant I had to involve Nina so I could find it first.' He gave Chase a hard look. 'I'm sorry. But it had to be done – we couldn't let the Russians find Excalibur on their own.'

'If you'd told us what was really going on, I'd never have got Mitzi involved,' Chase said bitterly.

'If Vaskovich thought you were going to give the sword

to him,' asked Nina, 'why the hell were Kruglov and the others after it too?'

'Like I said, Kruglov didn't trust me.'

'So now what?' said Chase. He pointed at the newspapers. 'Kruglov's all over the front pages; it's not like he can deny any of this. Christ, one of the coppers told me he killed some poor bastard in front of about five hundred witnesses.'

'You seriously think the Russians would hand him over?' Mitchell asked. 'The way relations are right now, with this polar territory dispute? He's the right-hand man of one of the most powerful men in the entire country, who also happens to be a personal friend of the Russian president. They'd never give him up, no matter how much diplomatic pressure was put on them.'

'So he just gets away with it?' Chase said in disbelief. 'He murders people, then gets to hide out in Russia laughing at us?'

'He's not even hiding. Mr Callum?' Mitchell turned to one of the other people in the room, the white-haired man whom Nina and Chase had met at the embassy the previous evening, and took a photograph from him. It was taken with a telephoto lens, showing Kruglov in the back seat of an SUV as it entered a gate set into a high wall. The figure beside him was only visible in silhouette, but it appeared to be Dominika.

'This was taken a couple of hours ago,' Mitchell said. 'It's Vaskovich's mansion, southwest of Moscow. We had our intelligence sources in Russia looking for

Kruglov as soon as we realised he'd left England.'

'How the hell did he get out of the country?' Nina asked.

'The guy used to be a spook. He knows all the tricks – and he's got Vaskovich's billions backing him up. If you've got money, border controls don't mean shit.'

'So your spooks knew where he was going, but couldn't bag him before he got there?' said Chase. 'Christ, and I thought MI6 were useless.'

'There wasn't time to arrange a snatch team,' Mitchell said defensively. 'Also, the CIA weren't happy about us running our own intelligence operation behind their backs.'

Chase made a disgusted noise. 'And now Vaskovich's got the sword? He's probably going to his base to blow up the world already!'

'He's not going anywhere,' said Mitchell. 'At least, not until tomorrow.'

'How do you know?' asked Nina.

'He's holding a party tonight, at his mansion. And not the kind he'd be willing to blow off, either,' he continued, forestalling the obvious questions. 'It's been planned for months, it's a way for him to consolidate his influence – all of the new Russian elite are going to be there.'

'You sure about this?' Chase said. Nina looked at him; she could tell he was formulating a plan.

'I was actually invited,' Mitchell told him. 'Although somehow I doubt I'm still on the guest list. But there's no way he'll cancel it, even now he's got Excalibur. In fact, knowing Leonid, he'll probably want to show it off.'

'So you know where he'll be tonight, and you know where the *sword'll* be tonight?'

'Yeah. Why?'

Chase shot him a humourless grin. ''Cause if he's having a party . . . I think we should crash it.'

23

MOSCOW

Although only a few degrees further north than London, the Russian capital was noticeably colder. Even the brief time Nina spent moving between the State Department jet and a waiting Lincoln Navigator left her feeling chilled.

'Should be here in winter,' Chase said as they were driven to the city. 'You think New York's nippy? It's like Bermuda in comparison.'

'You've been here before?'

'Couple of times, yeah. On business.'

'Is that how you met your friend, the one you called from the plane?'

Chase snorted. 'He's not my friend. He's a perverted scum-sucking little parasite who deserves a good kicking.'

'Oh, he's a he?' said Nina, raising an eyebrow in amusement. 'You mean there's actually a country where you *don't* have an attractive young woman on call?' She remembered the moment she spoke that there was indeed now such a country – Switzerland – and was about to apologise for her lack of tact, but a single, somewhat sad look from Chase told her she had been forgiven.

'Actually, I do know someone in Russia,' he said after the unspoken moment had passed, 'but she wouldn't be right for the job. This bloke is, though.'

'So who is this guy?' Mitchell asked. 'Sounds like you don't even trust him.'

'I wouldn't trust him as far as I could throw him, and last time I saw him he was such a fat bastard I'd have a job even lifting him. But as long as there's money at the end of it, he's more or less reliable. So I hope you brought your wad. He's a cash-only sort of bloke.'

'What's he called?' Nina asked. 'And what does he do?'

'His name's Pavel Prikovsky, and trust me, he really is a total *prick*ovsky,' said Chase. 'Used to be an officer in the GRU, Russian military intelligence. Ran into him a couple of times when we were on opposite sides before he went freelance to specialise in "executive protection".'

'Like you did,' said Mitchell.

'Not even fucking close,' Chase replied, offended. 'I looked after people. He *took care of* people, if you get what I mean. But that's how he got started, only he branched out into other stuff when he realised he could make a lot more money from the same clients without risking getting his head blown off. Now he arranges entertainment for rich guys' parties.'

Nina pursed her lips. 'By entertainment, I'm guessing you don't mean funny hats and balloon animals.'

He smiled sardonically. 'Not exactly.'

They drove down the highway, the traffic increasing as they approached central Moscow. Nina had never been to Russia before, and watched the city pass with interest. Most of it looked exactly how she'd imagined: a communist-built metropolis, grey and blocky and joyless, huge concrete apartment buildings dominating the landscape.

But there were surprises amongst the uniformity: churches with ornate spires and traditional onion-shaped domes of gold and oxidised green copper; giant Soviet bureaucratic monoliths designed to cow onlookers into insignificance beside the power of the state; and their modern equivalents, gleaming corporate skyscrapers and towering apartment complexes for the new Russian millionaires and billionaires. Moscow had leapt from relative poverty to become one of the world's most expensive cities within just a few years, yet it was clear that the vast majority of that wealth was concentrated in the hands of an elite few. Nina imagined Lenin would be spinning in his tomb so furiously that a generator connected to him could power half the capital.

They reached the heart of the city, the high walls of the Kremlin sweeping past before they crossed a bridge over the Moskva river and headed south. To her disappointment, she was only able to catch a glimpse of the colourful cupolas of St Basil's cathedral in the distance before it was lost to sight.

But she wasn't here for sightseeing. They continued south, eventually stopping outside a warehouse, its small yard surrounded by high fences topped with razor wire. Security cameras stared down conspicuously, covering every angle of approach.

'This is it,' said Chase. 'Wait here.'

He got out and went to the gate, looking up into the blank eyes of the cameras. Prikovsky was expecting him, but would undoubtedly make him wait, a crude attempt to show who was in charge. An intercom was mounted on a steel post beside the entrance; he pushed the button. Eventually, a woman answered in Russian.

'It's Eddie Chase,' he said impatiently. 'I know you're there, Pavel, so stop pissing about and let me in.'

Another pause, then a buzzer sounded. Chase pushed open the gate and waved the SUV inside, then headed for the warehouse door.

The driver remained in the Navigator, but Nina and Mitchell, the latter carrying a large briefcase, hurried across to Chase as he banged a fist on the door. It opened, a neckless man with a perpetual frown opening it. To Nina's alarm he was holding a small machine pistol. 'All right, put it away,' Chase told him, unimpressed. 'Just take us to the gaffer.'

The man sneered, then stepped back to let them in.

Nina took in the contents of the warehouse as he led them through it. Rank upon rank of boxes and crates displaying high-end Western brand names: big-screen TVs, computers, designer clothing, whisky, cigars, watches ... an emporium of riches.

'And I bet he doesn't have a receipt for a single one of them,' Chase said disapprovingly as they reached an office at one side of the packed space.

Waiting for them was Pavel Prikovsky, flanked by a pair of stunningly beautiful blonde women in short, tight dresses less than suited to the chilly environs. Slightly shorter than Chase, he was considerably broader, most of it round his waist. His figure wasn't flattered by the bulky fur coat draped over his shoulders. A fat Cuban cigar was jammed between his grinning lips, and the amount of gold jewellery he sported couldn't help but make Nina think of Mr T.

'Eddie Chase!' he boomed. 'Come here, let me kiss you!'

'Let's just make do with a handshake, eh?' Chase replied. Prikovsky cackled, then stuck out a hand so hairy it blended with the coat's cuff. Chase shook it with rather less enthusiasm than the Russian was showing.

'So, can I get you anything?' Prikovsky said. 'Cigar? Cognac?' He leered at one of the women. 'Companion-ship?'

Chase put an arm round Nina's shoulders. 'No thanks. I'm sorted.'

'No, you never did have any trouble with the women,

hmm? No money, that face – how do you do it?' He cackled again. 'And a celebrity, too! Dr Nina Wilde, I believe? Welcome to Moscow! I've heard all about your discoveries, Atlantis and Hercules. But you made a mistake.'

'Oh yeah?' said Nina suspiciously. Despite the Russian's seeming friendliness, everything about him made her want to cringe away.

'Yes, you went and told the US government rather than keeping the secret for yourself. Just think how much money you could have made from selling all that treasure!'

'It wasn't about money,' she said icily.

'*Everything* is about money, in the end.' He took out the cigar and jabbed it at Mitchell's briefcase. 'Like how much your friend here is willing to pay me to help you. So, what are you? CIA? DIA?'

'DARPA, actually,' Mitchell told him.

Prikovsky's face twisted into a gargoyle-like expression of disbelief. 'Really? I would have put money on you being in intelligence. I can usually spot my own kind.'

'Your kind live under slimy rocks, Pavel,' said Chase. Prikovsky didn't seem offended; if anything, he appeared amused. 'You want to do business, or what?'

'Oh, I always want to do business.' He clicked his fingers and said a single word in Russian, at which the two blondes turned on their high heels and left the room, closing the door behind them. 'You said you wanted to talk about Leonid Vaskovich.'

'That's right. He's having a party tonight, at his mansion. I want to be there.'

'And you think *I* can get you an audience with one of Russia's richest men?' Prikovsky asked in exaggerated surprise. Chase just stared at him. 'Ha, of course I can!' he boasted after a moment. 'My girls, they will be there tonight, and plenty of others too. When anyone in Moscow wants to party – anyone who matters, anyway – they come to me. Pavel Prikovsky always has whatever they need! I can get you an invitation, no problem.'

'I don't mean as a guest,' Chase said. 'I want to get in without anyone knowing about it.'

Prikovsky instantly became wary. 'Okay, now *that* is not so easy.'

'I know the layout of the building and the security system,' said Mitchell. 'I've been there. All we need is for someone to shut down the cameras long enough for Eddie to cross the grounds. Thirty seconds, tops.'

'My girls are not spies,' Prikovsky protested.

'I can tell them what to do through an earpiece—'

'No, no! Do you have any idea what would happen to them if they were caught? Vaskovich is a hard enough man, but his lieutenant, Kruglov, is a psychopath! He would kill them!'

'Yeah, we've met Kruglov,' said Chase. 'And I wouldn't mind meeting him again. One on one.'

'Then go to the front gate and ask for him! But I won't

put my girls at risk. It's too dangerous – and not just for them. Do you know what would happen to *me* if they found out I had helped you?'

Chase gave him a cold smile. 'Nothing you don't deserve.'

This time, Prikovsky was not amused. 'I agreed to see you out of, shall we say, professional courtesy, Chase. But this is not something I will help you with, however much money your friend has.'

'Then send me,' said Nina.

Chase wasn't sure he'd heard her correctly. 'What?'

'I'll go,' she said, Mitchell and Prikovsky regarding her with surprise. 'This whole thing's my fault – if I hadn't been suspicious of Jack in London, we wouldn't even be here.'

'No,' said Chase firmly. 'No fucking way.'

'Eddie, I don't want to do it, but it's the only way to get you inside. Unless Jack knows another way to shut down the security system?' Mitchell shook his head. 'I could go in with Pavel's other . . . girls, pretend to be one of them. Once I'm inside, Jack can guide me to where I need to go, and then I'll just hide until he's ready to pick us up in the chopper.'

'You are using a *helicopter*?' Prikovsky exclaimed. 'Expensive, dangerous, a high risk of disaster – I can tell this is an American operation!'

Chase ignored him. 'Are you out of your fucking mind? I'm not gonna let you do it.'

'We don't have any choice,' Nina insisted. 'If there isn't

somebody on the inside, you won't be able to get in without being seen – and you'll be killed.'

'Better me than you.'

'No. No, Eddie, it's not. You don't want to see me get hurt? Well, I don't want to see *you* get hurt.' She took his hands in hers, looking into his eyes. 'Eddie, we're getting married, we're going to be doing *everything* together – which means we share the risks. Either we both do this, or neither of us do. And if we don't do it, Vaskovich wins, and all the people who've died trying to stop him will have died for nothing. I know you won't let that happen. Well, I won't either.'

She could tell he was angry – but also that he was considering her words. Mitchell seemed about to add something, but she gave him an almost imperceptible shake of the head. This was a decision only Chase could make.

Finally, he looked at Prikovsky. 'If we did this – *if* we did it – could you get her in?'

'Yes, I can get her in,' said the Russian. 'It is getting her out that will be hard!'

'What about you, Jack? Can you get her to where she needs to go?' Mitchell nodded. 'And then get her out again?'

This time, his head remained still. 'I can't give you any guarantees, Eddie. But Nina's right – it's the only way to get –' he glanced at Prikovsky ' – the item back before Vaskovich takes it to his facility.'

'And there's no way we could get it back from there?'

'No. It's an old submarine base – but it's still in a closed military zone, and Vaskovich has very good connections with the Russian military. The only option would be to send in a SEAL team by submarine, and if they got caught, the state relations are between the US and Russia at the moment . . .'

'Shit,' muttered Chase. He looked at Nina. 'I don't want you to do this.'

'I don't either, but I'm going to have to. Because there's nobody else who can.'

'Then I'm going to have to let you, aren't I?' He let out a long, unhappy sigh. 'Buggeration and fuckery.'

'I know,' said Nina, squeezing his hands.

'If she is caught, I will tell Vaskovich that I knew nothing of this,' Prikovsky said quickly. 'Or that you held me at gunpoint and threatened to kill me. He would believe that, I'm sure. And by the way,' he added to Mitchell, 'I would like my money up front. All of it.'

'How much do you want?' Mitchell asked.

'I just told you – all of it! Everything you have brought – in your case and in your truck. In fact, I will have the truck as well! Tell your driver to take a taxi.'

Mitchell appeared surprisingly unconcerned about Prikovsky's demands, placing the briefcase on his desk and opening it to reveal crisp wads of hundred-dollar bills. The quick glance Nina got before Prikovsky turned the case round to riffle through its contents suggested there was probably the better part of half a million dollars within.

Half a million dollars – of American taxpayers' money. Being given to a man who seemed little more than a glorified pimp. Then there were all the other resources the mission had so far consumed . . . and the lives it had taken. 'It better be worth it,' she said quietly, only Chase hearing her.

Prikovsky snapped the case closed, his smile suggesting he was more than satisfied with its contents. 'Well, then. We still have a few hours before the girls go to the party, so there is time to get you ready, Dr Wilde.'

'Get me ready?' she echoed.

'You do not seriously think you would be able to get in looking like that, do you?' He looked disdainfully at her heavy coat, jeans and Reeboks. 'My girls all look amazing, like models – like *supermodels*! You will have to look the same.'

'Oh,' Nina said. 'Y'know, that might be a problem. I'm not really the supermodel type.'

Prikovsky grinned – or leered, though it was hard to tell with the cigar clenched between his teeth. 'No need to worry. Some makeup, the right clothes . . . Mario is incredible.'

'Mario?' hooted Chase. 'There's a proper Russian name.'

'He styles all my girls,' Prikovsky told him as he put the briefcase into a safe. 'We'll go and see him now.' He grinned again. 'In my shiny new truck!'

'Shut up,' said Nina, before Chase even had a chance to open his mouth.

It opened anyway – mostly in amazement. 'Bloody hell,' he finally managed to say. 'You look . . . whoa. Pavel was right – Mario really *is* incredible!'

Nina had spent the better part of two hours in an opulent salon, her hair being washed and styled, makeup applied to her face. She was not the only woman there – over a dozen others were also lined up before the huge illuminated mirrors, being worked upon and fussed over by two women apiece. Mario – who despite his name was about as Italian as Joseph Stalin – scurried back and forth along the line, brushing and plucking and tweezing and glossing, fixing every last detail of each makeover.

And though the overall look was a long way removed from anything Nina would have chosen herself, she was forced to admit it was indeed one hell of a makeover. She had spent a good portion of the time in a reclined position; when she finally sat upright, she experienced a bizarre moment of disassociation, as though someone else was looking back at her from the mirror. Someone who happened to be a model . . . though she wasn't prepared to go as far as supermodel. Mario wasn't *that* good.

It wasn't the heavy, smoky-eyed makeup or scarlet false nails or ultra-moussed hairstyle that aroused her ire, though. It was the outfit Prikovsky had provided for her – which, as she'd expected, provoked a wide-eyed response when she was presented to Chase and the other men.

'I look like a goddamn *hooker*,' she moaned. The sleeveless black rubber minidress was, she'd been assured, the product of some extremely expensive and exclusive designer in London – but that didn't alter the fact that it was also extremely tight and revealing. She had the horrible feeling that if she moved her knees more than a fraction of an inch apart, the entire skirt would twang up over her hips like an overstretched elastic band.

'You're *supposed* to be a hooker,' Chase pointed out.

'Hey!' said Prikovsky. 'My girls are not hookers. They are . . .' He thought about it. 'Escorts? No, courtesans. The courtesans of Pavel Prikovsky, that sounds better. Like the title of a great Russian novel.'

'Or that crappy American novel, *The Immodesty of Nina Wilde*,' Nina grumbled. 'Maybe this wasn't such a good idea.'

'No, no,' said Chase, smirking, 'I'm all for it now. You *are* going to dress like that after we're married, right?'

'That's it, I'm outta here.' Nina turned and tried to teeter back into the salon on her high heels, but found her way blocked by Mario, who clapped approvingly and ushered her into the lounge once more. He reached up, trying to remove her pendant, but she forcefully shook her head. He tutted, then spoke in Russian to Prikovsky, who laughed. Mario then bowed and returned to the salon.

'What did he say?' Nina demanded.

'He thinks your necklace looks cheap,' said Prikovsky.

Nina shot an offended look after the stylist. 'But he is very pleased with how you turned out, considering how little time he had to work with you. Oh, and also considering your age.'

'My *age*?' she shrieked. 'I'm only thirty!'

Prikovsky shrugged. 'Most of my girls are only twenty-two, twenty-three! You should be proud. You look . . . unrecognisable.'

'And that's a good thing?'

'In this case, yeah,' said Mitchell, who had been watching with quiet amusement. 'Honestly, if I didn't know you, I wouldn't have recognised you when you stepped out of there. So hopefully no one else will either.' He stood, taking a box from a pocket. 'Okay, time to mike you up.'

'What's that?' Nina asked, eyeing the object in the box. It looked like a small golden bullet.

'Earpiece. You ever watch that show, *24*? Just like Jack Bauer uses. It's two-way – you'll be able to hear me and Eddie, and we'll be able to hear you and what's going on around you. All you have to do is whisper.'

Chase stood for a closer look as Mitchell carefully slipped the bug into Nina's left ear. 'What's the range?'

'Only about two hundred metres. But that doesn't matter because you'll have the relay so I can hear, and once you get to the outer wall you'll be in range.' The device in place, he stepped back, quickly running an admiring eye over Nina's glossy curves.

'I saw that!' she snapped.

'Get used to it,' Prikovsky told her. 'You will get a lot more attention than that tonight.' He frowned as a thought struck him. 'Do you speak Russian?'

'*Nyet.*'

'Hmm. Still, not a problem. The girls are not there for conversation.' Nina could barely suppress a disgusted shudder. 'Okay, you're an American student here to learn Russian – and you're doing this because you need money to buy a dictionary. Ha!' He drew back a hand as if about to slap her on the butt, but stopped short on seeing Chase's stony glare.

'All right,' said Mitchell, adopting a commanding tone. 'I'll be waiting in the helo. It'll take me four minutes to reach the mansion from my takeoff point, so once you secure the item, that's how long you'll have to get to the extraction point. There's a balcony on the west side – it's not big enough to land on, but there's enough clearance for me to hover next to it so you can climb aboard. If you don't raise the alarm, we should be able to get clear before anyone realises what's going on.'

'And if we do raise the alarm?' asked Nina.

Chase reached into his leather jacket and drew out a massive silver handgun. 'Jack had a little present delivered while you were getting your cuticles done,' he said with definite glee. 'Desert Eagle, .50-cal Action Express. Would have preferred a Wildey, but I'm not complaining.'

Mitchell shook his head. 'Big, heavy, limited load, huge recoil . . .'

'Works for me. Anyone gets hit by this, they're done.' His smile disappeared. 'And if I see Kruglov . . .'

'Let's hope you don't need it,' Nina told him, gently pushing the raised weapon back down.

'Okay,' said Mitchell. 'Let's party.'

24

The girls left the salon in a small convoy of minivans driven by Prikovsky's men. Nina was in the last vehicle with three other young women, as carefully made-up and provocatively dressed as she was; none spoke English, but all seemed excited – in a somewhat calculating way – about the evening.

Excited wasn't the word Nina would have used to describe her feelings, however. *Tense* would have been closer. Or *nauseous*.

A voice in her left ear. Chase.

'Nina, if you can hear me, clear your throat.' She did. 'Okay, I'm not far behind you.' She glanced back, seeing headlights in the distance. 'I'll call you again soon as I get to the entry point.'

The lights dropped away. There was a faint crackle as if he had opened the line to speak again, but then it faded to nothing. Out of range.

She was on her own.

The minivan came to a stop at a gate with a high wall to

each side – the same wall she had seen in the background of the spy photo of Kruglov.

Vaskovich's mansion. The dragon's lair.

Security guards opened the doors and shone bright flashlights into the faces of each of the van's occupants in turn. Nina was the last to be checked. A chill swept over her, not solely from the night air. What if they recognised her, if she wasn't on the guest list, if Prikovsky had betrayed her . . .

The light swept down to her legs, paused for a moment – and flicked off. The guard leered, then shut the door. The minivan drove on.

Vaskovich's mansion lay directly ahead, at the end of a long drive surrounded by lawns. Nina leaned forward for a better look, impressed despite herself by the brightly lit edifice. It was as huge as she had imagined, but elegant where she had expected nouveau-riche vulgarity, a perfectly restored neo-classical building of the early nineteenth century, tall arched windows blazing with light.

The vehicles lined up outside more closely matched her preconceptions, however. Expensive, showy and mostly vulgar, a procession of stretch limousines and supercars. Valets drove them round the corner of the mansion after the occupants emerged. Nina imagined that a scratch on any of the vehicles would cost the careless perpetrator more than a docked pay packet.

The vans pulled up. More security guards in heavy coats lined the front steps, watching them. The girls got out, to be met by a man in a white tuxedo. He quickly spoke to each in turn before pointing to the doors above, reaching Nina last.

'Uh, I . . . I don't speak very good Russian,' she said in response to his instructions.

He frowned. 'You don't speak Russian? Oy! Pavel is getting lazy; I should send you home. What are you, American?' Nina nodded. He chewed his lip for a moment. 'Well, there are some Yankees in there. Easy to find – they're the ones who can't hold their drink. Stay with them. What's your name?'

'Nina.'

'Nina, okay. I'm Dmitri; if you need a private room, find me. The top floor is off-limits. Okay, shoo, shoo!'

Even with a coat over her outfit Nina was still freezing, and she was about to hurry gratefully inside when a blast of noise halted her mid-step. She looked up to see a helicopter sweeping over the mansion, swinging round to land on the lawn. But it was no ordinary helicopter; clearly military, black as the night sky and with two sets of rotor blades mounted one above the other on a single shaft, it was one of the most bizarre – and menacing – machines she had ever seen.

'What's *that*?' she asked.

Dmitri looked annoyed. '*That* is the new Deputy Defence Minister Felix Mishkin, showing off and ruining the grass! Go in, go, I will greet him.' He turned to watch the helicopter power down.

Nina clacked up the stairs on her heels, entering to have

her coat taken by another man in a white tux. A few groups of people were talking in the marble lobby, all men – and all taking the time out from their conversations to watch her strut past in her tight, shiny dress. Feeling horribly self-conscious as well as scared, she nevertheless remembered her role and smiled politely at them before going through the double doors into the next room.

Whether it was a ballroom or just a very large hall she didn't know, but it was clearly the hub of Vaskovich's party. A DJ on a platform in one corner pumped out thudding techno, but even this was overpowered by the hubbub of hundreds of voices all talking at once.

The air was thick with smoke, and everybody seemed to have a glass in their hand. The men were in tuxedos or more playboy-esque designer suits; the older women were formally dressed, the younger women showy trophy attachments to wealthy husbands . . . or 'entertainment', Prikovsky's girls having already spread out amongst the crowd.

Nina had barely taken five steps before a red-faced man in a straining tuxedo budded off from his group and blocked her path, treating her to a glassy-eyed smile as he spoke in slurred Russian. 'Hi,' she replied, her own smile fixed and fake as a pungent reek of aftershave assaulted her nostrils. 'I'm sorry, I don't speak much Russian. Er . . . *nyet Russki*? American.'

'Ah, American!' the fat man boomed. 'Pamela Anderson, *da*?' He cupped his hands in front of his chest as if holding a pair of beachballs, and laughed.

'Yeah,' said Nina, less than impressed. 'By the way, congratulations on *your* breasts – they're nearly as big as hers. Excuse me. Oh!' She flinched as a hand slid over her right buttock and squeezed it. She turned, expecting to see another drunken man, and was taken aback to find instead a drunken woman.

'So, you are American?' the woman said. She appeared to be in her late fifties, hard-faced and thin, but from her hairstyle and clothing apparently still thought she could pass herself off as two or three decades younger. 'How are you finding our country?'

'Just went through Poland and, ha, there it was!'

The woman let out a high-pitched, tinkling laugh. Her bony hand encircled Nina's wrist like a handcuff, and she pulled her into the crowd. 'Come, come, you must meet my friends.'

'I'm, er, supposed to go and see Mr Vaskovich,' Nina said desperately.

The woman laughed again. 'Then you are in luck – he is one of my friends!'

'Oh, he is? Oh. *Shit*,' she added in a whisper.

The woman led her through the room. Nina looked round, trying to get a feel for the mansion's layout. She spotted a staircase at the rear of the hall, polished marble and red carpet. Dmitri had said the top floor was out of bounds; that was presumably where Excalibur was being kept.

She heard a buzz in her left ear. '—an you hear me?

Nina?' Chase's voice was distorted by interference, at the very limit of the earpiece's range.

'Mm-hmm?' she said through closed lips, as loudly as she dared.

'I guess you can't talk, then. But I'm in position. Was that a chopper landing in the garden?'

'Mm-hmm.'

'Some rich bugger's always got to show off, don't they? All right, soon as you get a chance, find somewhere quiet so Jack can tell you what to do next.'

'O-ay,' she mumbled.

The woman glanced back at her. 'What?'

'Just, ah, clearing my throat. I'm a little thirsty.'

'I'll tell a waiter to bring you a drink. Come on, just over here.' She guided Nina around a knot of people—

And Nina found herself looking straight at Aleksey Kruglov.

He walked towards her, grimly purposeful. Three steps away, two, eyes flicking at her . . .

And gone. He passed so close that his sleeve brushed Nina's arm. But he hadn't recognised her, hadn't made the connection between the briefly glimpsed, seductively dressed escort and the dirty, scared archaeologist he'd seen in England. But she couldn't help glancing nervously back in case some suspicious synapse fired in his mind, finding common features of the two redheads and making him return for a closer look . . .

He kept going, disappearing into the throng. She gasped in relief.

The woman stopped, Nina almost bumping into her. She spoke in Russian to a slender, unassuming man in rectangular wire-framed glasses – who Nina realised with a chill was Leonid Vaskovich.

The man behind the entire plot. The man responsible for the murders of Bernd Rust, Mitzi Fontana, Chloe Lamb, and others whose names she didn't even know, collateral damage of his quest to gain the power of Excalibur. He was within arm's reach, unsuspecting, defenceless.

But there was nothing she could do. Her skin-tight latex dress had no room to conceal a weapon, even had she been able to pull the trigger. Chase could have – but he wasn't here. All she could do was paste on a smile to cover her fear.

Vaskovich responded to her companion with polite feigned interest, nodding before looking at Nina. He took in her sultry makeup, her fetishistic outfit, her bare legs and high heels – then turned back to the woman, uninterested.

Nina felt oddly offended, before realising that Vaskovich wasn't dismissing her specifically; he would have responded the same way to any of Prikovsky's girls. It was a seen-it-all-before look, the boredom of a billionaire who had long since indulged all his wildest fantasies. Despite being the host of the party, he seemed unenthusiastic about being there.

He spoke to the woman; she replied, then smiled at Nina. 'You said you wanted to meet Leonid Vaskovich? Here he is!'

'Vaskovich?' Chase said through the earpiece. 'Jesus, he's right there? Can you stab him with anything?'

Vaskovich regarded Nina again. 'Rozalina says you do not speak much Russian,' he said. His English, in contrast, was excellent. 'That is a shame. I hope you learn quickly . . .' He looked at her questioningly, waiting for her name.

'Don't tell him your real—' Chase began.

'Nina,' she replied automatically.

'D'oh!'

'Good to meet you . . . Nina,' Vaskovich said. He gave her a slightly puzzled look, as if struggling to remember a previous encounter.

'Likewise, Mr Vaskovich.' There was an awkward pause.

To Nina's surprise, Vaskovich then smiled, a flicker of genuine amusement twitching up one corner of his goatee beard. 'Well, I can tell you are not like most of the other young women I meet.'

'Really?' Nina asked, unsure where he was leading.

'Yes. By now they would be trying to get into my bed – or my wallet. But there is something different about you, I can tell. You are not a shark. It is a nice change.' For a brief moment, he seemed almost melancholy. 'Beautiful women always want me, but only for what I have, never who I am. And that long ago stopped being fun.' He sighed, then shrugged. 'Still. I hope you enjoy the evening.' He said something else to Rozalina before spotting somebody behind Nina. For the first time, his face actually revealed some enthusiasm. 'Ah, Felix Mishkin!'

Nina looked round – only to hurriedly turn away again as she saw Kruglov returning. With him was a man in his mid-thirties, hair slicked back, clad in a dark blue Italian suit. She remembered the name – he was the man who had arrived in the military helicopter.

Apparently Rozalina knew him too, as she kissed him on both cheeks. Nina was left to stand there, feeling exposed and isolated. But just as it struck her this could be her chance to slip away, she realised she was a topic of conversation, 'American' leaping out from Vaskovich's words.

'American?' said Mishkin. He looked at Nina, then said in a heavily accented mock whisper, 'Perhaps she is a spy, here to sleep with me to learn all my secrets!' He laughed at his own joke, Rozalina joining in.

Vaskovich managed a polite chuckle. 'Somehow, I don't think that is why she is here.' He continued in Russian, now almost excited about his subject.

'Nina,' Mitchell unexpectedly said via the earpiece, his voice even more distorted than Chase's. 'He's talking about his new "acquisition". He's got to mean Excalibur. I think he's going to show it to him, which means the sword is definitely in the building. Ditch the bitch and find somewhere we can talk – you've got to reach the security system so Eddie can get in.'

''Kay,' Nina said, disguising the word as a cough. Keeping her face averted from Kruglov, she spotted a waiter bearing a tray of champagne glasses through the crowd. 'Would you like me to get you a drink?' she asked Rozalina. The older woman seemed caught between staying with her catch and keeping in with her powerful companions, finally deciding on the latter. With relief, Nina moved away, heading for the waiter until she was out of sight and then making a beeline for the relatively empty area to one side of the stairs.

'How're you holding up?' Chase asked.

'I'm surviving,' she whispered. 'Although I nearly had a heart attack when I saw Kruglov. Oh, and I have a handprint on my ass.'

'Whose? If it's Vaskovich's, I'm going to have to revive the bastard after I kill him so I can kill him again.'

'No, it was that woman.'

'Really?' Chase sounded intrigued. 'A threesome, huh?'

Nina found herself smiling despite the situation. 'I don't think she's your type, Eddie. She definitely wasn't mine.'

'Can we stay on mission here?' Mitchell said impatiently. 'Nina, where are you now?'

'By the stairs in the main hall.' Looking up, she saw guards standing at the bottom of the next flight. She explained what Dmitri had said about the off-limits parts of the mansion. 'Crap, Vaskovich is coming.'

She crouched, pretending to tighten the strap on one shoe. Vaskovich, Kruglov and Mishkin ascended, the guards moving aside to let them through.

'If they're going to the top floor,' Mitchell said when Nina told him, 'I've got a fairly good idea where he's keeping Excalibur. Okay, Nina, you need to get to the back of the house. Are there any doors out of the hall that aren't guarded?'

She checked. 'In the middle of the west wall. Double doors.'

'They'll do. Go through them.'

Nina picked her way through the hall, trying not to attract any attention – which her outfit made a futile task. She didn't need to know any Russian to tell she was drawing lecherous comments. But she was almost at the door . . .

A hand suddenly clapped against her butt and squeezed it, sweaty flesh squeaking over latex. Nina choked back an obscenity-laden tirade and turned to see the fat man she had encountered earlier, two champagne glasses clutched clumsily in his free hand and an expectant grin on his florid face.

'Oh, hi,' she said through gritted teeth. 'You again.'

'Hello, Pamela!' he said drunkenly, before dropping back into Russian as his groping hand slowly clambered round from her backside towards her chest. He tried to push one of the glasses into her hand.

She reluctantly accepted it, realising that if he tipped it any further the contents would end up in her cleavage. 'Thank you. Hey! Easy, tiger,' she added, batting his wandering hand back down.

'What's going on?' Chase asked, in a voice that suggested punches would have been thrown by now had he been there in person.

'Nothing, just a very, very friendly man . . .' It occurred to her that she might be able to make use of the inebriated oaf. She clinked her glass against his, then indicated the doors. 'Do you want to go somewhere private?' He stared blearily at her. 'Private? God damn it. *Shhh*,' she said, putting a theatrical finger to her lips and glancing at the doors again. The message finally sank in, and he gave her a pop-eyed smirk, hooking a pudgy arm round hers and leading her into the next room.

The main hall had been standing room only; this was a lounge, guests chilling out on modern leather armchairs around glass tables. Nina saw the remains of a white line of cocaine on one. If anything, the sickly swirl of cigar smoke was even thicker. Trying not to cough, she peered through the haze, seeing a door at the rear of the room. A waiter bearing a tray of empty glasses hurried through. She nudged her companion towards it.

A brightly lit hallway was beyond – as was another tuxedoed guard, who with an expression of forced politeness moved to block their path. The fat man huffed and began what was almost certainly an outburst along the lines of 'Don't you know who I am?'

Nina shushed him. 'Dmitri said okay,' she told the guard, hoping he would understand two out of the three words. 'We get champagne?' She mimed holding a bottle and then flicking off the cork. 'Pop!' The guard regarded her dubiously. 'Dmitri said okay,' she repeated.

The guard finally stepped aside, saying something to the drunken man, who responded with a dismissive, '*Da, da.*' Apparently only the top floor was strictly off-limits. Nina saw another waiter coming back with a full tray. She tugged at the fat man's arm, leading him in that direction.

The scent of food replaced smoke. They were now in the mansion's kitchen and service areas, opulence toned down to mere elegance. A side room turned out to be for cold storage, walls lined with glass-fronted refrigerators filled with hundreds of bottles of champagne, more crates of vintage Dom Perignon and Krug waiting to be chilled. There was another door at the back of the room; it was ajar, darkness beyond.

Nina slipped free of the man and entered the storeroom, taking a bottle from one of the fridges and sliding a suggestive hand up and down its neck. The man chortled, downing the contents of his glass in one swig. She indicated the darkened room. He waddled to the door and shoved it open. Nina followed him inside—

There was a flat *dunk* as the champagne bottle came down on the back of his head. The Russian pitched forward and collapsed on some cardboard boxes. Nina hurriedly checked his pulse, finding it steady, then put the bottle down next to him. 'The pleasure was all yours,' she told him as she left. 'Okay, Jack, I'm alone. Finally. Where do I go?'

His voice crackled in her ear. 'Find the kitchen entrance, but don't go in – go past it. There'll be a door on your left when you reach a right turn.'

'Got it.' She strode through the hallways, waiters checking her out as they passed but doing nothing to stop her. Swinging double doors and the sizzle of cooking meat marked the kitchen entrance; she continued onwards until she reached the promised right turn. 'Okay, I'm at the door.'

'Go inside.' She did, finding herself in a small and chilly room with a heavy wooden exterior door opposite. A metal cabinet on one wall hummed ominously. 'There should be a junction box.'

'Got it. Won't it be locked, though?'

'Why?' Chase asked. 'It's the guy's own house.'

She tried the handle, and the cabinet indeed opened without any trouble. 'Huh. Okay, I see loads of complicated electrical stuff.'

'You need to find the switch that controls the security cameras,' said Mitchell. 'Don't worry about the labels being in Cyrillic, just look for one with the number 201. Don't push it yet.'

'How do you know all this stuff?' Nina asked as she scanned the ranks of switches and fuses.

'The company that installed the system emailed the plans to a subcontractor. We snagged them on the way. DARPA *created* the Internet, remember.'

'I'd better be more careful about what sites I look at while Nina's out, then,' said Chase. Nina wasn't entirely sure he was joking, but forgot about it when she found the right switch.

'Two-zero-one, got it,' she said. 'Now what?'

'Okay, here's what'll happen,' Mitchell told her. 'Pushing that switch will cut off power to part of the security grid. But the system's not stupid – if there's a fault, it runs a diagnostic and tries to reboot the affected sections. If they're not back up after thirty seconds, it goes into alert mode. So Eddie has twenty-nine seconds to get over the wall, cross the grounds and get inside the mansion – without being seen by any of the guards – before you push the switch back.'

'Two hundred metres in twenty-nine seconds?' said Chase. 'Piece of piss.'

Nina wasn't so certain. 'Eddie, are you sure you can do it?'

'I've got to, don't I?' he replied, more serious. 'I'm not leaving you alone in there.'

'Do you know the routes of the guards in the grounds?' Mitchell asked.

'What do you think I've been doing for the past ten minutes? I'm not watching films on my iPod here. I'm freezing my bollocks off in a tree!'

'Well, get ready to warm them up. Eddie, soon as you're clear to go, count down from three. Nina, when he reaches zero, throw the switch. I'll count down the seconds. Up to you, Eddie.'

Nina nervously raised her finger to the switch as Chase spoke. 'I can see the door, and the nearest guy's about to go round the corner.' She heard a rustling noise as he changed position. 'Okay, get ready. Three, two, one . . . go!'

She pushed the switch.

★

Chase sprang from the branch. The wall was topped by razor wire; his leading foot landed not on the brickwork but one of the metal supports for the bladed coils. It bent under his weight, the wires hissing metallically, but by then he had already jumped, flying through the air with his legs kicking.

He hit the ground—

And stumbled.

The earth was uneven, impossible to see in the low light. Momentum carried him forward, about to pitch him on to his face . . .

He threw out his hands. His fingertips hit cold ground, pain crackling through every joint as they took his weight for an instant. Then he launched himself forward like a sprinter at the starting line, still staggering but no longer falling. Two strides, and he regained his balance. How much time had he lost?

'Twenty-four. Twenty-three . . .'

Mitchell's voice in his headset pushed him onwards like an explosion. Over a hundred and eighty metres to go, no margin for error.

He was sprinting now, arms pumping like pistons. Nina had opened the back door for him, a dim rectangle of light. The lawn rolled past beneath his feet. Look to the right. No guard. Left—

Shit!

A figure at the corner of the building. Looking away from him – but for how long?

'Fifteen. Fourteen . . .'

Not even halfway. A hundred metres in twelve seconds. Could he do it?

In theory, yes, but this wasn't a running track—

The guard was still facing the front lawn. Despite the cold, Chase now felt heat racing through his entire body, exertion and adrenalin and fear.

'Seven . . .'

Fifty metres, forty, the ground just a blur. He pushed harder, *harder*, lungs burning.

'Three . . .'

Left. The guard was turning, about to walk down the side of the mansion.

Towards him—

'One—'

No time to slow. Instead Chase dived through the door, landing hard on the tiled floor at the instant Nina closed the switch. He skidded across the room and slammed against the far wall.

'Zero,' said Mitchell. 'Did you make it? Eddie, Nina – answer me, dammit!'

'He's here, he's here!' Nina gasped. 'Eddie, are you okay?'

'Shut the door,' he panted, weakly waving a hand. Nina closed it. 'Bloody hell, I must be getting out of shape. Two hundred metres never used to take me that long.'

'Did anyone see you?' she asked, dropping to her knees to help him sit up. His heart was racing; she could feel it pounding even through his layers of clothing.

'Give it five seconds, we'll know.' He took out his

Desert Eagle, hand shaking as he pointed it at the door.

Five seconds passed. Ten. Nothing happened.

He let out a long, relieved breath. 'Guess we're okay. Jesus.' He pushed himself to his feet, Nina assisting.

She kissed him. 'God, I'm so glad to see you.'

'Glad to be here. Oh, you've . . .' He indicated her red lips. 'You've smudged it a bit. Still, suits your cover – like you just gave someone a blow job.'

Nina decided not to tell him that he now had on almost as much lipstick as she did. 'I think Eddie's fine, Jack,' she said testily. 'What now?'

'For you, the best bet is to hide in plain sight – go back to the party. Eddie, I'll guide you up to the top floor.'

Nina peered out into the hallway. Nobody was in sight. 'Okay, it's clear.' She looked back at Chase. 'Good luck.'

Chase stroked her arm as he passed. 'See you soon.'

25

Mitchell's directions led Chase to a small staircase at the back of the house. He quickly climbed it.

If the mansion's uppermost floor were off-limits, there would be a guard. The question was, how would he respond to an unexpected visitor? The party was after all being attended by Russia's most rich and powerful people; being threatened by a goon wouldn't be appreciated.

If the guards were under orders to be polite but firm, that would give him an advantage. They wouldn't be expecting gatecrashers . . .

'Okay, I'm about to go in. I'll call you back in a minute,' he whispered into his headset before removing it and shoving it into his jacket. Earphones and a mike would raise the suspicions of even the most half-witted security guard.

He took a breath, then opened the door.

As he'd expected, there was a guard in the hallway, who hurriedly jumped up from a chair. Chase gave him a bleary look, pretending to be drunk and lost. The guard approached – then unexpectedly smirked.

Chase tensed, not knowing what had brought on the response. Had the guard somehow recognised him? Then the man touched a finger to his lips. Chase did the same, and found a smear of sticky red lipstick on his fingertip. No wonder the guard had been so amused. He looked like a geisha.

He smiled back – then punched the man in the stomach. The guard doubled over, wheezing. Chase whipped out his Desert Eagle and clubbed him on the back of the neck. He collapsed face first on to his chair with such force that his head ripped right through the rattan seat. He fell to the floor, the chair round his neck like some strange angular horse collar.

Chase dragged the unconscious man to the top of the stairs, closing the door behind him, then put his headset back on. 'I'm in.'

'Was there a guard?' Mitchell asked.

'Yeah, but he's sitting it out. So now where?'

'On the security plans, there was a room with extra systems, probably for a safe.'

'Wait, I'm supposed to crack a safe?'

'Not if Vaskovich's already opened it. Head for the front of the mansion.'

Chase got his bearings, then proceeded down the hallway. 'Eddie,' Nina's voice hissed through his headphones, 'that bitch who killed Bernd and Mitzi is here. So's the big guy, Bulldozer.'

'Do they know you're there?'

'I hope not! I'm staying as far from them as I can.'

'Any sign of Vaskovich?' Mitchell asked.

'No, but I'm kind of keeping my head down.'

'He could still be upstairs, then,' said Mitchell, sounding hopeful. 'Which means you've got a chance of catching him, Eddie.' The American issued more directions, Chase following them and arriving at a turn in the hallway.

He cautiously looked round it. A set of double doors a few metres away were half open, another guard standing outside them. His attention was more on the voices coming from within than on the corridor, curiosity having got the better of him.

Chase marched round the corner, gun aimed at the guard's head. The man took a moment too long to react, first caught by surprise and then involuntarily freezing in fear at the sight of the huge weapon pointing at his face. By the time he overcame his paralysis, two kilograms of hard steel had cracked against his skull, dropping him to the carpet as effectively as one of the Desert Eagle's bullets.

Barely breaking stride, Chase stepped over the fallen guard and kicked open the doors.

Standing before him were three startled men: Kruglov, Vaskovich and a third he didn't recognise. There was no mistaking what lay on the table between them, however.

Excalibur.

'Ay up,' said Chase, his gun locked on to Kruglov. 'Remember me?'

'Chase!' hissed Kruglov. His eyes narrowed. 'That bastard Mitchell. He got you in here, didn't he?'

'He's around. The sword's here,' he told Mitchell, before flicking the gun towards Vaskovich. 'Hi there. You don't know me, but I know you. You killed someone I cared about, and a lot of other people besides.'

'I didn't kill anyone,' said Vaskovich, eyes flinty behind his glasses.

'You didn't pull the trigger, but they'd all be alive if you hadn't told fuck-face here to get you this sword. Now me?' He thumbed back the Desert Eagle's hammer for emphasis. 'I pull my own trigger. If I'm going to kill someone, at least I've got the balls to take the responsibility myself.'

As he'd expected, Kruglov didn't react at all to the purely psychological effect of the hammer-click. Vaskovich flinched, but otherwise remained composed. The third man, however, gasped in fright before overcompensating with bluster. 'Who are you?' he demanded. 'How dare you threaten me! I am Felix Mishkin, Deputy Defence Minister of the Russian Federation!'

'I don't care if you're Yuri fucking Gagarin!' Chase told him. He aimed the gun at him; Mishkin instantly cringed back. 'Sit down and shut the fuck up.'

'I'm airborne,' said Mitchell over the headset, the whine of a helicopter engine partially obscuring his words. 'I'll be there in four minutes.'

'So how is Nina?' asked Kruglov. Chase whipped the gun back round at him. Vaskovich's eyes betrayed a flash of comprehension at the name, but Chase, his attention focused on the former KGB man, didn't notice.

'Better than you'll be in a couple of minutes,' Chase snarled.

A very small, calculating smile crept on to Kruglov's lips. 'What are you waiting for, Chase? Why not just kill me now?'

'You in a rush?'

'No, but you have us, you have Excalibur. There is no reason for you to wait . . . unless your escape route is not yet ready,' he concluded, the smile broadening. 'Go ahead and shoot.' Mishkin gabbled disbelievingly in Russian. 'He won't fire,' Kruglov told him, still speaking in English for Chase's benefit. 'Everyone in the building will hear the shot. He will never get out of the mansion, never mind the grounds.'

'You keep telling yourself that. In the meantime . . .' Chase stepped up to the table, gesturing for Vaskovich and Kruglov to back towards the open safe set in one wall. 'I'll be having this.' He picked up Excalibur.

'You are making a mistake,' said Vaskovich. 'Whatever Jack has told you about why I need the sword, it is a lie.'

'Well, it's funny, but after the experiences I've had with billionaires in the past, I don't believe a fucking word they say any more.' Chase stepped back, starting to feel vulnerable. Mitchell was still over three minutes away – and as long as he was holding the sword, he would be forced to fire the heavy Desert Eagle with one hand, reducing his accuracy. He would also have to drop the sword if he needed to reload with the spare magazine attached to his holster strap.

And there was something else, a growing feeling of *wrongness*. While Mishkin, now sitting, was trembling in fear, both Vaskovich and Kruglov were almost visibly growing in confidence as he watched. He glanced at the doors. Nobody there but the downed guard, no sounds of movement. But—

'Jack,' he said, voice taking on urgency. 'Those extra security systems in here – were they just for alarms? Or was there anything else?'

'I'm not sure,' came the reply over the helicopter noise. 'There might have been some data lines.'

'Data? Like to a computer?' He looked more closely at the yawning safe. 'Or from a *camera*?' There was a small circular hole in the top of the frame, only exposed when the door was opened.

He was being watched.

The men in the mansion's security centre had seen the whole thing – and to protect their boss would have ordered others to the room without raising a general alarm . . .

Chase looked through the doors. There was a very slight shadow being cast on the unconscious guard, someone pressed against the wall outside—

He snapped the Desert Eagle round and fired at a point two feet to the door's side. The noise was almost deafening, the recoil kicking his whole arm up and back as a hole exploded in the wall – followed by a pounding thump as the lurking man was blasted across the hallway into the opposite wall.

He wouldn't be alone . . .

Chase fired at the other side of the door. Somebody tumbled to the floor, blood spraying across the hall carpet.

Movement in his peripheral vision—

He spun back to face the Russians by the safe – and saw Kruglov dive at his boss and throw him down behind Mishkin's chair. The minister screeched, flinging up his arms in a pathetic attempt to shield himself from Chase's bullets.

Chase didn't fire. He couldn't blow away the Russian Deputy Minister of Defence to kill Kruglov, or even to stop Vaskovich's plans. Instead he ran for the doors, hearing movement outside. Gun in one hand, he swung Excalibur with the other—

Even without its weird glow, the sword was still sharp, hacking deep into the wrist of the guard who had been just about to shoot him. Before the man even had time to scream, Chase pistol-whipped him with the Desert Eagle and knocked him to the floor.

Nobody else was in the hallway, but others would be on their way. Nina and Mitchell were both speaking at once, the latter's shouts drowning out the former's frantic whispers. 'Eddie! What happened, what's going on?'

'If you can cut three minutes off your flight time, that'd be great!' Chase answered. 'How do I get out?'

'Back the way you came, but carry on past the stairs, then go left.'

Chase was already running. 'Shit – how's Nina going to get to the chopper now?'

The background noise from the hall had changed, party conversation turning to confusion at the gunfire. 'Eddie, Eddie!' Nina said as loudly as she dared. 'Dominika just ran upstairs! What do I do?'

'Nina,' said Mitchell, 'in about two minutes that whole place is going to be in total panic. You'll have to get out then – either meet up with Prikovsky's other girls, or just steal a car and head for the US embassy.'

'I don't know where it is!' Nina protested.

Chase was almost at the stairwell. 'I'm going back for her!'

'*No!*' Mitchell's transmission crackled as the shout briefly overpowered his microphone. 'If you go back you'll *die,* and Vaskovich will get Excalibur again!'

Chase reached the stairs, slowed fractionally – then continued past them. 'Shit!' Reluctant as he was to admit it, Mitchell was right. He arrived at the turn and went left. 'Nina, get close to the front door – soon as people start running, you go out with them!'

He heard a door crash open behind him. He twisted and fired at the guard who ran round the corner. The shot missed, blowing a hole in the wall, but it had the intended effect – the man jumped back into cover.

Mitchell directed him towards the balcony. Chase kicked open a door, firing another shot back down the hallway as he went through. The pursuing guard fell to the floor. Behind him was Dominika, wearing a black cocktail dress, hair now an acidic yellow.

Chase took aim. She saw him and dived, the .50-calibre bullet burning over her as she landed and grabbed the guard's gun. Before Chase had a chance to recover from the recoil she loosed off four rapid shots. He jumped backwards as the door frame splintered.

The room was a library. It was unlit, but enough illumination came through the arched French windows from the lights outside for him to see the balcony beyond. Mitchell had been right about there being enough clearance for a helicopter to hover beside it, but it would be tight.

No time to fiddle with the windows. Instead, he flung Excalibur at them as hard as he could. The sword smashed through, clanging down outside amidst the shattered glass and broken wood. Chase shielded his face and jumped at the broken hole. Jagged glass sliced against one side of his head, but his leather jacket took most of the damage. He shook off the fragments, then snatched up the sword and pointed the Desert Eagle back at the library's door.

No sign of the chopper. He glanced over the balcony's side. Dozens of expensive cars were parked below. On the front lawn, mostly hidden behind the mansion, was the glossy black tail of a helicopter.

A shadow in the doorway. Chase fired as another of Vaskovich's guards rushed through. The bullet hit his shoulder, spinning him like a top.

Dominika jumped through the door behind him, gun

blazing. The remaining windows burst apart. Chase dropped into a clumsy roll as bullets chipped the stonework of the balcony wall behind him. He fired a wild shot. The Russian woman rolled too, far more gracefully, dropping her now empty pistol and taking the wounded guard's weapon in a single smooth movement.

Only two bullets left in the Desert Eagle. Maybe Mitchell had a point about his choice of weapon after all . . .

The helicopter suddenly roared into view overhead. A gale scattered glass fragments across the balcony as it swept past, nose tipping up sharply in a hard braking manoeuvre. It wheeled round, turning side-on to the mansion and slipping back towards it.

Chase had lost sight of Dominika in the darkened library. But she was there somewhere, waiting to strike.

The helicopter, a small MD 500 with a rounded, almost egg-shaped fuselage, moved closer. Its strobing navigation lights lit up the balcony like silent explosions. He could see Mitchell in the pilot's seat, eyes flicking between him and the yellow-painted tips of the rotor blades, judging the distance to the mansion wall. Fifteen feet, ten, the blades perilously close to the wall . . .

Movement: acid-blond hair streaking past the broken windows—

Chase blasted off his penultimate shot as Dominika ran across the library, muzzle flashes searing a dotted line across his vision.

But she wasn't aiming at him.

The helicopter's aluminium skin buckled as bullets cratered the thin metal, the Plexiglas windows cracking. The aircraft lurched. Chase thought Mitchell had been hit, but he recovered, only startled. The American mouthed words at him, voice drowned out by the engine noise. *Come on!*

Chase looked back at the library. Dominika was in cover past the windows. He only had one bullet left. And she had a much bigger target to aim at.

The MD 500 swayed drunkenly, buffeted by its own backwash from the building as well as whatever damage Dominika had inflicted. It drifted away from the balcony despite its pilot's attempts to hold it.

Running out of time . . .

Chase vaulted on to the stone balustrade – and jumped.

Excalibur clutched in his left hand, he slammed against the helicopter's port landing skid, hooking his right arm over it. The Desert Eagle dropped away, spinning down to smash like a hammer through the windscreen of a Lamborghini parked below. The whole chopper was shaking from the impact, Mitchell battling to compensate for the extra weight swinging from one side.

Dominika sprang out of the library and emptied her clip into the helicopter's cabin.

A bullet slashed across the top of Mitchell's thigh. He yelled, reflexively jerking his leg against the anti-torque pedal. The MD 500 spun round anticlockwise, the cockpit for a moment head-on to the balcony, presenting him as a perfect target—

But the gun's slide had locked back. Dominika was out of ammo. The little helicopter kept turning before Mitchell fought past the pain and regained control of the tail rotor, countering the spin with the other pedal. The chopper had made almost a half-turn, its starboard side facing the balcony, hovering less than ten feet from the edge.

Chase hung from the port skid. He saw Dominika looking back at him. She dropped the useless gun, tensed . . . and leapt from the balcony.

She caught the starboard skid with both hands, swinging from it like a gymnast – and kicked Chase in the chest.

Air whooshed from his lungs as he was knocked back, the crook of his elbow slipping off the skid. He dropped, just managing to clamp his hand round the metal tube. His headset jolted loose, following his gun down to earth. Gasping, he swung helplessly, the sword a dead weight in his other hand.

Dominika pulled herself up, wrapping her legs around the skid as the MD 500 finally steadied and began to climb.

Gunfire crackled from below. Not pistols, but automatic weapons. A couple of shots hit the chopper's belly before the firing stopped – someone had spotted Dominika. Chase risked a look down. Guards were running round the corner of the mansion; he saw Kruglov amongst them, pointing up at him.

The helicopter kept rising, wheeling about to fly back

over the building. Chase saw the lights of Moscow in the distance as it straightened out. He fought against the blasting rotor downwash as he tried to pull himself up, glancing across at Dominika – who reached between her legs, under the hem of her dress, and pulled out a glinting knife from a sheath strapped to her thigh.

Nina stood in the lobby, a couple of dozen people crowding around her. A few seconds earlier, the noise of the helicopter coming through the earpiece had abruptly stopped, followed by gunfire from outside.

Had Chase been hit? She had no way of knowing. Vaskovich, Kruglov and Maximov had pushed through the nervous crowd shortly before, the host apparently telling everyone to remain in the building and stay calm. The guests had obeyed at first, but now some of them wanted to get the hell out of the place as quickly as possible. Several men near the exit came to a rapid agreement and threw open the doors.

It was as if a plug had been pulled from a bathtub: everyone surged for the exit, crushing together in the entrance before spilling outside. Nina fought to stay on her feet as she was jostled from all sides. Cold air hit her face, blowing away the fug of smoke. She was through the door—

A hand locked round her arm and pulled her fiercely aside. Maximov glared at her, a frown creasing the bandage covering his forehead. He dragged her across the steps as the fleeing guests hurried down them.

Vaskovich was waiting for her, flanked by a pair of armed guards. 'Hello again, Nina,' he said coldly. 'Nina *Wilde*. I thought there was something familiar about you – but you look very different tonight from your *Time* magazine cover.'

Kruglov ran up the steps. He glanced at Nina, eyebrows flicking up as he finally recognised her, then spoke to Vaskovich. 'Chase has the sword – he jumped on to the helicopter. I'm sure it was Mitchell flying it. And Leonid – Dominika went after him! She's hanging on the skid.'

Vaskovich looked across the lawn, seeing the military helicopter waiting on the grass. 'Where the hell is that idiot Mishkin? Get him here, now!'

Kruglov shouted orders, and barely fifteen seconds later Mishkin was escorted to the group by more guards. Nina saw that his once-slick hair was now dishevelled, and that he had a large damp patch running from his crotch down both legs. He stared wide-eyed and sweating at Vaskovich.

'That English bastard has just been picked up by a helicopter!' Vaskovich told him. 'I *must* have the sword back. Whatever it takes.'

'What am *I* supposed to do?' Mishkin asked, flustered. Vaskovich rolled his eyes, then pointed at his helicopter. 'Are you serious?'

'Is it armed?'

'I – I suppose—'

'Then tell your pilot to get the damn thing into the air! Now!' Mishkin turned and started for the chopper; he looked back as Vaskovich shouted after him. 'Don't shoot it down unless you have to – I don't want to risk losing the sword, and one of my people is aboard. But if anything happens to her . . .' He left the command unspoken. 'Just tell your man that recovering the sword is more important than anything else. Go!'

Mishkin nodded and ran across the lawn. The pilot was already in his seat, having sprinted for the helicopter at the first sound of gunfire, ready to respond. He listened to Mishkin's shouted orders, gave him a thumbs-up and closed the cockpit canopy, running through the emergency start-up sequence. The aircraft came to life, the stacked rotor blades starting to move.

They turned in opposite directions, their counter-rotation eliminating the need for a tail rotor and making the helicopter faster, more manoeuvrable. More deadly. It was no mere transport, but a gunship, a high-tech Kamov Ka-52 'Alligator' designed to hunt down and destroy whatever targets were offered it.

Including other helicopters.

Nina watched in horror as the war machine left the ground, hanging malevolently like a glittering black locust before turning and powering away after the other helicopter.

After Chase.

26

The MD 500 roared over the outskirts of Moscow. Glowing night-time streets swept past below, apartment blocks glinting like jewellery boxes in the dark. Chase would have found the view impressive – if it hadn't been unrolling beneath his dangling feet.

The helicopter wasn't holding a steady course, jinking as it flew. He didn't know if it was because of damage to the machine or its pilot. Without the headset he had no way to communicate with Mitchell short of climbing up and banging on a window.

And Dominika wasn't going to allow that.

She was wrapped almost cat-like round the starboard skid, the knife in one hand. The skids were about six feet apart, putting him just out of reach of her blade.

For now.

He hung by his weakening right hand, the sword in his left, pounded by the rotor blast from above and the slipstream as the chopper raced across the city. To get back up he would need to swing and hook a leg over the skid

– and when he did, he would be within range of Dominika at full stretch. All she had to do was stab an artery, slash a tendon, and he would fall.

But he had no choice. Much longer, and he would fall anyway . . .

He kicked, swinging Excalibur at the same time for extra momentum. His foot swiped out, well short of the skid, then fell back. He tried again, this time swinging higher, but still not high enough.

Dominika watched him, shifting position. Ready to attack.

Chase kicked again. His hand slipped slightly on the skid. This time the side of his foot banged against it – only to drop away again. He fell back down, palm slick with sweat against the cold metal. Another slip, further. He tried to tighten his grip, but he had nothing to push against.

And he saw a new danger, closing fast from behind. Another helicopter. Even against the dark sky he could see it had twin rotors, the ghostly circles of the blades pulsing with each flash of the navigation lights.

The only people who flew co-axial helicopters, he knew, were the Russian military. They'd sent a fucking gunship after him!

After the *sword*. The Kamov wasn't trying to stop them – it was tracking them. Wherever the sword went, it would pursue.

And the wounded MD 500 couldn't fly for ever.

His hand slipped again. If he didn't get a better hold on the skid in the next few seconds, he never would.

Swinging again, metal slithering through his fingers—

His right heel hooked over the skid. With the last of his strength, Chase yelled and pulled up his other leg. He just managed to sweep it over the landing gear as his grip finally gave way.

Moscow rolled inverted beneath him as he hung by his legs, leather jacket flapping violently around his shoulders. The empty holster and heavy spare magazine batted against his chest. Straining, he swung both arms and bent at the waist to pull his body up.

The sword clanged against the skid. He twisted his left wrist to hook the cross-guard round the landing gear. With a firmer hold, he was able to haul himself up, right hand clamping once more round the metal. He let out a breath of relief—

The tip of Dominika's knife stabbed into his forearm.

Chase lost his grip, injured right arm flailing in the wind. He looked across at Dominika. She was gripping the support connecting her skid to the fuselage with one hand, stretching out across the gap to jab at him again.

He pulled his bloodied arm away across his chest, the knife tearing another slash in the leather just below his shoulder. Another stab, falling mere millimetres short.

She switched her attention to the sword. With the cross-guard taking Chase's weight, he didn't dare move it until he could regain his grip with his right hand. Which he couldn't do as long as she had the knife.

And Dominika knew it. Her sour face for the first time displayed what was almost a smile beneath her wind-whipped yellow hair. She swung her blade at the sword, metal clashing against metal, jarring Chase's left hand.

Clang. Another hit. And another. The hilt began to slide through his grasp, a little more with each blow.

If the sword dropped, the gunship would go after it. If she caught it, Vaskovich had his prize. Either way, Chase would fall.

Clang. Clang. The sword jolted in his hand. His little finger reached the end of the hilt and clutched around nothing. Dominika stretched out further, loosening the grip of her legs to extend her reach. *Clang.* He felt his ring finger slip over the rounded end of the handle.

The Russian drew back her arm for a final swing—

And Chase tore the spare magazine from his holster strap and hurled it into her face.

Even though it only contained seven bullets, the .50-calibre magazine was still over half a pound of hard-edged steel and copper and lead cracking against the bridge of her nose.

Blood gushing from her nostrils, Dominika convulsed in pain, and her legs slipped off the landing skid. She screamed, her left hand wrenched from the support as she dropped – to catch the skid by her fingertips. Lighter than Chase, she was hit harder by the wind as she dangled precariously from the helicopter. The knife fell away as she tried to reach up with her right hand, but safety was just beyond her reach.

Chase stretched out his right arm, scrabbling for grip, finding it. He pulled himself back up and finally managed to hook an arm round the skid. Painfully dragging himself over the top, he looked across at Dominika.

She hung by one hand, desperately clawing with the other . . .

Clang.

Excalibur's gleaming edge was just an inch from her fingers.

Dominika turned her head towards Chase. He was now leaning across the gap just as she had done . . . but his blade was much longer than hers. Her eyes filled with terror as she realised what he was about to do. '*Nyet! NYET!*'

He stared coldly back, no mercy in his gaze as he slowly swung Excalibur away from her, the flat of the sword grating along the skid. He leaned closer so she could hear him.

'This is for Mitzi.'

The sword sliced back.

Dominika's severed fingers flashed through the beam of the helicopter's navigation light, then were gone, falling with the screaming assassin as she plunged hundreds of feet to burst on the unforgiving streets below.

But Chase's problems weren't over.

A laser-like streak of fire burned past, a harsh chainsaw rasp coming from behind. The Kamov was letting rip with its 30mm cannon. With Dominika gone, there was nothing to restrain the pilot.

But he wasn't trying to shoot down the MD 500. If he

had, it would have been destroyed already. He was aiming specifically at Chase.

'Shit!' Chase gasped. Only his helicopter's twitchy flightpath had saved him, the cannon shells passing less than a foot below as the MD 500 bobbed. But if even a single shell struck him, whatever body part it hit would instantly be reduced to a red mist – and Excalibur would fall.

The helicopter banked hard, almost throwing Chase from the skid. Mitchell had seen the tracer fire and was taking evasive action, rolling into a rapid descent.

The Kamov pursued. The MD 500 was nimble – but the much larger Alligator could match it move for move.

Chase knew what Mitchell was doing: if he dropped down close to street level, he could fly between the apartment buildings and use them for cover. Unless the Kamov's pilot was a psychopath, it would keep his finger off the trigger.

But they had to reach them first . . .

Another brief burst of fire lashed past, the shells arcing away into the distance. The helicopter continued its twisting descent. Chase struggled to keep hold, wrapping his arms round the connecting strut. He realised he was just below the cockpit door, the handle tantalisingly close.

The MD 500 levelled out, G-forces squashing Chase against the skid. An apartment block whipped past, its roof above him. Mitchell was flying down a street, barely clearing the streetlights and telephone cables as he weaved from side to side to make himself a harder target.

The Kamov was still behind them, but flying higher, waiting to pounce.

Chase pulled himself up, peering over the bottom of the large window in the oval door. Mitchell was on the opposite side of the cockpit, a smear of blood on his thigh, eyes fixed on the view ahead.

The Alligator's pilot had been deterred from firing, but he would still follow them wherever they went. And if they tried to land so Chase could flee on foot, he would have them.

Mitchell turned sharply, sweeping the helicopter round into another street. The movement banged Chase's head against the door. Mitchell glanced round at the unexpected noise, eyes widening in surprise as he saw him. The Kamov pursued, not fooled by its target's sudden change of course.

Although Mitchell could have reached the internal door release, he needed both hands to fly. Chase switched Excalibur to his right hand. Wind battering him, he stretched up for the handle with his left, fingers straining . . .

He reached it. The door popped open, banging against its frame in the slipstream. Chase jammed his arm into the gap, pushing his head and shoulder inside. 'Eddie!' Mitchell shouted. 'Where's the sword?'

'I've got it!'

'Then get in!'

'No! We need to take out that chopper!'

'Are you crazy?' yelled Mitchell as he made another sharp turn. The door swung open, then flapped back to bash painfully against Chase's shoulder. 'It's a goddamn gunship! This thing *isn't*!'

'You'll have to improvise!' Chase looked ahead, seeing taller, newer buildings rising above the old Soviet blocks. A long string of lights picked out the skeletal outline of a crane between them, another tower under construction. 'That crane! Drop me on top of it!'

'*What?*'

'It's the only way to get rid of him! Do it!' Chase hunched back down and slammed the door, cutting off Mitchell's objections mid-word.

The Kamov was still behind them, having moved to see what Chase was doing. He wondered what the pilot would make of the fact that he had deliberately shut himself out of the cockpit.

He had something else for him to think about. 'Hey!' Chase screamed, looking back and waving Excalibur out from the side of the helicopter as it ascended. 'You want this? Then come and get it, dickhead!'

A spotlight flashed into dazzling life on the Kamov's nose, locking on to Chase. The sword glinted in the harsh blue light.

The crane's long, orange-painted jib swept past, the MD 500 pivoting to fly almost sideways along its length. Chase looked down. He was at least two hundred feet up, the ground around the crane's base strewn with girders and concrete blocks and other things not remotely likely to provide a soft landing. 'What the *fuck* am I doing?' he asked himself as he leaned out from the skid—

And jumped.

The helicopter was only a few feet above the jib, but the impact as Chase slammed against the tubular metalwork was still like a baseball bat to his chest. One foot slipped. Clinging to a diagonal cross-member, he dropped, sliding down it like a fireman's pole, and thumped painfully to a halt straddling the lower horizontal beam.

Grimacing, he dragged himself back up. Mitchell's helicopter had peeled away, but the Alligator was still there, having overshot Chase when he jumped and now performing a rapid aerial pirouette to come back after him.

He stood upright, feet on the beam as he gripped the upper support. The top of the tall vertical tower was about thirty feet away. He started for it, Excalibur clanging against the orange metal as he moved crab-like along the jib.

A hot wind, reeking of burnt fuel, whirled around him. The Kamov drifted down on the other side of the jib, its blinding spotlight shining into his face. Chase lowered his head, using the upper beam to shield his eyes as he advanced. Through the glare he could make out the pilot in the cockpit – and the Alligator's cannon, mounted on the gunship's stubby starboard wing. It was slaved to the pilot's head movements, turning to track Chase, making ever finer adjustments to its aim. One shot was all it would take.

Only ten feet to go, less, but the cannon was locked on to his chest, the pilot grinning with expectant triumph—

The wind suddenly rose as Mitchell brought the MD 500 down on top of the Kamov.

The smaller helicopter's landing skids instantly disintegrated as they hit the gunship's upper rotor disc, but the blades themselves were also smashed, one shooting outwards like a javelin over Chase's head. Unbalanced, the Alligator began to spin, its tail swinging round . . .

Towards the crane.

Chase desperately leapt along the jib as the chopper veered towards him. He lost his grip on Excalibur, the sword falling away. But it was already forgotten as he threw himself at the tower—

The Kamov hit.

The whole crane shook as over nine tons of metal and composites slammed sidelong against it, swinging the jib round far faster than its screaming gears could take. Rapid-fire bangs erupted from the helicopter's rotor shaft as explosive bolts blasted all the remaining blades free, followed a fraction of a second later by a much louder detonation as the canopy blew off and the pilot shot skywards in his ejector seat on a trail of rocket flame.

With nothing to hold it aloft, the Kamov plummeted to earth, its momentum spinning it away from the base of the crane before it smashed into a pile of girders and exploded. Even dangling from the top of the tower, Chase felt the heat from the expanding fireball.

The entire crane was shuddering from the impact. A ladder ran down the centre of the tower, smoke from the burning Kamov boiling across it. Chase scrambled for a foothold, then squeezed through the framework to the ladder. Breathing the smoke wouldn't be healthy, but it was the only way down—

A sound like a shotgun blast above him. He snapped up his head – and saw one of the jib's diagonal cross-members shear loose at one end, the weld splitting under the strain.

Another strut broke, then another. The entire jib sagged, bending under its own weight. It was a chain reaction, each failed spar putting more and more pressure on the others.

Chase stared in horror, then desperately tugged his jacket's cuffs over his hands. The crane would give way at any moment . . .

With an ear-splitting shriek of tearing metal, the jib folded like paper, ripping apart where the helicopter had collided with it and spearing towards the ground. The tower lurched, the massive concrete counterweights extending out behind the operator's cabin pulling the whole thing over.

Like a giant redwood felled by a lumberjack, the massive crane slowly but inexorably began to topple.

The leather of his jacket covering his palms, Chase squeezed his hands round the outside of the ladder – and jumped off the rungs.

And fell.

Using his feet as guides against the vertical stiles, he plunged down the core of the shuddering crane.

The falling tower picked up speed, buckling. He was no longer falling vertically – the crane was leaning at five degrees, ten, the horizon rising above his line of sight as the ground rolled towards him.

The leather protecting his hands shredded as he sliced over the joints of each section of ladder, but he couldn't slow down – he was still too high to survive the fall.

Twenty degrees, thirty, metal twisting and tearing all around—

With an explosive boom of shattering concrete, the tower ripped away from its base.

Chase was still slithering down the ladder, but now he was on top of it as it hurtled towards the horizontal. He shot through the oily smoke, opening his stinging eyes to see the muddy ground rushing at him with increasing speed. Now he squeezed both hands tightly round the stiles. He felt the heat of friction through the leather as it tore and burned, slowing his descent, but maybe too late—

The crane smashed down.

The protruding counterweights hit first, sending a whipcrack ripple down the length of the collapsing structure. Chase bounced from the ladder and slammed against the framework above him, then thudded back down on to the rungs as the wrecked crane came to rest.

He lay unmoving, sprawled over the broken ladder. Concrete dust wafted over him. The echoes of the impact died away, for several seconds the only sound the crackle of the burning helicopter.

Then Chase coughed.

'Fuck . . . ing hell . . . *fire!*' he wheezed, dragging himself through the bent framework to lie in the mud. He was less than twenty feet from the crane's base, his descent having slowed as the tower toppled. But he had still hit the ground as if dropping face-first from over ten feet up, with all the pain that entailed.

The mere fact that he'd been able to crawl from the crane told him nothing major was broken, but there was a nasty throb in his left arm where it had been injured a year earlier. His head hurt too; he rubbed his forehead and realised he was bleeding, another deep slash to add to the one he'd received jumping through the window at Vaskovich's mansion.

The thought of the Russian cut through the fog of pain. Chase sat up. He had no idea what had happened to Nina. And as for Mitchell, and Excalibur . . .

Both the latter questions were answered within seconds of each other. A buzzing roar came from above as the MD 500 descended, the stubs of its wrecked undercarriage like broken insect legs. As he watched the helicopter drop into the construction site, he saw Excalibur sticking out of the mud near the crane's base like a gleaming grave marker. Which, for Chase, it almost had been.

Still breathing heavily, he hobbled to the sword. A moment of effort was all it took to pull it from the ground.

He had Excalibur.

But his body ached too much for him to feel

triumphant. Wearily, he turned to see the helicopter hovering unsteadily over a large pile of sand. Before Chase could wonder what the hell Mitchell was doing, the MD 500 dropped sharply, smacking down on its belly atop the soft pile. It squirmed deeper into the sand as the rotors kept spinning, but Mitchell had already shut down the engine and dived from the cockpit, rolling to the bottom of the heap and running as fast as he could on his injured leg towards Chase. Behind him, the helicopter wobbled, then finally tipped over. Its rotors thudded through the sand, kicking up a huge gritty spray before being brought to a stop.

'Bloody hell!' Chase cried. 'Took a bit of a chance, didn't you? You could've been puréed!'

'Can't wait around,' Mitchell said grimly, taking out a phone. 'I didn't have any other way to land, and there's already police and fire trucks on the way, I saw them from the helo. We've got to get out before they arrive. You okay?'

Chase indicated his torn clothing and bloodied skin. 'Oh, absolutely fucking top! What about Nina?'

'I don't know. You had the relay – I lost contact with her as soon as we moved out of range. Come on.' He called a number as he hurried towards the site's main gate, issuing rapid orders. Chase followed, the sword in his hand.

An hour later they were in an American safe house, an anonymous apartment in an equally anonymous block a few miles from the crash site. They had got clear just before the police arrived, hurrying through the darkened streets until being picked up by the same driver who had taken them to Prikovsky's warehouse – although his gleaming SUV had been replaced by a much more discreet old Volkswagen Golf.

'So do you know what's happened to Nina?' Chase demanded as Mitchell concluded another call. He himself had called Prikovsky, learning that while his girls had all left the mansion, Nina had not been with them. That didn't mean she hadn't got a lift back to Moscow with someone else, but his concern was rapidly growing.

'Not yet,' Mitchell snapped. 'Vaskovich is moving, though – his private jet just took off from Vnukovo airport. It's a safe bet he's aboard.'

'Probably doesn't want to be around when the Russians start asking why one of their shiny new gunships just crashed in the middle of Moscow. I bet that bloke Mishkin's wishing he hadn't taken the job. It'll be a bugger to explain.'

Mitchell was about to say something when his phone trilled. 'Yes,' he said, eyes widening as he listened to the caller. 'Yes, put him through. It's Vaskovich,' he added to Chase.

'Put it on speaker,' Chase said. Mitchell frowned, but did as he was asked.

There was a click of connection, then a voice came from the phone. Vaskovich. 'Are you there, Jack?'

'I'm here, Leonid,' Mitchell replied. The background whine suggested that the billionaire was indeed airborne in his jet.

'You've stolen something from me. You and Chase. I assume he's there.'

'Yeah, I'm here,' said Chase. 'If you're wondering where Dominika is, I dropped her off on the way back from your party. Sorry about messing that up, by the way. Seemed like quite a good bash.'

'Yes, it was,' Vaskovich said, clearly irritated behind his veneer of calm. 'But that doesn't matter. I'm having another party here in my plane. For a *very* special guest.'

A cold fear swept over Chase. He knew who Vaskovich meant. 'If you fucking hurt her—' he began, before Mitchell signalled him to shut up.

'Is she all right, Leonid?' the American asked.

'For now. You have something I want, I have something you want . . . or at least that Chase wants.'

'Let me talk to her,' Chase demanded. He glanced over at Mitchell, daring him to try to silence him, but the DARPA agent had a thoughtful, almost calculating expression.

Whatever he was thinking, Chase didn't care, forgetting about him as he heard Nina's voice. 'Eddie? Oh, thank God you're okay! I didn't know what happened, just something about a helicopter crash!'

'Yeah, just another day working for the IHA. Are you all right?'

'I'm fine. I'm sorry, they caught me on the way out.'

'There is a reason why *real* secret agents do not appear on chat shows,' said Kruglov sarcastically in the background.

'I recognised her,' said Vaskovich, 'but not soon enough, unfortunately. Her disguise was very effective. Still,' he went on, tone hardening, 'I have her now. I want the sword, Jack. Deliver Excalibur to my mansion within the hour and I'll release Dr Wilde. Otherwise, I may have to . . . *drop her off.*'

'Why the mansion, Leonid?' asked Mitchell, holding up a hand to cut off Chase's furious response. 'I assume you're on your way to Grozevny. Why don't we save you some time, deliver Excalibur to you there?'

Vaskovich laughed mockingly. 'Yes, I'm sure you'd love to see my facility at Grozevny, Jack. That was your plan all along, wasn't it? It's a good thing for me that Aleksey never trusted you.'

'I'm not going anywhere. Dominika shot me in the leg.'

'Are you okay?' Nina cut in.

'It's more than just a flesh wound this time,' Mitchell lied, giving Chase a faint smile. 'But I was thinking Eddie would be a better person to deliver it. He doesn't know anything about earth energy, or care either . . . and I'm pretty sure that if I tried to stop him getting Nina back, he'd kill me.' Another smile. Chase returned it, with just a hint of sincerity.

'Why should I trust you?' demanded Vaskovich.

'It doesn't matter, because I won't be there. Eddie will. And like you said, you've got something he wants. And you'll have what you need to make your system work, right there.'

Kruglov muttered something in Russian, clearly

distrustful, but after a moment Vaskovich spoke again. 'You have a jet?'

'Yes.'

'Then I'll arrange for the airspace to be cleared. But know this: if the plane goes off course, it will be shot down. If anyone other than Chase and the pilot are aboard, they will all die, and so will Dr Wilde. If Excalibur is not aboard, everyone dies. If there is any kind of deceit, everyone dies. And so will you, Jack. Don't think you are beyond my reach, even in America. Am I clear?'

'Pretty fuckin' crystal,' said Chase, scowling.

'I will arrange for your jet's safe passage,' Vaskovich said. 'Chase?'

'What?'

'You may not believe me, but I am a man of my word. If you bring me Excalibur, you will get to marry Nina. Whenever that may be. But if you betray me . . . you will both die.' There was a click as the line disconnected.

'You think we can trust him?' Chase asked.

Mitchell snorted. 'Doubt it. But it doesn't matter – I was lying too. I'll be on the plane with you.'

'Wait a sec – if they find you, they'll kill all of us.'

'Don't worry!' He gave Chase an enigmatic smile. 'I'll be aboard when it takes off – but I won't be when it lands.' He clapped a hand on Chase's shoulder. 'Come on. Let's go rescue your fiancée.'

27

The aircraft taking Chase and Mitchell north from Moscow was not the State Department plane in which they had flown to Russia, but a smaller Cessna Citation Mustang business jet, conspicuously lacking any kind of corporate markings. Chase suspected it was normally used for discreet, private transportation of US intelligence operatives.

A group of which Mitchell was now undeniably a member.

'So,' said Chase as Mitchell opened one of several plastic cases stacked in the jet's cabin, 'you were a spook all along, were you?'

'That a problem?'

'Depends on the spook. So the whole scientist thing, was that just a cover?'

'Hell, no,' Mitchell said firmly. 'I really do have a PhD in high-energy physics. Would never have been able to convince Vaskovich I'd be useful without it.'

'And how long's DARPA been running its own

intelligence operations behind everyone else's back?'

'A while. It's better if nobody else knows. We do whatever's necessary to ensure America has a decisive technological advantage over all other countries – and keep it that way.'

'By force.'

'If we have to.' Mitchell took a rifle from the crate – a weapon of a design Chase had never seen before. He tossed it to the Englishman. 'Case in point. Check it out.'

Chase turned the futuristic gun over in his hands. A cursory examination revealed it had two separate magazines, one flat along the top and the other set into the stock. The handgrip was positioned forward of both mags in a 'bullpup' configuration. 'Looks like something from *Judge Dredd*.'

'The XM-201 Advanced Assault Rifle, one of DARPA's new toys.' Mitchell brought out a second, identical weapon for himself. 'Two hundred rounds of caseless high-power propellant in the buttstock, and a top-mounted helical magazine with five twenty-round feeds for mission-variable three-point-six-millimetre munitions.' He moved a selector switch on his gun. 'Standard copper-jacketed, tungsten penetrator, explosive, or plastic non-lethals. Normal loadout is forty standard rounds and twenty of each of the others per mag, but I thought the plastics would be kinda pointless for this operation.'

'*Three*-point-six-mil ammo?' Chase asked dubiously. 'You won't get much stopping power with that.'

'You'd be surprised – although we haven't tested it on a

live human target. Yet.' He gave Chase a meaningful look. 'It's also got a three-round twenty-five-millimetre grenade launcher linked to a computerised laser range-finder. Just lase the target, tilt it up and the sights'll tell you when you're at the right arc angle. Viewfinder with ten-times scope and night vision here, built-in Identify-Friend-or-Foe system to cut down on friendly fire—'

'Now there's a gadget you Yanks actually need,' Chase said mockingly.

Mitchell shot him a sour look before continuing. 'Hold it in firing position.' Chase hefted the weapon and did so. Mitchell tapped at a small keypad set behind the sights. A green LED lit up with a bleep. 'There. It's now biometrically coded to your hands. Only authorised users can fire it. And if it falls into enemy hands, there's even a coded self-destruct signal that melts all the electronics to prevent duplication. Pretty cool, huh?'

Chase lowered the gun. 'Not really.'

Mitchell seemed surprised, even a little affronted. 'Your professional opinion?'

'Yep. All the gadgets mean it'll eat batteries, which means more crap you've got to cart about with you, fancy electronics are the first things to break in the field, this mag in the stock makes it too bulky, having switchable ammo paths into the receiver means it's more likely to jam, the carrying handle's too far forward and I bet it costs a fucking fortune. You've made a gun that does twice as much as an M-16 . . . for ten times the price.' He grinned. 'Typical American toy.'

Mitchell grinned back. 'Hey, how else are we supposed to keep increasing the stockholder value of our arms industry every quarter? Anyway, it's at least five years from service, maybe even ten. You know how much the brass hate change. Even for the better.'

Chase shrugged and put down the rifle. 'Think I'll stick with the old school, thanks.'

Mitchell shook his head. 'Not for this mission, you won't. There's another reason why I wanted these. When Vaskovich's earth energy system is running – which it will be as soon as he gets Excalibur – it puts out a *huge* magnetic field. You go in there with a gun made of steel, and it'll be pulled right out of your hand.' He patted the body of his XM-201. 'This baby's made of polymers and ceramics, nothing magnetic. And even the electronics are shielded. When the system's running, there's only one kind of gun that'll work in there. And we'll have them.'

'You'll have them, you mean,' Chase corrected. 'I don't see Kruglov letting me stroll in there with one of these. And speaking of that, how're *you* going to get in there?'

Mitchell indicated a case. 'Another DARPA toy.' He checked his watch. 'In fact . . . I should start prepping it about now, so give me a hand.'

The case contained what looked like a large, hard-shelled backpack. Mitchell slid the rifles into a compartment inside it, then climbed into a black one-piece flight suit and zipped it up. He donned the pack with Chase's assistance. 'Latest thing we devised for airborne special ops,' Mitchell told him as he fastened an electronic control unit to his wrist. 'And this one *is* going into service, within the year. It's a glidewing – we wanted to call it the Batwing, but we'd probably have some trademark problems if we did. Can carry a SEAL and all his gear. Once I'm in freefall, the wings extend – they're carbon fibre – and I can glide way further than I could in a HAHO parachute jump.' He put on a cheesy commercial announcer's voice. 'But wait, there's more!'

'Are these engines?' Chase said, seeing cylindrical protrusions on each side of the pack.

'Yep. Mini-turbojets, three hundred pounds of thrust between them. There's about fifteen minutes of fuel, but I can use them in bursts to gain height and glide. Then when I want to land, I just pop the 'chute. A good pilot can hit a fifty-foot target area from over a hundred miles away.'

'And you're a good pilot?'

'Not bad. The controls are very intuitive – just pretend you're Superman.' He smiled, then became all business. 'After I bail out, I can land in Vaskovich's facility without anyone even knowing. Then I'll come find you and Nina.'

'What about extraction? How are we getting out?' One of Vaskovich's demands had been for their jet to take off and return to Moscow immediately after delivering Chase – and being searched for uninvited guests.

'It's all taken care of. Trust me.'

Chase didn't like being left in the dark – especially when his and Nina's lives were on the line – but it was clear that Mitchell wasn't going to tell him anything else until he had to. Some kind of US incursion into Russian airspace would explain why he was being so secretive – Chase couldn't reveal information he didn't know.

Mitchell finished strapping on the pack, then took a full-face helmet from the case. 'Okay, I'll kick the cases out before I bail so nobody wonders what was in them – you'll have to close the door after I jump. Try not to fall out, huh?'

'And you remember to pull the ripcord *before* you hit the ground,' countered Chase with a grin. 'You know, for a navy man, you're not such an arsehole after all.'

'Oh, I'm an asshole,' said Mitchell. 'I'm just on the right side.' He clapped Chase on the shoulder, then donned the helmet as the pilot called a one-minute warning from the cockpit. 'Okay, here we go!'

Weighed down by his equipment, he moved to the cabin door as Chase brought over the empty cases and secured himself to the wall. 'Thirty seconds!' the pilot shouted.

'See you down there,' said Chase. He pulled the lever to open the hatch.

The noise and wind were horrific – even though it was slowing and descending, the Cessna was still cruising at over two hundred knots and nine thousand feet. Gripping the door frame, Mitchell booted the cases out, then hurled himself into the black void. He was snatched away by the slipstream, barely missing the jet's low wing as he fell.

Buffeted by the freezing wind, Chase pulled the lever to close the hatch. Shivering, he returned to his seat, hoping Mitchell knew what he was doing.

Ten minutes later, the jet was on the ground.

Vaskovich was taking no chances; before Chase was allowed to exit, three armed men came aboard and searched the aircraft. All they found were the pilot, Chase, and the aluminium case in his lap. After frisking him thoroughly for concealed weapons, they waved him out at gunpoint.

Even though the wind was low, the cold hit him hard. Grozevny was on the very rim of the Arctic Circle at the entrance to the Barents Sea, situated on the edge of the marshy tundra about a hundred and eighty miles from Archangel'sk, the nearest city. During the Cold War it had been a naval base, a hiding place for the Soviet Union's ballistic missile submarines. Now, that perverse non-conflict long over and the base's secrets laid bare for anyone with an internet connection and Google Earth to see, it had passed into the hands of one of Russia's new oligarchs.

As Chase stepped on to the runway he saw the cold sea off to the north, a cliff rising up along the curving coastline to the east. About a mile away, a long L-shaped jetty protruded into the waves from its base. He guessed the sub pen was under the cliff. Beyond it, the ground rose to a small hill, at the top of which was a brightly lit building, but it was too far away for him to make out any details other than its size, which was considerable.

More of Vaskovich's men surrounded the jet, weapons at the ready. Kruglov stood at the foot of the steps, Maximov beside him. 'Is that the sword?' Kruglov demanded, pointing at the case.

That Kruglov hadn't killed him on sight suggested Vaskovich intended to honour at least part of his deal. Chase opened the long case, revealing Excalibur nestled on a bed of foam within. 'Where's Nina?'

Kruglov glanced in the direction of the distant building, then indicated the nearer of two black Mercedes GL Class SUVs. 'Get in.'

Sandwiched between Maximov and another guard in the back seat, Chase was driven along a road on the coast. The view ahead confirmed what he'd thought: the jetty was indeed connected to the sub pen, a vast concrete arch set into the cliff face, lights blazing within. The jetty ran from the end of a dock on the pen's far side, a rusty crane overlooking the water.

To Chase's surprise, the dock wasn't empty.

The little convoy drove along a road at the base of the cliff and into the pen itself, giving him a grandstand view of the colossal vessel within. It was a submarine, a Typhoon-class ballistic missile boat, the largest type of sub ever built. As big as a Second World War aircraft carrier, only six Typhoons had been constructed by the Soviets, and just a single example remained in active service, the others either scrapped or supposedly held in reserve. Chase now knew where one had ended up.

But whatever the Typhoon's purpose here, it wasn't as

a weapon. The vessel wasn't seaworthy: a large section of deck aft of the squat sail had been removed to expose the twin pressure hulls within, dozens of heavy-duty electrical cables leading out from the hole to a pylon by a tunnel entrance on the opposite side of the dock. It wouldn't be going anywhere in a hurry – at least, not if it wanted to stay afloat.

The SUVs drove over a bridge at the dock's rear, then back along the other side of the sub to stop at the tunnel. 'So what's this?' Chase asked as he got out of the Mercedes. He mimicked Sean Connery in *The Hunt For Red October*. 'You going to shail into hishtory?'

Kruglov ignored him, directing him into the tunnel towards the lower terminus of a funicular railway rising out of the grim concrete cavern. The track was steep, ascending the hill above at a steady forty degree angle. A boxy carriage waited for them at one of the two gates.

Everyone entered the carriage, all guns pointed at Chase as it began to climb the track. He looked up the hill as they emerged from the tunnel. A second car was descending from the top of the track, the two linked by cables and counterbalancing each other. A road followed a long zigzag path up the hillside from the base, the funicular sometimes passing over, other times under it on its ascent. To each side, the hill was covered by what at first glance he thought was a forest of leafless trees . . .

'Christ,' he said, seeing what they really were. 'Your TV reception must be pretty crappy if you need that lot to get a decent picture.'

The 'forest' was man-made, metal: a vast antenna array stretching round the entire hill and on to the tundra beyond. The receiver for Vaskovich's earth energy station, Chase realised, like the American HAARP facility Mitchell had described, only on a much greater scale.

He got a better view of the large building on the hilltop as they approached. It was circular, with a domed roof resembling an observatory. More electrical cables were draped down the sides of the dome like morbid streamers, linking it to the array.

The funicular reached the upper station. Two more waiting SUVs took the group the few hundred metres across the freezing hilltop to the facility. Inside, Chase was hustled through the building's blank corridors to what resembled an airport's security screening station. Warning notices in Cyrillic plastered the walls; he had no idea what they said, but the stylised symbols accompanying them suggested danger from both high voltages and magnetism. A thick line of striped red and yellow was painted on the floor.

The station was manned by two men in orange overalls. When Kruglov stepped up to them, one man ran a sensor wand over his body while the other monitored the results on a screen. The machine bleeped several times. With a look of resigned annoyance, Kruglov emptied out his pockets, placing all his metallic belongings, including a gun, in a plastic tray. The first man ran the wand over him again. Satisfied with the result, he put the tray in a nearby locker and waved Kruglov over the painted line.

The process was repeated with the other members of the group. Chase went next, having to turn over his watch, keys, phone and – to his irritation – leather jacket. The teeth of its zip were steel, susceptible to magnetic fields. The titanium pins in his left arm initially caused some consternation, but once it was determined they were non-magnetic he was sent through. Presumably the plate in Maximov's skull was also non-magnetic; if not, he would get very attached to the machinery when it was switched on.

The one item that set off warnings yet was still allowed through was Excalibur. Carrying the case, Chase was led from the entrance into another room beyond, the facility's control centre.

Waiting for him was Nina.

The makeup and dress from the party were gone; she looked pale and vulnerable in a set of ill-fitting overalls. 'Eddie!' she called, relieved, but also worried. Vaskovich, standing beside her, was now in complete control.

'Hi, honey,' Chase replied. He was just as delighted to see her, but forced himself to remain outwardly cool. 'You okay?'

Nina made a sarcastic noise. 'Oh, *super* fine, really! Apart from the prison outfit.' She plucked at her baggy orange one-piece.

'Yeah, I think the black rubber number definitely wins out.' He turned to Vaskovich. 'I brought the sword. Now let her go.'

'Show me,' said the Russian. Chase opened the case.

Vaskovich regarded Excalibur with a look somewhere between awe and greed, then carefully lifted it from the foam, holding the polished metal up to the light. 'I wasn't sure if you would really do it. I have a hard time believing Jack would let it go so easily.' Suspicion crossed his face. 'Let's be sure he really has.'

He clicked his fingers, and one of the control room technicians hurried over bearing an electronic device. Vaskovich carefully placed the sword on a table; the technician clipped a pair of electrodes to it, then switched on the gadget. He watched its display for several seconds, then nodded to his boss.

'It really is Excalibur,' said Vaskovich, sounding almost surprised as he picked up the weapon again. 'A genuine high-temperature superconductor.'

'If I say I'm going to do something, I do it,' Chase told him.

'And so do I. You can have Nina back, Chase – after I test my system with the sword in place.'

'Don't seem to recall that being part of the deal,' said Chase icily.

'I think it was implied.' Vaskovich smiled slightly, then handed Excalibur to another technician, who climbed down a ladder leading through an opening in the floor. 'Take a look,' he said proudly, striding to the room's glass wall and opening his arms wide to encompass the much larger chamber beyond. 'This is what I have been working for. This . . . is the future.'

The control room overhung the edge of a huge

concrete-walled circular pit, a hundred feet across at its top and over twice as deep, narrowing as it descended. Overhead was the dome, the cables Chase had seen earlier hanging down through open louvres to the vast machine below. A hexagonal framework running down to the base of the pit supported a series of massive rings of electromagnets, suspended from electrical insulators. Outside the frame were three catwalks, one just below the level of the control room, a second midway down, and the third near the bottom of the apparatus. A small elevator platform was descending the framework, the technician taking Excalibur down to the lowest level. It was unmistakably some kind of generator, but on a truly enormous scale.

Chase wasn't impressed, however. 'Yeah. The future of war.'

Vaskovich shook his head. 'Do you know the purpose of war, Chase? The true purpose? It has nothing to do with ideology, or morality. It is about *resources*. Right now, it is all about oil. But there will be wars for other resources in the future – gas, uranium, even water. Control the supply of resources, and you control entire nations.'

'But you already do,' said Nina, stepping forward to join Chase and taking his hand. 'You control a huge chunk of Russia's oil and gas reserves. You already have that kind of power.'

'Oil and gas will not last for ever,' Vaskovich said. 'I know what governments say, even here in Russia: that peak oil production is a long way away. But I know the truth – we have already passed that point. The price will only go up from now on. You think over a hundred dollars for a barrel of oil is expensive? Soon it will be two hundred. Then three.'

'And you get to profit from it all,' Nina said scathingly.

To her surprise, Vaskovich responded with anger. 'No! What use is money if Russia freezes and starves? This is my country – my homeland! I will not let that happen!' He calmed slightly, looking back out over the generator. Below, the technician was carefully lowering Excalibur into a piece of equipment at the bottom of the pit. 'This will change all that. This will change the world – and Russia will take her rightful place as its leader.'

'By threatening to blow up everyone else with this thing?' Chase asked.

Vaskovich rounded on him, angry again. 'This is *not* a weapon! Whatever Jack has told you, it is a lie. This is a generator, a power station – which turns the earth's own natural energy into that power. It is clean, it is safe – and it is limitless. With more of these stations built on the points where the lines of energy converge, I can power the whole of Russia, for nothing. A productive use for my billions – my gift to my country.'

'Which won't exactly hurt your political ambitions,' Nina realised.

Vaskovich smiled triumphantly. 'Who wouldn't vote for the man who restored Russia to greatness? And it is a war Russia has already won. Anyone else who wants this technology will have to come to me – because I am the only person who has it.' He looked through the window. Excalibur in place below, the technician was ascending again. 'And now, I can make it happen.'

He issued an order in Russian. The technicians turned to their consoles, activating the system. Vaskovich's attention was on the machines; Chase surreptitiously looked round for any opportunity to escape. Kruglov and Maximov, he saw, were watching him. A corner of Kruglov's wide mouth twitched mockingly – the Russian knew exactly what he was thinking. He opened his jacket and revealed a knife, with a black carbon-fibre blade. Non-metallic. Chase mouthed 'Fuck off' at him, then returned his attention to Vaskovich.

A deep electrical hum rose in volume. The sharp tang of ozone filled the control room as the air took on a strange, almost tingling quality, literally charged. Nina flinched at a sudden lightning-flash from above, a crackle of electrical energy arcing between two of the cables descending from the dome. More bolts flicked across the generator as the power rose.

Vaskovich pointed out a particular digital indicator. It read 0.34, and rising. 'This gauge shows the system's power level,' he explained. 'Right now, all the power is coming from the submarine's nuclear reactors.'

'That's what it's for?' Chase asked in disbelief. 'You've got the world's biggest missile sub downstairs, and you're using it as a *generator*?'

'It produces nearly four hundred megawatts of power. But even if we fed all of Russia's electricity into it, it wouldn't be enough. Not without the superconductor.' He looked at the gauge again, which had now reached 0.47. 'The highest it has ever gone is zero point seven two. If it goes higher, then the superconductor is working – it is channelling earth energy into the generator. But it will still consume more energy than it produces . . . until the gauge reads one. That is the point where the process becomes self-sustaining.'

'And then what?' demanded Chase.

'And then . . . you can leave.'

Nina regarded him suspiciously. 'You're really going to let us go?'

'Your fiancé gave me his word that he would bring me Excalibur. I gave him my word that I would release you in return. I have what I want – there is no need for more violence.'

'Maybe you should've thought of that before you sent your little gang of psychos out to get it,' Chase snarled, with a hate-filled glance at Kruglov.

'If Jack had not been working against me, I would not have had to. He is as much to blame for what has happened as I am. For what it's worth, I regret the loss of life.'

'What, and you think saying sorry makes everything all right?' said Nina bitterly. 'You hypocritical bastard. Just because you send other people to do your dirty work doesn't mean your own hands are clean!'

But Vaskovich was no longer listening, his attention focused on the gauge. 0.68 . . . 0.69 . . . More electrical flares lit up the huge chamber, the hum of the machinery rising in pitch. 0.71 . . .

0.72 . . .

'It works!' Vaskovich cried, elated. The gauge now read 0.73, and kept climbing. He rushed over to one of the consoles, speaking in rapid, excited Russian to the technician. Despite herself, Nina found herself becoming caught up in the moment, willing the reading higher. It passed 0.90, 0.91. Vaskovich hurried back and leaned intently over the console, the digital figures reflected in his glasses. 0.96, 0.97 . . .

It stopped.

The gauge remained constant at 0.97. Vaskovich's face fell in confusion, then anger. He shouted an order to the technicians, jerking his hands upwards in an unmistakable 'More!' gesture. One of the men shook his head.

'What's wrong?' Nina asked.

'I don't know.' Vaskovich darted from console to console, shoving the technicians aside to work the controls himself, with the same lack of results. 'It should be working. The superconductor is channelling earth energy into the system – why isn't it working?'

'I know,' said a voice from above.

Everyone looked up to see Mitchell standing on top of the generator's frame, having descended by rope through one of the dome's louvres. He aimed his gun at Vaskovich, and fired.

28

The window shattered. Vaskovich's right thigh erupted with bloody holes as bullets ripped into it. The oligarch collapsed, screaming.

Chase was already moving, shoving Nina towards the ladder. 'Go!' he yelled, despite being unsure if there was another way out of the generator chamber. To reach the door of the control room she would have to pass Kruglov and Maximov, and he wanted to give Mitchell a clear field of fire.

Another burst of gunfire took out two of the technicians at their consoles as Mitchell descended the rope. Chase ran to pull him in through the broken window.

Nina scrambled down the ladder. Kruglov saw her go, pulled out his black-bladed knife and raced after her. She jumped to the catwalk below and looked round. A third of the way anticlockwise round the catwalk a walkway led to a passage set in the vast pit's concrete wall. She ran for it as Kruglov leapt down behind her.

Chase hauled Mitchell into the control room. The American fired the XM-201 again, a rapid sweep of shots killing another technician and taking down three of the guards. Maximov threw himself into the cover of another console as bullets seared past him.

'You miss me?' Mitchell asked. He indicated his shoulder: the second rifle was attached to the harness on his back. 'Brought something for you – oh, shit, look out!'

'Fuck!' Chase dived one way, Mitchell the other, as the console Maximov had been hiding behind was hurled through the window between them and crashed down into the pit. The huge Russian charged at them. Mitchell managed to get off another shot, blasting a chunk of shredded meat from Maximov's upper arm.

It didn't even slow him. Instead, he grinned and seized Mitchell in his massive hands, slamming him to the floor.

Chase jumped up. Mitchell was pinned down by Maximov – and both rifles were trapped beneath him.

And there was still another guard to deal with.

The surviving technicians were running for the exit, but the guard barrelled straight at Chase, intending to shoulder-barge him out of the broken window. Chase held his ground. He waited until the Russian was almost upon him, then feinted to the left. The guard instinctively moved to intercept him—

Chase instead ducked right, swinging a hammer-blow punch that smashed into the man's jaw. The guard reeled, throwing out his hands to stop his fall – only to impale his palms on the spears of glass. He fell through the window, dropping past Kruglov to plunge screaming into the depths of the pit.

Nina heard the terrified yell and looked back, fearful that it had been Chase. It only took a glimpse of the falling figure to see that it wasn't, but that glimpse also told her Kruglov was gaining. She raced for the walkway leading to the opening.

Chase ran back to help Mitchell. Maximov was choking him, thumping his head repeatedly against the floor. Lacking weapons, Chase snatched up a chair and smashed it over the Russian's broad back. The chair broke apart, pieces scattering, but Maximov just let out a grunting laugh.

'All right,' Chase growled, 'how about *this*?' He delivered a brutal kick to one of the giant's kidneys.

On anyone else it would have decisively ended the fight, but instead Maximov's back arched with pleasure. '*Daaaaaa!*' he gasped, insane smile widening in ecstasy.

Mitchell was turning blue, and Chase was out of ideas . . .

Wait!

If Maximov felt pain as pleasure, then . . .

'Can't believe I'm doing this,' Chase muttered as he moved behind Maximov and reached down to his sides, fingers outstretched – to tickle him.

It was as if the Russian had received an electric shock. He released his grip on Mitchell's throat and jumped to his feet, face twisted in rage. 'That hurt, little man!'

Chase backed away. On the floor, Mitchell gasped for air, moving weakly. The XM-201 lay across his stomach. *Come on, shoot the bastard!* 'No wonder you always look so fucking grumpy,' Chase said, trying to keep Maximov's attention off the gun. 'Must feel like a kick in the bollocks every time you have a wank.'

Through the window he saw Nina running along the catwalk, with Kruglov not far behind. Mitchell, groaning, rolled on his side . . . and the gun slid to the floor, forgotten as its owner struggled to breathe. *Shit!*

Chase looked from the rifle to Nina, to Kruglov, then back to Maximov. He was out of time. 'Ah, fuck it!' he spat as he launched himself at the Russian, ducking under his grasping hands to smash a fist into his stomach, hitting him again and again. 'This'll put a fucking smile on your face!'

'*Da*, little man!' bellowed Maximov, the sheer fury of Chase's attack actually forcing him backwards. He raised one arm, hand clenching into a fist. '*Do!*' The hand slammed on to Chase's back. '*It!*' Another blow knocked him to his knees. '*Again!*' The final punch dropped him to the floor.

Winded, Chase looked up through pain-filled eyes, and saw Mitchell struggling to all fours behind Maximov. The gun lay beside him, still forgotten.

But Maximov didn't know that . . .

Chase tipped his head back further, and smiled up at the Russian. Maximov stopped, confused. 'If you like pain,' Chase wheezed, 'you'll love this! Jack, *now*!'

Maximov's eyes widened. He whirled, expecting to see Mitchell pointing his gun at him.

Instead, he found the American kneeling at his feet.

Chase sprang up and rammed his shoulder against Maximov's backside, driving him forward. The huge Russian staggered, tripping over Mitchell – and toppled through the window. He fell past the first catwalk to bounce off the second level with such force that the walkway buckled, plunging into a nest of cables beneath it. He jerked to a stop, hanging upside down by one entangled leg, barely conscious.

Mitchell managed to stand, picking up his rifle. 'What happened?'

Chase didn't have the time or the inclination to explain. 'Give me a gun!' he snapped instead. Nina had just disappeared into a side corridor, Kruglov right behind her. Mitchell pulled the second XM-201 from his back. Chase grabbed it from him and ran painfully for the ladder.

'Eddie!' called Mitchell in a warning tone. Chase looked back to see him pointing at one of the large rings inside the still running generator. 'Don't damage the magnets!'

'What'll happen?'

'Bad things!'

'Good tip,' Chase said with a crooked smile before dropping down the ladder.

Nina ran along the concrete corridor to find herself in a room – with no exit. It was a storage area, the striped red-and-yellow line on the floor indicating the limit of the generator's magnetic field. Beyond it, at the far end of the room, was a rack of firefighting and other emergency equipment. Some of it appeared to be made of steel; presumably other, non-magnetic alternative metals were either unsuitable or too expensive.

She rushed to it and grabbed a fire axe. Kruglov's running footsteps behind her changed from the clang of the walkway to the flat slap of concrete. He was in the passage—

Nina spun and hurled the heavy axe at the entrance. It arced down, falling short of Kruglov – then suddenly changed direction in defiance of gravity as it crossed the painted line, instantly picking up speed and shooting down the corridor. Kruglov dived sideways with a startled yelp, the axe barely missing him as the intense magnetic field snatched it into the generator chamber. It slammed against one of the rings of electromagnets with an echoing bang.

She shook off her momentary amazement, looking for another weapon, but Kruglov was already back on his feet, the matte-black knife in his outstretched hand as he ran at her. '*Suka!*' he hissed.

Nina doubted it was a compliment. She tried to back away, but had nowhere to go. Trapped, she brought up her hands to protect herself. Kruglov sneered, moving closer – and Nina swung at him, managing to land a glancing punch against his chin as he jerked away in surprise. 'Yeah, fuck you too!'

Kruglov blew out an angry breath, then lunged again. She tried to twist his knife hand away from her, as Chase had taught her, but the Russian was ready. As Nina grabbed his wrist, he spun and drove his other elbow against her jaw. She cried out in pain, dazed. Kruglov wrenched his arm from her weakened grip, and cracked the haft of his knife down on the back of her head.

She staggered. Kruglov pulled her up in a choke-hold, pressing the knife against her ribs. He dragged her back down the corridor.

Chase stopped running and brought up his gun as Kruglov emerged from the passage, Nina held in front of him as a shield. He looked through the rifle's sight, trying to line up the crosshairs on the Russian's head. But Kruglov was a constantly shifting target behind his hostage – and Chase couldn't see where he was holding his knife. Even if he hit him, Nina might still be fatally wounded.

Kruglov reached the catwalk and slowly backed away around it. Chase advanced on him. 'Let her go, dickhead!'

'We've done this before, haven't we?' Kruglov responded with a cold smirk. 'You know I am willing to kill her. So drop the gun.'

Chase came to a standstill near the catwalk junction. He stood for a moment, the rifle still fixed on Kruglov . . . then tossed it to land at Nina's feet. She stared in shock at his surrender.

Kruglov glanced at the high-tech weapon. 'One of Mitchell's toys? I look forward to killing him with it.' He quickly slipped the knife back into its sheath and pulled Nina with him as he bent to pick up the gun. 'But you first.'

He groped for the rifle, eyes flicking down – and in the split second he was looking away, Chase winked at Nina. She looked back, confused, but already preparing herself for whatever happened next.

Kruglov straightened, the gun in his hand. Smile widening, he pointed it at Chase and pulled the trigger.

Nothing happened.

He tried again. The trigger clicked faintly, but the rifle remained inert. His smugness changed to anger as he realised he'd been tricked.

Nina took advantage of his distraction to twist and ram the point of her left elbow into his stomach. Kruglov jerked back, losing his grip on her.

Chase ran to tackle him. Kruglov batted Nina aside with the rifle, slamming her against the catwalk railing. His free hand swept over the gun, hunting for a safety catch or some other release mechanism—

It found the firing button for the grenade launcher.

Chase was still several feet away. He had no idea if the grenade launcher also had a biometric lock – Mitchell certainly hadn't programmed one with his handprint.

And the flash of uncertainty on his face was all Kruglov needed to know he still had a chance . . .

The Russian whipped up the XM-201 and fired just as Chase hurled himself on to the walkway leading to the storeroom. The grenade shot past him. It hit the main catwalk some fifteen feet away and exploded, ripping apart an entire section and sending it crashing down into the pit below.

The blast sent Chase reeling, almost flipping him over the safety railing. The grenade might have been small, but it was still powerful, enough to take down a wall. He looked back. Nina was pulling herself upright; Kruglov had an expression of almost maniacal glee on his face as he realised the full power of the weapon. 'Nina! Get to Jack!' Chase shouted, sprinting down the passage towards the storeroom entrance as the ex-KGB agent lined up a second shot—

Concrete shattered just behind him, knocking him off his feet. He hit the floor hard, bouncing over the painted line to end up sprawled before the equipment rack. Coughing, ears ringing, Chase looked round, and saw the room was a dead end.

A silhouette appeared in the entrance, shrouded in dust. Kruglov. And he knew Chase had no way out.

Chase stood to challenge him anyway. 'Fight to the end,' he told himself. He reached into the rack, hunting for a weapon, even if it was just a club.

He realised what some of the equipment was made from . . .

'I like this gun,' said Kruglov. 'It even has a little screen telling me how many bullets I have left. And how many grenades. I see I have . . . one. That should be enough.'

Chase faced him as he emerged from the drifting cloud of concrete dust, watching his expression intently. 'Well, you'd better use it, then. 'Cause if you don't, I'm going to shove it up your arsehole and pull the trigger.'

Kruglov merely smiled his oily, frog-like smile one last time. 'If you insist.'

His eyes narrowed in anticipation of the shot, finger tightening on the firing button—

Chase dived to one side.

The grenade barely missed him, streaking between the shelves to explode against the wall. The rack blew apart, equipment flying across the room—

Over the painted line.

The spinning pieces of steel all suddenly accelerated in mid-air, yanked inexorably towards the powerful magnets in the chamber outside – with Kruglov in their path.

The Russian screamed as the tools hit him, screwdrivers stabbing deep into his flesh, larger items smashing against him with bone-cracking force and sweeping him backwards down the passage. With a final cry he slammed against the generator – only for the cylindrical fire extinguisher that had buried its end in his abdomen to continue onwards and burst out of his back. Spewing blood, Kruglov slithered down the length of the cylinder impaling him, before gravity reclaimed its hold. He fell into the pit, smashing off the middle catwalk and spinning down to the bottom with a decisive crack of bones.

Chase didn't hear it; in fact, he couldn't hear anything except a disorienting clamour in both ears, the grenade explosion having all but deafened him. He opened his eyes to find himself crumpled almost upside down in a corner. A spanner was embedded in the wall just above him. Lumps of smashed concrete and pieces of equipment were scattered across the room.

He flopped on to his side and weakly clicked his fingers next to one ear. On the third try, he thought he heard a faint snap through the ringing. At least he hadn't been permanently deafened.

Kruglov was dead – but was Nina safe? He pulled himself upright and shakily crossed the room. The XM-201 lay in the passageway. He picked it up, then staggered along the walkway.

Kruglov's first grenade shot had destroyed a large section of the catwalk, too much for him to jump the gap; he would have to go the long way round to return to the control room. Nina looked down at him through the broken window. She shouted excitedly, but Chase had no idea what she was saying. He yelled what he hoped was 'I'm okay!' to her, then began the long plod round the catwalk.

'Looks like he's all right!' Nina told Mitchell, who was crouching beside the wounded Vaskovich.

'Great,' Mitchell replied, with an odd lack of enthusiasm. 'So, Leonid – you want to know why your system didn't work?'

Vaskovich, clutching his wounded leg, glared up at him through pain-clenched eyes. 'Go to hell.'

'Afraid I'm on the side of the angels. Seriously, though, aren't you curious?' He gestured at the generator, still flickering with bursts of electrical energy. 'You were so close, your people made it work despite all the disinformation I was feeding you about DARPA's system. And you even got Excalibur, you got the superconductor. But there was one thing you were missing, which even I didn't know about until we found the sword in England. Want to know what it was?'

'What?' Vaskovich gasped.

To Nina's shock, Mitchell pointed at her. '*She's* what you were missing. She's the key to making the whole thing work. Something about her body's bio-electric field – I'm not sure exactly what, but we'll figure it out. But without her to energise the sword, all you've got is a nice shiny antique.' He stood. 'Anyway, now you know.'

And before Nina realised what was happening, he shot Vaskovich in the heart. The Russian convulsed, then fell back, dead.

'Jesus Christ!' Nina screamed. 'What the hell are you *doing?*'

'My job,' he told her emotionlessly. 'The whole purpose of this mission was to terminate Vaskovich's operations, and secure Excalibur.'

'You knew all along,' she said, anger growing as her shock subsided. 'You *knew* he didn't build this place to use as a weapon.'

'Of course I knew.' He lowered the rifle and stepped over Vaskovich's body towards her, reaching into a pocket.

'Then why did you have to kill him? And all these other people?'

'Because we can't allow anyone but us to have this technology – for any purpose.'

'You've got your own system, haven't you?' she realised. 'DARPA's built a generator just like this one.'

'We have,' said Mitchell. He looked out of the window, seeing Chase about two-thirds of the way round the catwalk. 'Only problem is, it doesn't work either. But it soon will. Eddie! Eddie, can you hear me?'

The noise in Chase's ears had subsided enough for him to pick out his own name, even if the rest of Mitchell's words were unclear. He stopped and looked at the control room, cupping a hand to his ear to indicate that he had trouble hearing.

'Looks like he's a bit deaf,' said Mitchell. 'Let's see if he can hear *this*.'

He raised his rifle again, and fired.

Deafened or not, Chase could still tell when someone was about to shoot at him. He threw himself back out of the line of fire as a burst of explosive bullets detonated against the catwalk, spitting fragments of metal.

Nina lunged at Mitchell to knock the gun away. His left hand clapped against her arm and she felt a sharp stab of pain, followed by a spreading coldness. He pulled back his hand, revealing a plastic disc at the base of his middle finger held in place by a ring. A short spike protruded from its centre, smeared with her blood.

She stumbled back, numbness taking hold of her limbs. 'What – what've you done?'

'I need you to do something for me,' he said, his voice seeming to come from the end of a long pipe. 'But I didn't think you'd do it voluntarily.'

'You son of a . . .' she managed, before her knees buckled. She hit the floor, but didn't feel it, as darkness consumed her senses.

29

In cover behind one of the generator's supports, Chase cautiously peered at the control room, and saw Nina fall out of sight. 'Fucker!' he hissed, aiming at Mitchell and pulling the trigger.

No response. He switched to a different ammunition and tried again. Still nothing.

Mitchell shouted something. He strained to hear. 'IFF, Eddie!' called Mitchell, holding up his XM-201. 'You can't shoot at anyone carrying one of these! *You* can't, anyway – I disabled the lockouts on mine—'

Before he could finish, Chase aimed *above* the American and unleashed a stream of explosive bullets into the control room ceiling. The digital ammo counter fell from twenty to zero in little more than a second, the rifle vibrating in his hands like a chainsaw. Mitchell dived away from the rain of debris. Chase tracked him, switching to armour-piercing rounds in the hope that the gun's sensors would be blocked by the low wall at the base of the window and let him shoot Mitchell through it, but the weapon just clicked uselessly.

The screen suddenly flashed red. A pungent burning smell hit Chase's nostrils, and he tossed down the gun as acrid black smoke gushed out of it, the polymer frame sizzling and blistering. Mitchell had remotely activated the weapon's self-destruct, reducing its electronics to molten slag.

He ducked back behind the support, waiting for Mitchell to return fire now that he was defenceless. Nothing happened. An electrical flash from above, and he knew why – a line of electromagnets ran down the other side of the column. Mitchell was serious about not wanting to damage them.

Which might give him a chance to reach the control room. If he stayed close enough to—

A muffled thump gave him an instant's warning, just enough time to shield his face before a grenade blew out another section of catwalk ahead of him. Chase was knocked on his back by the blast. He scrambled back behind the protection of the magnets and saw he was completely cut off from the control room, trapped on the severed walkway.

Mitchell surveyed the scene, looking satisfied. He moved back across the control room and hoisted Nina over his shoulder.

Chase thought he was going to take her to the exit, but instead he climbed down the ladder to the same level as the Englishman, then boarded the little elevator leading to the bottom of the pit. Still carrying Nina, he began his descent.

Chase watched, powerless to stop them. He eyed the generator again. The vertical supports were separated from the magnetic rings by heavy-duty insulators, but he had no idea how much power was flowing through the rings themselves – and they were the only way he could reach the catwalk beneath the control room. One wrong step, and he would be fried.

The elevator passed the dangling, semi-conscious Maximov and reached the bottom of the pit. Kruglov's body lay to one side, but in the centre was the frame holding Excalibur. Mitchell carried Nina over to it. He put down his rifle, then manoeuvred her into position next to the sword. Taking hold of her wrist, he crouched, holding out her hand to touch the hilt . . .

'No!' Chase yelled, afraid she'd be electrocuted, but too late. Mitchell squeezed her limp fingers around the sword—

There was a dazzling flash of blue light as Excalibur glowed brilliantly. Above Chase, the size and frequency of the electrical arcs suddenly increased.

His eyes squeezed almost shut against the glare, Mitchell nevertheless kept his grip on Nina's hand. 'What do you think, Eddie?' he shouted, barely audible against the rising hum of the machinery. 'Pretty cool, huh?'

'What the fuck are you doing?'

'I'm making Vaskovich's system work. Too bad he didn't get to see it, but hey!' He lifted Nina's hand from the sword; the glow instantly vanished, but the noise of the generator remained constant. 'Yes! It's passed the threshold – I was right!'

He lowered Nina to the floor, then shrugged off his flat backpack and opened it. Inside was another piece of metal, which Chase recognised as the largest section of Caliburn. Mitchell carefully slid the broken blade into the frame next to Excalibur, the two swords touching. Then he brought Nina's hand back up to touch Excalibur. It glowed brilliantly once more – and Caliburn lit up too, though much less brightly. The electrical hum began to rise again.

Mitchell withdrew Nina's hand. The blue light disappeared, but the noise of the generator continued to climb. He grabbed Excalibur by the hilt and yanked it out of the system, leaving Caliburn in its place. The roiling electrical discharges kept flashing across the dome. He put the sword in his pack and pulled it over his shoulders, then bent to lift Nina, took up his rifle and returned to the elevator.

'Gonna have to say goodbye, Eddie,' he said when he reached the top level. 'It's nothing personal, but I can't leave anybody who knows what I was doing.'

'I honestly fucking don't!' Chase shouted back, keeping behind cover. 'So, you going to shoot me?'

'In a way. This whole place really is only one step away from being a weapon – the antenna array can draw in power, but it can also pump it out. Millions of watts of it. Now there's a superconductor in place – not as effective as Excalibur, but it'll do – and the reaction's become self-sustaining, the system will just keep on drawing in more and more earth energy. I'm going to let it all out – in one blast.'

'You're going to blow the place up?'

'Might as well get some empirical data for DARPA's own system! I'll set the array to heat up the ionosphere directly above, then fire the system's entire output into it – and the focused earth energy will bounce straight back down and destroy the whole facility.'

'Nice and neat,' Chase said sarcastically. 'What about Nina?'

'I'm taking her with me – I need her alive. At least, until I find someone else who can make the effect work. So long, Eddie.' He clambered back up the ladder, carrying Nina.

'Shit!' Chase searched desperately for some other way out of the generator room. Nothing presented itself. Above, he caught occasional glimpses of Mitchell as he operated the consoles. The intensity of the flashes above him increased, electrical bolts coiling across the machinery like liquid snakes.

He ran to the end of the broken catwalk. A twisted section across the gap hung down, a drooping tongue of grillework protruding from it. He might just be able to reach it . . .

He hurried back to give himself a run-up. A glance at the control room: Mitchell was no longer in sight. Was he still programming the system, or already fleeing with Nina?

Her name spurred Chase on. He ran. The floor clanged beneath him as he reached the edge of the damaged section and leapt across . . .

Falling . . .

Falling short.

He threw out his arms, clawed hands smashing painfully against the hanging section. One slipped away – the other hooked into the grille. For a moment he swung as the catwalk section buckled under his weight.

Then the whole thing tore loose and plunged into the pit.

The mid-level catwalk flashed past—

The plummeting walkway section crashed against it. The impact flipped him round, tearing loose his hold on the grillework and tossing him under the catwalk, still falling.

He hit a bundle of cables, tried to wrap his arms round it, failed. His hands slipped over the thick insulation, each successive line popping from his grip and bringing him ever closer to his death beside Kruglov below . . .

He caught the last cable.

Pain seared through his shoulder as he jerked to a stop. The cable bounced above him, shaking him like a doll. Gasping, Chase managed to bring up his other arm and secure himself with both hands.

For all the good it did him. He was still hanging over eighty feet up with nothing but concrete and metal to break his fall – and a countdown to destruction already ticking away above.

'Well, this isn't good,' he muttered.

Much to his surprise, he got a response: a groan. He twisted to see Maximov still hanging by one leg in another skein of cables above and to one side. The huge Russian blinked blearily, then focused on him – and his face twisted with upside-down fury. '*You!*'

'Yeah, me,' Chase said. 'Oh, shit,' he added as Maximov reached down, stretching for the cables beneath him.

His hand wrapped round the topmost of the bunch. 'You try to kill me. Now I kill you!'

'Nonono, *shit!*' Chase yelped as Maximov tugged at the cables, trying to shake him loose. 'This whole place is about to blow up!'

Maximov replied with what from his tone could only be the Russian equivalent of 'Yeah, whatever', pulling the cables harder.

'No, listen, you stupid bastard!' Chase cried with growing desperation as his hold began to slip. 'Mitchell's fucking betrayed us all!'

'Ha! Serve you right for trusting him!'

One of Chase's hands was jolted loose. 'Whoa, fuck!' he gasped. The pit whirled below him. He tried to regain his grip, but couldn't reach the juddering cable. 'Vaskovich is dead!' he shouted desperately, running out of ideas. 'And if you don't get out of here soon, you'll be dead too!'

That got a reaction, Maximov pausing mid-shake. 'The boss is dead?'

'Mitchell killed him! The whole thing was a set-up – he's killed everyone to cover his tracks. We're the only ones left – but if we don't get out of here, we'll be dead too! Look!' He pointed frantically up at the furious auroral display flashing across the dome. 'It's going to fucking explode any minute!'

Maximov's expression went from anger to concern. 'You not lying?'

'No, I'm not fucking lying! We're both going to *die* unless we help each other!'

'If I help you, how do I know you will help me?'

'You're ex-Spetsnaz, right? Special forces? I'm ex-SAS – special forces. Same job, just different bosses! You'd trust your squad mates – so trust me, please!'

The Russian considered this, sluggish thought processes almost visible on his face. Finally: 'What you want me to do?'

'Pull me up! Then I can climb up to the catwalk and pull *you* up!'

Another agonisingly slow moment of thought. 'Okay. I help you. But if you don't help me, I kill you! Even if I have to rise out of grave to do it!'

'Just pull me up, for fuck's sake!' With the cable no longer being shaken, Chase was able to reach it with his other hand. Maximov waited until he had a firm grip, then strained to lift the heavy skein until Chase could reach across and pull himself up the cables in the larger bundle above.

'Okay, let it go!' he ordered. Maximov released the cables. They dropped back down, and Chase braced his feet against them. With a foothold, it was a relatively easy task for him to scale the tangle of wiring until he reached the stability of the mid-level catwalk.

The vertical track of the elevator was not far away. He looked at Maximov, still entangled below. Part of his mind reminded him that he would have a much better chance of escaping alive if he left now, alone.

He ignored it. He'd given his word.

A metal bar lay on the floor a few feet away, a broken piece of the fallen catwalk. Chase grabbed it and ducked under the railing, extending the bar out below him with one hand as he gripped the handrail with the other. 'Hold this!' he shouted. The noise of the generator had risen to a piercing screech, energy crackling back and forth across the dome.

Maximov bent at the waist, trying to reach up for the bar. Chase strained to bring the end closer to his grasping fingers. He was just short, barely two inches away. 'Come on!'

'Can't – reach!' gasped Maximov, tendons bulging in his neck. He was so overmuscled that his own body was limiting his movement, unable to crunch any tighter.

'Can't reach?' Chase's voice changed to a mocking drill-instructor bark. 'Yes, you *can* reach, you great Russian pansy! Spetsnaz? *Shit*snaz, more like! Bunch of fur-hatted nancy boys, poncing about in the snow—'

With an enraged growl, Maximov lunged upwards, and his hand clamped round the end of the bar. 'Ha! Yes!' Chase cried, pulling back with all his strength to lift the Russian. Maximov gripped the railing, then reached down to unravel the wiring round his ankle before climbing on to the catwalk.

Chase ran to the elevator controls and hammered at the call button. The platform began to descend. 'Come on, come on!' he called to the Russian. 'Sorry about the Shitsnaz thing, by the way.'

'No problem,' Maximov rumbled. 'But maybe one day I tell you what we say SAS stands for, eh?'

The platform arrived; they jumped aboard even before it stopped, pounding at the controls. After an apparent eternity, it ascended again. Electrical arcs flashed past them, the very air seeming to tremble as the power built up.

They reached the top catwalk. Chase leapt from the elevator and rushed up the ladder to the control room, Maximov right behind him. Mitchell had gone, and so had Nina. The only people in the room were corpses.

And two soon-to-be corpses if they didn't get out, fast. *'Leg it!'* Chase yelled.

They raced through the checkpoint, Chase flicking an anguished look at the locker holding his belongings before running on to the doors, the darkness outside now pierced by unearthly flashes of light. They crashed through them and sprinted out into the cold.

The funicular station was ahead. The car they had ridden up in was gone, its empty counterpart just arriving at the summit on the adjacent track. Beyond it, great fluid coils of energy danced over the hundreds of antennas on the hillside, sparks spitting from their tips. He could see his own shadow ahead of him, not cast by the spotlights around the facility but by something far brighter, less stable, more deadly.

It was about to blow—

Chase reached the crest of the hill and dived headlong over it. With a blinding flash and an earth-shaking crack of thunder a wall of lightning blazed directly upwards from the antenna array, a sheath of unimaginable energy surrounding the entire facility.

The flash lasted only a moment, many of the antennas melting, but as Chase rolled down the scrubby hillside he was already protecting his ears, knowing there was more to come.

A spear of intense blue-white light lanced down from the heavens into the dome, which exploded into splinters as the beam seared through it to hit the machinery below.

All the remaining earth energy still in the system was released at once. The generator disintegrated, the force of the blast shattering the concrete walls of the pit and ripping a massive crater out of the hilltop. The circular building above was pulverised, the shockwave reducing the entire structure to rubble in a split second and hurling it outwards in a huge swelling ring of destruction.

The force of the blast hit Chase through the ground itself, a colossal *whump* from within the hill knocking him into the air in a shower of soil and stones. He landed hard on a leg of the road below amidst a blizzard of churned earth, having just enough time to realise that he was almost beneath the steeply sloping trackbed of the funicular and roll into whatever protection it offered before the shattered remains of the generator building fell round him.

A cloud of choking dust swirled downhill. The ground shook again, a continuous bone-shaking drumming like an artillery barrage as debris smashed down all around.

Then it began to fade.

The rain of rubble fell to a drizzle. Chase sat up and coughed, squinting through the dust as the cold wind from the coast gradually wafted it away. The entire hillside was spotted with fires where molten metal from the twisted, blackened antennas had dripped on to the grass.

He stepped out from beneath the track. The slope above him was shorn to the bare earth, the topsoil and grass blown loose by the explosion. Below, the lights of the dock still shone brightly. The submarine pen had been built to withstand anything short of a direct nuclear strike. There were other lights closer to him: a vehicle on a lower leg of the road, lying on its side.

He heard a muffled Russian curse. 'Hey!' Chase shouted, scrambling down the hillside to the source of the swearing. 'Thingy, Bulldozer! You okay?'

Maximov was slumped against one of the track's supporting girders, covered in dirt. He dizzily raised his head and peered at Chase. 'Oh. Is you.'

'Can you move? Are you hurt?'

He grinned. '*Da*. What was that? It was like . . . fire from God!'

'It wasn't God, it was Mitchell. But I'm going to kick his arse straight *to* God when I catch him. You still with me?'

Maximov nodded, and Chase helped him stand. 'What are we doing?'

'Going after Mitchell. He's kidnapped Nina and stolen the sword – and I'm not going to let that bastard have either of 'em. Come on.'

They picked their way down the hillside between the fires and warped antennas, following the funicular railway. The sea breeze had by now cleared most of the dust, giving Chase a better view of the base. He saw movement on the jetty.

'Shit!' Even though the figures were only tiny at this distance, Chase knew there was only one person who would be carrying another over his shoulder – especially when the person being carried had long red hair.

It was clear where Mitchell was taking her. A couple of small boats were moored at the far end of the wooden pier. The DARPA agent's escape route wasn't by air, it was by sea.

He had to go after him – or stop him from leaving with her.

'We'll never catch him!' Maximov said, but Chase was already thinking otherwise as they reached the overturned car. It was another Mercedes GL Class, a man whom he recognised as one of the control room technicians hanging bloodily through the broken windscreen. He had escaped Mitchell's onslaught and tried to drive to safety, only for the SUV to be flipped over by the subterranean shockwave. As they got closer he realised the engine was still running, fumes putt-putting from the exhaust.

'How strong are you?' he asked the Russian. 'Are you like Arnold Schwarzenegger strong?'

'Arnie? He is girlie-man compared to me!' Maximov said proudly, flexing his massive arms.

'Great! Then you can help me tip this thing back over!'

They reached the Mercedes, Chase grabbing the front wing and Maximov taking hold of the back as they forced the two-ton SUV back on to its wheels. 'You will never get there in time. The road is too long,' Maximov protested as the vehicle tipped over and bounced upright.

Chase opened the dented door and dragged out the driver's corpse. 'We don't need roads.' He climbed in and fastened the seatbelt. The cabin was strewn with broken glass and the airbags hung limply from their compartments, but everything else appeared to be working. 'Coming?'

Maximov squeezed into the Mercedes and gave Chase an uncertain look. 'Can we make it?'

'We have to.' Mitchell was now about a third of the way down the jetty. Chase pointed the SUV down the hill. 'Let's off-road!'

He stamped on the accelerator.

The Mercedes leapt off the edge of the road and bounded down the steep, bumpy hillside. Chase yanked the wheel back and forth to guide it through the antenna forest.

The next leg of the road was coming up fast. Chase swerved, hitting the frost-cracked asphalt in a shower of soil. The SUV shot over the edge of the embankment, airborne for a moment . . . then slammed down on top of the funicular line.

He aimed the car straight down the steel track. Maximov swore again, bracing himself against the dashboard. Chase glanced at the jittering speedo. Over sixty kilometres an hour and quickly picking up speed – and his foot wasn't even on the accelerator.

But he couldn't slow down, not yet. Mitchell was now over halfway along the jetty with Nina.

The track was perfectly straight, heading to a vanishing point at the bottom of the tunnel. The semicircle of light was partially obscured by a dark box – the funicular car, blocking his path. And there was a gap between the two tracks, making it impossible for him to swing into the open lane.

He looked to the side. Just before the tunnel was a concrete expanse running to the edge of the cliff. Some kind of fuel storage, tall cylindrical tanks lined up along it.

No choice—

Now he braked, pushing the pedal down as hard as he could and turning sharply. Tyres and brake discs shrieked in unison. There was a horrific bang as the wheels crossed the steel track, then the GL Class was clear, slithering sidelong down the rough slope before flattening a chain-link fence and hitting the concrete so hard it almost flipped over.

Chase frantically spun the wheel to apply opposite lock. The SUV wavered on two wheels for a moment before thumping back down on all four – heading right for one of the fuel tanks.

He yanked the wheel back the other way. The Mercedes

skidded, spinning round . . . and stopped. It was actually touching the white-painted tank, the door panel bent inwards.

Maximov winced when he saw how close they had been to an explosive collision. 'Next time, I drive.'

'No, this is where you get out,' said Chase. 'Unless you want to go swimming.' He jerked a thumb towards the low wooden fence at the edge of the cliff.

Maximov's eyes widened. 'You are mad!'

Chase threw open his door. 'Mad? I'm fuckin' *furious*!' He quickly reversed past another fuel tank, and sliced the door off the Mercedes with a crunch of tearing metal. 'Seriously – out!'

The Russian had no further arguments, hurriedly flinging open his own door and rolling out. Chase didn't even wait for him to close it, instead slamming the SUV into gear and flooring the accelerator. The tanks flicked past as he picked up speed, the black sea coming into view over the edge of the cliff.

As did the lights at the end of the jetty.

Chase adjusted his course, aiming straight for them – then ploughed the Mercedes through the flimsy fence and off the edge of the cliff at over eighty kilometres an hour.

He threw himself out as the GL Class rolled in mid-air, the water rushing up fast. He had barely enough time to twist into a dive before hitting the freezing sea just short of the jetty.

The SUV continued onwards without him. A fraction

of a second after Chase splashed down, it nose-dived into the pier and exploded, blasting the end of the wooden structure to pieces – and cutting the shocked Mitchell off from the boats, knocking him on his butt less than thirty feet away.

He dumped the unconscious Nina on the planks and jumped up, staring in disbelief at the burning wreckage before looking at the water. Only one person could have been driving the SUV. 'Eddie!' he roared, unslinging the XM-201 and running to the jetty's edge to point the weapon at the expanding splash below. 'Fuck you, Eddie! *Fuck you!*'

Stunned by the cold, Chase was only just struggling to the surface when the water above him erupted with sizzling spears of metal and froth. Cheeks bulging as he held in his breath, he desperately swam back downwards as Mitchell kept firing into the dark water. The 3.6mm bullets only reached a depth of a few feet before the water slowed them to a non-lethal speed, but they were still hot, a couple like cigarette burns against his shoulders.

Mitchell exhausted the twenty rounds in his current load. He was about to switch the gun to different ammo when he remembered he had something more powerful.

Chase was already expecting it. He swam deeper, heading for shore as fast as he could—

The 25mm grenade smacked into the water, sank four feet deep – and detonated.

A spherical shockwave blasted outwards at the speed of sound. Its upper half reached the surface in a fraction of a second, sending a huge plume of white spray into the air. Beneath the surface, the shockwave continued to expand, much more powerful and deadly in dense liquid than in air.

However fast he swam, Chase had no chance of outrunning the blast. A grenade tossed into a swimming pool could kill everyone in it through hydrostatic shock alone – his only chance of survival was to be moving directly away from the epicentre, feet towards it to spread out the impact along his body, as the shockwave swept past him. If it hit him squarely, he would be dead, organs ruptured . . .

The blow was horrific, a crushing pressure pummelling him from all sides and knocking him into an uncontrollable tumble. Air was forced from his lungs. He spun limply into the darkness.

Above, Mitchell surveyed the foaming surface for any sign of life. Nothing. He waited a little longer to be sure, then shouldered his rifle, picked up Nina, and hurried back towards the submarine dock.

30

Chase had no idea which way was up. Freezing salt water stung his eyes as he forced them open. No sign of any lights showing the way to the surface, nothing to be heard except the hiss of billions of tiny air bubbles swirling around him.

He was running out of air. In the SAS, he had been able to hold his breath underwater for over five minutes, but without regular training his capacity would have decreased, and he didn't know how much air the explosion had driven out of him. All he knew was that there wasn't much left, pressure rising in his chest and his heart beating faster . . .

A new noise – a deep, booming splash. Close by. *Mitchell's last grenade.* He braced himself for the explosion—

It didn't come. Instead a huge hand locked round his arm and pulled him to the surface. He burst out of the water, gasping for air, and saw the grinning Maximov beside him. 'Did – did you jump off the cliff?'

'If little man like you can do it, hey! No problem for big Russian like me.' He swam for the jetty, pulling Chase after him. 'Mitchell went in the dock with your wife.'

They reached one of the pilings and clung to it. 'She's not my wife. Well, not yet.'

'No? So when is wedding?'

'Why does everyone keep asking that?' His breath regained, Chase climbed up the piling. He heard echoing gunfire from the sub pen – explosive rounds. What was Mitchell shooting at? A few seconds later came a much louder detonation. The last grenade.

Maximov dragged himself from the water. 'What is he doing?'

'Dunno, but we've got to get in there.' Aching all over, Chase shook off some of the water soaking his clothes. The cold sea wind was already slicing through him; if he didn't get into cover soon he'd be at risk of hypothermia.

They limped down the jetty, the pen's brightly lit interior coming into view. The Typhoon's broad black bow rose menacingly above the water, the squat sail set way back behind the ranks of missile tubes. Chase saw people running along the opposite side of the dock. He guessed Mitchell's gunfire had prompted them to flee, but there was no sign of the American himself—

The submarine started moving.

Only slowly at first, but the rising wash of water over its bow was unmistakable as it angled away from the dock. Mooring lines hung limply down the side of the hull – Mitchell had used explosive rounds to sever them.

An echoing crash came from the sub as a gangway slid loose and fell into the water. Further aft, smoke drifted across the dock. The aftermath of the grenade explosion, Chase realised: a bollard had been blown apart, all the lines connected to it shredded.

The Typhoon was free – but Mitchell hadn't cut the power cables running from the sub's reactors through the hole in the hull. They slackened as the submarine slid past the pylon on the dockside, but it wouldn't be long before they pulled taut again.

The vessel's stern came into view, its giant propellers churning up the water on each side of the high rudder. The screws were mounted inside metal rings to shield them from damage by objects in the water, putting paid to Chase's faint hopes of entangling them in the cables.

And his chances of even getting aboard the sub were rapidly diminishing. By the time it drew level, it would be too far from the dockside for him to jump on to the casing – and if he fell in the water, he would be swept into the screws. The protective rings were more than large enough for him to be dragged inside and torn apart.

No way to get aboard . . . except for the crane at the end of the dock.

It was turned away from the submarine, jib pointing along the jetty. But if it could be brought round . . .

'Can you turn this?' Chase asked, running to the crane. Its paint was scabbed with rust, the machine apparently unused for some time. But there was a crank at its base that still seemed to be in fair shape.

'*Da*, but why?'

'Because I need to get on that sub.'

'What if it is too short?'

'Then I'm fucked! Come on, turn it!' He started scaling the rusty frame.

Maximov released the brake, then gripped the crank and strained to turn it. 'It won't move!'

'Shake it loose!'

With a growl, Maximov pushed and pulled at the recalcitrant crank. It screeched horribly, then began to turn. 'It's moving!'

'Great, keep it up!' As Chase ascended, the jib slowly rotated, flecks of rust falling on him like sharp-edged snowflakes. He looked across at the Typhoon. The bow had already passed him, the massive submarine picking up speed.

A crunch of metal echoed inside the pen. Some of the electrical cables had torn loose from the sub, but others were holding firm, the pylon buckling as they were pulled taut. Sparks flew as the cables twisted against each other, then the pylon's legs gave way and the whole thing crashed to the dock, dragged along as the submarine moved into open water.

'Come on, come on!' Chase yelled. The jib had turned through about thirty degrees, but he needed it to go much further. He reached the jib, clambering along its top as Maximov kept working the crank. The Typhoon's missile tubes rolled past below. 'Faster!'

Maximov roared as he pushed harder. The jib picked up

speed, but Chase realised he was out of time. The submarine's sail had almost reached him, and by the time he got to the end of the jib and climbed down the cable the stern would have passed.

Instead he ran along the jib.

One slip and he would fall to his death. But he kept running, feet clanking along the weather-worn metal until he reached the end – and leapt from it, arms and legs still pumping as he flew through the air . . .

Chase slammed against the rear end of the sail, slithering down the steep black wall to crash on to the rounded hump at its base. He rolled painfully down it, ending up skidding on his back down the wet stern. Barely missing the edge of the hole cut in the hull, he picked up speed on the sloping casing, one of the churning propellers rising out of the water just ahead—

His hand bashed against a recess in the hull. He reflexively grabbed it, swinging around with his feet just short of the enormous bronze blades. Freezing spray sluiced over his body. Gasping, he pulled himself forward.

An ominous crack. He looked towards the sail . . .

Another overstretched power cable ripped loose from the reactor. Chase ducked as it whipped over his head and tore a chunk as big as a man out of the rudder before splashing into the sea. The pylon was still being dragged along the dock, sweeping up smaller objects as it went.

It reached the crane. Maximov, who had been watching Chase's battle for survival in frozen fascination, suddenly realised the danger he was in and fled along the jetty as the wrecked pylon crashed into the crane behind him. The Typhoon was now moving at near running pace, the impact shaking the crane to its foundations. Another cable tore free in a shower of sparks – but the remainder were firmly secured, thirty thousand tons of submarine jolting as if it had run into a wall.

With an earsplitting screech, the crane was wrenched from the jetty and toppled over. It fell into the water, pulling the pylon with it. Both broken structures sank, sweeping the cables across the submarine's stern.

Chase pulled himself up and vaulted them as they sliced over the recess. 'Jesus!' he gasped, seeing them pile up against the ring shrouding the propeller. The safety feature had done its job – not that it helped him. The Typhoon was now clear of the dock and heading out to sea at an increasing pace.

He staggered up the stern and reached the gap in the casing. The Typhoon consisted of two long titanium pressure hulls mounted side by side like a catamaran, enclosed in an outer steel shell. Looking down, he saw where the inner hulls had been cut open to facilitate the decommissioned vessel's new life as a mobile nuclear power station, cables running through them. Some of the gaps were large enough for him to fit through. He dropped into the opening.

Behind him, unnoticed, water crept up the stern as the weight of the wreckage being dragged behind the submarine pulled its back end lower and lower, waves sloshing towards the hole in the hull . . .

Chase slipped through a gap to land on the deck beneath – and found himself facing a huge radiation warning symbol on a bulkhead. He instinctively clapped both hands protectively over his groin and looked for the quickest possible way out of the reactor room.

An open hatch led forward. He moved through it, the low thrum of the driveshafts turning the screws fading behind him. There were no other sounds of activity. Presumably the sub only had a skeleton crew, just enough to operate the reactors rather than actually take it out to sea. Either they had got off, or Mitchell had killed them.

He guessed the sub's control room would be under the sail, where its commander could use the periscopes. He headed forward until he found a ladder to the next deck, and crept up it.

The faint sound of someone talking reached him. Mitchell. Chase couldn't make out what he was saying, but from his clipped tone it sounded as though he was issuing orders. Was he sending a radio message?

He quietly advanced through what turned out to be the sonar room, seeing the first physical sign of Mitchell's presence, a splatter of blood on one of the pale cream walls. A few more steps and a body came into view, a man slumped over a hatch entrance. A large wrench lay beside him. Chase picked it up – any weapon was better than none – and peered through the hatch.

It was the control room. Two long tubes ran down from the ceiling through large circular holes in the deck to the level below: the sub's periscopes, both lowered. At the front of the room was a pair of seats before banks of instruments and almost aircraft-like controls. Another corpse was slumped in one, blood trickling down the seat back. Mitchell must have forced the luckless sailor to get the sub under way before killing him.

Chase couldn't yet see Mitchell – but he could see Nina. Still unconscious, she lay in a corner beneath a bank of computer screens. He watched for a few seconds until he was sure that she was breathing. Then he heard movement from the other side of the room, and slowly leaned further round the hatch.

Mitchell stood before what he assumed was the communications console, his back to him. The XM-201 was propped beside him. As Chase watched, the American unzipped the pack containing Excalibur and took out the sword to examine it.

Chase assessed the situation. If he could get close enough, he could smack Mitchell over the head with the wrench and knock him out – or kill him, either was fine. But the rifle was within easy reach of the DARPA agent, and apart from a faint hiss of static from a radio the control room was all but silent. It would only take one footstep, one slap of wet clothing, for him to be heard.

There wasn't much choice. He couldn't wait for ever – Mitchell definitely wasn't planning to sail the Typhoon all the way back to the States. Someone was meeting him, either a ship or another submarine.

Hefting the wrench, he stepped through the hatch and moved behind the nearer of the two periscopes. Glancing through the hole in the deck he could see the handgrips and eyepieces in a compartment below, ready to rise at the push of a button. Mitchell was about ten feet away. Close enough to rush him?

A small noise caught Mitchell's attention. Chase ducked back, but it wasn't him the American had heard. The sound had been a faint scrape of metal. Mitchell stared intently at a piece of equipment resembling a weighing scale, low-tech in the computerised control centre. Chase realised it was a mechanical inclinometer: a weighted pendulum, a simple but near-foolproof way to determine the sub's angle of climb or descent. As he watched, the pointer slowly moved. The Typhoon's bow was gradually rising – or the stern was sinking.

A chill ran through Chase as the implications of that hit home, but then Mitchell took a step closer to the inclinometer, Excalibur still in his hands. His eyes were fixed on the pointer.

Chase saw his chance and crept round the periscope behind him.

Mitchell turned, about to put Excalibur down on the console – and his eyes locked on to Chase's, reflected in the sword's polished blade.

Chase jumped back behind the periscope as Mitchell snatched up the rifle. He expected gunfire, but nothing came. He quickly realised why. Even if Mitchell switched to armour-piercers, shooting the thick titanium casing of the periscope would result in a potentially lethal spray of ricochets.

But he only needed take a few steps round the periscope to have a direct line of fire.

'God *damn*, you're persistent, Eddie!' said Mitchell, dropping Excalibur on the console and moving towards him. A couple more steps and he would be exposed—

Chase slapped his hand on the periscope controls.

With a hiss of hydraulics, the metal tube rapidly rose into position. Chase dropped, hurling the wrench under the bottom of the periscope. It cracked into Mitchell's knee and clanged to the floor.

Mitchell staggered back in pain. Chase rushed at him. The rifle came back down, but too late, as Chase tackled the taller man at the waist and slammed him back against the console. Excalibur spun to the deck and dropped into the hole beneath the raised periscope.

Chase swept out an arm, knocking the XM-201 from Mitchell's hand. He was about to drive his fist into Mitchell's crotch when a knee rammed into his face. His nose cracked, hot blood gushing over his lips.

'Oh, you fucker!' Chase roared, whipping up his head and catching Mitchell under his chin. The American's jaw snapped shut, and he spat out blood. Chase punched him twice in the stomach, doubling him over, then smashed a fist into his mouth and knocked him backwards. '*Not* such a – *fucking* pretty boy – *now*, are you?' he shouted as he delivered three more brutal blows to Mitchell's face, his own knuckles splitting with the force of the punches.

But Mitchell was far from down, an arm snapping up to

block Chase's final attack. The heel of his palm hit the Englishman's jaw like an axe, and as Chase reeled Mitchell kicked him in the stomach and knocked him back against the periscope. He hit one of the handgrips, the tube spinning round and pitching him to the deck.

Face swollen and bleeding, Mitchell shot Chase a look of rage, as if about to leap at him and continue the attack with his bare hands – before diving for the fallen rifle.

Sprawled on the floor with no cover, there was only one place Chase could go—

Bullets clanged around him as he threw himself into the hole and smashed down on the unyielding floor of the periscope compartment below. He scrambled forward as Mitchell ran to the edge of the opening and kept firing, ricochets pinging and sparking off the bulkheads. He was now moving uphill, the Typhoon undeniably tilting down at the stern. But that was far from the forefront of his mind as he reached an open hatch – and saw something few Westerners had ever seen.

The Typhoon's missile bay stretched out before him, three decks high and the better part of two hundred feet long. He was on a narrow catwalk round the uppermost level, looking down at the ten pairs of launch tubes sandwiched between the two cylindrical pressure hulls. Even though the tubes were empty, the whole dimly lit chamber exuded menace, a symbol of fearsome destructive power.

But a much older force of destruction was also in the room with him. Seawater sloshed through the aft hatches on the bottom level, foaming waves creeping forward as he watched. The lowest deck was already flooded, water gushing through the hole in the hull, and the deluge would only speed up as the ever-growing weight dragged the stern deeper under the surface.

A thump behind him. Mitchell had just jumped down from the control room. Chase rolled under the heavy hatch and kicked it with both feet. It slammed shut on Mitchell's rifle. Something cracked. The American forced his way through the gap, snarling down at Chase and swinging the XM-201 round to point at him—

Click.

Mitchell's finger tightened round the trigger, but no bullets emerged. He tried again, then fumbled with the ammo selector. It refused to move, the mechanism damaged.

'Told you it'd break!' Chase shouted, delivering another forceful kick and crushing Mitchell against the jamb. He let out a gurgling groan. As Chase prepared to strike again, he pulled back into the periscope chamber. The hatch clanged against the frame.

Chase stood, wiping blood from his face. The submarine was now tilting down by about ten degrees at the stern, the leading edge of the water halfway along the missile bay. Dealing with Mitchell was rapidly becoming a secondary priority – he had to find a way to get himself and Nina off the sub.

With luck, Mitchell would now have a few cracked ribs. Chase swung open the hatch – and jerked away as Excalibur slashed at his head.

If Mitchell had been hurt, he wasn't showing any signs of it. He thrust again, Chase leaping aside to avoid taking the sharp tip in his face.

Mitchell advanced, expression furious beneath the blood. Chase jumped back as Excalibur stabbed at his abdomen. Another attack, this one slicing upwards from groin to chest. Chase grimaced and retreated more quickly. He glanced over his shoulder, only to see that the catwalk came to a dead end at a large control panel.

Mitchell saw it too, a mocking sneer on his split lips. He jabbed at Chase's chest, forcing him back still further. Chase saw nothing he could use as a weapon or to fend off the blade. He was literally about to die by the sword.

He reached the control panel, trapped. Mitchell drew back Excalibur for a killing thrust—

The deck trembled, a deep metallic groan echoing through the submarine. Wind suddenly blew around the huge chamber, water surging through the hatches with much greater force than before. Something clanged back and forth across the missile bay with a sound like a rifle shot – a rivet popping loose under the strain.

The bow had risen out of the water, nothing supporting it as the stern continued to drop, causing the massive vessel to flex.

It was going to sink, very soon.

Mitchell gripped the handrail to steady himself, and struck.

31

Chase was no longer there.

He flung himself off the catwalk. The blade ripped his wet shirt, slicing a gash in his shoulder as he fell – to plunge into the water flooding the chamber.

Even with the water to cushion his fall, he still thudded against the deck, the impact knocking the breath from him. The force of the incoming water swept him against one of the missile tubes. He grabbed a pipe and pulled his head above the churning surface, coughing.

He looked up, seeing Mitchell glaring down before the American hurried back to the hatch. He hesitated, then turned and ran up the catwalk towards the bow, the sword glinting in his hand.

Chase knew why Mitchell had paused. He had boarded the submarine with two prizes, but considered only one of them irreplaceable. He was taking Excalibur, leaving Nina to drown.

Chase dragged himself through the water until he reached a ladder, and climbed it, freezing water streaming off him. More almost animalistic moans sounded around him. The submarine was still dropping at the stern, the flood now at the missile bay's forward bulkhead.

He was on the catwalk. The thought of going after Mitchell didn't even occur to him; instead, he ran back to the periscope compartment and went through the hatch at its rear to find himself at the base of the control deck ladder once more. A cold, sinister wind blew past him – air being displaced by the rising water.

By the time he entered the conn, the Typhoon was tilting up by over fifteen degrees, loose objects sliding down the deck. Nina was still in the corner. Chase searched the room for a first-aid kit. He spotted a small cabinet marked with a green cross and pulled out a plastic case before going to her. He pawed through the Cyrillic-labelled contents before finding what he was after: smelling salts. He cracked the ampoule under Nina's nose.

No reaction for a moment. Then:

'Gah! Wha' the, what, *shit*!' she mumbled, trying to squirm away from the stinging vapour before blearily taking in Chase's battered, blood-streaked face. 'Oh, my God, Eddie! Are you okay?'

'You should see the other guy,' he said with a pained grin.

A long, mournful groan rolled through the room, followed by a series of rifle-shot cracks as more rivets broke. The submarine shuddered, the pointer on the inclinometer rising faster. Nina surveyed her surroundings, then tipped her head in bewilderment to match the angle of the room. 'We're on the submarine,' Chase told her.

'Why?'

'Long story. But we need to get off it, because it's sinking.'

'*What!*'

'Yeah, I thought that'd wake you up.' He helped her stand.

'Well, how *do* we get off it?'

'I don't know.'

'Can we get up into the, what's it called, the conning tower? Maybe there's a life raft!'

'Worth a try,' Chase decided. He had seen another ladder aft of where he had entered the control deck; the only place it could go was into the sail. 'Watch your step – the whole thing's going down at the arse. This slope's only going to get worse.'

'Where's Jack? And Excalibur?'

'Last I saw, he was running for the bow, with the sword.'

'Why didn't you stop him?'

He shot her a look and cupped his hands as if comparing two weights. 'It was a tough choice – you know, bit of tin, woman I love!'

'Oh, all right – aah!' Nina's foot slipped, and she stumbled down the tilting deck to hit the aft bulkhead, now well on its way to becoming the new floor. Chase gripped one of the plotting tables and made his way to her as she peered through the hatch. 'Er, Eddie?'

'Yeah?'

'I can see water. That's supposed to be on the *outside*.'

He looked past her. Water was indeed rising up the floor of the sonar room. The ladder he'd seen was already submerged. 'Buggeration and fuckery! Okay, Plan B.'

'You have a Plan B?'

'No, but if you do that'd be bloody fantastic!'

More loose items crashed on to the deck. The radio handset on the communications console swung on its coiled cord. The submarine was now close to thirty degrees down by the stern, and the rate of tilt was increasing. The inclinometer clanked as it reached its limit.

Nina jumped away from the hatch as a first wave splashed through it. 'Okay, how about we close this?' She slammed the heavy metal door and spun the locking wheel a couple of times, then pointed at the dangling microphone. 'What about that radio? Can we call for help?'

'Call who? The Russians won't be able to reach us in time – assuming they don't shoot us on sight for sinking one of their nuclear subs!'

'Maybe not, but they might be able to tell us how to get out of this thing.'

'If they speak English—' Chase began, but Nina cut him off.

'Is that a phone?' she asked, jabbing a finger at the piece of equipment mounted next to the radio. It looked like a later addition to the control room, not as utilitarian and military in design.

'Yeah, a satphone.'

'Great!' She battled her way across the room, using the firmly secured legs of the plotting table as steps before clambering over the periscope to reach the console.

'Who you gonna call?' Chase asked as he followed, confused.

Nina resisted the near-automatic urge to cry 'Ghostbusters!' in response. 'Someone who knows about submarines! What time is it in New York?'

Chase looked at his wrist, but saw only skin; his watch had been confiscated at Vaskovich's power station. 'I dunno – late afternoon?'

'Hope he's still in the office . . .' She picked up the receiver and held it to her ear, then pushed a green button on the phone. She heard a bleep. 'Yes!' She dialled a number from memory and waited, adjusting her precarious position as the room tilted around her.

A click, then a hollow hiss of static. 'It's working!' she cried on hearing a ringing tone. Another few seconds and she got an answer from the IHA's receptionist in New York. 'Lola! It's Nina Wilde. This is an emergency – I need you to put me through to Matt Trulli at UNARA right now!'

To her credit, Lola didn't waste time asking any questions, but immediately dialled Trulli's extension. Another ringing tone, two rings, three . . .

'Hello?' said Trulli.

'Matt! It's Nina!'

'Hey, what's up?'

'Oh, nothing much. Just that Eddie and I are trapped aboard a sinking Russian submarine.'

Even with the time lag of a satellite link, a reply was a long time coming. 'Really?'

'Yes! Really! You said you'd been on a Russian sub – so tell us how to get off this one!'

'I've been on *a* Russian sub, but they're all different. What kind is it?'

'A . . . a *big* one! Eddie, what kind of sub is this?'

'A Typhoon,' Chase told her.

'A Typhoon,' she repeated. 'We're in the bridge and we can't get to the ladder behind us because it's flooded!'

'When you say bridge, do you mean the observation deck in the sail, or the main control room?'

'What?' Nina shook her head in exasperation. 'The second one! Matt – we are *going to die*! Get us out of here!'

'I've never been on a Typhoon – I was aboard a Sierra!' Trulli protested. 'I've read about 'em, though. Hang on, let me think.'

Nina gave him exactly three seconds. '*Matt!*'

'Okay, okay! If you can't get up into the sail, there're supposedly escape pods on each side of the control deck.'

'Supposedly?'

'The Russians don't exactly put the plans on the Internet! But there are big hatches in the hull, and everything I've read says they're for escape pods.'

'Okay! Great! How do we get to them?'

'I dunno! If there's no direct access to the sides, you'll have to go forward or aft and double back to them.'

Nina glanced at the aft hatch. 'Going back's out. This thing's sinking ass first.'

'Then you need to go forward.'

She looked ahead – and up. The forward hatch was now above her, the floor at forty degrees from the horizontal. 'Yeah, I was afraid you'd say that.'

'Nina!' Chase warned, pointing at one of the panels in front of the dead sailor. He had realised it was a depth gauge some time ago, but ignored it, with the Typhoon on the surface. Now, though, it was starting to tick down . . . and with increasing speed. The sheer volume of water in the stern section was outweighing the buoyancy provided by the remaining air in the bow. 'We're going down, and not in the good way. Time to go!'

'Matt,' Nina said, 'if you're right about this escape pod, you're going to get *such* a great thank-you present from us both.'

'And if I'm wrong?'

'Then it was nice working with you! Bye!' She dropped the handset and pulled herself up the consoles.

Chase was right behind her. 'Escape pod?'

'Hopefully. He says there's one on each side of the control room.'

'Shit, then they're probably flooded by now.'

'There you go with that British pessimism again! Stop it!'

The forward hatch hung open. Nina braced herself against a console and stretched to grab its frame. Chase pushed her up from below until she was able to wriggle over it, then climbed after her. They found themselves in a narrow passage running across the sub; a closed hatch led forward, but Nina was more interested in the routes to the left and right, which as Trulli had suggested headed back along each side of the control room. 'This way's not flooded,' she said, looking left.

'This way is!' Chase yelped as seawater reached the top end of the other corridor. The sub was now at a forty-five degree angle, walls turning to floors, the water flowing with increasing force along the welded corner where the two joined.

'Oh boy.' Nina ran left and looked down. 'Eddie! I think I've found it!'

Chase joined her. The hatch at the far end of the corridor was closed, keeping out the water – however temporarily. About ten feet below them was another hatch set in the side wall, this one hydraulically operated. A large button on a panel beside it glowed with a green light. 'Great, but we've still got to get to it,' he said as the water gushed past their feet and spewed into the passage like a waterfall.

One side of the passage was lined with protruding metal boxes – electrical switchgear. Chase climbed down them until he reached the level of the hatch, then leaned across. Water splashed over him from above. Some of it sprayed into the boxes, causing a bang and a flash of sparks. Nina shrieked. Chase winced and shifted his grip to something he hoped was non-conductive, then pushed the button.

The hatch hissed open. Through it Chase saw another, smaller hatch opening more slowly, beyond it a white-painted cylindrical chamber. 'Is it the escape pod?' Nina asked.

'Either that or a Portaloo. Come on!'

Nina gingerly descended. The water was coming faster now, rushing down the steeply sloping floor to churn against the bulkhead below. More spray found its way into the electrics – something further down the passage exploded, sending a cloud of smoke swirling up past Chase. Flames crackled briefly before the rising water extinguished them.

Chase brought up a hand to help Nina, directing her towards the open hatch. 'Come on, quick—'

The entire submarine shook, titanium and steel groaning as if in pain. A wave burst over the top of the corridor, hundreds of gallons of freezing water cascading down on them. Hanging halfway across the passage, Nina was hit by the deluge and slipped, sliding down the sloping deck.

Chase's hand flashed out, snagging the baggy sleeve of her overalls. A seam tore, but he clenched his fist tighter round the bunched material as Nina swung below him. Water drenching her, she managed to clamp her hand round the edge of the hatch and shakily pull herself back up. 'Thanks,' she gasped.

He gave her a relieved smile. 'Didn't want you to miss the wedding.'

'Uh-huh. And when's that going to be, exactly?'

'Oh, don't fucking start,' Chase moaned, pushing her

through the hatch. He followed as more water gushed down the corridor, the dying submarine moaning around them.

Nina had already found a control panel by the hatch, helpfully annotated with diagrams beside illuminated push buttons. She hit each in turn.

The inner hatch rumbled shut, closing with a clang. Nothing seemed to happen for a nerve-racking moment – then the escape pod trembled as its compartment flooded. The hatches on the Typhoon's outer hull retracted, and with a thunderous bang of compressed air the pod was blown free of the stricken sub.

Nina was thrown against Chase as the pod abruptly righted itself. A digital depth gauge rapidly counted down to zero, and before they had a chance to recover a whoosh of spray over the hull and a bobbing motion announced that they had reached the surface.

Deeper booms and thumps came from below as the Typhoon finally hit the seabed. Nina looked worriedly at Chase, pushing her sodden hair off her face. 'What about the sub? What if the reactors explode?'

'They won't,' Chase assured her. 'That's not how they work. And sub reactor casings are tough, they should be able to recover them without too much crap leaking out.' He stroked her cheek, then took in the pod's interior. As well as the hatch through which they had entered, there was another in the ceiling with small portholes set beneath it. 'I think this is the bit where M and Q are supposed to catch us having a shag.'

Nina huffed. 'Y'know, freezing seawater doesn't really put me in the mood.'

'Does wonders for your nipples, though.'

'Hey!'

Chase chuckled tiredly, then levered Nina off him and stood, pointing at a protective plastic cover over another panel at one end of the pod. 'See if there's a radio under that.'

Nina lifted the cover as he looked through the portholes. There was indeed a radio beneath it – and more besides. 'I think this thing's got an engine,' she told him. 'There's a wheel and a compass.'

'See if you can start it.' Chase peered out towards the shore. The glaring lights of the sub pen stood out clearly against the dark cliffs – as did the burning hilltop where Vaskovich's facility had stood, a thick pillar of smoke and dust lit from below by the flames. 'Jesus. Jack really fucking wrecked the place.' He wondered what had happened to the DARPA agent; Mitchell hadn't run for the Typhoon's bow out of panic. He'd had a plan. Chase turned, looking out to sea.

Something in the distance stood out against the horizon, a barely discernible line of white in the dark water. Waves washing against a floating object.

The clatter of an electric starter was followed by the low chug of an engine. 'Pretty neat, huh?' Nina said.

'Yeah. Are there any binoculars down there?'

She searched the compartment beneath the controls, finding a medical kit as well as what Chase had asked for.

'Let me fix those cuts,' she said, handing him the binoculars.

'In a minute.' Chase scanned the horizon. 'Well, fuck me.'

'What is it?'

'Jack's got a ride home.' Through the binoculars, he could now see the cause of the line of waves – another submarine. A faint red light lit up an open hatch from below, figures moving around it to pull an inflatable life raft out of the water. Though Chase couldn't make out the face of the figure climbing from it, the sword he was holding was a dead giveaway.

Once Mitchell was aboard, the other men dropped the raft back into the water and climbed through the hatch. A wash of reflected light briefly passed over the sail as it closed, letting Chase pick out the number 23 painted on the black metal before it vanished in the darkness. The sub began to move; he tracked it until it disappeared under the surface, which it did with surprising speed.

'The bastard had a sub waiting for him,' he told Nina. 'Soon as it's clear of Russian waters, he'll probably get picked up by a chopper and taken to . . . well, wherever the fuck he's going with Excalibur.'

'God.' Nina sat, rubbing her hands over her arms to warm them. 'The whole thing was a set-up, right from the start. And Jack was, what, a *quadruple* agent? The *hell*? Shit,' she added as a thought struck her, 'I bet he was the one who got Vaskovich to kill Bernd – that way he could be sure I'd help him find the sword.'

'It's not over,' said Chase, eyes narrowing. 'He was going to take you with him as well. He'll want to get you back; he needs you to make his own system work. And his *is* a weapon.'

'Jesus. So what do we do?'

Chase looked through the portholes again. 'First thing we do is get back to shore.'

'It'll take a while,' said Nina, examining the controls. 'This thing's not exactly a powerboat. The speedo only goes up to five!'

'Well, it'll give you time to patch me up.' Chase sat heavily on one of the bench seats.

Nina turned the pod towards the sub pen, then took the medical kit and sat beside him. 'You know, you were right about Jack. He *was* after my body. Just in a really weird way.'

'Yeah. I can't believe I got jealous of that arsehole. Sorry about that, by the way. Ow.'

Nina finished dabbing one of his cuts with antiseptic. 'Apology accepted. Just don't do it again, huh?'

'Oh, I won't. Next time some bloke tries to chat you up, I'm just going to lamp the bastard.'

Nina laughed, a little uncertainly. 'Wait, no, really?'

'Nah, I'm just—'

'Taking the piss, gotcha. Anyway, you don't need to worry about other men.' She gently kissed his cheek. 'Thank you.'

'For what?'

'For everything. I just realised what you were trying to

tell me in London, at the embassy. About not wanting to lose me.' She kissed him again. 'Thank you.'

'What made you realise?'

Nina smiled. 'Oh, y'know, just that you'd sink a nuclear submarine to save me. Most women don't have a fiancé who'd do that. So I'm pretty sure I've found the right one.' She applied a plaster to his face.

Chase lifted an eyebrow. 'Only *pretty* sure?'

'Well, there *is* still that whole won't-talk-about-his-past deal . . .'

'You know I can't. Official Secrets Act and all that.'

'I don't mean the SAS stuff,' she said with a pointed look.

'Right.' Chase sat in contemplative silence as Nina continued to patch up his injuries, waiting for him to find the right words. 'The thing . . .' he began, and hesitated.

'It can wait,' she assured him. 'We're not exactly in the ideal surroundings here.'

'No, I need to get this out. The reason I never talked to you about my family is . . . because it *hurts*. There, I said it.' He let out a breath. 'It's nearly twenty years ago, and it still fucking hurts. My mum was dying of cancer right in front of me, and my dad . . .' Chase's fists clenched. 'My dad had a fucking *affair*! He was with some other woman while my mum was dying. So after she did, I just left. I didn't want anything to do with him.'

'So that's why you never talk about him.'

'Your dad was a role model,' Chase said, voice bitter.

'Mine was everything I *didn't* want to be. I never talked about him 'cause I didn't want to be reminded of him . . . and I didn't want to think that I might be anything like him.'

Nina had paused in her treatment to listen; now, she gave a final dab to his last cut. 'I don't think you are,' she whispered, kissing him.

He returned it. 'Thanks.' It was only a single word, but it told Nina the depth of his gratitude.

They sat against each other as the lifepod continued its sluggish voyage home.

To their surprise, they weren't met by armed and angry Russians as the pod finally bumped against the jetty. Instead, Chase opened the top hatch to find Maximov waiting for them. 'It's okay, he's on our side,' he assured Nina as he helped her out. 'I think.'

'Uh-huh,' Nina said uncertainly.

'What happened to submarine?' Maximov asked. 'Whole front end came out of water like – like *whale!*'

'Well, it's sleeping with the fishes now,' Chase told him. He saw a handful of people waiting at the dock's cavernous entrance. 'What's going on?'

'They were going to fly away in the boss's jet.' The big Russian grinned menacingly. 'I persuade them to stay, wait for army or navy or whoever to arrive.'

'But we've got to get out of here,' said Nina. 'Jack's got the sword. We need to go after him.'

'Can you get us back to Moscow?' asked Chase.

Maximov looked puzzled. '*Da*, in jet. But I said, we wait for army to arrive.'

'No, seriously, that would be a really bad idea. You know who they're going to blame for all this? *Whoever they find.* You're Russian, you know the drill – bag everyone in sight and worry about who actually did anything later. And if we're all under arrest, we can't stop Mitchell getting away.'

'You have point,' said Maximov. 'Okay, I take you to plane, get you back to Moscow.'

Nina shivered. 'Anywhere, as long as it's warm.'

The lights were on in Pavel Prikovsky's warehouse, but it was far from warm. The gate was open, the door ajar.

'Stay in the car,' Chase warned Nina. Vaskovich's jet had been equipped with a gun cabinet; the fact that it had a combination code presumably known only to Vaskovich and Kruglov made no difference to Maximov, who simply ripped off the door. Both men drew their weapons and cautiously advanced across the yard.

Chase peered through the door, seeing one of Prikovsky's men lying in a pool of blood. It had coagulated; whatever had happened had taken place some time ago. It couldn't have been Mitchell, then . . . but it could have been men acting under his orders.

The warehouse was silent. Chase held up three fingers as a signal to Maximov, mouthed a countdown, then burst through the door, the Russian covering him. He swept his gun from side to side. No movement. No life.

They made their way through the stacks of boxes to Prikovsky's office, passing another corpse slumped against a forklift, his chest a ragged mess of bullet holes. Prikovsky was slumped over his desk, dead eyes staring at the door as they entered. 'Oh, Jesus,' said Chase softly. Prikovsky had hardly been a friend, but he had still come through for him, and this was his reward. The Russian had been shot in both legs, but the actual cause of death was easy to see: a metal pole protruding from his back, plunging down through his chest and the table below. Someone had held Prikovsky in that position in order to impale him, leaving a very clear message.

Chase knew he was the intended recipient. A piece of paper had been taped to the pole, three words printed on it in large bold capitals.

CALL YOUR SISTER.

'Shit,' Chase whispered, filled with utter dread. He hunted for a phone, and found one that had been knocked from the desk by Prikovsky's struggle.

'What does it say?' Maximov asked.

'The fucker's going after my family!' Snatching up the phone, Chase dialled 44, the international dialling code for Britain, then Elizabeth's number. He waited anxiously for the connection to be made, the phone to start ringing . . .

The answer came on the second ring. 'Lizzie!' Chase snapped. 'Are you okay? Is Holly all—'

'Eddie, oh, my God!' Elizabeth cried. 'They took her, they took Holly!'

'Who? Who took her?'

'I don't know, they wore masks! They said they were watching, that if I called the police or spoke to anyone else they'd kill her – that I had to wait to hear from you!'

Chase smashed his gun down on the desk, splintering the wood in his barely contained fury. 'Mitchell, you fucking little shit, talk to me! I know you can hear me!'

A click, then a familiar voice on the line, an eerie electronic distortion behind it. 'Hello, Eddie.'

'Let Holly go, right now,' Chase barked. 'Or I *will* fucking kill you.'

'Save your threats, Eddie.' There was another noise under Mitchell's voice, the whine of an aircraft's engines. He was no longer aboard the submarine.

'It wasn't a threat. It was a *promise.*'

'Don't waste my time and I won't waste yours. I want Nina. Or rather, I need Nina. I know this is kinda drastic, but I needed to show that I'm one hundred per cent serious.'

'By kidnapping a teenage girl?' Chase cried. 'The British government'll go apeshit!'

'The British government will shut the fuck up and do as they're told, like always. But they won't even need to hear about this if you do what I tell you. Bring me Nina, and you get your niece back.'

'Eddie, what is it?'

Chase whirled to see Nina standing in the doorway. 'That fucker's kidnapped Holly!'

'Is that Nina?' Mitchell asked as she reacted with shock. 'Put her on, Eddie.'

Tight-lipped with anger, Chase put the phone on speaker. 'She's here.'

'Nina, hi. I'm sure you've guessed what I want already, but I'll tell you anyway so there's no ambiguity – I want you to turn yourself over to my people. In return, I'll let Eddie's niece go.'

'Your people?' Nina said in disgust. 'Kidnappers and killers? I'm ashamed to be an American right now. DARPA'll be finished when this gets out.'

Mitchell almost laughed. 'You still think I actually work for DARPA? I didn't realise you were so naive.'

'A black project,' Chase growled.

'Blackest of the black. This is way too important to be put in the hands of any official agency. Or politician.'

'So you've just unilaterally declared yourself the guardian of American interests?' Nina asked, appalled.

'Someone has to do it. But I'm not here to debate idealism versus realpolitik – I'm here to do a job, and for that I need you. Get back to England. Once you're there, call this number again. We're monitoring it; I'll hear you. And then we can make the exchange.'

'No!' Chase shouted. 'You want me to trade my fiancée for my niece? Fuck you! I can't – I can't make a choice like that!'

'I can,' Nina said quietly. 'I'll do it.'

'*What?*'

'I said I'll do it.'

'No you fucking won't!'

Her voice was firm. 'I have to. And you know it. It's the only way to get Holly back safely. She's your niece . . . and she's going to be mine too.' She took his hand. 'She's going to be part of my family, Eddie. And you have to do whatever's necessary to protect your family.' She turned to face the phone. 'Jack, we'll do it. I'll do it. If I have your absolute assurance that Holly will be released unharmed.'

'You have it,' Mitchell replied. 'Now get to England. And make it soon.' The line went dead.

Chase swept the phone off the table. '*Fuck!* I don't fucking believe him, he'll kill her anyway. He can't risk anyone finding out what he's done.'

Maximov grunted. 'The man is a shit. I should have crushed his head! But at least you know he is not all-powerful, or he could have left men here to wait for you.'

'Powerful enough,' Nina said, worried. She shared a look with Chase, a look that betrayed their fears for Holly . . . and each other.

32

England

The New Forest covered over two hundred and twenty square miles, a national park beginning ten miles east of Bournemouth that contained some of England's oldest heaths and pastures. But it was in one of the swathes of forest that gave the region its name that Nina and Chase now waited, Elizabeth's car parked in a clearing. Chase had checked the area in satellite photos; the nearest house was over a mile away, the spot Mitchell had selected for the exchange as isolated as it was possible to get on the densely populated south coast.

Night had fallen. The only illumination came from the car's headlights, casting stark shadows across the ground. Chase surveyed the trees, but couldn't see anyone.

He knew they were not alone, though.

'I hear something,' said Nina, looking northwards. It

took a few more seconds before Chase was able to pick it out, his hearing still not fully recovered from the pounding it took in Russia. But the whine and chatter of an approaching helicopter was unmistakable.

It came in low, a flickering light through the trees before it swept into the open, turning side-on to the car as it descended. A man leaned out of a door, directing a circular antenna at them.

'Get rid of the gun, Eddie.' Mitchell's voice boomed from a speaker as the chopper hovered just above tree level. The antenna was part of a millimetre-wave radar system, showing the helicopter's occupants exactly what Chase and Nina were carrying under their clothes. 'And Nina, that thing in your left pocket, I assume it's a tracker. Ditch it. Then both of you step away from the car.'

Chase tossed his pistol beside a fallen log as Nina reluctantly took out the piece of electronic gear and placed it on the car's roof. They walked further into the clearing. Another few seconds as the man concluded his radar scan, then the helicopter touched down in a miniature hurricane of dust and leaves, the rotors still whirling at takeoff speed.

Holly stepped out fearfully, Mitchell lurking behind her. 'Uncle Eddie!'

'Holly, are you okay?' Chase shouted.

'She's fine,' Mitchell said. 'Nina, walk toward me. I'll send the girl. Careful, now.'

Nina took a step, then paused and looked back at Chase. 'Eddie . . .'

'I'll find you,' he said softly. Then, with a not entirely convincing attempt at a casual smile: 'By the way, you doing anything next May? Maybe around the fourteenth?'

Her answering smile was entirely genuine. Loving. 'I am now.'

'Don't miss it.'

'Don't let me.'

'Enough with the schmaltz,' Mitchell's amplified voice snapped. 'Nina, get over here, now.'

With a last glance at Chase, Nina walked towards the helicopter. Holly came the other way, desperate to break into a run. As they passed each other Nina whispered, 'Do whatever Eddie tells you.'

She reached the helicopter and looked back. Holly had just met Chase. 'Get in,' Mitchell shouted from the cabin. Trying not to show her fear, Nina climbed inside. The radar operator grabbed her wrists and handcuffed them, then shoved her down beside Mitchell.

The engine noise immediately rose, the helicopter ascending. Nina stared out of the window at the two figures on the fringe of the headlight beams as they fell away. 'Get us to the jet,' Mitchell ordered the pilot. 'I want the other helo fuelled and ready by the time we reach Scotland. We've got a lot of work to do – I want a full test of the system by tomorrow night.'

'What about Eddie and Holly?' Nina demanded.

'I said I'd release Holly unharmed,' said Mitchell with a hard expression. 'After that . . .'

Nina's eyes narrowed hatefully. 'You son of a bitch.'

'I do what I have to do.' He sat back as the helicopter picked up speed over the dark forest.

The sniper was less than two hundred feet from Chase, but at thirty feet away he would still have been invisible, even in daylight. Draped in multi-textured layers of mottled camouflage, he blended perfectly with the scrub and bushes of the forest floor. Even his rifle looked more organic than manufactured, the brown-painted barrel and its fat suppressor wrapped in twigs to break up its shape, the telltale reflective lens of the scope concealed beneath drooping leaves.

He flicked them away, taking in the full view through the sights. The crosshairs were almost perfectly centred on Chase's head. He raised himself higher on his elbows as he adjusted his aim and prepared to fire. Chase was moving slightly, talking to the girl, but not enough to throw off the shot.

With the helicopter gone there was hardly any wind, and at such a close range the effects of the suppressor and ballistic drop on the bullet would be negligible. He took them into account anyway, lifting the crosshairs fractionally to just above Chase's eyeline. The bullet would hit the dead centre of his skull, and blow it apart.

After Chase, he would move on to the girl, who would be so shocked that she would be paralysed, easy prey. Two targets, two shots, two seconds.

Two deaths.

He braced himself, holding his breath to minimise the movement of his body, making the final delicate adjustments to his aim, finger caressing the trigger . . .

Firing—

As Chase ducked.

The silenced shot hissed over Chase's head and thumped against a tree. The faint click of the sniper rifle's action told him the direction from which the shot had come, but he already knew.

'Jesus!' said Peter Alderley's tinny voice in his right ear as he threw Holly to the ground beneath him. 'Could you leave that any later?'

Chase didn't reply, rolling into the partial cover of the log and dragging Holly with him. 'Stay here!' he hissed as he grabbed his gun and crawled on his belly through the leaves and mud to the other end of the fallen trunk. If the sniper were any good – and Chase didn't doubt it – then he would already have reloaded and be seeking to re-acquire his target, surprised by his apparent precognition or not.

'He's still in place,' Mac said over the earpiece. 'Tracking left, looking for you.'

'Wait, he's doing something with his gun,' Alderley added. 'He just switched something on, maybe night vision or thermographics.'

Chase didn't need to see the radar image the two men were viewing somewhere inside MI6's London headquarters; he could picture it perfectly in his mind's eye. The sniper would be lying behind cover, a log or a tree stump, somewhere with direct line of sight through the trees to the original position of his targets. He wouldn't move unless he absolutely had to.

Which meant Chase had to *make* him move. The synthetic aperture radar satellite orbiting some three hundred miles above could see through tree cover and even the ground, but it could only keep its unnatural gaze on one particular spot for a limited amount of time before its trajectory carried it out of sight. If he hadn't located his enemy by the time the satellite passed out of range, he would be left blind.

And then dead.

'One minute to range limit,' said Alderley. 'Come on, Chase, nail the silly bastard, he's just lying there!'

'Never faced a sniper, have you?' Chase growled as he reached the end of the log. The next available cover was behind a tree maybe ten feet away – ten feet in which he would be completely exposed. 'Talk to me, what's he doing?'

'Switching aim between each end of the log,' Mac told him. 'Waiting for one of you to move.'

'Which end's he aiming at now?'

'Yours.'

Chase hated himself for what he was about to do, but knew it was the only chance of saving himself and his niece. 'Holly,' he said in a loud whisper. 'When I say now, very quickly stick your hand out from the end of the log and then pull it back again. Okay?' Although confused and scared, she nodded. 'Okay! Ready, set, *now*!'

Holly thrust her hand out into the open.

Chase was already moving even as she pulled it back into cover, bursting out from behind the log towards the tree. The *thwack!* of the bullet striking wood and the soft clack of the rifle reached him simultaneously. Holly screamed as smashed bark rained over her.

'Stay down!' Chase yelled. Even the best snipers in the world needed a moment to reacquire a target after the jolt of firing, and the flash of his movement between the trees would force the other man to change his aim, slowing him further.

But not by much.

Chase slammed against the next tree a split second before a bullet did, broken wood spitting at his face.

'Forty seconds,' Alderley announced, voice tense.

'Where is he?'

'Five o'clock from you, about forty metres,' Mac told him. 'Aiming at your cover.'

'Left or right side?'

'Left.'

Gun raised, Chase jerked to the right, exposing his arm and shoulder and drawing the sniper's aim, then immediately lunged back to fire two shots round the left side of the tree. Another rifle bullet smacked into the trunk, his adversary thrown off by the return fire, just as Chase had hoped.

He sprang from cover once more, this time not stopping. The undergrowth crunched beneath his feet as he ran between the trees, curving round towards the sniper's position—

'Thirty seconds!'

'He's moving, you've spooked him!' Mac cried at the same moment. 'Going right from his original position, crawling – no, he's up, he's on his feet.'

Chase reached another tree, throwing himself against it. 'Position!'

'Four o'clock from you, still moving right, still moving – shit! Eddie, he's going for your niece!'

'Twenty!' Alderley said. 'Chase, move it!'

Chase risked a look. He could see nothing moving in the unreal half-light from the car's headlamps. 'No visual! Where is he?'

'Coming up to your three o'clock, still moving – no, he's dropping, taking aim—'

'Shit!' He ran directly for the still unseen sniper, gun held out ahead. 'Guide me in!'

On the radar image, his outstretched arm would act as a pointer, letting Mac direct him towards his target – if he was fast enough. 'Left!' snapped Mac. Chase turned slightly, trees flicking past. 'Left, left – straight, straight!'

'Ten seconds!'

Chase fired, and kept firing into the undergrowth ahead.

No hits, and he was running out of bullets and time—

'He's moving!' Mac said. 'Changing aim, changing aim!'

No need to ask who the new target was. Chase was down to three bullets, two, one—

'He's hit!' shouted Mac. No triumph, just an immediate warning. 'Gun, gun, gun!'

At close range a sniper rifle was a liability, but it wasn't the man's only weapon. Chase saw a flicker of movement ahead, a bush that wasn't a bush shifting, a glint of light catching dark metal—

He fired his last shot.

'Contact lost!' Alderley almost gasped. 'Chase! Did you get him, did you get him?'

'Yeah, I got him,' Chase announced, kicking the pistol out of the sniper's hand. But there was no threat: his last bullet had hit the man in the neck, tearing out a ragged chunk of muscle and tendons that now hung gelatinously by a flap of skin, blood gushing blackly over the camouflage. He was still moving weakly, but he would be dead within a minute or two even if Chase had been inclined to do anything to save him.

There was an audible exhalation of relief through the earpiece. 'In that case,' Alderley said after a moment, 'you can expect a bill from Her Majesty's Government for the satellite time. Should only be about, oh, a million pounds or so.'

'They can knock it off the reward for recovering Excalibur,' Mac said. 'Eddie, are you all right?'

'Fine,' Chase replied, turning his back on the dying sniper and hurrying back to the clearing. 'Holly, are you okay? Holly?'

He found her still lying by the log, trembling. 'Holly,' he said, crouching to take her hand, 'it's okay. Are you all right?'

She slowly looked up at him, tears running from her wide eyes. 'Uncle Eddie?'

'Hi.' He managed a smile. 'Come on, love. Let's get you back home to your mum.'

He lifted her carefully to her feet. She hugged him and pressed her face into his chest, sobbing.

'It's all right,' he assured her. 'It's over.'

But he knew it wasn't.

'I take it the sniper's not talking,' Mac said in his ear, following the same line of thought. 'Peter and I can deal with the local police for you, but how are you going to find Nina now?'

Chase guided Holly to the car, face set. 'There's still someone else. I'm going to have words.'

Hector Amoros jolted awake, sitting upright and reaching across to switch on a lamp.

'Ay up, Hector,' said Chase coldly from the chair he had pulled up beside the bed. He had a gun in his hand, not aiming it directly at the director of the IHA, but needing only the smallest movement of his wrist to do so.

'Eddie!' Amoros exclaimed. 'What are you – how did you get in here?'

'Ways and means. I wanted a chat while you were still in London. About your mate Jack Mitchell.'

Amoros's expression tightened a little at the name. He

looked more closely at Chase as his eyes adjusted to the light of the hotel room. 'My God! What happened to you?'

Chase indicated the cuts and bruises on his face. 'Like I said, Jack Mitchell. Turns out he wasn't what he said he was.' Now the gun pointed at Amoros. 'But you knew that, didn't you? Right from the start.'

'I don't know what you—'

'Don't! Don't even fucking *try* to deny it. Jack set this whole thing up, getting the IHA involved so that he could find Excalibur before the Russians did. And with him being a navy man, and you being a navy man, you were great mates right off the bat. You'd do anything to help each other out, right?'

'That's not what happened,' Amoros said firmly. 'I might be retired from the navy, but if the Pentagon asks for something it's still my duty to give it to them. Most of the IHA's funding comes from the United States. You know that.'

'He who pays the piper, right?' said Chase with a sneer. 'Well, you know what tune he's playing now? It's called "I've kidnapped Nina and stolen Excalibur so I can build a big fuck-off WMD."'

Amoros sat straighter, shocked. 'He's kidnapped Nina? What are you talking about?'

'Kidnapped Nina, tried to kill me – and my niece. Because he didn't want to leave anyone alive to talk about this black-ops superweapon he's built.'

'And you think I had something to do with it?' Amoros asked.

Chase regarded him with flint-hard eyes. 'If I did, you'd already be dead.' Amoros tensed, knowing he meant it. 'But you know more about Jack than you've let on. I want to know where he is.'

'All I knew about Mitchell was that he was ex-Special Forces intelligence, now supposedly working for DARPA, and that I'd been told to give him total co-operation in the interests of national security. That came from the highest level at the Pentagon.'

'Well, it seems Jack doesn't take his orders from the Pentagon. Seems he doesn't take them from *anybody*. He's got his own little black operation, and he tells the Pentagon what to do.'

'What do you mean?'

'He got picked up from Russia by a sub. An *American* sub, inside Russian territorial waters.' Amoros reacted with clear surprise. 'I saw the hull number,' Chase went on. 'I looked it up – SSN-23, Seawolf-class attack sub, USS *Jimmy Carter*. Mitchell's old boat. And funnily enough, it's been modified for Special Forces operations. Be a bit of a coincidence if it just happened to be there.'

'There's no way he could have that kind of authority,' protested Amoros. 'Even black projects report to *somebody*.'

'Doesn't seem to bother him much. He had a little rant about what he was doing being too important to leave to politicians. The bastard's gone rogue, Hector – and he's got Nina, and the sword, and everything he needs to make his weapon work. I've seen one like it in action; it's pretty fucking nasty. So I need you to help me rescue her – and stop him.'

'How? I don't know where he is.'

'Someone does,' said Chase, leaning back in the chair. The gun drifted away from the former admiral, very slightly. 'He might be running a black project, but he's using regular military assets as well. Intel and civilian ones an' all. The sub, helicopters, jets, cars, even the weapons he's requisitioned – there'll be a paper trail, somewhere. Somebody at the Pentagon knows how to find him. You must still have lots of old mates there. Get on to them.'

Amoros shifted uneasily. 'That would mean I'd be revealing knowledge of a black project I wasn't cleared for. I wouldn't just lose my post for that – I could go to prison for it.'

The gun moved back. 'At least you'd still be alive to go to prison.'

Amoros stroked his beard, considering it. 'I'll . . . make some calls.'

33

The Norwegian Sea

Nina jumped from the bunk as the cabin's steel hatch was unlocked and swung open.

'Whoa, now,' said Mitchell, his open palm snapping up to intercept her fist just before it smacked into his face. He closed his fingers round it and forced her arm back down. 'Guess it's true about redheads having a bad temper.'

She narrowed her eyes in pain as he squeezed her hand; then she lashed out with one foot at his kneecap. He jerked back, her heel barely missing him. 'I'm going to kill you,' she promised.

'No you're not,' Mitchell replied, unconcerned. 'Let's go.'

'Go where?' The initial helicopter flight the previous night had been short, transferring to a private jet at

Southampton airport that then flew the length of the country to Wick, on the northeastern tip of Scotland. Another, larger helicopter was waiting for them there, quickly taking off and pounding northwards over the dark wastes of the North Sea, the flares of oil platforms below the only markers of the passage of hundreds of miles. Eventually even these fell behind, nothing outside except blackness.

Until a ship appeared ahead, a blazing beacon of lights in the void. It seemed to be a cargo vessel, the main deck loaded with stacked containers. The chopper landed on a pad overhanging the stern, and Nina was bustled through the ship to the windowless metal cabin. After being released from the cuffs, she had been left by herself.

Her fear for Chase and Holly gradually gave way to a simmering fury. Despair would get her nowhere. What she had to do now was stop whatever Mitchell was planning, and make him pay for everything he had done.

'To Excalibur,' said Mitchell. 'It's in place, the system's ready . . . there's only one thing we need.'

'Me.'

'Yup. Let's go.'

There were two large men accompanying Mitchell, one with a pair of handcuffs attached to his belt, but they weren't needed; Nina was all too aware that even if she broke away from her escorts, there was nowhere for her to go. Instead, she examined her surroundings for anything that might help her as they descended through the superstructure. A momentary glimpse through a porthole told her it was again dark outside, a whole day having gone by.

They passed below the level of the main deck and continued to descend. 'So I'm guessing this isn't a regular container ship,' she finally said, faux-conversationally.

'You got that right,' Mitchell answered. 'By the way, this is the *Aurora* – I didn't get a chance to welcome you aboard last night. Guess my manners are slipping. Made entirely out of non-magnetic steel and titanium. It's DARPA's latest toy.'

'I thought you didn't work for DARPA.'

He smiled. 'DARPA paid for it – only they don't even know it. That's the great thing about having an agency where most of its budget is off the books. It's hard to challenge the construction of something if no one even knows it exists.'

'So you're basically just stealing money from the government.'

'Hardly.' His expression became colder. 'When it comes to the defence of the United States, any expenditure is justified. And any price is worth paying.'

'Including murder?'

'Maybe you should ask Eddie about that,' he said sarcastically. 'He didn't exactly go around handing out candy and flowers while he was defending *his* country.'

'He's nothing like you.'

'Yeah, you're right – because he just did what he was told, went where he was sent. Killed who he was told to kill. I'm being active. I'm taking care of threats to my country before anyone even knows they exist. You should be thanking me for what I'm doing.'

Nina laughed incredulously. 'Y'know, I really don't think I want to be indebted to you. Or anyone like you.'

'Then it's a good job we never ask for those debts to be paid. What the hell would you know about making sacrifices for a greater cause, anyway?' He shot her a scathing look as they continued down another flight of stairs. 'My work cost me my marriage, but I'd do it all again, because it has to be done. What've you done? Poked around in the mud finding trinkets. And don't give me any crap about it being for the benefit of humanity – it was all for your own personal glory, don't try to deny it.'

Nina snorted. 'A little defensive there, Jack, ain'cha? All those lonely nights getting to you?' Mitchell ignored her, prompting her to let out a self-satisfied 'Hah!' under her breath as they reached the bottom of the stairs.

He went to a large metal door and pushed a button beside it. It slid open with a hydraulic hiss. 'This is it,' he said, directing her inside.

Nina stepped through to find herself in a control room, surprisingly similar to the one at Vaskovich's facility. There was even a view through a large window out at another huge piece of machinery . . . but where the Russian generator had been built vertically, descending into the hill, this one lay horizontally, running along the length of the cavernous hold. The rings of electro-magnets, more of them than in the Russian system, receded hundreds of feet into the distance. Knots of cables wrapped around everything like black veins gave Nina the feeling of being inside a monstrous bio-mechanical ribcage.

At the far end of the hold, spotlights picked out a gleaming silver cross at the bottom of the final ring.

Excalibur.

'This is *our* earth energy generator,' Mitchell announced proudly, 'and it's better than Vaskovich's system in every way. For a start, it's mobile; the lines of energy aren't limited to dry land. They occur at sea, too, and we can move the ship to wherever the flux convergences are the strongest.' His smugness increased when he saw that Nina was unable to conceal her awe at the scale of the structure. 'So what do you think?'

'I'd be a lot more impressed if it hadn't been designed to kill people,' she said acidly, taking his smile down several notches. She turned to a large screen on one wall which displayed a map of the North Pole, the shapes of the continents distorted around it. She located the United Kingdom near one edge of the map and looked polewards from it, seeing a green circle marked with longitude and latitude co-ordinates in the sea at the edge of the Arctic Circle between Norway and Iceland. 'So that's us, huh? I take it we're not freezing our asses off in the middle of nowhere without a good reason.'

'Damn straight.' Mitchell went to one of the consoles, waved the technician manning it aside, and entered commands into the computer. More symbols appeared on the map: groups of green circles and red triangles in the open ocean between Russia and the polar icepack. 'The red symbols are Russian warships.'

'Red Russians? Gee, that's original.'

'I didn't pick the colours. But the green symbols are the two carrier strike groups we've deployed in the Arctic Ocean, the *Enterprise* and the *George Washington*. I know you haven't exactly seen much CNN for the last week, but I'm sure you remember that the Russians are being kinda belligerent about their territorial claims at the pole. There's a lot of oil and gas up there, and they want it. They want it all.'

'And you don't want them to have it,' said Nina, realising. 'You're going to sink their ships, aren't you? You're going to use this thing to blow them out of the water without anybody ever knowing who did it.'

'Not exactly.' Mitchell's smug look disappeared, replaced by one of grim determination. 'I'm going to use it to sink one of *our* ships.'

'*What?*' Nina gaped at him. 'You want to blow up an *American* ship? Why?'

'If one of our carriers gets attacked, it'll automatically be assumed that it was by the Russians, and the other ships in the strike group will retaliate. We'll take out the bulk of the Russian polar fleet, including their carrier, the *Admiral Kuznetsov* – their only carrier.'

'But – but the Russians have *nukes!*' Nina cried, horrified. 'If you do this, it'll escalate into World War Three!'

'No. It won't. The Russians don't want Moscow to be nuked any more than we want to see New York go up. So after the initial skirmish, the hotlines'll get *real* hot for a while, then things'll gradually cool off. But the job'll be done – the Russians will be out of the game. After that, there'll only be one power in the Arctic. Us. *We'll* control the resources up there, not them.'

'But what if you're wrong? What if the Russians don't back down?'

'Then,' Mitchell said in a chillingly matter-of-fact tone, 'we'll have to deal with them. But it won't come to that. The loss of the *Enterprise*'ll make it obvious to the world that we were the victims.'

Nina was appalled. 'You were an American naval officer! How can you even *think* about attacking one of our own ships?'

'The *Enterprise* is fifty years old, and about to be decommissioned and scrapped anyway. This way, at least she serves a purpose for the good of the country.'

'And what about the crew?' Nina demanded. 'There must be thousands of people on an aircraft carrier!'

'Over four thousand.'

'And are their deaths for the "good of the country" as well?'

'I'm not taking this lightly,' Mitchell insisted. He indicated the other people in the control room. 'None of us are. But when those sailors signed up they took an oath to serve and protect the United States of America, and by securing those resources from the Russians that's exactly what they'll be doing. It's all about power – the power to protect our future.'

'Yeah, I'm sure their families'll see it that way,' Nina said angrily. 'You really think the American people would approve of what you're doing?'

'Yes!' said Mitchell. 'Yes, I do. They want security and stability and cheap gas and *American Idol*, and they don't want to get their own hands dirty to have it. I'm the one who gets my hands dirty, I have to live with it. But I *will* live with it. Just like all the others who've been doing the same thing for sixty years. Because we know we're *right*.'

'My God,' Nina said despairingly. 'You're worse than Vaskovich. You honestly think you're some kind of patriot, don't you? You know what you *actually* are? Completely fucking batshit insane!'

Mitchell regarded her silently for a long moment, then went to a locker and took out one of the futuristic-looking assault rifles she had seen him use in Russia. Before Nina realised what he was doing, he shot her in the thigh.

She dropped to the floor, screaming and clutching the wound. The 3.6 millimetre bullet had gone cleanly through her right leg, Mitchell deliberately aiming to miss the bone and any major arteries – but it was still agonising. 'Jesus Christ!' she shrieked. 'What the *fuck* are you doing?'

'It's just a scratch, a flesh wound,' he replied with cold sarcasm. 'I only need you *alive*. I don't need you *unhurt* – and to be honest, I've had enough of the sound of your voice.' He put down the rifle and turned to the startled occupants of the control room. 'Stick a Band-Aid on that wound, then get her into position. It's time.'

★

'How much further?' Chase asked over the incessant buzz of the propellers, surveying the darkness below.

Amoros checked the plane's instruments. 'It can't be much further, if it's where my contact said it was.' He gave Chase a look of concern. 'Eddie, we're getting close to the fuel limit. If we don't find this ship in the next ten minutes, I'm going to have to head for land.'

Chase wanted to order him to stay out for as long as it took them to locate Nina, but knew it was pointless. The Piper Seminole that Amoros had managed to wangle from another UN agency had already burned through more than half its fuel; even landing in nearer Norway rather than returning to Scotland would be cutting it fine.

But he was sure Nina was out here. Amoros had made use of his Pentagon connections to probe more deeply into the recent actions of Jack Mitchell, and though it had taken several frustrating hours the name of a ship had eventually been provided: *Aurora*. Chase suspected that whoever gave Amoros the name had put their entire career on the line by doing so, but the former admiral had a lot of good friends in the military – and a lot of favours he could call in.

The *Aurora* itself, when they looked up its details, seemed unremarkable: a container vessel of slightly under nine hundred feet in length, registered to a Panamanian shipping company – almost certainly a front. Why Mitchell would have taken Nina aboard, Chase wasn't sure, but Amoros's sources suggested that he had.

So Chase was going aboard too.

If they could find the *Aurora* in time.

'I don't know what you think you're going to do,' Amoros said, glancing across as Chase gave the pair of pistols he was carrying a final check, then attached a sheathed combat knife and two hand grenades to the webbing round his chest. 'There'll be an entire crew aboard, not just Mitchell.'

'They won't have any problems if they stay out of my way,' Chase told him. 'I'm just there to get Nina.'

'And then what? Put a gun to the captain's head and tell him to turn for port?'

'If I have to. I'll figure it all out when it happens.'

Amoros was about to offer his opinion of Chase's tactics, or lack thereof, when he spotted something in the distance. 'I see a ship. Eleven o'clock.'

'Got it.' Chase scanned the cold sea through a pair of powerful binoculars, quickly picking out a cluster of lights in the ink-black void. 'Container ship, could be the *Aurora*.' The barely discernible flag at the stern looked Panamanian, but it was hard to be sure. 'Get in closer.'

Nina's leg was being bandaged, but she was offered no painkillers. Her body fought her mind, wanting to shut down to find relief from the burning in her thigh, but she refused to cave in to it, doggedly resisting unconsciousness.

'Is she ready?' Mitchell asked impatiently.

'Almost,' replied the man securing the last of the bandages.

'Bring the reactors up to stage one power. We've wasted enough time.'

'Reactors?' Nina asked. 'This thing's nuclear?'

'From decommissioned Los Angeles-class subs. The generator needs a lot of power at start-up, just like Vaskovich's.' Mitchell turned to one of the technicians. 'Once we're steady at stage one, deploy the antenna array. Then charge up the magnets—'

'Sir!' called another man from across the room. 'Radar contact changing course, coming straight for us.'

'On screen,' Mitchell snapped, facing the large display on the wall. The map zoomed in on a smaller area around the *Aurora*'s position. A yellow square was slowly moving towards it from the south. 'What is it?'

'Propeller aircraft, course track suggests it came from Scotland.'

'Identify it!'

'Got the transponder code, checking the tail number . . . It's a United Nations plane, sir. Attached to the Oceanic Survey—'

'Son of a bitch,' Mitchell hissed under his breath. 'It's Chase, it has to be.' Nina's heart jumped at the name. 'Someone at the Pentagon's been talking to Amoros. God *damn* it!'

Even through her discomfort, Nina managed a smile. 'Oh, you're in trouble now.'

Mitchell glared at her. 'Get her into position,' he ordered. 'And take down that plane!'

★

Chase finished fastening his parachute straps and used the binoculars to take another look at the ship. It was now close enough to show that the flag was indeed that of Panama, and after a moment the name painted on the bow finally came into focus.

Aurora.

'That's it!' he said. 'Okay, fly over it, I want a closer look.' He glanced at the altimeter and saw that the Seminole was at slightly over seven thousand feet. When he was ready to jump, he would get Amoros to descend by a couple of thousand; he had no way to judge the wind, and wanted to minimise the chances of being blown away from the freighter.

He looked back through the binoculars. The *Aurora* took on greater clarity as they approached. There was a helicopter on a pad behind the superstructure, which was unusual – most ships of the type would use the space for additional cargo – but the rest of the vessel seemed normal, high stacks of multicoloured containers filling its huge main deck.

Movement caught his eye: someone emerging from the superstructure and crossing to the edge of the open wing bridge . . .

He wasn't going for a smoke.

'Shit!' Chase gasped. '*Incoming!*' Amoros stared at him in disbelief. 'They've got a Stinger!' The man was hefting the tubular anti-aircraft missile launcher over his shoulder, lining up the heat-seeking head on their plane . . .

'Jump!' Amoros shouted. 'Eddie, go!'

'But—'

'*Go!*'

With a last look at Amoros, Chase pushed open the door and flung himself out. The freezing wind was like a blow to the chest; he tumbled through the air before throwing his arms and legs wide to stabilise himself. The ship rolled into view, a splash of floodlit colour amongst the darkness.

Orange light flared from the wing bridge. A Stinger missile leapt from the launcher, a spot of fire at the head of a column of smoke.

The Seminole had already banked away, Amoros turning hard in an attempt to break the Stinger's lock. Chase knew his chances weren't good. The Stinger could take down fighter jets – a civilian twin-prop would be an easy target.

The missile spiralled upwards as Chase fell, its sonic boom pounding him as it passed. He turned his head to track it—

The Stinger hit the Seminole's port engine and exploded, the wing blowing apart in a swelling fireball of burning fuel. The cabin windows flared white as an inferno swept through the fuselage, then the remains of the aircraft rolled in flames towards the hungry sea below.

Chase had no time to think about Amoros. He was dropping fast, and the *Aurora* was still some distance ahead. He had no choice but to deploy his parachute –

but if he was seen he would be an easy target, and he might still fall short of the ship . . .

He pulled the ripcord. Nylon hissed out of the pack, blossoming above him into a dark rectangle. The harness snapped tight round his chest and shoulders.

Had it slowed him enough? Or was he already too low?

He guessed he was at about four thousand feet, but in the darkness it was difficult to be sure. He pulled the control cords, trying to give himself as much forward momentum as possible.

All he could do now was hope.

'Got it!' the technician said. 'Target is going down. It's on fire.'

'Monitor for distress calls,' Mitchell ordered. 'If there are any, jam them.'

Nina's brief elation turned to horror, part of her mind now wanting to follow the desire of her body and simply switch off to escape a new pain: loss. But again she refused to surrender.

If Chase was gone . . . then *she* had to stop Mitchell.

Somehow.

'It just hit the water,' said the technician a few seconds later. 'No radio messages.'

'Keep monitoring just in case. And deploy the antenna array.' Mitchell pulled Nina roughly to her feet. She gasped in pain. 'You wanted Excalibur?' he said. 'It's yours – for the rest of your life.'

★

Chase willed the parachute to stay aloft. He was almost in range of the slowly moving *Aurora*, just a few hundred feet away, but was still losing height too rapidly. He strained to hold his position, trying to eke out every last foot as he aimed for the containers . . .

They *moved*.

For a moment he was stunned, unable to take in what was happening. The container roofs were opening, each swinging up and round in a mechanical ballet like some monstrous transformer toy. More mechanisms came to life within, gleaming metal spears rising up and extending as their upper sections sprouted into giant alien sunflowers.

The entire top layer of containers was nothing more than a disguise for an antenna array, smaller than the one surrounding Vaskovich's facility but more dense, more complex, hundreds of glittering collectors ready to draw in the earth's own energy . . . then unleash it.

And Chase was falling right into them.

He pulled the cords, trying to swing away from the antenna field towards the stern. It meant travelling further and running the risk of falling below the level of the deck, but it was better than being impaled as he landed. 'Come on, come on, *shiiiiit*—'

Too low, moving too slowly . . .

He thrust his feet out as he swept into one of the still-deploying antennas with a rattling clash of metal. The parachute swooshed over him, already collapsing as he was brought to a near-stop – the antenna was stronger than it looked, bending but not breaking.

He fell, grabbing for one of the extended 'petals' to stop himself dropping into the pitch darkness inside the container. It twisted under his weight, creaking and screeching at its hinge, but didn't give way. Half tangled in the parachute cords, Chase crashed against the antenna's column. He flung his arms round it, sliding down as if on a fireman's pole before hitting the metal floor.

The parachute was caught in the antennas, flapping in the wind. He pulled the release and shrugged off the harness, then drew one of his guns with one hand, a small torch with the other.

What looked on the outside like a collection of individual containers was revealed as nothing more than a framework supporting a façade. The whole array was now fully raised, extending high above the open roofs. Chase directed the torch at the floor, which turned out to be a solid deck. That meant the containers below were fake too, a shell with something hidden inside. The antenna array gave him a pretty good idea what. The whole ship was a floating version of Vaskovich's earth energy facility.

Only Mitchell had designed this one for destruction, not production. And if the antennas were now in position . . .

He ran through the metal forest towards the aft superstructure, hunting for a way in before anyone aboard realised they had a visitor.

★

Mitchell and his two guards half carried, half dragged the struggling Nina along the length of the hold, the generator's magnetic rings hanging threateningly overhead. Excalibur waited for them at the far end on what Nina now saw was a platform mounted on a crane arm that would lift it up to the centre of the ring. 'You'll be staying with us for a while,' Mitchell told her. 'At least until we can find someone else who can energise the sword.'

'Gee, I feel so special,' Nina snapped. 'Didn't you think about testing your own people before moving into kidnapping? You know, keep it in the psychotic, traitorous family.'

'I did. Nobody worked. I would have gone wider, but trooping hundreds of people through the ultra-secret weapons platform and asking them to hold King Arthur's sword to see if it glowed might have raised a few questions.'

They reached the platform. Excalibur had been diligently polished, not a speck of dust on it. It rested point down in a black frame of carbon fibre, held in place by a clamp round the cross-guard. And there was another clamp, larger and more box-like, open and waiting round the hilt. Nina felt a chill. Inside the clamp was an indentation . . . just large enough for her hands to fit inside.

Mitchell saw her growing look of horror. 'Yeah, I thought you wouldn't hold it voluntarily.' He nodded, and the two men pushed her closer.

Nina struggled to wrest her arms from their grip, keeping her fists clenched. 'If you think I'm gonna stick my hand in that thing—'

Another nod. The man to her right punched her injured thigh. The resurgent pain hit Nina so hard that she almost blacked out. By the time she started to recover, it was too late – her hands had been prised open and placed round Excalibur's hilt, and the clamp closed with a decisive *snick*.

'No!' she cried, trying to pull free. 'Lemme go!' But the box was tight round her wrists, hard edges cutting into her skin. Both hands were pressed against the cold metal of the sword, and the blade was shining brightly. Charged with earth energy, the molecules along its edges aligned into a single line of sharpness, it could cut through almost anything.

But that didn't help her. The clamps round the guard and hilt held it in place in the frame, locked solid.

Nina wanted to kick Mitchell, but the pain in her wounded leg was too intense for her to move it. All she could throw at him was spit and invective. 'Fuck you.'

Mitchell irritably wiped away the glob of her saliva from his left eye, and was about to operate the platform's controls when an urgent voice crackled over the walkie-talkie of one of the guards. He took it from the man and listened, eyes slowly widening first in surprise, then sudden anger. 'Find him and kill him!' he snarled. 'Now!'

Nina's eyes widened too, with something she hadn't

expected to feel again – delight. 'Eddie, huh? You're screwed now!' she crowed.

'There are forty people on this ship—'

'Tough luck on them.' Stung, Mitchell hit the controls to elevate the platform. Trapped, alone, Nina was lifted to the centre of the vast generator.

34

A hatch at the rear of the fake containers led into the superstructure. Chase went through it, gun covering the passage beyond. No sign of anyone. So far, so good—

An urgent, honking alarm sounded, a voice booming over the PA system: 'All hands, intruder alert! Repeat, intruder alert!'

Not so good. The parachute must have been spotted.

Chase drew his second gun, a Heckler and Koch USP Expert now in each hand. It wasn't his preferred choice of weapon, but the .45-calibre bullets would be more than adequate at close quarters.

Not knowing Nina's location, he decided to start with the most logical place. If Mitchell planned to fire the weapon, he needed both Nina and Excalibur to make it work, and the hold was the only place large enough to house the earth energy generator. He prowled the corridors until he found narrow stairs leading down, and started to descend—

Someone was running towards him.

Caught halfway down the steep flight, Chase hooked his arms over both banisters and slid down the stairs with his guns held out in front of him. An armed man was below; Chase fired twice, knocking him back in a spray of blood. He reached the end of the banisters and clanked on the deck, seeing another man and taking him down with a single shot to the head before spinning at a sound behind him and blowing away a third.

He hurried forward. Though an open hatchway at the end of the corridor he saw more stairs leading down—

A man leaned out from behind the hatchway and fired at him. The bullet zipped past Chase's head as he threw himself sideways, shooting back. Both shots clanged uselessly against metal.

Shadows darted across the wall beyond the hatch, more men on the stairs—

He fired another shot to encourage them to stay back as he looked for cover. There was a hatch in the wall – he pulled it open, using it as a shield as more gunfire spat from the end of the corridor. The hatch jolted as bullets slammed into it, coin-sized dents erupting across the metal.

Shouts from behind. More people were coming after him.

He was about to be pinned down . . .

With no other choice, he jumped through the door and slammed it behind him.

The room beyond was a storage area. Some of the stacked equipment resembled the magnets of Vaskovich's generator, and he also saw a pack containing a glidewing like the one Mitchell had used to reach Grozevny. But he didn't care about the room's contents – only that there were no other exits.

Unless—

A large duct emerged from the ceiling, feeding fresh air into the enclosed hull – with another vent in the wall below it. Chase raised both guns and blasted the vent cover to pieces. He jumped on a pile of boxes and bashed the broken louvres away, then clambered inside.

The duct was wider than he'd expected, and he felt a warm breeze against his face as he scrambled along it. It wasn't so much for ventilation as for cooling, to let hot air out. He heard the hatch being thrown open behind him. More shouting as men burst into the room and found nothing but hardware – but it wouldn't take a genius to figure out where he'd gone.

He aimed one gun back at the vent entrance, moving as quickly as he could towards the light coming through grilles in the duct floor ahead. Another shout – someone had seen the open vent. He glanced backwards. A head appeared in silhouette within the rectangular opening. A shot from the USP, and the head disappeared in several different directions at once.

A fusillade of bullets would come along the vent at any moment—

He reached the first grille, getting a brief sense of a cavernous space beneath before smashing at it with his pistols. The thin metal immediately buckled. He kept striking it until one end broke away from the frame and it swung loose.

There was a girder several feet below. Not much, but it was all he had. He dropped through the hole as shots ripped into the duct walls just above him.

He hit the beam and slithered down it, the metal tilted at a steep angle. One of his guns spun away to the floor far below as he grabbed the support, both legs hanging over a long vertical drop.

Pulse pounding, he saw he was hanging from the framework supporting a horizontal copy of Vaskovich's system. One of the huge rings of electromagnets was suspended from the other side of the beam by massive insulators. More rings stretched away along the length of the hold to—

Nina!

She was slightly below him at the far end of the generator, trapped on an elevated platform with Excalibur. He wanted to call out to her, but couldn't, unwilling to give away his position.

Though it wouldn't be long before he was found.

He pulled himself up, finding a foothold. The generator didn't seem to be active yet – but with the antenna array deployed, it wouldn't be long. Could he sabotage it?

The gear attached to his webbing clinked against the support. An idea formed . . .

'What the *fuck*?' Mitchell ran to the control-room

window, staring in disbelief at the figure climbing down a support beam. 'He's in here!' He snatched a headset off one of the technicians and yelled into its microphone. 'Security! He's in the hold, on the generator! Get your asses down here, *now*!' Grabbing the XM-201, he raced down the steps to the deck.

Chase saw him coming as he jumped from the frame and stood beneath the magnetic ring. He had his remaining pistol in one hand . . . and a grenade in the other, fingers lightly gripping the safety handle. He held his arms wide to make sure Mitchell could see what he was holding. There was still a chance he might just shoot him anyway, but as he'd hoped the American was being cautious, not wanting to risk any damage to the generator.

'Hey, Jack!' he called as Mitchell drew closer, rifle raised. 'Nice boat!'

'Put the pin back in, Eddie,' said Mitchell angrily.

'I dunno, I'm curious. You said bad things'd happen if the magnets got damaged – sounds like it might be worth seeing. Or you could let Nina go and we'll just leave.' He looked up at the platform. Nina had seen him by now, watching the distant scene play out.

'That's not really an option.' Mitchell clicked the ammo selector to a new position and took more precise aim. 'I can blow your whole arm off at the shoulder, Eddie – and who knows, your hand might even keep hold of the spoon. Even if it doesn't, the magnets will survive, they're tough.'

'So tough that you need a room full of spares?' Chase

countered. 'Let Nina go, or I blow this place to buggery.'

'And you with it?'

'If that's what it takes.'

Mitchell shook his head. 'No. I know you by now, Eddie. You're all about the mission, just like me – and your mission's getting Nina out of here alive. If you blew yourself up, your mission'd fail, and I know how much you hate that.'

'We'll see.'

Mitchell just smirked. Other men ran up behind him. Some were armed with XM-201s, others with more conventional sidearms. Mitchell glanced at them, then erupted in anger. 'What the hell are you doing? Non-magnetics *only* in here! Get out!' Realisation crossed his face, and he turned back to Chase. 'You were reported as carrying two guns, Eddie. Where's the other one?'

'No idea,' Chase answered truthfully. 'I dropped it, could be anywhere. No telling how much damage it might do if it gets pulled into the magnets, eh?'

'Spread out,' Mitchell ordered his men, keeping his gun aimed at Chase. 'Foreign object sweep. There's a gun around here somewhere – find it.'

Chase adopted a casual, not-a-chance expression, but it wasn't long before one of the men called out and recovered the fallen USP from behind a skein of cables. 'Bollocks,' he muttered.

'Nice bit of improvisation, Eddie,' Mitchell said, 'but it didn't work. You've got nothing. Now put the pin back in.'

With a resigned shrug, Chase flipped the grenade round in his hand to reveal that the pin had been in place all along, hidden by his thumb. 'Worth a try.'

'Search him.' Two men went to Chase and frisked him, taking his few remaining belongings. 'Okay, get those out of the field limit. Move it, Eddie.' He jerked the XM-201 towards the control room.

'Not going to kill me?'

Mitchell smiled. 'Oh, hell yes. I just don't want any bullets flying around in here. Go on.'

Chase looked helplessly up at Nina, then started for the control room, Mitchell tracking him with his gun. All but one of the other men exited the hold ahead of them, the last also aiming a rifle at Chase as he followed him to the stairs. 'So what're you going to blow up? Iran? Russia? Venezuela?'

'Close with the second one,' said Mitchell as they entered the control room. 'Are we at stage one power?'

'Yes, sir,' a technician answered. 'We're at the convergence point of five flux lines, and already drawing zero point three seven from them. Everything is green.'

'Then fire it all up. Full power.'

The technicians worked their consoles in unison, the deck trembling as a thrumming electrical rumble began to rise. Mitchell moved to watch one display in particular, a digital readout of the system's power, just like the one in Russia. It climbed smoothly past 0.50 as power was fed in and the magnetic field increased in strength, channelling more earth energy through the system.

Through the superconductor. Through Excalibur.

Chase could still see Nina at the far end of the hold, pinned in the bull's-eye of the last ring. The sword glowed ever brighter in front of her. Unable to shield her eyes with her hands, she turned her head away from the glare.

A bolt of electricity sizzled across one of the nearer rings, dancing between the magnets. Other flashes built up around the generator, the sharp smell of ozone hitting Chase's nostrils. 'Will she be okay up there?'

'I wouldn't have put her there if it was going to kill her. I need her alive.' The gauge ticked rapidly past 0.80. 'Confirm antenna alignment.'

'Confirmed, sir,' a man replied. 'Ionic reflection is calculated and set, and we have target lock.'

Mitchell nodded. 0.90 flicked past, 0.95 . . . 'We've reached threshold!' he exclaimed, banging a fist on the console as 1.00 came and went without pause, the numbers climbing at an increasing pace.

'Confirmed!' said a technician with equal excitement. 'The process is now self-sustaining, and rising along the predicted curve.'

'Magnetic field status?'

'Firm, and also rising.'

'Keep it going,' Mitchell demanded. 'Ready firing sequence.'

Chase watched Nina as electrical flares crackled around her, and then his gaze moved across to the support beam on which he had landed after dropping from the duct.

Staring intently at one particular spot, he whispered, 'Come on, come *on* . . .'

Mitchell looked sharply at him. 'What was that?'

'Oh, nothing,' Chase said. 'Just that, you know I had a hand grenade when you found me?'

'Yeah?'

'When I came into the hold, I had *two*.'

Mitchell whirled to stare up at the beam, opening his mouth to issue a frantic command—

Too late.

Chase's other grenade had been hanging by its pin from a hook supporting part of the generator's miles of wiring. As the magnetic field rose in intensity, the grenade's steel casing was pulled towards the nearby ring of electro-magnets, dangling perpendicular to the floor below. At first the pin held, but as the invisible force grew stronger and stronger, it began to bend . . . before breaking.

The grenade shot across the gap and smacked against a magnet, its safety handle springing loose and clanging beside it. The fuse counted down the seconds, three, two, one—

The explosion blew the electromagnet to pieces. Shattered fragments were snatched up by the intense magnetic field and whirled around the generator to slam into other components, tearing them from their supports. Massive electrical arcs seared across the hold, sparks and flames gouting into the air where they struck.

Another magnet overloaded and exploded, debris smashing the control-room window. Mitchell dived behind a console – and Chase spun and drove his fist into the face of the stunned man guarding him, mashing his nose up into his brain with a hideous crunch.

He grabbed the dead man's XM-201 as he fell. It was useless to him as a rifle, the biometric lock in place. Instead he stabbed at the button of the grenade launcher.

The grenade shot across the control room, hitting a console in the opposite corner. Technicians were sent flying by the blast, one man backflipping through the broken window like a rag doll. Chase ran for the door, firing another grenade to take out a second set of controls. He saw Mitchell scrambling across the floor and was about to send the final shot at him, but a nearer console blocked his aim – if he fired, he would be caught in the blast himself. Instead he jumped through the door and unleashed the last grenade at the big screen on the wall, the computer map vanishing in a storm of pulverised liquid crystal.

He raced down the stairs into the hold. The man who had been blown out of the window was draped brokenly over the first ring above him. Chase ignored the gruesome sight and sprinted along one side of the generator, tossing the rifle away.

Shielding his eyes from the arc-welder brilliance of the electrical bolts, he ran towards the platform holding Nina.

★

'Shut it down!' Mitchell screamed at one of the surviving technicians. 'It's overloading, shut the goddamn thing *down!*'

'I can't!' the man protested. 'It's self-sustaining! The system's locked into its last command – it's just going to keep on building up power until it blows. The only way to stop it is to take out the superconductor!'

'Or the person holding it,' Mitchell growled, looking through the swirling smoke towards the far end of the chamber. The glow of Excalibur was clearly visible – as was Nina, still locked to it.

He hunted for his gun. It lay under a burning console, flames blistering its casing. 'Maybe you were right about it being too easy to break, Eddie,' he said, before darting to the window. A glance down into the hold told him that Chase had abandoned his stolen XM-201, his handprint not in the gun's memory.

But Mitchell's was.

'Do whatever you can to stabilise the system,' he snapped at the technician as he ran for the door.

The temperature was rising fast as more bolts of electricity sizzled across the generator, but what Chase hadn't been prepared for was the smell. The stench of burning paint and melting plastic assaulted his nose and eyes, everything the arcs touched outside the magnetic rings instantly flashing into flames. Some of them came too close for comfort as he ran along the hold, forcing him to stop until they died away. His vision was blotched by vivid after-images of nearby strikes.

He held back as another bolt stabbed at the wall, molten blobs of metal spitting out from it, then dashed past and reached the crane. 'Eddie!' Nina warned from above. 'Jack's coming after you!'

Chase looked back. Mitchell had retrieved the rifle and was running along the hold in pursuit. But he held his fire, not wanting to risk hitting another magnet and making the situation worse.

There was a panel near the platform's base. Chase worked the controls. With a hydraulic whine, the platform descended. Nina came into full view as it dropped the last few feet. He saw the bandage on her right thigh. 'Jesus! What happened?'

'That son of a bitch shot me, that's what happened! Get me out of this thing!'

Hunching down out of Mitchell's line of fire, Chase climbed on to the platform and examined the clamp round Nina's hands to find a catch. He pushed it; the restraint sprang open. Nina pulled out her hands and Excalibur's light instantly disappeared. But the generator kept working, electricity zapping angrily around the hold. She reached into the frame to release the sword, unlocking the clamp holding it in place.

'What're you doing?' Chase demanded.

'We can't let Jack have it! He was going to blow up the *Enterprise*.'

He looked confused. 'The starship?'

'Yes, the starship,' she snapped sarcastically. 'The *aircraft carrier*! He was going to blame it on the Russians to start a war!' The clamp open, she pulled Excalibur from the frame, the blade lighting up once more. 'Oh, shit!'

Chase saw Mitchell running towards them, not far away now – but his line of fire was still partially blocked by sections of the generator. 'He won't shoot the mag—'

Mitchell fired.

Some of the spray of bullets bounced off the generator, but they didn't damage it, hitting with dull thumps rather than sharp metallic cracks.

Others hit softer targets.

Chase felt as though he'd been kicked in the stomach. Another painful blow slammed into his right shoulder as he was knocked backwards, instantly numbing the limb. Nina took a glancing impact to her side, her injured leg buckling. She lost her balance and fell off the platform. Excalibur skittered away across the deck.

Plastic bullets, Chase realised – the XM-201's non-lethal ammunition option. Gasping, he rolled over, right arm hanging limply. He gripped the now-empty frame that had held Excalibur with his left and began to haul himself up.

Mitchell's boot smashed into his back, felling him again. The American jumped on to the platform and delivered another vicious kick, then clubbed him with the rifle. 'Come on, you fucker!' he screamed. Another kick. Chase groaned in pain. 'See who's the best now, won't we?'

He stamped on Chase's chest, grinding a heel into his

ribs. Breathless, Chase tried to twist out from under him, but with only one arm couldn't get enough leverage. Mitchell loomed over him, huge electrical arcs crackling around the ring above him like a malevolent halo.

But Chase wasn't finished yet.

With a strangled roar, he smashed his fist into the only vulnerable target he could reach, the back of Mitchell's knee. Mitchell lurched forward as his leg bent, and Chase delivered another punch, this time straight up between his legs into his groin.

Mitchell doubled over with a groan, stumbling against the frame. The pressure on Chase's chest eased and he rolled from the platform to the deck. He looked up—

A boot smashed into his face, cracking the back of his head against the floor. Sickening stars exploded in his vision. Mitchell's foot stamped down again, this time on his left forearm. Agony erupted from the old wound. Chase screamed.

Mitchell brought up the rifle and aimed it into Chase's face.

He switched the ammo selector. No plastic bullets this time, just pure metallic death as his mouth contorted into a sadistic leer of victory.

A flash of light filled Chase's eyes.

35

B ut it wasn't from the gun's muzzle.
Instead it was a streak of brilliant blue-white that sliced down to chop the XM-201 cleanly in two. The front half of the rifle barely missed Chase's head as it clattered to the deck – with Mitchell's severed right hand still clenching the grip.

'How's *that* for a flesh wound?' Nina shouted.

Mitchell screamed, clutching the stump of his wrist as blood fountained from it. He stumbled back against the frame.

Nina swung Excalibur again. The blazing sword stabbed straight through Mitchell's abdomen and embedded itself deeply into the carbon fibre frame behind him, only stopping when the cross-guard hit his stomach. She let go – and the weapon's glow vanished, leaving him transfixed, unable to pull the blade out of the frame.

'You wanted power?' cried Nina, hobbling to the platform's control panel. 'Try fifty million volts!'

She hit the button.

The platform started to ascend towards the fierce bolts of earth energy lancing back and forth within the magnetic ring. 'No!' Mitchell shrieked, desperately tugging at the hilt with his remaining hand. It didn't move. *'No!'*

He crossed the streams.

The entire ring lit up with a surging storm of lightning. Mitchell burst into flames, instantly incinerated by the concentrated power searing through his body. More electrical arcs spat outwards, burning into the walls and ceiling with blinding force.

Nina pulled Chase aside as a bolt hit the controls, blowing the machinery to pieces. The platform plunged back down in a column of fire, scattering debris in all directions.

More explosions shook the hold. 'Are you okay, Eddie?'

He spat out blood. 'Right as rain.' A siren wailed, echoing through the vast space. 'I think we should be fucking off home about now.'

'No arguments there.' As Chase stood, Nina saw Excalibur lying amongst the smoking remains of the platform. The blade lit up again as she lifted it and shook off a lump of what looked horribly like barbecued ribs.

Chase put an arm round her waist to support her. 'Let's go!'

More energy stabbed at the walls as they made their way back down the hold. The few people still alive in the control room had gone; the siren was apparently an evacuation warning. One of the magnetic rings behind them tore from its supports and fell to the floor with enough force to shake the entire room. Other components blew apart, sections of the supporting framework collapsing.

An especially bright flash was followed by an ominous creak of metal. 'Oh, that can't be good,' said Nina, looking back at a molten spray spitting from a gash down one side of the hold.

Chase held her more tightly as he increased his pace towards the exit. 'I think we're about to get wet.'

'Not again!'

The gash burst open, metal peeling back like tin foil as seawater spewed into the hold, thousands of gallons of freezing Arctic water rushing through the widening gap. The air filled with explosions of sparks as the generator shorted out.

Fire above, water below, a wave surging along the hold after Chase and Nina as they raced for the exit. Pain stabbed through Nina's leg with every step, but she forced herself onwards. She could hear it thundering towards them like a tsunami, about to sweep them away—

They reached the hatch. Chase flung Nina through just as the wave hit, a chill spray biting at them as the water dashed against the bulkhead. He braced himself and pushed his back against the hatch to force it shut against the force of the flood. It clunked against the frame; Nina dragged herself up and pulled the lever to secure it. She slumped to the deck, panting.

'Sorry, love,' said Chase, taking her by the waist again and leading her along the corridor, 'but we can't hang about.' He nodded at the sword. 'Why don't you leave that thing, let it go down with the boat?'

'They could still find it if they salvage the ship.'

'Fair enough. But how about I keep hold of it? That way I don't have to worry about you accidentally chopping off my leg.'

She handed the sword to him as they reached a flight of stairs leading upwards. Despite her best efforts to keep the weight off her injured leg, Nina still winced in pain at every step. 'Ow, oh, ow! Son of a – oh, if Jack wasn't dead I'd kill him again!'

'I didn't say thanks for that, by the way,' said Chase.

'You don't need to.'

'Yeah, I do! You saving my life isn't something I ever want to get all blasé about.'

'In which case, thank *you* for saving *me* – again! What's that, ten times now?'

'Altogether, or just this time?'

'Y'know, most couples don't actually lose count of that kind of thing . . .'

They kept climbing. More creaks echoed through the ship, distant thumps of explosions still rolling up from the hold. And there was another noise, an engine . . .

'Fuck!' said Chase. 'There goes the chopper.'

'Well, it's not as though we could have flown it. And hijacking it might have been a problem without any guns.'

'I've got a bloody sword! Just hope there's some boats left.'

They finally reached the level of the main deck. By now it was clear the ship was beginning to sink, tipping down at the bow. Chase opened a hatch and stepped out into the cold wind, leaving Nina leaning against the bulkhead. 'Shit!' The lifeboat davit was empty, cables hanging limply down to the water. Below, a large orange boat bobbed away from the freighter, a strobe light blinking on its fibreglass roof.

He hurried across the deck to check the opposite side. The other boat was still on its cables, almost in the water. He could have jumped on to the nearest cable and shinned down into the boat, but Nina couldn't, not with her leg.

'What is it?' Nina asked as he ran back to her.

'You saw *Titanic*, right?'

'Oh . . .'

They both lurched as the *Aurora* shuddered. The tilt of the deck was now more apparent, and increasing.

'Okay, okay,' said Nina, thinking out loud, 'we're on a ship, with no lifeboats. There must be something else that floats. What floats?'

'A witch,' Chase answered. Nina gave him a surprised look. 'What? I never said I didn't *watch* any Monty Python.'

'Great, but unless you've actually *got* a witch, and preferably her broomstick, that doesn't help much!'

'No broomsticks,' said Chase with sudden hope, 'but I

know where there's *something* that can fly. Wait here!' He dropped Excalibur at her feet and ran back into the ship, sliding down the stairs on the banisters.

'Eddie, where are you – *Eddie!*' Nina shouted, but he had already gone. Frustrated, she waited for him to return. After a minute, Excalibur slowly slid along the deck to clink against the forward bulkhead.

'Two sinking ships in three days,' she muttered as she awkwardly bent to retrieve the sword. 'Eddie! Whatever you're doing, now would be a good time!'

Chase ran back up the stairs. 'Yeah, I'm coming!'

Nina saw he was carrying what looked like a large suitcase with a harness attached. 'What's that?'

'Our way off. Maybe. Come on, we need to get to the top deck.'

Five more painful flights, and Nina slumped with relief against a bulkhead – only to realise she was standing at an angle. A nearby porthole gave her a view of the antenna array, silver flowers picked out by spotlights . . . and beyond them, waves crashing over the top of the mock containers at the bow. It was the Typhoon all over again – only this time they weren't even close to shore.

She looked back at Chase, who was fastening the harness round his body. 'What *is* that thing? A parachute?'

'More like a jetpack.'

'A *jetpack*?'

'It's how Jack got to Vaskovich's – I just hope it's as easy to fly as he said. If you're bringing the sword, there's a compartment in the back – stick it in there. But don't poke any holes in it!'

Nina limped to him and found the compartment's cover, opening it and gingerly dropping Excalibur inside. The glow disappeared as she let go, the blade clanking harmlessly against the polycarbonate interior. She closed the cover as Chase secured the harness. The ship shuddered again, a mournful metallic moan running through the hull. 'Okay,' he said, indicating an exterior hatch, 'get outside.'

Nina still wasn't sure what he had in mind, but limped through it to find herself on the ship's port wing bridge, extending out over the side of the hull. Far below, she saw one of the lifeboats moving away, an orange lozenge picked out by a flashing beacon. Ahead, the sea continued its advance over the containers. The *Aurora*'s stern was out of the water and rising higher, the huge freighter being dragged nose first under the black ocean.

Chase held up a length of rope. 'Wrap this round me, and then round you. Do it a couple of times and tie it as tight as you can. Trust me,' he added, seeing her expression.

'Okay,' she said dubiously, threading the rope between his lower back and the case as he fastened a small control unit round his wrist. 'So you know how this thing works?'

'Sort of. Jack showed me. Okay, more told me than showed me, but I got the gist.'

'I'll take your word for it,' Nina said nervously. She

brought the rope around herself and Chase for a second time and pulled it tight, squeezing them both together as she knotted it.

He wrapped his arms round her, plodding to the edge of the wing bridge. 'We need to get up on the railing. Can you manage?'

'I'll have to, won't I?' Looking down as Chase lifted her, Nina used her left heel to push herself up on each bar of the railing. He followed, one heavy step at a time. She gritted her teeth as her leg wound pressed against Chase's thigh, but managed not to cry out.

'Good lass,' said Chase as they balanced precariously on the top rail, leaning against a post for support. 'Okay, let's see if I can get this thing started.'

'Before you do . . .' Nina said.

'What?'

She kissed him. 'Just in case I don't get another chance.'

He smiled. 'Hey, I finally committed to a wedding date – I'm not going to bloody miss it!' He returned the kiss, then examined the control unit as Nina clung to him. 'Okay. Let's see . . .'

He touched a button. The pack's sides sprang open like the shell of a beetle taking flight, black carbon-fibre delta wings popping out and unfolding before each section then telescoped outwards with a clack.

Chase was impressed by the speed and precision of the deployment, the total wingspan almost ten feet. 'Pretty cool. All right, engines.' He poised his finger over the next control. 'Hold on really tight,' he warned Nina.

'Because when I push this button, it's going to feel like a kick up the arse, and we'll go over the edge!'

Nina squeezed her eyes shut. 'Do it.'

Chase leaned forward and pushed the button.

The four miniature jet turbines screeched to life, the heat from their exhausts instantly blistering the paint on the railing as Chase and Nina fell. The wings flexed in the wind as they dropped, picking up speed—

Downwards. They were plunging parallel to the side of the ship, decks flashing past them.

Chase shifted position, arms outstretched as he arched his back, trying to level out. If he could build up enough speed for the wings to generate lift . . .

The black water rushed towards him, patterns of light from the ship shimmering over it. Still dropping, too fast—

The reflections started to slide under him as the engines reached full thrust and drove them away from the *Aurora* with increasing speed.

It still wasn't enough. They were past the level of the main deck, plummeting the final metres towards the ocean—

They levelled out, the wings abruptly bending upwards as if coming to life. Nina shrieked as the ropes pulled tight around her. Chase desperately leaned back as hard as he could, face pounded by the freezing wind rasping at his skin.

Ground effect, he realised. At very low altitudes, any kind of wing traps air between itself and the surface below, giving extra lift.

But would it be enough to keep them out of the water?

His eyes were streaming in the rising wind. Something shot past to one side: the lifeboat, a barely glimpsed blur of colour falling behind . . .

And below.

They were gaining height!

Chase strained to hold his position as Nina hung beneath him, the thrust from the engines combined with the angle of the wings just enough to put them into a shallow but steady climb. He squinted at the control unit, watching a digital altimeter gradually count upwards. Remembering how much fuel Mitchell had told him the glidewing carried, he struggled to work out how high they could go before it ran out. Nina could have done the calculations in moments, he knew, but the roar of wind and engines would have made it hard to get the information across – and from the way she was shivering, she had other things on her mind. Like temperature, and gravity.

About three thousand feet, he worked out. He would be able to see to the horizon over sixty miles away – assuming there was anything to see. Mitchell wouldn't have wanted any other vessels close enough to observe when he fired the earth energy weapon. The question was, could they glide for long enough to reach anything that might be out there?

The glidewing kept climbing. A thousand feet, and rising. Chase felt Nina's heartbeat thudding against his chest. Rapid, scared . . . but gradually slowing.

Not because she was calming down. Because she was starting to freeze in the bitter wind.

'Stay with me!' he shouted. Her hand squeezed his side. But exposure would take its toll soon enough – and even he couldn't withstand it for ever. It had been years since he had trained for such conditions.

Minutes passed, the altimeter still rising, the jets howling. Not much fuel left. Chase wiped his eyes, realising his tears had frozen on his face. He could barely feel his own touch, nerves numbed.

Three thousand.

A red light flashed on the wrist unit. A fuel warning. One minute left, or thirty seconds, or ten? He didn't know. But the powered part of the flight was almost over, only a long glide down into the blackness remaining . . .

Lights!

Off in the distance, a little constellation of blue and yellow. In the overcast utter darkness it was almost impossible to judge how far away it was, but Chase doubted it was anything less than twenty miles. Could the glidewing carry them that far?

No choice but to find out the hard way. He banked, lining up with the ship.

The engines stuttered, then cut out. The only noise now came from the wind.

He felt Nina's hold on him loosening. 'Nina, stay awake!' he yelled. 'There's a ship, we can make it!' He didn't know if that was true, but if he'd unwittingly lied, she wouldn't have a chance to call him on it.

The altimeter was counting down now. He leaned back as much as he could, trying to maintain height, but without the engines descent was inevitable.

Two thousand feet. The lights still distant, but getting closer, the constellation taking on tantalising form. Smaller than the *Aurora*, maybe nearer than Chase had thought. A trawler?

Closer. Fifteen hundred feet. Nina was now held as much by the rope as by her own efforts, grip weakening, heart slowing. He had no feeling in his face, barely any in his outstretched hands. A thousand feet. The spaces between the lights began to fill with solid colours, the ship fading in from the blackness as if in a movie. Five hundred. Closer. Four hundred, three . . .

Nina went limp. He fought to hold his position as her arms and legs dangled in the slipstream, slowing them. Two hundred, one, dropping fast—

The ship rushed at him, a mast springing out of the darkness directly ahead. Chase twisted, losing lift. Something on the deck, a pile of nets and glistening silver within. He aimed for it, last chance before overshooting and plunging into the waters beyond—

They slammed into the nets. The wings cracked and broke off, but Chase had already wrapped his arms round Nina to protect her as they slithered through a huge pile of fish, scattering freshly caught cod everywhere. The other side of the net was being winched up off the deck; they skidded up it before rolling back into the flapping shoal.

'Bloody hell!' Chase gasped. His sense of touch might have been numbed, but his sense of smell was working all too well. 'Stinks!' The net stopped. He looked round to see a group of shocked fishermen staring at him.

Nina moved feebly in his grip. 'Nina! Are you okay? Nina!'

'Eddie . . .' she whispered drowsily, moving again – this time to rest her head against his chest with an expression almost of contentment, eyes closed. It didn't last long, though. Her nose twitched, and she frowned. 'What's that smell?'

Chase laughed in relief, hugging her. He looked back at the trawlermen as they clambered on to the net. 'Ay up, lads!' he said. 'You going anywhere near England?'

36

England

' So it's my great honour to be here with the
... discoverer of King Arthur's tomb, a woman who
has rewritten the history books more than once ... Dr
Nina Wilde.'

'Thank you, Prime Minister,' said Nina, blushing at the
applause as she limped to take his place at the microphone. Her wound had been treated and she had been
assured of a full recovery in time, but it was less than a
week since it had been inflicted, and the leg was still stiff
and painful.

The small stage on which they stood had been set up at
the foot of Glastonbury Tor. Behind it, a cordon marked
the entrance to the tomb, a full-scale archaeological survey
now under way. She looked out across the crowd, which
was larger than she had expected; as well as the inevitable

press corps and the entourage of police, security and bureaucrats accompanying Britain's Prime Minister, there was also a throng of ordinary people, wanting to witness one of those rare moments when myth was revealed as fact.

But for all the faces looking up at her, Nina's attention was fixed only on one. Chase stood near the stage. Despite all the cuts and stitches on his face, he still managed a grin as he clapped. With him were Elizabeth, Holly and his grandmother, and Mac. She smiled back, then lifted her head to the crowd.

'Thank you,' she repeated, waiting for the applause to die down. 'I'm honoured to be here. But the first thing I should say is that I didn't discover the tomb alone – I had lots of help from other people. And unfortunately, too many of them are no longer with us. Great treasures from the past can inspire awe and wonder, but they can also inspire greed and violence, which cost some of my friends their lives. Before I go on, I'd like to take a moment to remember them.'

She looked down, hands clasped in front of her. The noise of the crowd fell almost to nothing, birdsong from the surrounding countryside briefly the only sound. Then she raised her head again, seeing Chase giving her a sad but appreciative smile. She returned it, then continued.

'Thank you. The Prime Minister just said I've rewritten the history books – and I know that for some people that can be a very frightening thing, when everything they thought they knew gets turned on its head. And I've been guilty of that myself; I've had my own preconceived beliefs. But I've also learned that, sometimes, having your beliefs challenged is the only way that new discoveries can be made, that knowledge can be advanced. And because of that challenge, I'm here with you today as what was once just legend now becomes something greater: truth. A truth that has yet to be fully explored, but the path starts here – at the resting place of Arthur, king of the Britons.'

More applause, even cheering. But Nina was once more looking only at Chase, and his expression of pride.

'So why weren't you up on stage, Uncle Eddie?' Holly asked.

'Ah, you know me,' Chase said modestly. 'Camera-shy.'

'Not from me, you're not.' She held up the phone Chase had bought her and took a picture of him and Nina. 'I want a good picture of my hero.'

'I don't think it's possible to take one,' said Elizabeth, but with humour in her voice. 'Eddie, I'd say thank you, but I don't think it would be enough. You saved . . .' She tailed off, overcome by emotion.

Chase put his arm round her. 'It's okay, Liz . . . E-lizabeth.' They both smiled. 'I mean, come on. You're family. What else would I do?'

'Maybe you should go and see Dad, tell him that.'

'Let's not get ahead of ourselves!'

Chase's grandmother bustled up to them. 'Come here, my little lambchop. I'm so proud of you!' She reached up and pinched his cheeks.

'Ow. Ow, Nan!' Chase protested. 'You'll pop a stitch!'

'Oh, don't be silly.' She kissed him, then turned to Nina. 'And I'm so happy you've finally set a date!' She kissed Nina as well. 'Welcome to the family!'

'Don't forget to send Peter Alderley his invitation,' said Mac mischievously.

'Alderley can f—' Chase began, before looking at his grandmother and niece.

'Find one in his mailbox soon?' Nina suggested.

Mac chuckled, then stepped closer, lowering his voice. 'By the way,' he said, glancing across at the Prime Minister as he spoke to a TV news crew nearby, 'there are some people in London – and Washington – who are rather keen to find out what happened to Excalibur.'

'Lost at sea,' Nina and Chase quickly replied in unison. 'Went down with the ship,' Nina added.

'Glug glug,' Chase said, making a spiralling downwards motion with a finger.

'Hrmm.' Mac regarded them both intently for a moment, then his face creased into a wry smile. 'Terrible shame. Still, probably for the best. So what are you going to do now?'

'We're going back to the States,' Nina told him. 'I have to make a full report to the IHA and the UN. And we need to see Hector Amoros's family.'

Mac nodded sympathetically. 'I wish you all the best, then. Are you heading back to Heathrow? I could give you a lift.'

'That's okay,' said Nina. 'We've got a rental car.'

Chase grinned. 'And we're going to take the scenic route.'

They stood at the edge of a small lake deep in the English countryside, sunshine giving the rolling green landscape a hazy glow, peaceful and romantic. There was nobody else in sight, no cars or houses, just trees and fields and birds drifting through the warm air.

'It's beautiful,' said Nina. She moved closer to the bank, looking down to see her reflection in the rippling water. A little fish rose almost to the surface to peer up at her, then darted into the safety of the depths with a flick of its tail.

'It's nice,' Chase agreed, 'but not as good as Yorkshire. God's own county – I'll have to take you up there.'

'Maybe next time.' She regarded the view for a moment longer, then turned and picked up an object wrapped in a towel.

'Sure you want to do this?' Chase asked.

'Not entirely. Something of this historical importance should be in a museum. But . . .' She shook her head. 'We can't let anyone like Jack get hold of it again. And besides, according to legend Excalibur ended up in a lake, waiting to be found again when the time was right. It feels appropriate.'

She unwrapped the towel, revealing Excalibur gleaming within. The blade glowed almost imperceptibly when she took the hilt, no invisible lines of earth energy nearby. After regarding the reflections in the metal for a moment, Nina carefully handed the sword to Chase. 'Me?' he asked. 'Oh, I get it – if you're King Arthur, then I'm the loyal knight who casts away the sword, right?'

'No,' Nina said with a smile. 'You can throw a lot further than me, that's all!'

Chase laughed, then weighed the sword in his hands before drawing back one arm to throw it. 'Sure?'

'Yes.'

'Okay.' With a grunt, he hurled the shining weapon out across the lake. It spun end over end, sunlight flashing from the blade, and arced down to land with a splash some distance from the shore, dropping out of sight into the deep waters beneath. 'Huh. You know, I almost expected someone's hand to pop out of the water and grab it.'

'Some moistened tart, maybe?' Nina asked him, grinning.

'Yeah, that's enough Monty Python,' Chase said, taking her hand and starting the walk back to their car. 'So, we'd better start thinking about the wedding, I suppose. I know – how about getting married in Vegas by Elvis?'

She laughed. 'Keep thinking.'

Epilogue

Washington, DC

The white-haired man handed the folder to the man seated behind the desk and stepped back respectfully. 'That's everything we've got so far, sir.'

'The ship?'

'Based on the GPS track of its last known position, it's approximately eight thousand feet down in the Norwegian Basin, just inside the Arctic Circle. Reachable, given time, but there's no way to tell how much would be recoverable.'

'What about the sword?'

'According to Dr Wilde and Chase, it went down with the ship. Whether that's true or not is another matter, but considering her public profile right now, rendering them for interrogation might be a problem.'

'Damn it. Mitchell should have had the superconductor

analysed and duplicated *before* testing the weapon. He rushed it, and we lost everything!'

'With respect, sir,' the white-haired man said, 'he was acting under your orders. He wanted to take advantage of the stand-off with the Russians, and you personally authorised him to sink the *Enterprise* as a false flag—'

'I *know* what I authorised!' A fist banged on the desk. 'We would have eliminated the Russians as a competitor for polar resources for a decade, but now all that's gone because of some – some *archaeologist* and her Limey boyfriend!' He flicked through the pages inside the folder, stopping at a pair of photographs: Nina and Chase. He threw the folder down on his desk with a slap. 'All right, Mr Callum. You can go.'

'Yes, Mr President.' The white-haired man nodded, then marched crisply from the Oval Office.

President Victor Dalton turned to look out across the White House's rose garden beyond the high armoured windows. Jack Mitchell had known that failure would see him castigated as a rogue agent misusing DARPA's black budget for his own ends. Like a true patriot, he had accepted the risk and taken that responsibility in order to protect the man whose orders he was actually obeying. There would be no link to the White House . . . but that didn't change the fact that the operation had failed. The earth energy weapon had been destroyed, and Dalton's long-term plans had been derailed.

He scowled at the photographs of Nina and Chase. 'I won't forget this,' he promised them.

If you enjoyed THE SECRET OF EXCALIBUR,
turn the page for an exclusive extract of Andy
McDermott's explosive new novel

THE COVENANT OF

GENESIS

Coming soon from Headline

Prologue

Oman

For all that the Arabian desert was traditionally supposed to be devoid of life, there was far too much of it for Mark Hyung's liking. A cloud of flies had been hovering in wait as he left his tent just after dawn, and now, three hours later, they had seemingly called in every other bug within a ten-mile radius.

He muttered an obscenity and stopped, removing his Oakleys and swatting at his face. The flies briefly retreated, but they would resume their dive-bombing soon enough. Not for the first time, he cursed himself for volunteering to come to this awful place.

'Got a problem there, Mr Hyung?' said Muldoon with barely concealed contempt, pausing in his ascent of the steepening slope. The bear-like Nevadan was a thirty-year veteran of the oil exploration business, tanned and

583

leathery and swaggering. Mark knew Muldoon saw him as just some skinny fresh-from-college Korean kid from California, and rated him little higher than the desert flies.

'No problem at all, Mr Muldoon,' Mark replied, replacing his sunglasses and taking out a water bottle. He took several deep swigs, then splashed some on his hand and tilted his head forward to wipe the back of his neck.

Something on the ground caught his attention, and he crouched for a better look. The object was familiar, yet so out of place it took him a moment to identify: a seashell, a fractal spiral chipped and scuffed by weather and time. 'Have you seen this?'

'Yeah,' said Muldoon dismissively. 'Find 'em all over. This used to be a beach, once. Sea was higher than it is now.'

'Really?' Mark was familiar with the concept of sea level changes due to climatic shift, but until now it had only been on an abstract level. 'How long ago?'

'I dunno; hundred thousand years ago, hundred and fifty.' Muldoon gestured at the low bluff ahead, their destination. 'This woulda been a nice resort spot. Cavegirls in the raw.' He chuckled lecherously.

Mark held in a sigh. No point making his relations with the old-guard oilman any worse. Instead, he returned the bottle to his backpack. 'Shall we go?'

Sweating in the hundred-degree heat, they trudged across the sands for another half a mile, finally stopping near the base of the bluff. Muldoon used a GPS handset to check their position, then spent a further minute confirming it with a map and compass as Mark watched impatiently. 'The satellites are accurate to within a hundred feet, you know,' he finally said.

'I'll trust my eyes and a map over any computer,' Muldoon growled.

'Well, that's why we're here, isn't it? To prove that computers can do a better job than anybody's eyes.'

'Cheaper-ass job, you mean,' Muldoon muttered, just loud enough for Mark to hear. He folded up the map. 'This is it. We're two thousand metres from the spike camp, just like you wanted.'

Mark looked back. Barely visible through the rippling heat haze were the tents and transmitter mast of their encampment. Two other teams had set out at the same time, also heading for points two kilometres away, to form an equilateral triangle with the camp at the centre. 'In that case,' he said, taking a quiet relish in his moment of authority, 'you'd better get started, hadn't you?'

It took Muldoon an hour to prepare the explosive charge.

'No way this'll be powerful enough,' he said as he lowered the metal cylinder containing fifteen pounds of dynamite into the hole he'd dug. 'You need a couple hundred, at least. Shit, you'll be lucky if any of the other stations even hear it.'

'Which is the whole point of the experiment,' Mark reminded him. He had set up his own equipment a safe distance away: a battery-powered radio transmitter/

receiver, connected to a metal tube containing a microphone. 'Proving that you *don't* need a ton of explosives or a drilling rig or hundreds of geophones. All the simulations say this will be more than enough to make a detailed reflection map.'

'Simulations?' Muldoon almost hissed the word. 'Ain't no match for experience. And I'm telling you, the only results you'll get will be fuzz.'

Mark tapped his laptop. 'You would – without my software. But with it, four geophones'll be enough to map the whole area. Scale it up, Braxoil'll be able to cover the entire Arabian peninsula with just a couple of dozen men in under a year.'

That was hyperbole, and both men knew it, but Muldoon's disgusted expression still said it all. Traditional oil surveys were massive affairs involving hundreds, even thousands, of men, laboriously traversing vast areas to set up huge grids of microphones that would pick up the faint sonar echoes of explosive soundwaves bouncing off geological features deep underground. Mark's software, on the other hand, let the computer do the work: from just four geophones, three at the points of the triangle and the fourth in the centre, it could analyse the results to produce a 3-D subterranean map within minutes. Hence Muldoon's displeasure: long, labour-intensive – and very well-paid – surveys would be replaced by much smaller, faster and cheaper operations. Not so good for the men who would have to find a new line of work, but great for Braxoil's bottom line.

If it worked. As Muldoon had said, everything was based on simulations – this would be the first proper field test. There were hundreds of variables that could screw things up . . .

Muldoon carefully inserted the detonator into the cylinder, then moved back. 'Okay, set.'

'How far back should we stand?' Mark asked. 'Behind the radio?'

Muldoon let out a mocking laugh. 'You stand there if you want, Mr Hyung – I won't stop you. Me, I'm gonna go all the way up there!' He indicated the top of the bluff.

Mark's own laugh was more nervous. 'I'll, ah . . . defer to your experience.'

The two men climbed the hillside. The bluff wasn't tall, but on the plain at the southern edge of the vast desert wasteland called the Rub' al Khali – in English, the Empty Quarter – it stood out like a beacon. As they climbed, Muldoon's walkie-talkie squawked with two messages. The other teams had also reached their destinations and planted their explosives.

Everything was ready.

After reaching the top, Mark gulped down more water, then opened his laptop. His computer was linked wirelessly to the unit at the foot of the bluff, which in turn was communicating with the main base station at the camp, and through it the other two teams. The experiment depended on all three explosive charges detonating at precisely the same moment: any lack of synchronisation would throw off the timing of the arrival of the reflected sonar waves at the four geophones, distorting the geological data or, worse, rendering it too vague for the computer to analyse. 'Okay, then,' he said, mouth dryer than ever. 'We're ready. Countdown from ten seconds begins . . . now.'

He pressed a key. A timer on the screen began to tick down.

Muldoon relayed this through his radio, then dropped to a crouch. 'Mr Hyung,' he said, 'you might want to put down the computer.'

'Why?'

''Cause you can't cover both ears with only one hand!' He clapped both palms to his head. Mark got his point and hurriedly fell to his knees, putting down the laptop and jamming his fingers into his ears.

The charge exploded, the noise overpowering even with his eardrums protected, a single bass drumbeat deep in his chest cavity. The ground beneath him jolted. He had involuntarily closed his eyes; when he opened them again, he saw a plume of smoke rising from the base of the bluff. In the distance, two more eruptions rose above the shimmering haze in seeming slow motion. After a few seconds, the thunderclaps of the other blasts reached him.

A fine rain of dust and tiny pebbles hissed down round the two men. Mark picked up the laptop again, blowing dirt off the screen. The first results were coming through, the geophones confirming that they were receiving sonar reflections. It would take a few minutes to gather all the data, then longer for the computer to process it, but things looked promising so far.

Muldoon peered down the slope. 'Too close to the surface,' he grumbled as he wiped sand from his face.

Mark stood beside him, examining the incoming data intently. 'It's working just fine.' He flinched as another tremor passed beneath his feet. 'What was that?'

'Can't be the other charges, they weren't powerful enough . . .' Muldoon tailed off, sounding worried. Mark looked up, concerned. The shuddering was getting worse—

The ground under his feet collapsed.

Mark didn't even have time to cry out before the breath was knocked from him as he dropped down the slope amidst a cascade of stones and dust. All he could do was try to protect his face as he bounced off the newly exposed rocks, pummelled from all sides—

Something hard hit his head.

The first of his senses to recover, oddly, was taste. A dry, salty taste filled his mouth, something caking his tongue.

Mark coughed, then spat out a mouthful of sand. The back of his head throbbed where the stone had hit him. He tried to sit up, then decided it was probably a better idea to remain still.

A muffled sound gradually resolved itself into words, a voice calling his name. 'Mr Hyung! Where are you? Can you hear me?'

Muldoon. He actually sounded genuinely concerned,

though Mark's faculties had already recovered enough to realise the sentiment was professional rather than personal. Muldoon's job was to look after the specialist; an injury on his watch would reflect badly upon his record.

'Here,' he tried to say, but all that came out was a faint croak. He spat out more revolting dust, then tried again. 'I'm here.'

'Oh, thank Jesus.' Muldoon clambered over loose stones towards him. 'Are you hurt?'

Mark managed to wipe his eyes. He grimaced at the movement; he was going to have some real bruises tomorrow. 'I don't think so.' He turned his head to see the slope down which he'd tumbled. 'Wow. That's new.'

Muldoon looked up, surprise on his face as he registered the change in the landscape. The landslide had exposed a large opening in the side of the bluff, a deep cave. 'Lucky you didn't fall straight down into it. It'd probably have killed you.' He held up a water bottle. 'Here. Can you move?'

Mark gratefully took the bottle, swallowing several large mouthfuls, then gingerly moved his legs. 'I think I'm okay. What about the computer?'

Muldoon held up the screen, which in addition to being cracked was no longer attached to the rest of the machine. 'I don't think the warranty'll cover it.'

'Damn,' Mark sighed.

Muldoon helped him up. 'Sure you're okay?'

'My knee hurts, but I think I'm fine apart from that.'

'I dunno.' Muldoon examined the back of his head.

'You've got a big cut there, and if you were knocked out you might have a concussion. We could call for the chopper to come pick you up, get you to hospital in Salalah.'

'I'm fine,' Mark insisted, even as he spoke wondering why he wasn't taking Muldoon up on his offer of an immediate trip out of the desert. 'Can you see the rest of the laptop? I might be able to recover the data on the hard drive.'

Muldoon snorted, but turned to hunt for it. Mark looked the other way, towards the cave entrance. It was hard to believe that the relatively small explosive charge could have opened up such a large hole.

Unless the gap had been there all along . . .

That thought was brushed aside as he spotted the rest of the broken laptop just inside the cave entrance. 'Here,' he told Muldoon, limping towards it. It looked battered, but unless the hard drive had actually been smashed open it ought to be salvageable.

He crossed into the shadow of the cave and picked up the computer. Eyes adjusting to the low light, he examined the casing. It was more or less intact, dented but not actually broken. The experiment might not be a total loss after all.

Cheered slightly by the thought, Mark glanced deeper into the cave . . .

And was so surprised by what he saw that he dropped the laptop again.

★

Muldoon clapped Mark on the back. 'Well, son, I had my doubts about you . . . but you're gonna make us all very rich.'

'Not quite how I planned, though,' said Mark.

'Doesn't matter *how* a man gets rich, just that he does!'

Muldoon had joined him in the cave, and been equally stunned by what lay within – though he had recovered from his amazement rather more quickly, radioing the rest of the survey team to demand a rendezvous, right now. One of the other men had a digital camera; once they too had overcome their astonishment and obtained photographic proof of their discovery, they returned to the camp to send the images back to Houston via satellite.

Mark couldn't help thinking events were moving too fast for comfort. 'I still think we should inform the Omanis.'

'You kidding?' said Muldoon. 'First rule of working out here: never tell the Arabs about *anything* until the folks at home have okayed it. That's why the company has all those high-powered lawyers – to make sure our claims are one hundred per cent watertight. And that's just for oil. For *this* . . . Jesus, I don't even know where to start. We're gonna be famous, son!' He laughed, then ducked into the tent housing the communications gear.

'Maybe.' Mark drank more water, not wanting to get his hopes up. For a start, he was sure that Braxoil would take full control of his discovery. The Omani government would certainly also lay claim to anything found within their borders.

But still, he couldn't help fantasising about the potential fame and fortune . . .

He finished the water, then followed Muldoon into the tent. The survey team's six other members were already inside, flicking through the digital photos on another laptop. Debate about exactly what they had found was still ongoing, but the overall consensus was much the same as Muldoon's: it was going to make them all very rich.

'Of course,' said one of the men, a New Zealander called Lewis, 'since it's my camera, that means copyright on the photos is mine.'

'Company time, company photos, fellas,' said Muldoon.

'Yeah, but personal camera,' Lewis insisted.

'Guess we'll have to let the lawyers work that out.'

'If anyone ever bothers getting back to us,' said a laconic Welshman, Spence. 'I mean, we sent the things three hours ago.'

'What time is it in Houston?' Mark asked.

Muldoon looked at his watch. 'Huh. After ten in the morning. Still no reply?'

Lewis switched to the laptop's email program. 'Nothing yet.'

'Check the satellite uplink,' Mark suggested. 'There might be a connection glitch.'

Lewis toggled to another program. 'That explains it. No connection.'

Mark raised a puzzled eyebrow. 'Wait, *no* connection? You didn't log off, did you?'

'You kidding? Soon as we get an answer, I want to read it!'

'Weird. As long as we're logged into the Braxoil network, we should be getting *something*. Here, let me . . .'

Lewis gave up his seat to the computer scientist. After a minute Mark leaned back, more puzzled than ever. 'Everything's fine at our end, we're still transmitting. But we're not getting anything back. Either the satellite's down, which is pretty unlikely . . . or someone at the other end's blocked us.'

Muldoon frowned. 'What do you mean, blocked us?'

'I mean, cancelled our access. Nothing we're sending's getting through, and nobody can send anything to us.'

'The hell they can't.' Muldoon picked up the satellite phone's handset. He entered a number, listened for several seconds, then jabbed with increasing anger at the buttons. 'Not a goddamn thing!'

'Try the radio,' suggested an American, Brightstone. 'Call Salalah. The guys there can patch us through to Houston.'

Muldoon nodded and moved to the radio, donning a pair of headphones. He switched the set on – and yanked off the headphones with a startled yelp, making everyone jump. *'Jesus!'*

'What?' Mark asked, worried.

'Beats the hell out of me. Listen.' He unplugged the headphones. An electronic squeal came from the radio's speaker, the unearthly sound making Mark's skin crawl.

'Oh, shit,' said Spence quietly. Everyone turned to him.

'You know what it is?' Mark asked.

'I used to be in the Royal Signals. That's a jammer.'

Muldoon's eyes widened. '*What?*'

'Electronic warfare. Someone's cutting us off.'

That prompted a minor panic, until Muldoon shouted everyone down. 'You're sure about this, Spence?'

The Welshman nodded. 'It's airborne. The pitch is changing too fast for it to be on the ground.'

There was a sudden rush for the door, the eight men spreading out to squint into the achingly blue sky. 'I see something!' yelled Brightstone, pointing north. Mark saw a tiny grey speck in the far distance. 'Is that what's jamming us?'

'Where are the binocs?' Muldoon asked. 'Someone—'

An ear-splitting roar hit them from nowhere. Mark had just enough time to see a pair of sleek, sand-brown shapes rush at him before the two aircraft shot less than a hundred feet overhead, sand whirling round the men in their barely subsonic slipstream. In what seemed like the blink of an eye, the two planes had shrunk to dots, peeling off in different directions.

'What the fuck was that?' Muldoon yelled.

Spence stared after the retreating aircraft. 'Tornados! Those were Saudi Tornados!'

'But we're forty miles from the border!'

'I tell you, they were Saudi!' They watched as the two fighters came about. One them appeared to be turning back towards the camp. The other . . .

Mark realised where it was heading. 'The cave!' he cried, pointing at the distant bluff. 'It's going for the cave!'

Even as he spoke, something detached from the fighter, two dark objects falling away. Then another, and another, arcing down at the bluff—

The hillside was obliterated, the explosions so closely spaced that they seemed to have been caused by a single giant bomb.

'Jesus!' someone shouted behind Mark as a churning black cloud swelled cancerously across the face of the bluff. The sound of the bombs hit them, shaking the ground even from over a mile away.

The Tornado banked sharply north, afterburners flaring to blast it back into Saudi airspace at Mach 2.

The second Tornado—

Mark whirled to find it.

He didn't have to look far. It was coming straight at him, bombs falling from its wings—

The encampment vanished from the earth in a storm of fire and shrapnel.

The Hunt for Atlantis

Andy McDermott

A LOST CIVILISATION

The hunt for Atlantis has obsessed many minds. No one knows this better than archaeologist Nina Wilde: it dominated her parents' lives, and now it dominates hers.

A DANGEROUS QUEST

Nina believes she knows where Atlantis is: and when reclusive billionaire Kristian Frost offers her the funding to find it, there's nothing to stop her. With the help of Frost's daughter, Kari, and ex-SAS bodyguard Eddie Chase, the hunt begins . . .

A DEADLY SECRET

But Giovanni Qobras, the leader of the shadowy Brotherhood of Selasphorus, will do all he can to stop them. Nina and her team find themselves in a frantic race across the world to find the lost city before Qobras finds them. For contained within Atlantis is a secret that could destroy civilisation for ever . . .

Hurtling along at breakneck speed, THE HUNT FOR ATLANTIS is the most exciting adventure thriller you will read this year.

Praise for Andy McDermott:

'Adventure stories don't get much more epic than this' *Mirror*

978 0 7553 3912 9

headline

Run the Risk

Scott Frost

A MURDER; A BOMB EXPLOSION; A PARTNER LYING IN INTENSIVE CARE

When Lieutenant Alex Delillo's partner almost dies in a bomb explosion, Alex is catapulted into the middle of an incendiary and deadly game being played with ever-increasing stakes.

The annual, televised Rose Bowl parade is two days away and all indications suggest the bomber is intent on making the parade his final target. As the clock ticks down, Alex is closing in on her prey when the unthinkable happens and the bomber takes the most important person in Alex's life hostage as collateral.

Almost paralysed by fear, Alex will have to use all her skill if she is to find the bomber, before he forces her to make a choice that will change her life forever . . .

Acclaim for Scott Frost's NEVER FEAR

'*Never Fear* is as tough a crime novel as I have ever read, with a plot that twists and turns like a snake on crack. A classic crime novel' *Independent on Sunday*

'Frost's combination of psychological depth, complex plotting and an evocative Los Angeles setting will have fans of intelligent suspense counting the days until his next book' *Publishers Weekly*

'A fast read . . . Frost has definitely set himself up to become the next big thing in action thrillers' *Shotsmag*

978 0 7553 3392 9

headline

Die For Me

Karen Rose

A SECRET CELLAR

A multimedia designer is hard at work. His latest computer game, *Inquisitor*, heralds a new era in state-of-the-art graphics. But there's only one way to ensure that the death scenes are realistic enough . . .

AN ISOLATED FIELD

Detective Ciccotelli's day begins with one grave, one body and no murder weapon. It ends with sixteen graves, but only nine bodies and the realisation that the killer will strike again . . .

A LIVING HELL

When it's discovered that the murder weapons are similar to those used in medieval torture, Ciccotelli knows that he's up against the most dangerous opponent of his career – let the games begin . . .

A killer obsessed with the past, victims tortured to death, and all in the name of a game – DIE FOR ME is Karen Rose's most chilling thriller to date.

Acclaim for Karen Rose:

'Karen Rose's COUNT TO TEN takes off like a house afire. There's action and chills galore in this non-stop thriller' Tess Gerritsen

'Rose delivers the kind of high-wire suspense that keeps you riveted to the edge of your seat' Lisa Gardner

978 0 7553 3706 4

headline

Power Play

Joseph Finder

THERE ARE FIVE RULES TO MAKING A POWER PLAY

RULE 1:   FIND YOUR TARGET –
The billion-dollar Hammond Aerospace Corporation

RULE 2:   ISOLATE YOUR HOSTAGES –
In a remote Canadian hunting lodge

RULE 3:   MAKE YOUR RANSOM DEMAND –
Opening bid – $100 million

RULE 4:   USE VIOLENCE IF NECESSARY –
One dead . . . so far

RULE 5:   TAKE THE MONEY AND RUN

WARNING: *Rule 5* may not be possible – especially if Jake Landry is one of your hostages. He may seem quiet but push him too far and you'll live to regret it – if you're that lucky.

POWER PLAY is the brilliant new novel from the author of *PARANOIA* and the award-winning *KILLER INSTINCT*.

Praise for POWER PLAY:

'Joseph Finder is one of the best thriller writers around, and POWER PLAY is his best yet' Harlan Coben

'I dare you to read the first page. You won't be able to stop' Tess Gerritsen

'A real blood-pumper, which surprises on every page' *Independent on Sunday*

978 0 7553 4207 5

<u>headline</u>

Now you can buy any of these other bestselling
Headline books from your bookshop
or *direct from the publisher*.

FREE P&P AND UK DELIVERY
(Overseas and Ireland £3.50 per book)

The Hunt For Atlantis	Andy McDermott	£6.99
The Tomb of Hercules	Andy McDermott	£6.99
Count to Ten	Karen Rose	£6.99
Nothing to Fear	Karen Rose	£6.99
Die For Me	Karen Rose	£6.99
Scream For Me	Karen Rose	£6.99
Never Fear	Scott Frost	£6.99
Run the Risk	Scott Frost	£6.99
Point of No Return	Scott Frost	£6.99
Immoral	Brian Freeman	£6.99
Stripped	Brian Freeman	£6.99
Stalked	Brian Freeman	£6.99

TO ORDER SIMPLY CALL THIS NUMBER

01235 400 414

or visit our website: www.headline.co.uk

Prices and availability subject to change without notice.